Maiden's End

Maiden's End

Josephine Boyle

St. Martin's Press
New York

MAIDEN'S END. Copyright © 1988 by Josephine Boyle. All rights reserved. Printed in the United States of America. No part of this book may be used or reproduced in any manner whatsoever without written permission except in the case of brief quotations embodied in critical articles or reviews. For information, address St. Martin's Press, 175 Fifth Avenue, New York, N.Y. 10010.

Library of Congress Cataloging-in-Publication Data

Boyle, Josephine.
    Maiden's end Josephine Boyle.
       p.   cm.
    ISBN 0-312-03391-5
    I. Title.
PR6052.093M35   1989
823'.914—dc20   89-35112
                                                           CIP

First published in Great Britain by Judy Piatkus (Publishers) Ltd.

10 9 8 7 6 5 4 3 2

For Anne Dewe. Thanks a lot.

Chapter 1

They would be home soon, and they would bring friends with them. There was no point in going to sleep.

It was quiet; quiet for London, that was, although the complaint of traffic toiling up the hill was a constant roar in the background. That never disturbed her. For her, as for all citydwellers, the sound was subliminal, so permanent that she didn't even notice it. There would be a disturbance, but the time for it was not yet. In half an hour, perhaps, the front door would be flung open and noise would flood into the house, Petra's voice protesting through it, 'Quiet, please, darlings, you'll wake Virginia!' She always made that token gesture of maternal concern, like a superstitious crossing of the fingers, but no-one ever took much notice.

Her daughter pushed back the duvet and got out of bed, padded across the carpet, drew aside the curtain and stared out of the window. Far below, on the other side of the broad, black gulf which lay behind the house, a million lights sprang out and danced away into the distance, mile after mile of glittering wakefulness, spreading from the foot of the northern slopes into the busy fever of the West End, across the Thames and on into the interminable sprawl of the southern suburbs.

All those lights, all that pulsating, wasted electricity. All those great power stations feeding millions of watts of the stuff into things which its users regarded as so indispensable – lights, televisions, cinemas, theatres, restaurants, pubs – fuel for activities which continued far into the night, when you would have thought the only reasonable thing required was sleep.

The child shivered. It was cold in the bedroom. The central heating had switched itself off at ten as usual, although Sandy knew perfectly well that they would still be up in the small hours. It was his one meanness, a compulsion left over from youthful hard times, ridiculous when set beside his extravagances.

There would be the usual protests when they came in ('God, Petra, this place is like a morgue, can't we have some heat?'), and then Sandy would go into the kitchen and there would be the click of the switch and ticking in the radiator beneath the window. They would be shivering and complaining as the first drinks were poured and only become comfortable an hour later, by which time they would be too stoned to notice the temperature, anyway. Virginia knew all the progressive scenes of the farce; the clink of bottles and glasses, the increasing decibels of the conversation and laughter, the feet stumbling up the stairs, the noisy bang of the lavatory door, perhaps the sound of retching, perhaps the creak of the bed in the spare room.

But at the moment it was quiet, and she stood brooding in solitude.

Down there, in the fairyland of lights, other mothers and fathers sat companionably in front of their televisions, holding hands. Other children slept peacefully, knowing that they would wake to the sort of weekend depicted in commercials – morning tea, a jolly family breakfast, a walk on the Heath with the dog, a properly cooked lunch, a cosy afternoon in the garden; togetherness for all the family.

All those millions of people in the sparkling city were enjoying the things from which she was excluded. Down beyond the dark, separating gulf, real life was going on, and she was missing it. People were smiling at eath other across glass-crowded tables, meeting eyes, touching hands, promising each other things she could only dream of, perched high above in her ivory tower.

They laughed. They lived. They knew.

They knew about love.

Down there, in the darkness of the lane, they kissed and embraced and learnt all the things which no-one would ever want to teach her. Over there, in a half-timbered block of council flats on Holly Lodge Estate, Angela Parker necked and more than necked with her achingly desirable Wayne, and Virginia was cut off from it all, an outsider, a pariah, a kind of cripple.

She gazed down into the black void. It looked so empty, so threatening, now, but it wasn't, really. In daylight it revealed itself as merely a desirable open space, one of the lungs of London; the park, where birds clustered round your feet like loving friends and where squirrels were so tame that they would take scraps from your fingers; and beyond the park, the cemetery, another carefully protected reserve, not of present recreation, but of past rectitude. It was a cavern of mystery at night, but by day Virginia's favourite place, despite Sandy's personal claim upon it.

'I went straight there from the station,' he said, 'and gave him an earful.' But that story only came out when he had been drinking a lot. Sober, he kept it to himself.

Virginia loved the cemetery. It was a place of peace, of permanence, of duty done and work accomplished. They had such security, the dead. They were untouchable, superior, because now they *knew*, as none of the living knew, even those who claimed so confidently that they did. It must be nice to be dead, with no worries, no struggles, no pain, a winner at last, because everyone was afraid of you. Virginia wasn't afraid of those dead, as many of her friends were. She envied them.

At the turn of the stairs, the grandfather clock struck quarter past eleven. Not long now. The clock had stood there all her life, except for those few alarming hours when it had been dissected like a carcase, torn apart into body, head, brain and entrails and carted out on to the pavement, where it stood in its pitiful dismemberment for all the world to see while Petra raged at the men who had been sent to remove it. They had been indignant, bringing up all the usual arguments in support of their actions. 'I'm only doing my job, Mrs.' 'It's down here on my list, clear as day.' There had been phone calls and shouting and rows, and by the evening the clock had been carried inside again and up the stairs, reassembled and left to catch its interrupted breath.

Virginia, frightened by the violence done to its venerable dignity, had felt that it suffered from shock. It now had a breathless, jerky catch to it, like an asthmatic, and had stopped altogether the following day. Not until Sandy investigated and rebalanced the wedges which made it level did it return to its old reliability, and he had only done that because Virginia pleaded that he should. That silent symbol of disrupted time was more than she could bear, among so many other changes.

Now it happened: the key in the lock, the bang of the door being thrust back against the wall, the laughter, the loud voices.

'Shut up, Boris, Virginia's asleep.'

'Sorry, darling.' Crash!

'Hell, look where you're going.'

'Christ, Sandy, get out into that kitchen and switch the boiler on. I want to wrap myself round a radiator.'

'Wrap yourself round me, Sam, I'll warm you up.'

Raucous laughter and the sound of a playful slap.

'Rod, darling, put the electric fire on, will you?'

'O.K., Petra.'

Virginia didn't move. Behind her the gust of icy air slid in under the door and bit at her back. Outside, a flurry of snow drifted across the window, making the clear, sparkling landscape look like Christmas, although it was nearly March. The spring was slow to come this year and the earth huddled beneath suppressing frost.

She heard the gurgle of water moving in the pipes and laid her cold hands on the radiator, waiting to feel the warmth creep in. Come along, she urged it, I'm frozen. Hurry up, spring, I'm sick of winter. Oh please come to me, life, I've been waiting for you so long.

The last visitor left as the clock struck two thirty. Virginia heard the voices coming up the stairs. Sandy sounded drunker than usual and Petra tired and unemotional.

'Oh, leave me alone, Sandy.'

'But you're looking absolutely lovely, tonight, Petra. I've been leching after you all evening.'

'No, you haven't, you've been all over Samantha. Anyway, you're probably incapable.'

'I am not!' He sounded petulant, like a little boy who has been denied sweeties.

'Of course you are, you're pissed as a newt.'

'Oh, come on, Petra – '

Virginia pressed her hands to her ears and started to count. One, two, three –

At fifty she took them away and listened. Someone was thudding out of the bathroom and along the landing. The bedroom door slammed. The voices started up again. She covered her ears. One, two, three, four –

This time she counted up to two hundred.

Now it was quiet. She got back into bed and slid down under the duvet. The clock struck. Three o'clock in the morning on Saturday, the first of March.

'Happy birthday, Virginia Blackie,' she said.

The letterbox clattered, then there was the rush of envelopes collapsing on to the mat. She jumped out of bed, opened the door and ran downstairs. The house was warm now; the heating had been left on all night.

In the white-painted hall, with its stripped pine doors, the cold, bright light from the glass in the front door illuminated the scatter on the ground. She knelt and gathered them up, studying the addresses eagerly. There were a lot of brown envelopes bearing the brittle type of the computer; circulars, ingenuously personalised Grand Free Draw offers, bills. Saturday, as Petra said, was a Crap Mail day.

But there were also more exciting envelopes, some garishly coloured, in non-standard shapes and sizes, and with Virginia's name on them. She studied them as she went into the living room, searching for the familiar writing.

She rattled back the curtains and the reflected whiteness of newly-fallen snow slammed in, surprising the half-empty glasses, the tumbled cushions on the floor, the ground-in scatter of crisps and ash and peanuts across the carpet.

She sat down and sorted the letters through again, hoping that she had missed it, but it wasn't there. Her face fell as she started to open her cards. First, a flowery piece of sentimentality from Granny Davison, with a rhyme on it. *'To a Dear Granddaughter'* was embossed in gold. And inside:

'To one who brings me hours so sweet,

*Who turns each cloud to shine,
Whose youthful face stirs memories dear
Of days which once were mine,
A little girl whose loving ways
Are all the world to me,
A happy birthday, dear, and many
Joys in years to be.'*

A five pound note was enclosed. Granny never actually bought presents – she couldn't get to the shops, and the cost of posting anything from the Midlands was beyond her purse anyway.

A glamorous teenager in disco gear danced frenetically across the next one. *'Have yourself a ball!'* it instructed her. That was from Angela. It was all right for her, she never had any problem about that, with her looks. Still, it was a nice card – she felt quite flattered to be associated with it. She put it up on the mantelpiece, right in the middle.

There were three more from schoolfriends, one from Granny and Grandpa Blackie in Herne Bay, one from Aunty Mary and Uncle Tony and a big envelope which had been ruthlessly bent down the middle to get it through the letterbox. She drew out the glossy sheet with its clever, simple drawing. A dazed, pink elephant in boxing gloves and shorts hung over the ropes and smiled at her through a cloud of stars.

'I'm just knocked out it's your birthday!' Petra's bold, wild handwriting scrawled all over the inside in felt tip pen. *'Who's a big girl, then? Lots of hugs and kisses, darling, and all the best for a very happy birthday, from Petra and Sandy. Your present's under the sideboard.'*

Virginia went and pulled it out, a big, very heavy box wrapped in gold and pink candy stripes and tied with pink plastic ribbon bowed like a chrysanthemum.

It was a video. There was one wired up to the television already, but this was for her own set, another amenity for her private territory. She already had a hair dryer, heated curlers, a coffee machine, a sandwich toaster, a record player and a huge ghetto blaster. It had almost got to the point where she need never leave her room at all. If she wanted to, she could live her entire home life shut away from Petra and Sandy, and let them get on with their bickering and their parties and their awful friends in the rest of the house.

There was a note tucked inside the box, with the guarantee and book of instructions.

'*Look in the airing cupboard!*'

There was no sound from their bedroom and Virginia opened the airing cupboard quietly, searching through the piles of sheets and towels beneath stalactites of Sandy's socks. There it was, tucked behind the tank. She lifted out the parcel, feeling the flowered paper warm and crackling dry under her fingers. Down in the sitting room, she tore it open.

She hadn't smiled when she opened the video; it was much the sort of thing she'd expected, another expensive electrical luxury. But now, her face broke into ecstatic wonder as she held up the lovely things; a waist slip, chemise and briefs in pink and white, with bows and lace and all the insignia of womanhood on them. And a bra – a real bra in white satin, with pink lace butterflies set into the cups. Her very first bra.

She gathered up the box and rushed for her room, tore her nightdress over her head and sorted out the unfamiliar straps and fastenings. The bra closed around her as she hooked it together, then she looked eagerly into the glass, prepared to see a new, grown-up Virginia at last.

The plain, thin face stared back, framed by short, mousy hair. Below it, the infantile body, with its few sparse pubic hairs, mocked the swell of the empty cups, flapping like uninflated balloons upon her chest. It was too big. Petra had bought the wrong size. It was so like her to fling pounds and pounds away with the careless signing of a cheque, but not to have bothered about whether it would fit. The shop would change it, though, wouldn't it? She took if off and looked at the label. Thirty-two A, about as small as you could get. She looked at herself, all her feeling of maturity draining away. Her chest was as flat as a board, with only the swollen pink nipples sticking out above its corrugation of ribs.

It wasn't fair. Angela was months younger than her and she wore a thirty-six. All her friends wore bras, flaunting their figures around the school changing room and boasting about the awful inconvenience of having periods. Perhaps she wasn't going to grow up at all. Perhaps she was some sort of freak, a curiosity, doomed to remain a skinny child all her life. ⟩ trembling, she pushed the clothes back into the box, n bothering to try on the other things. Among the tissue another note emerged. '*Now look in the larder.*' She ⌐⌐ ⌐ed it without interest. She couldn't face any more disappointments yet.

She covered herself quickly with baggy jumper and jeans and sat down on the bed, her knees drawn up beneath her chin. Somehow, she had expected that this birthday would change everything, bringing the new self that she longed for, but it was still the old Virginia Blackie who met her this morning, and she despised her.

Petra got up at eleven, rushing round in a dressing gown with her curly black hair tumbling over her shoulders. Virginia, who had been eating toasted cheese sandwiches and drinking coffee in her room, came down and hovered in the doorway.

'Hello, Mummy.'

'Oh, Virginia, *please* don't call me that, it makes me feel old, 'specially this morning. Oh, for God's sake, there's red wine all over the settee! I bet that was Candida, silly slut, she was out of her tree. How on earth am I going to get it out?'

'Thanks for the video.'

'What? Oh, the video. Glad you like it, darling. Happy birthday.' Petra gave her a quick peck and started to collect the glasses. 'Did you find the other things?'

'Yes, thanks. They're nice, and the card. I didn't get one from Daddy, though.'

'I expect he'll bring it round with his present. He never could catch the post. Oh no, some cretin has burnt a hole in the carpet. God, what a shambles!'

She went out into the kitchen and rummaged in a cupboard, looking for cleaning rags.

'Hey, your present from Aunty Mary is still in here. Didn't you see my note?'

Virginia wandered in.

'Oh yes, sorry, forgot to look.'

'Forgot to look? A bit blasé, aren't we?' Petra's head was aching and her mouth tasted foul. She filled a glass with water and downed it in one.

'Is Daddy coming round?'

'I don't know.'

'You did remind him, didn't you?'

'I expect I did,' said Petra vaguely, 'but he'd hardly forget your birthday, would he?'

'He might,' said Virginia, 'you know what he's like.'

'I certainly do,' said Petra. She opened the larder door, revealing the birthday cake in its festive splendour of pink and blue icing. Beside it sat another package.

'Good heavens, Virginia, you haven't opened this one either. What's the matter with you? After I've taken the trouble to write little notes so you can have a lovely time searching for them, you don't even bother.'

She thrust it into Virginia's hands.

'Go and open them both now. Upstairs, so you're out of my way. I've got the hairdresser at twelve, and I'll never get this place straight before this afternoon.'

'You shouldn't make so much mess,' said Virginia in a flat voice, gathering the parcels into her arms.

'Tell that to Sandy. He's like a lumping great kid, sometimes. I don't know why I put up with him.'

'I do,' said Virginia under her breath, 'he's a stud.'

It was Angela's word, not hers, but it was a good description. Angela, with her precocious body and mind, had summed up Sandy as soon as she saw him.

'Mmm, not bad, really. Pretty unsubtle and obvious, of course, but some women like that.'

'I suppose they do,' Virginia had said, but she couldn't see it herself.

By tea-time the house was amended, and Petra smartly dressed and crowned with new burnished copper highlights. Virginia's four friends arrived, banishing the dullness of the winter afternoon with flying beads, plastic hair ornaments, at least ten earrings, shriekingly coloured trousers which would have better fitted their younger sisters, and upper garments so fashionably unstructured that they might have been made for their fathers. They filled the living room with chatter, giggling and exuberance, and Virginia, cheered up by a new dress, joined in, although she made regular obsessive trips to the front window.

The meal was well advanced before Sandy made his first appearance of the day, a trifle shattered but with his image properly defined by expensive, pegtop slacks and an immense lump of designer knitwear. He stood just inside the door and surveyed the attractive crowd of jailbait, hands thrust into his belt, golden head well back, a broad smile upon his face.

He was a big man, with the tan of one who has spent part of the winter abroad and the build of one who spends money on a regular workout. He leant against the doorpost, pushed one knee forward and posed, like Henry the Eighth presenting himself for the admiration of his female courtiers.

'Hi there, girls! What a roomful of glamour! How are you all, sweeties?'

He advanced into the room with the swing of a cowboy entering a bar, moving round the table and planting kisses on cheeks, finally coming to Virginia. She held her face up reluctantly and tried not to breathe in the heavy odour of aftershave and tobacco which hung about him like a miasma.

'Happy birthday, darling. Like your present?'

'Yes thanks, Sandy.'

He put his hand on her shoulder, his grip hurting her ill-covered bones.

'What an age, eh? I'm beginning to feel quite an old man.'

They laughed politely at the absurdity of the idea, but Virginia thought that he *was* looking a bit of a wrinkly today, and serve him right.

'Why hasn't Daddy come?' she asked Petra, easing herself out of Sandy's grasp.

'Oh, goodness, I don't know. I expect he'll turn up sooner or later. Now come along, blow out your candles. They'll be dripping on to the icing in a minute.'

'I wanted to wait till Daddy came.'

'Well, I'm afraid that's just too bad. Come on, darling, blow.'

At ten, Virginia showed the girls out of the front door, shivering in her short sleeves as she admitted the cold air. Sandy insisted on kissing them all again and gave Angela a not-quite-avuncular squeeze, a little too near her breasts. He had taken off the sweater and his open-necked shirt revealed a gold Capricorn birth sign medallion, held half an inch away from his chest by pale, curly hair. Angela smiled wickedly at Virginia as he went back into the living room, where a relieved Petra was pouring a vodka and tonic.

'Medallion Man,' she whispered.

They started to giggle, then fall about, then roar, throwing themselves against the wall and the open door while Virginia joined in, the pent-up force of her bitter disappointment bursting out in hard, angry mirth which contained both pleasure at the putting-down of Sandy and pain that her home should contain a figure of fun for her friends to laugh at.

The girls tumbled down the step, waved from the gate and were gone, their screeching hysterics echoing down the snowy street as they made for Highgate High Street. Virginia closed the door and went into the living room.

'I'm going to ring Daddy,' she said defiantly.

'All right, if you want to, but I don't suppose he'll be in.'

He wasn't. The bell rang repeatedly, beseechingly, on and on into the emptiness of the flat. After several minutes she put down the receiver and went upstairs. She stared resentfully at the photograph on her mantelpiece.

He might at least have remembered something as important as her sixteenth birthday.

Chapter 2

The woman on the next bench was talking to herself. The words rose and fell with the tide of her thoughts, sometimes little more than a murmur, sometimes increasing to a shout of defiance at the world and the oppressors who inhabited it.

Virginia looked straight ahead, pretending not to notice, afraid that if she caught her eye the local loony would come over and talk to her. She sat huddled up inside her coat and stared across the path at the row of naked trees, the privet-shrouded railing which backed them and the small, solemn classical pediment beyond.

He was late again. He would turn up; she had phoned to remind him that morning and not even Derek Blackie could forget an appointment that quickly, but he wouldn't be on time. She knew him too well to expect that.

She had used up all the food she had brought for the birds and they had abandoned her long since, taking their cupboard love away to where the woman was armed with a whole plastic bag full of white, sliced bread. The despised remnants of Petra's left-over lasagne lay on the ground, the square corners of the pasta too hard for even a starving sparrow to attempt, let alone one which was never short of man-provided scraps.

'Bastards!'

The woman's voice burst out in a sudden access of rage at her tribulations, and Virginia looked anxiously to her right down the path towards the gate, longing for him to appear and take her away from this disturbing situation.

A man was coming, but it wasn't him. As he came closer she saw that he was young, hair close-cropped around his ears and the back of his head, but with a long thatch on the crown, straight-topped like Frankenstein's monster. He looked nice, but then, to Virginia all young men looked nice. They were the most desirable objects in the world. She studied him for as long as was safe, then looked back quickly at the pink mausoleum behind the hedge as he drew near.

'Morning,' he said as he reached her, having been fully aware of her examination.

'Hello,' she said, her eyes flickering up to his and then away again, as if she couldn't have cared less. Her fists clenched inside her pockets with excitement.

'Cold enough for you?'

'Yes.' How did you answer a question like that? No would have sounded just as silly.

'Too cold to sit here, anyway.'

'I'm waiting for my father. We're having a day out.'

'Great! Where are you going, the Zoo?'

'No,' she said, humiliated, 'I'm miles too old for the stupid Zoo.'

'Oh, sorry. Have a nice time.'

He had barely stopped as he passed her. His words had been kind, but they were just the friendly greeting of a man to a child, a skinny, plain little girl who looked as if she would enjoy the Zoo.

'What we want is a proper government with a proper prime minister,' the woman told the pigeon on her arm angrily. 'Not her! Not a bleeding woman!'

'Hello, Patsy,' shouted the young man as he passed her, knowing that she was deaf. 'How are you today?'

'None the better for seeing you, mate,' she retorted, and he strode on, laughing, a nice, friendly young man who would pass the time of day with anyone, even Virginia.

There he was at last, turning in at the gate, hurrying towards her with his side-to-side, bobbing gait, his hands in his pockets, his thin face poking out of his turned-up collar like that of a small, anxious animal. She got up and ran forward, throwing her arms around him with joy.

'Hello, Daddy!'

'Hello, darling. Been here long?'

'Ages,' she said, with the scolding tone which he always

seemed to provoke in the people around him. 'You are *hopeless*, Daddy. You'd think you'd never heard of clocks.'

He put both arms around her and kissed her affectionately. 'How's my little girl?'

'All right. Where are we going?'

'Well, I don't know. Where would you like to go?'

She felt disappointed at once. Always she built these meetings up in her mind and was let down by them. Always she saw him taking charge of the day and whisking her off to some carefully planned treat. 'I've got something really special for you today, Ginnie. We're going on a river trip/ rollerskating/ to a theatre/ for a meal in a big restaurant. . . . ' Always the day collapsed instantly into indecision, wasted hours of aimless wandering and snatched meals in Wimpys or McDonalds, with nothing left at the end to boast about to her friends or, more importantly, to Petra. She could have made the plan herself, but she wanted it to be a free, unsolicited gift from him, a spontaneous loving gesture. She longed to be able to return home in triumph, bringing news of exciting adventures, but instead she would slink into the house, trying to avoid her mother's suspicious questioning.

'Well, where did he take you today?'

'Oh, nowhere in particular. Just about. Just for a walk.'

She looked up into his face, so surprisingly young-looking for his forty years, with soft, mousy hair falling over the grey eyes which were the matrix for her own. He was very like a child himself, but oh, she loved him so. It had always been he who played with her when she was little, who pushed her out in her chair, who listened to her questions and answered them as best he could. Petra had always seemed too busy.

'We could go for a walk while we make up our minds.'

'All right,' he said, 'though it's pretty chilly. Are you wearing enough?'

'I am a bit cold, but you could put your arm round me.'

'That's right, so I could,' he said indulgently, and they strolled down towards the gate and into the lane. Even here, he hesitated and looked left and right.

'Which way?'

'This way,' she said, pulling him to the left. 'Let's go into the cemetery.'

He laughed incredulously, but obeyed the pull of her arms, clasped around his waist.

'What, again? We've been there lots of times. You're a funny little girl, aren't you? I've never heard of a kid before who likes tombstones so much. What's the attraction?'

'Oh, I don't know. It's all so settled there. No surprises. I know where they all are and they don't change. Not like living people, they change all the time.'

They turned left again immediately through an open iron gate and started to walk down the slope between heavy, solemn monuments. An elderly couple were clearing snow from a grave and arranging a bunch of shivering flowers in a vase. Derek looked around him uneasily. He didn't care for graveyards himself; life was enough to cope with, without disturbing thoughts of death as well.

'You are a funny little kid,' he repeated.

'I'm not a kid. I'm old enough to be married.'

'Oh no you're not, darling, not yet. Not till you're sixteen.'

'I *am* sixteen,' she said stiffly, her heart sinking. 'My birthday was yesterday.'

He stopped short and clapped his hand to his forehead.

'Oh no! Oh, darling, I'm so sorry, it went clean out of my head. I've been so busy, I didn't realise that Saturday was the third already.'

'The first,' she said. 'My birthday is the first.'

'Yes, of course, the first. Oh, why didn't Petra remind me? She knows I've got a head like a sieve.'

'Didn't she?'

'No, I'm sure she didn't. If she'd only given me a ring I'd have gone straight out and got you a card, you know I would, don't you? I wouldn't let my little girl down.'

'No.'

'And I haven't got you a present. Look,' he released her and started fumbling in his inside pocket, pulling out his wallet. 'Here you are, buy yourself something nice. Something special. It's a special birthday, after all. Mustn't let this one go by without making a splash, must we?'

'No. Thanks, Daddy.' She tucked the notes away without looking at them, heavy with hurt.

'That's all right, darling,' he said, pleased with himself.

'Well now, what have you been doing?'

'Nothing much. Let's walk down here, please. I want to show you Fireman Burton.'

She led him off the carriageway on to a long, straight, narrow path, dropping downwards between rows of close-packed graves. As it got lower, the stones became more neglected, the snowy path shadowed by trees and stained with dead leaves. Occasionally, clumps of bulb spikes pushed their way up from between broken stones. On she drew him, with the eagerness of one going to visit old friends, and now the graves began to disappear under ivy and purple-leaved brambles, and the dates on the stones were older, back in the last century. At last she stopped, pointing into the middle of the crowded ground to where a white monument stood up above the jumble.

'There he is! Isn't it lovely? Come and see it properly.'

They threaded their way through the fireman's neighbours, trying not to tread on them but finding it impossible. Every square inch was occupied by the last resting places of the dead. Derek felt uncomfortably that he should apologise for stepping on their buried heads, and experienced a creeping thrill of horror as he was forced to do so.

Virginia looked with delight at the stone monument. On it lay a fireman's helmet, axe and hose. With affectionate gentleness, she brushed the mantle of snow off the carving.

'That's awful!' Derek protested. 'Right over the top. Who on earth was he?'

'He died in a fire at a theatre. Isn't that sad? I imagine him sometimes getting out of his grave at night and putting on his helmet and picking up the hose and watering the flowers on the graves with it. Don't you think that's a lovely idea?'

'No, I don't! I think it's pretty sick.'

'Oh, it's not! I only found him the other day and I was dying to show him to you.'

Her face fell. It was as if she had introduced him to a new friend and he had disappointed her by not liking him. She had been deeply touched by the story of heroic Fireman Burton, gleaned from a leaflet on sale by the gate. She could love someone like that devotedly. Did he have a wife and children? The poor, poor things. Oh, it was so sad, and yet so wonderful.

'Just think how brave he must have been. I'm glad you're not a fireman, Daddy, I should be worried about you. I much prefer you being a company director, it's so nice and safe.'

She hung on to his arm, comforting herself with the thought of his safety. She needed safety, any sort of safety. When she found it she clung on to it.

'Not as safe as all that, darling,' he said, a spasm of unease moving in his face. She didn't notice. 'Can't we get back to the main path? It's so messy here,' he said, looking down at his polished shoes, although what was really disturbing him was the knowledge that he was standing only six feet above something quite loathsome. His buttocks contracted at the thought.

'All right,' Virginia sighed, 'we'll go and see the other fireman.'

She led him back along a little path and out onto a broad, straight carriageway. Derek knew that one, she had shown it to him before. It was much more his idea of how a grave ought to look, if there had to be such things, just a large, plain, white cross.

'He's the one in *Iolanthe*, you know,' she explained.

'I know, dear, you told me. Now let's go somewhere more cheerful, look at the shops or something like that.'

'I want to see the piano first.'

Farther down the carriageway, they found it standing like a piece of furniture left out in the garden.

'You like this one, don't you?' said Derek, regarding it, as always, with fascinated incredulity. It made Fireman Burton's memorial look conventional.

'Not like it, exactly, I feel sorry for it. I keep thinking that the damp must be ruining the strings and making the keys stick.'

Derek laughed.

'It reminds me of the clock, that time it was out on the pavement for hours. It looked so lost. It's awful to feel lost.'

'Clocks don't feel anything, silly, and that was years ago. What a funny thing to remember.'

'It was yours, wasn't it? Grandpa gave it to you. You should have had it. I wouldn't have minded if it had gone straight to you, but they shouldn't have left it out in the street like that, as if nobody wanted it. I cried.'

'Did you? Good Lord!'

Derek felt puzzled by his daughter, as he often did. He put his arm around her and walked her off the grass, back on to the carriageway.

'It didn't matter. I haven't got room for it in the flat, anyway.'

'But it's yours! He's your father.'

'No, no, not really, it was a wedding present. If Petra liked it, there was no reason why she shouldn't keep it.'

'She doesn't like it, she only wants it because it's old and valuable.'

He gave her a little shake of reproval and tried to turn her uphill. 'Now, now, don't talk about your mother like that.'

She pulled the other way.

'We haven't seen the dog yet.'

Near the broad gates at the bottom of the road, the blunt stone face poked out of the obelisk. *'Her faithful dog, Rex.'*

She reached up and fondled its nose while he watched glumly, then they turned left and walked along the bottom edge of the cemetery, where the graves were more modern and better spaced, and where, although they seemed to watch Derek and Virginia's progress like a crowd of solemn, staring, silent people, they were set well back from the path. They turned the corner and started the uphill climb. Every now and then, Virginia stopped at a favourite friend; a philanthropist, a devoted married couple, a child's grave with a heartrendingly sentimental inscription. The settled headstones nodded to left and right, as though discussing them as they passed.

At the top, where the road rounded the bend towards the way out, it was Derek who stopped, cocking his narrow, foxy little head backwards to peer up at the huge, craggy one on his left. In the snow around the immense, grey marble plinth lay wilting offerings of flowers; wreaths, sprays, posies, dying in their scarlet like bloody sacrifices. On the other side of the path, a few earnest young people were leaning against more reserved monuments, gazing at their hero and paying their respects.

'Well, there he is,' said Derek. 'Can't say I care for him much.'

'I rather like him,' said Virginia.

'Whatever for?'
'Because Sandy hates him.'
'Oh, does he?'
He looked again at the frowning colossus, his mouth spreading into a grin. Then he walked up the little path, stretched out his hand and patted the cold stone.
'Hiya, Karl,' he said.

Derek paid for the meal with his Access card. It was an expensive restaurant, the sort that charged you a pound for a portion of peas, because it was served in a hot, stainless steel dish and topped with a knob of butter. He had seemed reluctant when she stopped outside it, urging him to enter, having decided desperately that the only way she could get things from him was to demand. But he had indulged her, helping her off with her coat as if she were Joan Collins in *Dynasty* and ordering the overpriced food with what seemed to her enviable sophistication.

He left her at the front door.
'Won't you come in, Daddy?'
'No, darling, I've got to ring someone. Anyway, your mother –'
She kissed him goodbye passionately.
'Till next time, Daddy. You won't forget, will you? The same place, in two weeks' time.'
'No, of course I won't forget,' he assured her.
Oh yes, she thought, you might, but I won't let you. I'll ring you in the morning as usual. I couldn't bear it if you forgot all about me and left me alone in the park, with the mad woman and the betraying birds and squirrels and the patronising kindness of beautiful young men.

Sandy was sitting on the settee surrounded by what looked like Crap Mail, while Petra smoked urgently, her eyes fixed on the television screen.
'Gosh,' Virginia said loudly, throwing her coat down into a chair, 'I'm full to busting! I haven't eaten so much for ages.'
Petra looked up.
'Junk food, I suppose.'
'No, we went to La Calinda. It was dreamy. Absolutely brilliant. Toyah Willcox was there.'

Well, a lady who looked very like her was there. Near enough to make the identification pardonable.

'I hope he didn't let you eat too much rich food so that you're sick.'

'I didn't eat anything silly, like *moules marinières*. I had *chicken a la crême*, and it was superb. I haven't tasted anything so nice in years.'

Petra gave a tense, overacted laugh.

'Oh dear, half-starved, are we? Poor little Virginia.'

'I bet you didn't have *chicken à la crême*,' said Virginia defiantly.

'We had escalope of veal,' said Sandy, raising his eyes from the pile of brown envelopes and coloured foolscap sheets, 'and it was absolutely delicious, as Petra's cooking always is. So you had a nice time, sweetie, that's good.'

'It's good as long as she isn't ill,' snapped Petra. She seemed angry, as if something outrageous had happened to her, as if she had been insulted. She didn't look at Sandy, even when she addressed him.

She was often sulking at him now — it was like being back in the days before Daddy left. Sandy had moved in soon after, although he had been around for ages before that, and there had been a long honeymoon period, with the two of them billing and cooing in a way which made Virginia feel sick, pressing her hands over her ears in the small hours so that she would hear nothing from the bedroom next door. When the relationship started to sour, as all Petra's relationships eventually did, she had been glad at first, delighted that Sandy's big, muscular attractions had proved no more lasting than her father's small, slight ones. But bad atmospheres are uncomfortable to live with, and now she got away from them as much as possible, shutting herself into the privacy of her bedroom in mixed elation and depression at their disharmony.

She sat down, still acting the sated helot, anxious to play Derek's unusual generosity for all it was worth.

'We had a marvellous time, but then, I always do with Daddy.' She flung the words at them like a challenge.

'Jolly good, sweetie,' said Sandy, his eyes on the folder in his hand. 'No, this is definitely the one, Petra, I'm sure of it. Absolutely splendid. Just what we're looking for.'

'What you're looking for, you mean!' said Petra.

'But you'll love it, I know you will. If only you'd come and see it, it's got such potential. You don't want to spend the rest of your life in London, do you?'

'Yes, I do.'

'But we need fresh air, space, room to live and breathe as God intended.'

'God!' muttered Petra. 'You make me sick, sometimes, Sandy. You're so bloody sentimental.'

'What's sentimental about God?' Virginia demanded aggressively.

'Oh, don't start arguing, Virginia, I'm tired.'

'You always are,' she said resentfully, and went out of the room and upstairs, disappointed by their lack of reaction to her exciting evening. She switched on the television and sat in a morose sulk before the garish, stupid programme. She'd had a lovely time, though, hadn't she? She was sated with the meal she'd consumed; more than sated, to be honest, uncomfortable. She had Daddy's money to spend, too. She'd buy something really brilliant with it and flaunt it in front of them.

Down in the living room, she could hear her mother's raised voice, though not her words.

'It's my house!' Petra was protesting. 'If you don't like living here you can get out of it. I don't have to come with you.'

He slid an arm like a tree branch around her shoulders.

'Our house,' he said. 'I bought Derek out, remember?'

'Oh, I know,' she said, wriggling irritably in an effort to shake him off. He reacted no more than if she were an insect. If she had actually slapped his face, the idea might have crept into his brain that her wishes were not in accord with his, and he would then have released her with hurt surprise, but subtlety of perception was not his forte. 'If I don't want to sell, you can't. It's in both our names and we both have to agree.'

Sandy laughed and drew her tighter into his embrace.

'Look, Petra, I really want this house, it's what I've always dreamed of. I don't want to move there on my own, I'd far rather you came with me and we worked on it together.'

'*Worked* on it? What is it, a ruin?' Petra looked round the warm, perfectly appointed luxury of her living room with horror. 'You mean it's got no electricity and no running water and a cesspit in the garden?'

'No, of course I don't. At least, it's got a septic tank, but it's well away from the house. You have to expect that in the country. I don't suppose many rural houses have proper drainage, unless they're on a main road.'

'You want to be an English country landowner, don't you?' said Petra with contemptuous recognition.

'Why not?' asked Sandy, 'I can afford it. It's the trend now, Petra, lots of people are moving out of London and living civilised lives. Pete has just bought a place in Bucks.'

'Oh, *that's* it, is it? Don't want to be one down on Pete Goate, do you? Must keep up the image, mustn't we? Well, if that's it, what's wrong with Highgate? I should have thought that was trendy enough for anyone.'

'If it was one of the Georgian places, yes, but this is only Victorian, and a bit naff, to be honest.'

'Naff! Do you know what houses in this street are fetching now, Sandy? Do you know how much Derek spent on the place?'

'But I want *this* house, Petra,' said Sandy with serene certainty. 'At least come and see it. We'll go down next Saturday. The agent was so helpful.'

'He's probably desperate to get rid of it. I bet he couldn't believe his luck when you turned up.'

'Just come and see it,' he insisted. He pulled her against him and started to try and placate her in the way which had once worked so immediately, but which now took much longer.

Upstairs, Virginia pulled the notes out of the pocket of her jeans and counted them for the first time. Ten pounds. Ten grotty pounds. She'd expected at least thirty. Ten pounds! What could she get for that?

If people loved you they gave you things, and a small gift meant small love. Only ten pounds, that was all he loved her. That was all she was worth to him, while Petra and Sandy showered her with expensive bribes.

She looked at the mean little horde and started to cry. The self-pitying tears ran down her cheeks and dropped on to the notes. She cried harder, more angrily, squeezing out the salt drops and letting them fall on to the creased paper, then pressing the notes to her eyes so that they became sodden and finally tore into damp pieces. She tore them even further, then ripped them meticulously into shreds, smaller and smaller, until that exposure of her father's lack of love for her was totally destroyed. Then she took the incriminating evidence to the window and flung it out, where it disappeared into the dark gulf containing one of the only two certainties of life.

Down in the living room, the couple eventually achieved that contact which goes by the name of making love.

Chapter 3

Miss Hibbert was giving Virginia a 'little chat'; not a telling-off, she didn't believe in them. She preferred to make subtle appeals to her pupils' better natures by means of wistful regret and hurt reproach.

It was such a pity that you didn't take more trouble with your work when you had such a good brain; it wasn't as if you were one of the slower girls. She was so dreadfully disappointed in you. There was no reason why you shouldn't sail through your O-levels if you would only apply yourself, but you just didn't seem to care, did you? And your writing, dear, whatever had happened to your writing? Why, it was barely legible. There, for instance, all that crossing out and writing in — it was impossible to make out what you were trying to say. And examiners just hadn't the time to stop and work it out like she did, they'd go straight on, and if they couldn't read it they couldn't find out how much you knew, could they?

Your mocks had been quite terrible, hadn't they? If you didn't pass you'd have to start all over again, instead of going into the sixth form, and that would be such a pity, wouldn't it? She was sorry to go on at you, dear, but she was only thinking of you — she did so want you to do your best. And think how *deeply* disappointed your parents would be if. . . .

Virginia stared down at the messy, red-corrected sheets, ignoring the interminable, sorrowful whine which was Miss Hibbert's idea of psychology. Frankly, her dear Miss Hibbert, she didn't give a damn. She had problems far more pressing than stupid O-levels. At that moment, for instance, she was worrying that the next term was going to bring the dead give-away of swimming lessons. Perhaps she could talk Petra into giving her excuse notes for colds or rheumatism or other fictitious aches and pains.

Miss Hibbert paused, feeling a sudden pang of pity for the subdued child before her and bringing her homily to a kindly close, unaware that her pupil's dejection was caused by the knotty problem of how to keep up the myth of physical maturity before her already nubile friends.

'Now you're going to try really hard next term, aren't you, Virginia? Promise me.'

'Yes, Miss Hibbert.'

'Good girl. I'm glad we've had this little chat. Run along, now.'

Obediently, Virginia ran along, if her customary sulky drift could be so described. She put on her outdoor clothes, picked up the moral blackmail of her loaded brief-case and walked slowly home.

The snow had gone, although the day was damp and miserable, and it was definitely warmer. Perhaps spring was coming at last.

She scraped her shoes along the gritty, salt-whitened pavements, eyes fixed on the ground in front of her, ignoring everything but her own gloomy thoughts. Fancy Daddy being so mean. Fancy him forgetting her birthday, she never forgot his. Fancy her being sixteen years old, old enough to be married, and not having periods. Fancy being sixteen and still looking like a kid of twelve. Fancy having friends like Angela with boyfriends like Wayne, and her having no boyfriends at all.

How desperately, cruelly unfair to be Virginia Blackie, with divorced parents who didn't care about her at all and a stupid great lump like Sandy for a step-father.

Poor Virginia Blackie, oh poor Virginia.

She'd show them all one day. She'd suddenly blossom and become incredibly, fantastically beautiful and then they'd be sorry. They'd take notice of her then, eager to bask in her reflected glory and success, but it would be too late. She wouldn't forget how they'd treated her in the past, oh no. She'd be aloof, withdrawn, smiling to herself secretly while they tried to make up to her for their past neglect. She'd got them all down in her mental black book, all the disappointments, all the slights, all the painful hurts and humiliations they had inflicted on her so heedlessly. Even when boys started to look at her with new eyes she wouldn't take any notice of them if they'd laughed at her in the past. Not even Wayne. How she hated Wayne! 'Hello, Angela, got skinny Ginnie with you?' 'Hi there, Virginia, thought it was Samantha Fox for a minute.' 'Give us a kiss, Virge, you gorgeous lump of flesh, you.'

She hated him with all the bitterness of rejected adoration. He figured largely in her daydreams. 'I fancy you really, Virge, I just go with Angela to be near you.' Just you wait, Wayne, just you bloody well wait! When I do grow up I won't have anything to do with you, even if you *kill* yourself for love.

The rain started to fall, gusting against her shivering, shrunken body like the whole spiteful, unjust world.

Spring wasn't here yet, not by any stretch of the imagination.

Virginia slouched downstairs and into the living room. It was nearly eleven o'clock, but she was still in her dressing gown, her hair ruffled and her pale, infantile face crumpled with unwashed sleep. She didn't know why she'd bothered to get up now, there was nothing interesting to do. The only good thing about Saturday was that there was no school. She might go down to the cemetery, she supposed. It was peaceful there, with no-one to nag at you or tell you you ought to be out enjoying yourself. Yes, she'd go to the cemetery. The dead offered companionship without making judgements.

'And about time too!' Petra greeted her, standing there with her coat on. 'God, you look a mess!' Judgements like that, for instance. 'How you can waste half the day in bed beats me. When I was your age I had too many interesting things to do to waste time like that.'

It was not true, as the brief effort of casting her mind back would have told her; long, adolescent lie-ins had been as much a part of her life as anyone else's, but then, her adolescence had been cut unnaturally short, and the intrusion of an unplanned, unwanted baby, demanding attention with the insistence of a tyrant queen, had eliminated further self-indulgence and sold her into the slavery of feeds, winding and nappies.

Virginia slumped down in front of the television and clicked the switch.

'Now turn that off, Virginia, you know we're going out. I told you last night.'

'Where?' demanded Virginia, not moving. It was Saturday Superstore, pretty stupid, really, but they often had pop groups on, with deliciously dreadful young men on whom to build erotic daydreams. That one for instance. She'd have *him* when she became beautiful.

'Sandy's taking us out for a drive,' said Petra shortly. She didn't look a lot more excited about it than Virginia. She'd had to change her weekly hair appointment to nine o'clock, and was still disorientated from the effort of rising early at a weekend.

'How pathetic!' retorted Virginia. 'Who wants to go for a drive in March?'

'He does. Come along, darling, let's get it over. You can watch television when we get home. Or go out with your friends. Have you got anything fixed for tonight?'

'Of course not,' said Virginia bitterly.

The traffic was heavy on the Great Cambridge Road, as motorists flooded out of London on the first reasonably mild weekend of the year. Cars full of bouncing, obstreperous children made for the country, caravans waved their rears dangerously in front of Sandy's Volvo, elderly couples sat stolidly in the front seats of Fords and hugged the centre of the road at a steady thirty miles an hour as he hovered behind them, trying to get past.

Petra sat in the front seat, regarding the passing suburbs with dislike while the stereo pumped out the classical music which Sandy loved. Behind, Virginia stared out of the window, enclosed in the new daydream she had adopted to shut out the boring parts of her life — lessons, family meals, silly television programmes she couldn't be bothered to turn off.

A Victorian fireman, tall, strong and handsome in his smart uniform and gleaming helmet, was rescuing her from terrible danger. Like a guardian angel sent from heaven to snatch her from her peril, he leant his ladder against her bedroom window and climbed up, heedless of the flames. He swept her into his arms and carried her down the long descent to the ground, gripping her to his breast with tenderness and passion, not letting her go even when they reached the bottom, despite the attempts of his colleagues to take her from him.

'That's the M 25 below,' said Sandy.

Petra glanced up at the huge, unignorable motorway sign.

'Is it really? I'd never have guessed.'

They slid off the roundabout and continued northwards. Virginia looked vacantly at the outskirts of Cheshunt.

The fireman was gazing into her face. 'You're beautiful,' he murmured. His commanding officer was at his side. 'Put her down now. You're a brave fellow, you've saved her life, but there's work to be done.' 'No,' said the fireman, 'never. She's the loveliest thing I've ever seen. I'll never let her go as long as I live.' The officer fell back, wiping a tear from his eye. 'God!' he muttered to another fireman. 'You don't often see love at first sight, but this is it, or I'm a Dutchman.'

'That's Haileybury College over there. Client of mine is sending his son there.'

'Wow,' said Petra.

The road swept up on to concrete stilts, crossed the river, then curved round Ware to rejoin the old A10; dead straight to near Puckeridge, curving to the left, then dead straight again; the Roman road; the Saxon road of Ermine Street.

He cradled her in his arms. 'Virginia,' he whispered, 'my beautiful Virginia! I've been waiting for someone like you all my life. Say that you love me, Virginia. Say that you'll be mine. I'll look after you, I swear it. I'll love you and cherish you and give you my children – '

Virginia wriggled in the back seat, feeling a blush flooding up over her face and looking quickly at Sandy and Petra as if they could read her thoughts. But firemen had such dangerous lives, look at poor Fireman Burton. She didn't want to be widowed young, she wanted someone who would die long after she did, so that he could mourn at her grave. She pictured her monument among the others in the cemetery; a sorrowful angel, with hands held wide in pity and blessing above her buried coffin.

'*Sacred to the memory of Virginia ---, dearly beloved wife of---, devoted mother of ---, deeply missed by all. Her* sweetness made this dark world a brighter place for those who were privileged to know her.'

Oh yes, that was beautiful. The sentimental tears sprang to her eyes and she smiled the sad, resigned smile which had so moved the people gathered around her deathbed.

'I suppose we fall off the edge of the world soon.' said Petra.

'Here we are,' said Sandy as he crossed a bridge by a needle-spired flint church and slowed down. The car behind hooted.

'You're holding everybody up.'

'I want to park close to the agent's. Look, there it is.'

He came to a halt and the car behind gave a long, exasperated blast. Petra pointed impatiently.

'Look! Car Park!'

The car park was behind the Co-op. Petra stayed where she was until Sandy came round to open her door.

'Put the catch down on the back doors, will you, Virginia?' She dragged herself back to reality. She did as she was told, got out and surveyed the tarmacked space with distaste.

'Where's this?'

'Buntingford.'

'Where's Buntingford?'

'Hertfordshire. It's an old country town, very historic.'

'What, Victorian?'

'No, centuries older than that. This is part of the real old England,' said Sandy, regarding the tatty backside of the High Street with delight. It was a row of irregular, bits-and pieces buildings, looking as if they had been built ad hoc as their successive owners required further room. They mostly had. 'Come on, girls, this way.'

Virginia followed them into the noisy, claustrophobic funnel of the High Street, resenting her presence in this dirty, run-down old town. The shops were small, old-fashioned, boring. The buildings were neglected and dull. What on earth had they come here for?

Sandy stopped at a shop with bow windows and an upper floor so close above them that it looked little more than a loft.

'Look, Petra, there it is in the window.'

Petra, drifting along the narrow pavement in a cool personal cloud, came and glanced at the small, carefully-angled photograph. Her expression didn't change. She looked at the photograph, looked at Sandy, looked up at the sky, looked unimpressed. Sandy went in alone.

Back in the car, he recrossed the bridge, turned down a side road on the right and entered the maze of lanes beyond.

'What are we doing here?' asked Virginia, peering out at the close-set hedges.

'Nothing,' said Petra, 'apart from indulging one of Sandy's whims.'

'What whim?'

'A sentimental foreign illusion about the English rural ideal.'

'Oh for Petes's sake,' said Sandy, sudden irritation at the barb letting the slip through.

Petra laughed. 'For Petes's sake! Did you hear that, darling? For Petes's sake!'

'Where are we going?' Virginia whined. 'You haven't told me yet.'

Petra turned round as Sandy steered the car down a steep slope which had suddenly appeared in the lane ahead, plunging into the dip as if he was taking a dive out of the modern world into a time unimaginably remote.

'Well, darling, we are going in pursuit of a dream, a romantic dream.' Her voice was amusedly detached. 'We are going to see a half-ruined dump which should have been pulled down years ago, because dear Sandy fancies becoming a country gentleman with a stately home and an estate. That's where we're going.'

Virginia sat very still, trying to understand what her mother was talking about.

'But we've got a home.'

'Oh yes, we've got a home, a home which millions of people would be only too glad to have. Millions of *English* people, that is. That's not good enough for you, is it, Sandy? You want to be one of the landed gentry. You want to go back to the good old days of Buchan and Galsworthy, when a *real* Englishman had a few acres around him in which to slaughter the animal population.'

The road reached bottom then swung up again sharply, while the car groaned and whined at the challenge. Sandy leant forward, shoulders hunched, apparently oblivious to the barrage of spiteful innuendo from his left. A crossroads appeared ahead. He slowed, looked both ways, then eased across into a narrow lane between bare hedges on the other side. Within yards the road dipped again.

Virginia tensed, insecurity starting to grip her like a fist.

'We're not going to move, are we?'

'No, we're not,' said Petra. 'Not if I have anything to do with it.'

'You just wait until you see it,' said Sandy soothingly, as the car slid down into a deep hollow and nosed its way round a corner, then another, zig-zagging through the secret places of the countryside like an explorer of the British Empire opening up the dark depths of the African Continent.

'But I don't want to move!' Virginia cried. 'I don't want to leave our house. I want to stay in Highgate.'

'Hear, hear!' said Petra. 'We've got to humour him, but I have no intention of moving out into this bloody wilderness, so don't worry, darling. I promise you, Virginia, we are definitely *not* moving out of London.'

Virginia relaxed. That was all right, then. She began to look at their surroundings with more interest, the superior interest of a person who was definitely *not* going to have to live in it. The car dipped up and down, turned left and right, nosed its way through the mysterious lanes in pursuit of an England which lived only in the minds of foreigners. What a ghastly place. Who could possibly live here without going mad? Why, they hadn't passed a house in miles, let alone a shop or a cinema. What on earth did you do with yourself? She congratulated herself on her lively, urban home environment. Gosh, it must be *awful* to live out here.

'Not far now,' said Sandy. Petra lit up a cigarette and sat puffing it with her eyes closed.

The road started to climb again, up out of yet another hollow, up, up, while the engine howled and protested and Sandy changed down into low gear. The hedges closed in on them. The road was little more than a gravel track now, only one vehicle wide. At last it levelled out and there was a sudden glimpse across a lower stretch of hedge, still unleafed but studded with the first blackthorn blossoms. Fields rolled away to their right, mile upon mile of brown earth studded by an occasional solitary, naked tree.

'My goodness,' said Petra, 'how lovely. The Sahara Desert. Just where I've always wanted to live.'

When they came to the signpost, they hadn't realised that there was a track there at all. Only when Sandy turned into the narrow entrance did they see its pale thread bisecting the bare, muddy expanse. Not even the words on the white finger made them believe that anything could possibly lie at the end; not even the smudge of evergreen trees ahead, on the very roof of Hertfordshire, convinced Petra and Virginia that this was a place where human beings had voluntarily chosen to live, had really settled, had built a dwelling and surrounded it with a screen against the upland winds, until Sandy drove into its dark shelter and drew up in front of the neglected frontage.

Petra stared out of the windscreen, shocked out of her studied, disinterested detachment at last.

'Bloody hell, Sandy!' she exclaimed.

Maiden's End had never been beautiful – it had not been intended to be. The man who built it in the second half of the eighteenth century was, unlike Sandy, no romantic with dreams of a rural retreat and an idyllic life. He was a gentleman farmer, the owner of a tumbledown timber house in a hollow, surrounded by a stagnant moat from which all water was drawn and into which all waste eventually drained. The parliamentary enclosure of the high boulder-clay plateau between Stevenage, Buntingford and Ware had given him the chance to build again in the centre of his new land, and he had built without sentiment; a hard, brick box of a house, for use, not show. A semi-basement, a ground floor, a first floor and a floor of attics, the walls chopped off impatiently above the attic windows by a brick parapet, the attic ceiling only inches below the leads, so that the sun and snow passed their extreme temperatures straight through to the suffering servants trying to sleep beneath.

The black front door, fully nine feet high, was reached by a flight of stone steps and surrounded by a stone doorcase which had no damned nonsense such as ornament about it, and was the only place where John Maiden had employed anyunnecessary expense, stone being hard to come by in Hertfordshire. The rest of the frontage was plain stock brick, with two large sash windows on either side of the door, five slightly smaller windows on the first floor and five much smaller windows on the attic floor. In the semi-basement, two grubby windows peeped over the edge of the muddy driveway on either side of the steps.

It had the detail and proportions of a child's drawing of a house, but it was not homely or cosy. The lack of a pitched roof made it look as if it had been scalped, and it was too big. Much too big. It was like an institution.

Dumbstruck with dismay, Petra and Virginia sat staring through the windscreen at the rearing, weather-fouled slab of brick while Sandy got out eagerly and pulled the keys from his pocket.

The two in the car remained silent, listening to the restless sough of wind in the pines which enclosed them on all sides. The ash on Petra's cigarette grew, trembled, then fell on to her pink jumpsuit. She brushed it off, took the last drag and stubbed it out in the ashtray on the dashboard. Then she got out like a sleepwalker and leant on the car roof, disbelief in every line of her beautifully made-up face.

Virginia started to laugh.

'He's *mad!* He's absolutely stark, raving bonkers, Mummy! He *can't* want to live here!'

The concrete confirmation of the unreality of Sandy's dream filled her with joyous relief and she hurried out of the car, eager to share her laughter with Petra. Of *course* Mummy couldn't live here – Petra with her London ways and her expensive life-style and her smart, sophisticated friends. She stood beside her, still laughing, waiting for Petra to join in and drown the whole preposterous pipedream in a scornful tidal wave of ridicule.

The huge front door was yawning wide now, and she saw Sandy pulling at the shutters inside a window on the left of it. The house opened one of its eyes and studied them like a newly-awakened giant.

She looked at her mother, ready to catch her smile, but Petra wasn't laughing. Virginia tugged her arm, still forcing the laughter out of her lungs and looking up into her face,

as if mirth was a cold she was trying to give her.
'Isn't it awful, Mummy?'
Petra suddenly jerked back into life.
'Don't *call* me that, Virginia. You're not a baby now.'
She marched towards the house and up the steps, with the air of one who is about to put a decisive end to a child's game which has got completely out of hand.
'Sorry, Mum – Petra – ' Virginia's laughter died.
The house swallowed Petra as if it was taking a pill. It almost seemed likely that the sharp medicine would work on it like a dose of salts, and that within minutes it would pull itself together, realise what a fool it was being and shrink into the sensible, reasonable form of a well-maintained residence in Highgate.
Virginia looked up at the blinded eyes of the other windows, round at the hissing heights of the dark trees, down at the muddy floor of weeds and dead leaves and felt suddenly not alone, but watched. She rushed across the drive, up the steps and into the house, calling: 'Where are you, Petra? Sandy! Petra! Where are you?'
The words echoed across the hall to the high, arched window beyond. In front of it wide, dusty stairs wound up into the well. She hardly looked at them before gratefully catching up the clue to the whereabouts of her mother. Petra's voice protested in the booming space of the room on her left.
Virginia hurried in to find the couple standing in a big, panelled room with a naked floor and a ceiling as high as a church hall. The panelling had been painted a sickly pale pink, and in its centre squares patches of flowered wallpaper attempted to turn the barnlike bareness into a cosy modern living room and seemed embarrassed by their failure.
'Just look at the proportions!' Sandy was insisting. 'And look at that fireplace. Imagine it with a log fire in it.'
Virginia, the creeping frost of possible change beginning to shrink her like a worm on a path, looked at the looming overmantel on the far wall, the mantelshelf the size of a sideboard and the choked mouth of the chimney, filled with rubble, soot and what looked horribly like a dead pigeon.
'Look at the mess!' said Petra.

'But try to imagine it with the panelling stripped and polished and the cornice picked out with gold. It would look a dream.'

'A nightmare,' said Petra inevitably.

'And velvet curtains with gold cord tiebacks.'

'That would certainly come in handy when I wanted to hang myself.'

'We could have all our friends down for weekends. I can just see a long table down the centre of the room.'

'And all of you under it.'

'Silver on the sideboard.'

'And me cleaning it.'

'We can get help from the village.'

'*What* village?'

'Might even get a couple to live in, there's plenty of room.'

'For God's sake, Sandy, have you gone mad?'

He laughed and put his arms about her, unaware that there was precious little left of the attraction she had once felt for him.

'It's only eighty thousand, isn't that marvellous? We could get four times that for Highgate, we'd be quids in. A mere eighty thousand pounds!'

'I'm not surprised, who'd want it?' She struggled to pull away and he held her tighter. 'Is that why you picked this one? Because it was dirt cheap? I might have known.'

'Now, now, Petra, come along, darling –'

Virginia turned her back on them and stared at the fireplace. It *was* a dead pigeon. She turned again, then backed a few steps, putting the wall behind her. Her eyes still avoiding the embarrassing embrace, she glanced out of the door, then away. She looked up at the ceiling, where frayed wires protruded from the centre moulding, and looked down again quickly. She looked to left, to right, to the windows, to the floor, and always she found she could not hold her gaze, because she had the impression that if she looked one second longer the thing she beheld might suddenly become inconceivably dreadful.

Panic welled up in her and she closed her eyes. I don't want to live here. I can't live here. I'd rather die than live here.

There was a sudden angry outburst and then the sharp,

echoing cracks of feet walking out of the room. She opened her eyes and saw Petra and Sandy crossing the hall and opening the door on the other side. She fled in pursuit, grabbing Petra's arm as they stopped and surveyed another immense, dim room, this one stretching from front to back of the house, with two tall, shuttered windows at each end. Sandy pushed back the front pair and the full light shone pitilessly on to the same pathetic attempts at cosification; dirty, pastel paint, silly patches of wallpaper, a paltry little square of worn, mottled, rubberback carpet adrift like a boat in the centre of the floor. Pinned to the panelling beside the fireplace was a 1979 calendar issued by a firm of tractor manufacturers and far away, down at the other end of the room, was a broken 1950s easy chair, too useless for the last owners to bother to remove.

Virginia held on grimly to Petra while they followed Sandy round the house on a resentful guided tour. He enthused, he raved, he pointed out the potentialities; the lovely big bedrooms, the roomy bathroom with its old-fashioned suite tucked shyly into one corner, the *untouched* basement kitchen with its picturesque range and *original* dresser, the invaluable extra guest space provided by the attics — Oh God, the attics!

The approaching stairs were hidden behind a scarred, painted door on the first floor landing, and the dirty skylight shadowed rather than illuminated them. Then, the narrow corridor, the low, stained ceilings, the uneven floors, the large mouseholes — Oh no, *rat*holes!

'And just look at this, girls!'

Sandy opened the last door in the corridor and revealed a ladder. They climbed up and he shot a bolt. There was a shaft of light, air, then the flat expanse of the sprung, leaking leads, like a ship's deck surrounded by the surging, dark green waves of the trees.

'Now look at that view!'

Hertfordshire spread, swelled, dipped, in a dizzying sea for miles around.

'No,' said Petra.

'I've got the name of a decent local builder from the agent's. Very good firm, they tell me, thoroughly reliable and quite reasonable. I've already had a word with them and they could start almost at once.'

'No.'

'And the bank say they'll give me a bridging loan until the other house is sold. The sooner we get started on it the better. We'll probably need the whole summer to get the outside work done and –'

'No!'

'Now come on, darling –'

'No, no, no!' screamed Petra, stamping her foot. 'No, do you hear me? I am not leaving a comfortable house in London to bury myself in a mausoleum in the sticks!'

'Neither am I!' Virginia shouted, shivering in the centre of the leads. She had refused to follow them to the parapet, although the relinquishing of Petra's warm, human arm had left her with a dreadful sense of isolation. She turned, turned again, as if warding off an approaching danger. The treetops rotated slowly before her eyes, rustling and whispering with secrets too terrible to be told out loud.

'How can I see Daddy if I'm living out here?' she wailed.

Chapter 4

'Daddy?'

'Hello, Ginnie.'

'Daddy, I've been trying to get you for days. Where have you been?'

'Away on business.'

'I want to see you.'

'Of course, darling. On Sunday, as usual.'

'Not on Sunday, now.'

Derek Blackie fidgeted with the piles of paper on his desk and threw an apologetic glance at the man sitting opposite.

'Afraid not, darling. You know it's only supposed to be fortnightly. I'll see you Sunday, all right?'

'But I want to tell you about something. It's terribly important — I just don't know what to do. Please, Daddy!'

The man glanced at his watch, recrossed his legs and looked up at the office ceiling, with the overacted patience of one who wasn't feeling patient at all.

'Sorry, Ginnie, I'm busy just now. Surely it can wait?'

'No, it can't. I *must* see you. How about this evening?'

'I can't manage this evening, I've got an appointment. Can't your mother deal with it?'

'No, I don't think Petra knows what to do, either.'

Derek felt irritated.

'Petra? What do you mean, Petra? She's your mother, not the au pair. Look, I'll try and ring you tonight from a phone box, how's that?'

'No, I can't talk about it at home, Sandy might hear.'

The visitor made a sudden movement which meant that he

38

was a very busy man who wasn't going to waste much more of his valuable time. Derek winced and responded hastily to the hint. He looked quickly through his diary.

'All right, I can meet you for an hour after school on Friday, but for goodness' sake don't tell your mother. It's only a couple of days away.'

She agreed reluctantly.

'In the park at half past four?'

'Yes. Must go now. 'Bye, darling.'

He put the phone down and smiled placatingly.

'Sorry about that. My daughter. The difficult age, you know. Always seem to be in trouble, don't they?'

'Like father, like daughter,' said the man with a mirthless smile. 'Now, Mr. Blackie, about these figures.'

Petra heard the ting of the phone going down as she opened the front door. Virginia, in school hat and coat, was sitting on the floor in the living room, pulling at the frayed edge of the burnt hole in the carpet.

'Hello, had a good day?'

'No, I've had a rotten day,' said Virginia sulkily.

'Well, that makes two of us. Who was that on the phone?'

'It was a wrong number.'

Virginia rose from the floor and went upstairs.

Petra flung her handbag on to the settee and poured herself a vodka and tonic. She was furiously angry, both with Sandy and with that fatuously useless solicitor.

He had been so helpful before; so cunning in the way he had exploited the law for her benefit, manipulating, extorting, standing up for her rights, grinding Derek down with his expertise so that she would end up in full possession of the things she had come to take for granted, things acquired by no initiative on her part save for that single act of carelessness and her impatient endurance of the next ten unsatisfactory years.

It had all been so simple before, why couldn't it be now? Why was the business of grabbing a house so much easier than the business of keeping it? Why should Sandy have his dream and she not be allowed to hang on to hers?

She had been absolutely confident when the interview started.

'I want a mortgage on the house. It's a good property, as you know. My husband is thinking of getting somewhere out in the country, but I don't want to move from Highgate so I thought I'd buy him out.'

'How much does he want for his half?'

She frowned. 'Oh well, he's put a provisional price of three hundred and fifty thousand on it, but I'm sure we could beat him down. About a hundred and fifty, probably.'

'I see,' he wrote the figures down neatly on the pad in front of him, 'and what is your income, Mrs. Matheson?'

'Income? I haven't got an income, I don't work.'

'But you will be getting a job, I presume?'

'Oh – yes.' She suddenly realised that she had never thought about how the mortgage would be paid off and felt unbearably foolish.

He raised his eyebrows and laid down his pen.

'It might be advisable to get that settled first, if you are contemplating a separation.'

'It's not a separation,' Petra said, surprised. 'I just want to take over full ownership of the London house.'

'But you are getting a job?'

'Well – of course.'

'Good, good. But even so, Mrs. Matheson, I'm afraid it might be rather difficult to get a mortgage in your name only. If you and your husband were taking one out jointly it would be a different matter, but for a married woman there is always the possibility of a pregnancy –'

'Oh no there isn't!' said Petra strongly. 'That's completely out of the question.'

He smoothed his balding male head, smiling at the unpredictability of the female condition.

'Well, yes, that may be your intention, but accidents happen, you know, and finance companies aren't in the habit of taking risks against something as uncertain as nature.'

'Haven't they ever heard of birth control?' she asked, amazed. 'You'd think it was a myth.'

'I am afraid, Mrs. Matheson,' he said doubtfully, 'it very often is. I'm rather afraid that you may have to rethink your plans. Why not get your husband to come in and see me, and we'll see what we can do? If he were to guarantee the payments it might be a different matter. In that case there would, of course, be no trouble. I believe he is in quite comfortable circumstances, isn't that so?'

Petra glared angrily at the vodka bottle, then topped up her glass before sitting down. She didn't want a separation. Sandy was all right, fully able to provide her with the comfortable, supported life she liked, still attentive, still competent in bed, when she could forget her irritation at his personal idiosyncracies and allow him to get on with it. He was beginning to bore her a bit, but that was marriage.

It was sickening to be confronted so unexpectedly by your financial impotence. Sandy couldn't force her to sell, the joint names on the deeds made that impossible, but he would almost certainly be able to rustle up the money to buy his ghastly dream house anyway, and that really wasn't a very good idea. He spent freely and so did she, and no matter how much there was coming in from the lucrative world of advertising, there were always the bills. Many people she knew had their comfortable life-style supported by a large overdraft, set hopefully against the security of a regular future income, but she would much rather not be in such a situation. She wasn't used to it.

A mortgage was different, of course, and she *could* find a job, but she'd never actually worked in her life and didn't particularly fancy starting now.

She frowned, looking down at the carpet which had cost fifteen pounds per square yard not long before Derek had given up trying to please her and moved out. It was all his fault, really. If he had been different she would never have needed Sandy, and there would have been no divorce. The remedy for their emotional impasse had been in his own hands, if he had only cared to grasp it. All he would have had to do was to become what she wanted. It wasn't much to ask of the man who had trapped her into marriage, that he should change his character to suit her.

If only she hadn't come down from Peterborough for that weekend at Kate's. If only they hadn't gone to that club and met Derek. If only she had known that a degree from the L.S.E. and cleverness in business matters were not necessarily a guarantee of psychological strength, and recognised that the assertiveness of Derek in courting display was only an act, hiding the wavering, diffident personality underneath. If only she hadn't had too much to drink; if only she hadn't gone back to his grotty little office so that he could show off the business he was starting to build up.

And if only she hadn't, in her alcoholic haze, mistaken his importunity for passion, instead of discovering weeks later, when it was too late, that it had merely been opportunism.

She lit a cigarette and lay back on the settee, wallowing in dissatisfaction. Men were hell; men were useless. Even big, butch Sandy, with his ringing, confident voice and his swaggering extraversion, had turned out to be not much more than a great kid, once you had him to yourself.

Only sixteen, she'd been. Only sixteen! God, it made you sick. It wasn't fair, it just wasn't fair. Her life had been ruined.

She got up and wandered round the room, touching her possessions; the Heal's curtains, the expensive German fitted furniture, the modern painting which she didn't honestly like much, but which Derek had said was such a good investment. It would all be completely useless at Maiden's End — none of it would fit in. Had Sandy thought of that? And why the hell should she give up, not only her house, but also her furniture?

No, she was *not* going to move. There had to be a way out of this.

He was there, waiting. Amazed, Virginia ran down the path, arms flung wide in gratitude.

'Daddy, you're early! Oh, how lovely!'

He got up and kissed her.

'Well, I've taken time off from work, you know, so I hope this is as important as you say.'

'Oh, yes, it is! Daddy, something absolutely dreadful has happened, you must stop it!'

'What is it? Come on, sit down. Tell Daddy.'

She started to sniff ominously.

'Now, now,' he said quickly, 'it can't be that bad.'

'Yes it can,' she said, and burst into luxurious tears.

Derek comforted her for a while but then began to feel anxious, for two very good reasons. First, a passing couple were giving him accusing stares, as if he were a child molester.

He wished Virginia was not so emotional. It had been a plus once, when she was a bright, demonstrative little girl, now it was definitely a minus. Over the last few years that affectionate child had gradually changed into an anxious, clinging waif, given to sudden storms of tears and unreasonable, obsessive demands. It was only to be expected, he supposed. Divorce was always hard on children, and it had been such a noisy, messy, bitter divorce; Petra had made sure of that.

'Now come on, Ginnie, stop crying, dear. How can I help if you won't tell me what's the matter?'

Virginia turned tragic eyes upon him and exploded her terrible bombshell.

'It's Sandy. He wants to move. It's a horrible big house right out in the country, all old and broken-down and I hate it. And if we move out there I may never see you again!'

The extravagant overstatement of her case set her crying again, sobbing so bitterly that the couple looked back over their shoulders, faces dark with renewed suspicion.

'Ginnie,' said Derek hastily, his second anxiety taking the upper hand, 'if you go home looking like that and your mother finds out that you've been with me, you certainly won't ever see me again. You know what happened before. She'll get on to the solicitor and have our meetings stopped. I had to go to court to get them back last time, you know. Please, darling, try to calm down and we'll talk about it quietly.'

'But I won't be able to see you, will I?' she wailed. 'It's miles from anywhere, there's not even a bus near it.'

'Where is it? Amersham, Chigwell, somewhere like that?'

'No, miles further than that. It's near a boring town called Buntingford. It took ages to get there.'

'What, right up in Hertfordshire?'

Derek felt extreme annoyance but, conscious that he couldn't afford to give her emotion full rein, hid it. He controlled his anger and tried to sound positive.

'Well, it might be near the main line. You could come down to King's Cross and I'd meet you. It could be much easier than you think.'

Virginia looked up, alarmed. She had expected that he would be as full of consternation as she was.

'But I don't want to live in the country.'

'Lots of people do, even ones who work in London. I mean, Sandy does, so it can't be that isolated.'

She looked almost disappointed as her tears subsided. It suddenly occurred to him that she might rather enjoy being unhappy, but he pushed the unkind suspicion away with shame.

'How does your mother feel about it?'

'She's furious. She's trying to talk him out of it.'

Derek relaxed thankfully, all worry gone.

'Well, she certainly will, if I know Petra. If you ask me, Ginnie, you're making a mountain out of a molehill. Be honest, it's all just a distant possibility, isn't it? There's nothing definite at all. You'll see, in a week or two it'll all be forgotten and you'll have got yourself into a state about nothing. Aren't I right?'

'I suppose so.'

'Of course I am. Now I really must get back to the office, and you must go home or your mother will wonder where you are. Don't tell her, will you? It's important that you don't, you understand that, don't you?'

'Yes, Daddy.'

'Good girl. See you on Sunday, and we'll see how things are then.'

'All right. 'Bye.'

He watched her walk away towards the gate, head bowed, mopping herself up with the end of her scarf. Good Lord, you'd think Petra would make sure she'd got a handkerchief. Still, she'd never been the motherly type. Guilt nagged at him as he rose from the seat and walked back to the car. The thought of Petra always brought guilt.

He'd always known she didn't love him, but he'd thought it would turn out all right if they worked at it. He had determined that it should, that he would make up to her for being an irresponsible man of twenty-four who had unforgivably put a sixteen-year-old in the club. It was the decent thing to do, to marry her and give the child a name. His parents had brought him up always to do the decent thing, as they invariably did themselves. The shame of his having done something so utterly indecent as to father a child outside wedlock could only be wiped out by his doing the decent thing.

He had put every penny he could raise into a run-down house

in a good district and done it up himself, painting woodwork, stripping doors, sanding floorboards. He had bought her everything she wanted – not always immediately, but as soon as there was the money for it. (Derek was very careful with money, a trait of character which was not always helpful in business, where all expansion is achieved on tick. His parents would have starved rather than live on tick.)

He had tried so hard. His guilt about what he had done to her forced him to greater and greater indulgences with which to win her affection, but she was not to be won. She wore her wrongs like holy stigmata and accepted his offerings without granting the absolution which they were intended to buy. Strangely, he had never blamed her for that, although whatever he did he was aware of reproach, of rejection, of subtle denigration.

And at last, of Sandy. She hadn't bothered to hide the affair, rather held it up before him in triumph as final proof of his failure. Derek, weakened by his guilty conscience, finally capitulated and gave in to Sandy.

What really hurt was that he also had to give him Virginia, except for a few hours each week, and there was always the threat that he might lose even that. No, you couldn't get the better of Petra, she always got what she wanted. Sandy had probably found that out by now. It would all blow over, and he had plenty of other really important things to think about.

Like the account books.

As he got into his car, the last party of the day was being shown out of the enormous iron gates on the other side of the lane. They were talking animatedly to each other, their faces bearing expressions of thrilled, stunned amazement. The old West Cemetery always had that effect on people. The totally unexpected impact of funereal splendour, solemn, overgrown decay, rather gruesome historical anecdote and sheer Victoriana was enough to stimulate the most phlegmatic of men. They went over to examine the chapels with their boarded-up windows, opportunistic hanging-gardens-of-Babylon decoration and carved label – London Cemetery Company.

Rod Singleton, hanging back for a few words with the guide, recognised the small, disconsolate figure turning uphill. Poor kid, she did look low, even worse than when they had exchanged those few words in the park. And wasn't that Derek Blackie getting into that car? Must be Petra Matheson's daughter. He couldn't remember ever seeing her closely before, just an occasional resentful shadow at the top of the stairs when they all crowded into Sandy's house for *après*-pub gatherings. He'd thought she was older than that.

'Look, I'm doing a couple of tours tomorrow and I'd like to show them a newly-cleared area so they can get an idea of the work in hand. Is that feasible, or is it too dangerous? Don't want one of them ending up with a broken ankle.'

'Depends how many there are. Five or six would be all right, but more could be difficult.'

'Right, I'll see when the time comes. Have they found Mrs. Bilston yet?'

'No.'

'O.K. Thanks.'

Rod walked away from that evocative, beautiful ruin which occupied so much of his free time. He was a member of the Cemetery Friends and his voluntary work there included not only weekend guiding but also clearing, labouring and help with paper work, anything which would advance the day when the great necropolis would return to its original condition, a well-tended, respected, peaceful sanctuary for the dead.

He had plenty of time for voluntary work these days. Even a man with a degree had difficulty in finding a suitable job, particularly if it was an arts degree.

Confounded waste of time and money, Rodney. You should have gone into the army like I told you.

He often wondered whether he would ever break free of that nagging, disapproving inner voice.

Virginia was still crying when she got home. She'd tried to stop, she really had, but every time she managed to control herself the memory of Derek's indifference in the face of disaster came into her mind and started her off again. She had pictured the touching scene when she broke it to him so often these last two days; his pained shock, his blind despair, his broken cry of 'Oh no, they can't take you away from me, not my Virginia! Not my little girl!' The reality had been an awful let-down.

Of course, she had known in her heart of hearts that that sort of thing wasn't Derek at all, but the hope that he might have hidden emotional depths had been a seductive one. It was the sort of reaction she had experienced, so why shouldn't he feel it too? Her love for him was so passionate that she had every right to expect equal love in return.

She finally pulled herself together outside the gate and walked in with her head down, but by ill luck Petra was in the hall and noticed her swollen face at once.

'What's the matter?'

'Nothing.'

'Of course it isn't nothing! Tell me, Virginia, what's happened?' Her stomach sank. 'You haven't been bothered by someone, have you? Some man, I mean? Tell me, darling, quick!'

'No, of course I haven't. I just hurt myself.'

'Where?'

'Out in the street.'

'No, where on you? Show me.'

'It doesn't show,' Virginia said desperately. 'A bruise on my arm. It won't have come up yet.'

'Well, at least let me see it.'

'No! Don't fuss, Petra. I'm all right.' She tore herself away and ran up to her room. Petra pulled an exasperated face. That child! One minute she was demanding attention, the next she was brushing it off like an impertinence. You couldn't win.

Virginia ate her dinner in sullen silence and then escaped again. Safely locked in her room, she let herself go completely, wallowing in misery, sobbing into her bedspread until it was soaked. Oh, Daddy, you don't love me enough, Daddy; I love you so much and you don't care at all. And Mummy, you pretend you do, but you don't really, it's just an act. And Sandy, you're horrible and I hate you! You want to take me away from my home and lock me up in a horrible frightening house like a princess in a tower. Nobody loves me, nobody cares about me, I'm all alone.

Virginia had an infinite capacity for self-pity.

At last she was cried out. She tried to continue, but had to recognise that she was now only acting. She raised her face and stared out at the night sky, mulling over her wrongs with the enjoyable masochism of one putting their tongue into an aching tooth.

Some day I'll be loved. Some day I'll get the appreciation I deserve.

She walked slowly to the window, very aware of the tragic expression on her face.

He climbed the ladder, his glowing eyes fixed on her through the smoke. 'I'm here, Virginia! I'll help you. Put your arms around me.'

Comforted, Virginia floated away on the wings of fantasy.

In the next bedroom, a pool of water had started to collect in the centre of Sandy and Petra's bed.

Chapter 5

Sandy Matheson stirred in the bed and came immediately to full consciousness, with the fearless, unquestioning acceptance of the new day which is the privilege of the unimaginative. He stretched out an arm to clasp Petra. She was snuggled down under the quilt, only her black curls showing. He pushed his hand under her protesting form and pulled her against his shoulder, where she settled down again, grumbling, and went back to sleep.

He looked across at the window and saw with pleasure that it was sunny outside. Good, just what he needed. The builder would be able to make a proper examination, inside and out, and the estimate would be in his hands within days.

He would insist that it should be – he was in a hurry. With luck, the house would be ready to move into by the summer, and they would be fully organized and comfortable before the next winter set in.

He felt gloriously happy. His dream come true at last; a desirable period residence in a rural district, admiring friends coming down for weekends, healthy tramps round the grounds in green wellies, really stylish, high-class entertaining.

'Alexander Matheson, Maiden's End, Hankey Green, Buntingford, Herts.' A good name and an impressive address. He could see it printed on his stationery now.

He rose slightly to take the Estate Agent's folder off the bedside table and saw the duvet.

'Oh hell, not again!'

He looked up at the ceiling then sat up fully, dragging his arm from beneath Petra so that she bumped back against the pillows and came to with an annoyed exclamation.

'Petra, it's happened again. Look! Where the hell is it coming from?'

She struggled up and peeped over the edge of the quilt, rubbing her eyes.

'What?'

'The water. All over the bed. It's soaked!'

She pulled a dropped strap up on to her shoulder, regarding the stain with sleepy irritation.

'You must have spilt your drink last night.'

'I didn't bring a drink up here.'

'Well, I certainly didn't do it.' Her feet felt a cold shock.

'Good God, the bed's full of it, it's soaked right through to the mattress!' Angry, she jumped out and pulled back the bedding, throwing the folder on to the floor. He retrieved it quickly and put it on the bedside table. 'You'd better go and look in the roof. The tank's probably leaking.'

'No, it can't be that, there's no stain on the ceiling. Anyway, I've got to get off. The builder's meeting me at the house at eleven.'

'Well, *I'm* not going to go crawling about up in the loft! I'll have enough to do getting this mess dried out before tonight. And I've got my hair appointment at twelve.'

'But aren't you coming?'

'No, I am not coming. One look at that monstrosity was quite enough, thank you. You go and play your games by yourself, I'm not interested.'

Sandy made for the bathroom, giving her a hug on the way.

'You'll love it when it's finished.'

'No I won't.'

'Silly girl,' he said patronisingly, and left her stripping off the electric blanket.

'That's *that* done for,' she said, and flung it in the general direction of the wastepaper basket.

Sandy sang along with the stereo. Marvellous! Real English stuff, the perfect accompaniment to the awakening countryside all around him. The magnificent final chord of Elgar's First Symphony swelled through the car as it turned in obedience to the fingerpost.

He switched off the tape deck and drove across the exposed track, seeing the red and white paint of the builder's van bleeding through the dark mass of trees ahead. As he brought the Volvo to a smooth halt beside it, a square, red-faced man in a woolly hat and an imitation sheepskin coat came round the side of the house, carrying a pencil, a notepad and a flat, leather- covered drum of steel tape.

'Mr. Hargreaves?'

'That's right.'

'Matheson.' Sandy's hand shot out of his genuine sheepskin sleeve and shook Hargreaves' pudgy, broken-nailed mitt. 'Well, what do you think? Got immense potential, hasn't it?'

'Needs a fair bit of repointing,' said Hargreaves doubtfully, 'and there's some rising damp round the back. And I don't like the look of that coping, the brickwork's rotten. Up there, see? And I reckon you're going to need a few new window frames. How much were you thinking of spending?'

Sandy waved his hand expansively.

'Whatever it needs, old chap. Just put it all down and we'll discuss the price later. Have you finished examining the outside? Had a good look?'

'Yes,' said Hargreaves gloomily.

'Splendid. Come inside, then. I know exactly what I want, so you just tell me how we set about it.'

Hargreaves followed Sandy into the hall, noting the crumbled limestone round the door. He looked at the skirting.

'Rats,' he said. 'They had rats in a place I did over at Standon. Filthy mess.'

'Now this room,' said Sandy, striding into the dining room, 'I want completely stripped. All the paint and wallpaper off, right down to the natural wood, then sealed and varnished.'

Mr. Hargreaves tapped the nearest panel.

'You get a lot of rot hiding under panelling. Did one like this a few months ago at Westmill. When we started scraping, the wood folded up like paper.'

He walked over to the fireplace and studied the rubble. 'Flue could do with relining.' He started to write.

Sandy stamped on the floorboards.

'This floor seems to be O.K. I think we'll just sand it down and seal that as well. I like a polished floor. I saw one at a client's house in Surrey recently; absolutely beautiful. These old houses are a joy, aren't they? Good materials, good workmanship, solid as a rock.'

Mr. Hargreaves went over to a suspicious dip under the window and did his own bit of stamping, then scribbled busily.

'Same in the drawing room,' said Sandy, leading the way across the hall.

Mr. Hargreaves followed him around the house, with more interest than Petra and Virginia but little more enthusiasm, except for the tide of expense rising inexorably upon the pad.

Sandy flung open the bathroom door.

'This will need a new suite, of course, plus shower. And I'd like the loo partitioned off, in fact, a separate room with its own wash basin, if you can manage it. There's a little dressing room next to the master bedroom which could be made into another bathroom *en suite.*'

'Wrong side of the house. We'd have to bring a whole new pipe off your mains.'

'There's no mains at the moment – pipe's broken. The Water Board are looking at it next week. It's sealed off over near Hankey Green.'

Mr. Hargreaves gave an intake of breath.

'Electricity?' he asked, looking up at the dangling light bulb and across at the brass switch by the door which looked not later than 1920.

'Having it completely rewired. Electrician's coming about midday.'

'Who you having?'

'Carter's of Buntingford.'

'Ah!'

'All right, are they?' Sandy asked with slight apprehension.

'Oh yes, fine,' said Hargreaves, whose hesitation had been personal, not professional. 'Bit messy, but they'll do a safe job. Still, you're not going to be bothered about mess, are you? Don't suppose you'll be moving in for a good while.'

'Well, I thought during the summer.'

Mr. Hargreaves sucked a sibilant hiss of doubt through his teeth and shook his head.

'I don't know about that, Mr. Matheson. You see, we don't know what we're going to find when we start pulling the place apart. Could be dry rot, woodworm, anything. We did a place over at Stocking Pelham a couple of years back which looked a walk-over until we started, but it turned out to need a whole new roof – the rafters were riddled with beetle.'

'Oh well, no trouble like that here, the roof's flat.'

Mr. Hargreaves hissed sharply again, as if he had stubbed his toe. He followed Sandy up the ladder and out on to the leads, where he ignored the magnificent view and kicked destructively at the erupting grey flaps.

'There's your main trouble. You've got the rain going straight through into your attics, where that fallen plaster is, and it's probably gone down into the floor beneath. What you're going to need is the whole of your leads stripped off and new ones laid. Do you know what lead costs now? It's a wonder all this lot hasn't been nicked, but I reckon no-one knew this place was here. Of course, you could have asphalt instead – be cheaper?'

'Anything, anything,' said Sandy cheerfully. 'I told you, money's no problem. I fully realise this is going to be a costly job. I'm not going into this with my eyes closed, you know.'

Mr. Hargreaves rather doubted that, but scribbled obediently. More money than sense, some people. Still, it was his business, there was no accounting for tastes. He followed Sandy down through the house, potential trouble meeting his professional eye at every turn. By the time they got to the basement the pencil was worn right down. He took a sharpener in the shape of a vintage car out of his pocket and prepared for more writing on the wall.

'Now the kitchen I want restored as nearly as possible to its original state. I don't want to spoil it – all I want is a genuine, unpretentious country kitchen.'

'You going to cook on that thing?' asked Mr. Hargreaves, staring with incredulity at the iron range.

'Why not?'

'I prefer electricity, meself.'

Sandy laughed and slapped the top of the range affectionately. The rust came off on his hand and he looked at it, disconcerted, then drew out his handkerchief and cleaned up.

'Solid fuel was used for centuries, Mr. Hargreaves. If it was good enough then, I don't see why it shouldn't be good enough now.'

Mr. Hargreaves tried to picture the unfortunate woman who was going to have to use the thing. Probably one of those back-to-nature types, all rush matting, herb gardens and bake-your-own-wholemeal-bread. He'd done a conversion job for a woman like that over at Baldock, and she'd been daft enough to want the cushioned vinyl taken out of the kitchen so that she could walk on a freezing Victorian tiled floor laid straight onto the earth. There was no accounting for tastes.

As Sandy showed him out, Kevin Carter's van pulled up and the handsome young electrician got out. Hargreaves greeted him distantly, then, pulled into irresistible intimacy by the ties of trade, raised an expressive eyebrow and put his thumb down, unnoticed by Sandy.

'Ah, Mr. Carter, how do you do? Lovely old place, this, isn't it? I want a complete rewire and plenty of double plugs. I know exactly what I want, so you just write it down and tell me the damage. Goodbye, Mr. Hargreaves. Let me have the estimate by the middle of next week, won't you?'

Hargreaves looked up at the broken fanlight above the door. There'd been one of those when they did that cottage over at Benington — the bars crumbled as soon as they tried to put the glass in. The price of the new one had been astronomical.

His pencil jabbed away at the notebook, then he went round the back to take another look at the rising damp. Its rise had been so spectacularly successful that it had already achieved the level of the staircase window.

No, there was definitely no accounting for tastes.

Sandy walked into the house in Highgate as the grandfather clock struck seven. From the kitchen came the idiot babble of Radio One, Petra's constant companion as she went about her household chores. He went into the living room and picked up the telephone, dialled, then stood humming the Big Tune from Sibelius Two, which had accompanied him most of the way back from Hertfordshire.

'Hello? Philip?'

He waited, smiling mouth open, for confirmation. It came.

'Sandy Matheson here, Philip,' he stated, in the triumphant

tone of one announcing profits up by a hundred per cent and a bonus. 'Sorry to ring you at home, old man, but I couldn't get back to the office in time to do it yesterday. Big promotion down at Milton Keynes for Taggart's. What's the news on the loan?'

He listened intently, picked up a cigarette from the box on the table and lit it with a table Ronson which had all the panache of a sports trophy.

'No, it won't be for long, say three months at the most. My agent's got a buyer in mind already. No, no mortgage. Yes. No, no problem there. No, she's quite keen really. A bit doubtful about the condition of the place, but that's only lack of imagination, you know what women are like. If there're a couple of doorknobs off, they think they're moving into a slum.' He laughed loudly. 'What? Oh God, yes, marvellous investment, could be a half a million job when I've got it as I want it. Sort of thing an Arab would give his chief wife for. Well, that's great, Philip. I'll be in touch early next week. Get it moving for me, will you? Great! You and Caroline must come round for dinner again before we go – haven't seen your lovely wife for yonks. Right. *Ciao*, Philip.'

He put the phone down and made for the drinks, humming Sibelius again. 'Ta ta ta, Ta ta ta, *Tum* te Ta!'

Petra came in, dressed up to the nines in the full fashionable palette of cerise, jade green, royal blue and black, and with diamanté earrings gleaming through her hair.

'Well, has it fallen down yet?'

He laughed, generously spilling his pleasure on to her, despite her sulks. 'No, my sweet, and it isn't going to. The builder was quite impressed. He's got it all down in black and white and we'll know the damage next week. The loan's O.K., too. I've just been on to Philip Collingwood. It's all moving, Petra, everything's absolutely hunky-dory!'

'What a stupid expression,' said Petra. 'Nobody says that now. Did you learn it from an American film in a fleapit in downtown Bucharest?'

'Budapest!' said Sandy sharply, before he remembered himself.

Petra grinned. It never failed. Sandy normally swanned along like a self-satisfied bulldozer, flattening everything and everybody in his path as if they didn't exist, but a snide reference to his origins always got him on the raw.

Eastern Europe is no place for incipient entrepreneurs, with a drive towards free enterprise. Sandy had lived his early youth in a state of repressed frustration, seeing no remote possibility of ever fulfilling the talent for making money which he knew lay within him. He was not alone in his loathing of the system under which he and his countrymen lived, but he had no idealistic dreams about building a new, free society in Hungary's green and pleasant land. He just wanted out. When the chance did come, even as his contemporaries were flinging their courageous defiance at the invading Russian tanks, Sandy was making a daring escape across the border to Austria, hotfoot for the decadent West.

His real name was Sandor. The diminutive had been given him by his first English acquaintances, not as a token of intimacy but for more patronising reasons, a xenophobic putting-him-in-his-place as an outsider with funny ways and a funny accent.

There are two paths open to the immigrant. Either he can cling to his identity and become a professional foreigner, squeezing the last bit of exotic charm out of the fact that he sticks out like a sore thumb, or he can take on the protective colouring of his surroundings, ruthlessly destroying every clue to his background and becoming more native than the natives.

Sandy had decided on the second option. His musical ear made the learning of a new language easy, and his accent had, within a remarkably few years, become impeccable. He was also a born actor and he had learnt his part to perfection, copying the models around him in every particular, from vocabulary, life-style, opinions and habits down to the correct number of buttons on his Savile Row sleeves.

Tucked away in his wardrobe was a library of reference books, gradually acquired. *U and Non-U, The English Gentleman*, even *Class* and *The Sloane Ranger's Handbook*. No-one had ever seen them, not even Petra, for they were locked in an old briefcase and the key never left his keyring, but they had been regularly consulted and Sandy now knew exactly what he was doing in every department of his public and private English life. In consequence he had become a raging success in both. Even the inevitable setbacks had been only temporary, because he possessed the ability to discount them and carry on with confidence undiminished. Marriage had come late, after an extended, man-about-town, bachelor spectacular, but he had no regrets about it. He had never regretted anything he had done. Regrets were for the weak and unsure, for people who stopped and looked at themselves, who tried to put themselves in the other man's shoes.

'You'd better get changed,' said Petra.

'Changed?'

'Yes, we're going to Marjorie's party, don't you remember?'

'Lord, yes, it'd slipped my mind. What's she celebrating this time?'

'Her decree's come through.'

'Oh, jolly good. How about Virginia? She won't mind being left alone, will she?'

'Of course she won't.'

'Where is she?'

'Up in her room. Isn't she always?' said Petra crossly. 'You'd thing we'd got Aids or something.'

Sandy looked shocked.

'Oh, for God's sake, Petra, don't be so tasteless. Remember poor Trevor.'

'Oh Lord, yes, I forgot. Sorry. Still, it's his own fault, shouldn't put himself about so much.'

Sandy frowned and finished his drink, unpleasantly sobering thoughts disturbing his complacency.

'I managed to dry out that mattress, but the electric blanket was ruined. I had to buy another. For goodness' sake be more careful tonight, you're bound to be stoned out of your mind when we get home. Now do hurry up, we don't want to have to park out on the Heath.'

They left just before eight. Virginia was summoned from her retreat to hear Petra's last-minute instructions. She stood halfway down the stairs, kicking at the banisters and shrugging off the homily.

'Now get yourself a proper meal, won't you? There's plenty of stuff in the fridge. And don't stay up half the night, you're looking really washed-out these days. And just look at your hair!'

She pushed impatiently at the straggling locks.

'Why don't you take an interest in your appearance, Virginia? It's not as if you hadn't got nice clothes to wear. Do make an effort!'

'What for? I never go anywhere interesting.'

'Well, of course you don't, the way you look. No-one's going to ask you out looking like that. Why not ring Angela and ask her round?'

'She's going out with Wayne.'

'Come along, Petra,' said Sandy, 'I thought you didn't want to be late?'

'Goodbye, darling.' Petra's lipsticked mouth kissed half an inch away from her cheek. 'And remember, bed by eleven.'

'Well, don't wake me up again at two,' Virginia shouted as the door slammed.

She slouched into the kitchen and opened the fridge, surveying its generous but uncooked plentitude without interest. She wasn't hungry; she'd been stuffing crisps and sweets all afternoon. She shut the door and turned to the biscuit tin. There were two Penguins among the plainer sorts. She took them out, left the tin open and went into the living room, switching on the television. A manic idiot with a sequinned dinner jacket and carefully-styled hair told her a few blue jokes which had the studio audience screaming with shocked delight but which left her cold. She clicked the switch in her hand. Wildlife. 'The jackdaw starts courting his mate the year before he becomes fully mature, and they will remain faithful, devoted and attentively affectionate for the whole of their lives.' Lucky old them. Click. Golf. Click. Men in orange life-jackets drove their paddles into swirling masses of white water; 'The canoeists are in the pink of condition, every one with his heart set on this prestigious prize — ' Click.

The folder was lying on the coffee table. She opened it and recognised the picture with a lurch of revulsion. It was a clever photograph, done on a brilliantly sunny day, just far enough away from the house to give an impression of period charm without revealing its condition. The shutters were open and the house was fully awake.

'An impressive period property with excellent potential for conversion into a desirable gentleman's residence, standing in

two acres of grounds offering privacy and seclusion. Within easy drive of main line into King's Cross. A wealth of period features, including original panelling and charming old-world kitchen. Enjoying magnificent views across surrounding countryside. In need of some modernisation.'

Her despair welled up. I don't want to go; I hate it, it's a horrible house. Why can't I stay here with my nice room and my friends and my Daddy? Daddy! Daddy! I want my Daddy!

She rushed for the phone. He was in.

'Daddy!'

There was an imperceptible pause, then Derek's weary voice said, 'Hello, Ginnie.'

'Daddy, you're home! Can I come and see you?'

'Er, no, darling, I'm afraid not. I've had a pretty tough week and I'm going to turn in early.'

'But it's only eight o'clock. I can come over at once. I'll get a bus, it won't take more than half an hour.'

Derek groaned inwardly.

'No, darling. Look, I've got a bit of a cold and I don't want to give it to you – '

'I don't mind, I think I've got one already. Listen – ' She snuffled into the receiver, making her voice sound thick.

'Well, then, it's silly to come out, isn't it? You get yourself up to bed with some aspirins and a hot drink. Ask your mother to bring you one up.'

'But I'm alone,' she whined, 'they've gone to a party. I'm all on my own, Daddy.'

'Sorry, darling, the doorbell's just rung. Have to go, I'm afraid. Look after that cold. See you tomorrow. 'Bye.'

Virginia slammed down the receiver and burst into tears, kicking angrily at the furniture. She ran upstairs and shut herself into her room, turning on the radio at full volume so that she could cry as noisily as she liked without provoking unwanted investigation from nosy, well-meaning Mrs. Goodison next door. She needn't have bothered. The Goodisons had gone to the theatre, the children were asleep and the au pair was on the floor in the lounge with a devastatingly attractive Swede she had picked up at Berlitz.

Eventually, Virginia crawled into bed, fully clothed. She opened the second Penguin and munched it from one end to the other, wiped her chocolatey fingers on the quilt cover, then closed her eyes and switched on her lovely daydream.

Once again the fireman climbed through the window into her room, where she stood trembling amidst the wreathing smoke.

'It's all right, lady, you're safe now. Just put your arms around me.'

She looked up into his eyes as he swept her off her feet, and felt his strong muscles tensing under his uniform. Half-fainting, she lay back against his shoulder and allowed herself to be carried down the ladder, her pale cheek pressed to the hard, shining buttons on his tunic.

Of course, she knew that it would more probably have been a case of the fireman's lift, but the picture of herself slung across his shoulder like a sack, with her bottom in close proximity to his left ear, was so unappealing that she had discarded authenticity in the interests of romance.

Above, the first flames shot out of the window and she murmured pathetically into his ear, 'My parents! Save my parents! They're in the front bedroom!'

He drew in his breath.

'God! Poor devils! It's too late, I'm afraid. The front of the house is a raging inferno.'

She gave a tragic moan of despair and fell into a deep faint at his feet, though not before a satisfying picture of a screaming, dying Petra and Sandy had flashed before her mind's eye.

The fire chief hurried up as the young man knelt down and gathered her into his arms.

'The poor child! Who'll look after her now?'

'I will,' he said. 'I will.'

Sandy made another stab at the keyhole. Petra, who had had to drive home, snatched the key from his hand and allowed him to stagger into the hall. She stopped short, sniffing.

'Smoke! My God, it's smoke!'

She shut the door quickly, sober enough to remember that draughts could send smoke flaring up into flame. Sandy pulled himself round with the automatic pilot of the real pro.

'It's coming from upstairs.'

'Virginia! Oh God, Virginia darling!'

But it was not in Virginia's room. She was peacefully asleep, quite unaware of the flames which were creeping across Petra and Sandy's bed.

Chapter 6

Sandy put the phone down and sat back with a satisfied smile. Marvellous what a really nifty solicitor could do if you leant on him. Still, Sillitoe knew better than to treat him like just another client — there was too much valuable work to be had from Matheson Hummerstone Vickers Goate. You didn't mess *them* about, least of all Matheson.

He pressed the button on the intercom.

'Yah, Sandy?'

'Send Mr. Taggart in, will you, Sarah?'

'Yah. Will do.'

He rose from behind the black glass top of the desk and held out his hand, introducing it carefully between the Anglepoise and the potted palm.

'Hello, Mr. Taggart, great to see you. Well, I hope you were quite satisfield with the launch. I thought it went absolutely marvellously, myself; absolutely bloody marvellous. *Ideal Home* should do a very useful piece on your product, and the Sunday supplements will be running a full-page ad.'

'Yes. Good,' said Mr. Taggart, easing his fat, untrendy form into the squashy leather cushions and sinking inches below the level of Sandy's alert, upright, black swing chair, which was precisely the position in which Sandy liked business contacts to be. Sandy looked down at him, beaming, and opened a shining black box.

'Cigarette?'

'Thanks.'

'Light?'

'Ah! Yes, thanks.' Mr. Taggart stopped struggling to extrude the lighter from his condensed trouser pocket and accepted the proffered spurt of Design Centre-approved flame, which sat awaiting the call of duty upon Sandy's desk.

'Now you've given final approval on the commercials, haven't you? We're putting them out on Channel Four. We thought that was definitely the appropriate marketplace, a more selective, exclusive audience, you know.'

Mr. Taggart looked doubtful.

'It doesn't have very high viewing figures, does it?'

'Well, not as high as ITV, no, but we're not going for the masses, are we, more the upmarket field. I don't think your average council house owner is likely to buy an electric cocktail shaker. No, what we want is the executive type, the Home Counties, ambitious upwardly-mobile with an interest in gracious living.'

'Yes —'

Mr. Taggart flicked his ash in the general direction of the ashtray on the desk, which was slightly too high up to allow the action either comfort or accuracy.

'What time will it be going out?'

'Oh, prime time. A little pricey, of course, but you said you wanted a real hard sell, didn't you?' Mr. Taggart looked alarmed. 'Or perhaps I misunderstood you when you came to that conference? We had to push pretty hard to get the slot, but if you're getting cold feet —'

'No, no,' said Mr. Taggart hastily, 'I'm sure you know what you're doing. What programmes will it be slotted into?'

'To start with, first showing halfway through the seven o'clock news. Another at eight thirty, during a documentary about Nicaragua, then a final burst at ten, just before the big film.'

'What is it?'

'A very prestigious Italian classic about a Neapolitan prostitute under the protection of the Mafia.'

'Oh. Do you think our potetntial customers will be staying tuned for that?'

Mr. Taggart thought that he certainly wouldn't. He'd be switching over for *News at Ten,* or already absorbed in the film on BBC 1.

'Oh, I *think* so, don't you? I mean, the sort of person we're targetting is really into the basic realities, a sophisticated, totally aware, socially-conscious man with an eye to what is going on in the real world. I've got the programme schedules for the other three channels that night, and all that's on offer as an alternative at the relevant times is a sitcom called *Pigs in Muck,* a game show called *Blow your Top,* an *Arena* on modern ballet and yet another showing of *The Sound of Music.* Hardly irresistible options.'

'No.' Mr. Taggart quite liked game shows, and Mrs. Taggart would certainly insist on seeing *The Sound of Music* for what was probably the sixth time. 'I can't help feeling that, even so, we might lose quite a few viewers – to the ballet, for instance. Ballet is quite a strong interest for a lot of – er – upwardly-mobile people.'

'Not modern ballet, Mr. Taggart. It's not *Swan Lake,* or something pretty like that. I mean, one doesn't go much for bony, semi-nude dancers hurling themselves around in an attempt to portray the class struggle, does one, or perhaps I'm wrong?'

He waited, the willing, ready-to-be-corrected smile drilling like a laser across the desk at his client, while irritation started to niggle at his inner psyche. Why the hell did he have to deal with these geriatrics? He normally dealt with Taggart's son, who fully understood his motivation, and he was open to new, creative concepts, not stuck in a world where the acme of good advertising was a cute cartoon character like the Bisto Kids.

'*The Sound of Music* is quite a competitor, though. I mean, if the choice lay with me, I must admit I'd go for Julie Andrews; charming woman. That film's a real crowdpuller.'

Sandy smiled artificially and lit a cigarette.

'Well, Mr. Taggart, you could be right, but until the powers-that-be come to their senses and instruct the BBC to accept advertising, I'm afraid we can't fight that one. Pity, but there it is. What you must understand is that this is a totally new departure for you. It's all very well advertising toasters and electric kettles and electric blankets on the proles' channel, but this product is designed to appeal to a totally different market.'

'Perhaps we should have stuck with the basic family lines,' said Mr. Taggart uncomfortably. 'I'm not altogether happy with this one, I must admit. I mean, cocktails went out years ago, didn't they?'

'But they're in again, didn't you know? Haven't you noticed all those fun pubs springing up everywhere? It's the in thing, cocktail bars.'

'Oh really? It wasn't my decision, actually. Alistair thought it up. I much prefer the tried, mass-market ranges. I mean, we've sold thousands of our see-through kettles and Happy Cook Foodmixers. And the Cosibed electric blankets are a constant sale. That was a very nice commercial you did for us over Christmas, by the way – Mrs. Claus tucking Santa up with one in his sleigh. Very imaginative idea, I thought.'

'Yes, well, we like to fit the image to the product,' said Sandy. Stupid old buffer, you just loved those darling little Scottish gnomes, didn't you, although Trevor practically threw up when he was drawing them. Oh God, Trevor! An unpleasant wave of distress surged up and left a stranded highwater mark of irritation.

'Yes, I'm glad you liked that, Mr. Taggart. By the way, I *don't* know whether I ought to mention it – after all, I am committed totally to your products, you know that – but my wife purchased one of your blankets last week and I'm afraid it turned out to be faulty; practically incinerated our nuptial couch, in fact. We got a replacement, but even so I must admit to being just a teensy bit apprehensive about it, even now.'

Mr Taggart was horrified. 'Good Lord! I'm terribly sorry, Mr. Matheson.'

'Sandy, please.'

'Of course – er – Sandy. Did the retailer examine it? We've never had trouble like that before. Although, come to think of it, we did have a little hiccup with the Byo-Rithmic Massager, but then that was one of Alistair's ideas as well, and I must say I was deeply disturbed when I found it was being stocked by Sylvia Spring's sex shops. . . . It appeared that shocks were being applied along with the soothing, deep-muscle massage, but we sorted it out. One of the girls on the assembly line just wasn't up to the job; her wiring was nowhere near the standard we require –'

Mr. Taggart was now on the defensive, a situation with which Sandy was completely happy. He laughed and waved his hand in confident elimination of all doubts about the reliability of Taggart's Electrical Products.

'No, no, don't worry about it. Just a chance in a million, I'm sure. Just thought I'd mention it.'

' *So* sorry, Mr. Matheson – I mean Sandy. Oh dear, what a pity. Look, I'll reimburse you for your loss. How much was it?'

'Oh no, no – well, it was, let me see, and then there was the new mattress – '

Mr. Taggart went for his wallet. Sandy watched his embarrassed fluster, smiling.

'No, no, Mr. Taggart, it's all covered by the house insurance.'

'Well, if you're sure – '

'And I take it you're quite happy about the arrangements for the commercial, now that we've talked it through?'

'Oh yes, yes. Absolutely. I'll leave it entirely in your hands.'

'Jolly good, George,' said Sandy.

' – absolutely no improvement at all, dear, and you did promise me faithfully to try harder. And you didn't even bother to do your homework last weekend, did you? A whole day late handing in your essay, and even then it was only two pages long and very, very badly written. It's such a sin to waste these precious years, you'll never get the chance to lay up educational treasures again. Do you remember what St. Paul said in his letter to – '

Oh no, not St. Paul! Don't let her start on about St. Paul again. Stop her quick. Say something.

'I couldn't do it on Sunday, Miss Hibbert, I had to go and see my father.'

'Well yes, dear, that's all very well, but he wants you to pass your exams, too, and I'm sure he would have understood if you had told him how important it was. After all, St. Paul tells us that – '

It was a lie; she hadn't seen him. His cold was too bad for him to come out; in fact it felt like this 'flu which was going around, and he'd got to be fit for work next day. 'Perhaps next week, darling. I'll have a word with your mother and arrange it. She really can't object to that.'

'But I wanted to talk about the move, Daddy. I'm sure Sandy means it, he's been down there again and taken a builder with him.'

'Yes, but these things take months to settle, and nothing's definite until the contracts are exchanged. It could fall through at any time. A week certainly isn't going to make any difference, and I promise we'll talk about it then.'

'I don't want to wait a whole week. I want to see you now!' pleaded Virginia.

Derek closed his eyes, longing for the solace of his bed.

'I can't, darling, I really am feeling ill. Look, put Petra on and we'll arrange about next weekend.'

'She's not up yet. They went to a party last night and got back late and had to sleep in the spare room, because their bed caught fire.'

'There's passion for you,' said Derek bitterly.

'What?'

'Never mind. Is she still against the move?'

'Yes, but Sandy isn't taking any notice.'

'He will, he'll have to. He won't be able to stand up to Petra. I'll ring her later. See you next week.'

Miss Hibbert droned on, the bespectacled eyes in her round, earnest face shining with missionary light beneath her heavenly crown of plaited, grey hair.

'Now you've got all the holidays to catch up, Virginia, and I'm sure you're not going to let me down this time. It's Easter, the time of new life and new hope, and I want you to think of yourself as a lovely spring flower, pushing up out of the dull, cold earth towards the sun. Open your buds and bloom, dear, show us all how beautiful you can be. You can do it, I know you can.'

'Yes, Miss Hibbert.'

Angela met her in the cloakroom.

'Was she cross?'

'No, it was just the usual emotional blackmail.'

'Evil, isn't it? All that making you feel guilty. Really screws you up. Just our luck to be taught by a Plymouth Sister. Anyway, cheer up, term's over, we're free. I'm going to lie in all tomorrow. What are you doing over Easter?'

'Nothing, really, except Sandy wants us to go down to the

house again,' said Virginia with sullen resentment. 'Oh, Angela, I don't want to go. It's awful there. Like the House of Usher. Honestly, it's really scary.'

Angela's eyes widened. 'Gosh, it sounds absolutely foul!' Prurient interest stirred in her susceptible soul. 'I suppose I couldn't come too, could I?'

'Oh yes! Oh please,' Virginia exclaimed with gratitude. 'I wouldn't be half so afraid if you were there. Are you sure you don't mind?'

'Not a bit,' said Angela cheerfully, 'in fact I'd love to see it. It could be really exciting if it's as doomy as you say. We might even see a ghost.'

'Don't!' said Virginia, her stomach giving a sickening lurch. 'Oh, you are horrible, you've made me feel worse than ever now. Oh, Angela, you beast!' she shouted, as Angela went off into delighted giggles. 'It's not funny! You're not going to have to live there. You're horrible! I hate you!'

Angela subsided, repentant.

'Sorry, Virge, I was only joking, honest. You do lose your cool quickly these days, don't you? Anyway, all empty houses look doomy, specially if they've been for a long time. Once it's been done up and furnished it could be really nice. You know how good your mother's taste is, much better than mine's. Our flat's like the home life of Queen Victoria.'

'She won't have anything to do with it. She says that she's going to stay in London, no matter what. Sandy just laughs and takes no notice, as if she didn't really mean it, but she does. He doesn't care a bit about how she feels. I think he's the most selfish, insensitive person I've ever met.'

'Mm,' agreed Angela, but with a speculative gleam in her eye. 'Do you think they're breaking up, then? Is she going to leave him?'

'I don't know – I suppose they could be, but I don't see how Mummy could keep herself on her own.'

'Can't she get a job?'

'I don't think she can do anything,' Virginia admitted. 'She never has. She married straight out of school at the same age I am now. She was desperately in love with Daddy,' she added proudly, 'and just gave up everything for love. It's quite tragic being a woman, isn't it?'

'I'll say it is,' said Angela, 'I've been doubled up the last couple of days. Do you get bad periods?'

'No,' said Virginia, 'I'm lucky. No trouble at all.'

She made her usual telephone call on Sunday morning. Derek clung on to the table and eased his aching body down into a chair.

'Oh, darling, I'm sorry, no. I've been feeling like hell all week, and I must stay in bed today. I'm as weak as a kitten.'

'Oh, poor Daddy! I'll come round and look after you.'

'No, you might catch it. As soon as I'm well again I'll let you know.'

'But we're going down to the house again on Good Friday. It really is going to happen, I'm sure. Oh please, Daddy, can't you do something quickly?'

'Ginnie,' groaned Derek, 'at the moment it's as much as I can do to walk. Please, do be patient. I'll do something next week, I promise. Now I must get back to bed. Goodbye, darling.'

'Goodbye, Daddy. Get well soon.'

The longed-for day suddenly yawned with emptiness. She couldn't even cry this time. The estate agent's brochure was on the table and she flung it across the room, then sat on the floor by the telephone, another dreary, endless, frustrating week stretching away before her into eternity. At last, when the first sounds of movement thudded in the room above, she went and put on her coat and let herself out of the front door.

In a cloud of angry disappointment, Virginia walked down Swain's Lane to the cemetery.

Petra found the folder on the floor when she came down. Sandy followed her in as she was throwing it into the wastepaper basket.

'That's right, sweetie, shan't be needing that again.'

She gave a gasp of delighted relief. She *knew* he'd come round.

'I should think not,' she said triumphantly. 'Oh Sandy, I'm so pleased. I knew you'd come to your senses.'

She went over and hugged him as he sat down and opened the paper.

'We've exchanged contracts.'

Petra stiffened, aghast.

'You can't have done! Not already!'

'It's been in the solicitor's hands for weeks. I've just been waiting for the loan.'

'You mean you've been doing it all behind my back? You never told me a thing about it until it was practically settled? That's unforgivable, Sandy!'

'Oh come on, darling, don't get in such a state. I wanted to surprise you – '

'Surprise me! *Surprise* me!'

'Now calm down, Petra,' he said easily. 'When it's all done up you're going to love it. The builders will be starting tomorrow.'

'Oh, don't be such a liar, you only saw him a week ago. No builder starts that quickly.'

'I gave Hargreaves an advance payment as soon as the money came through. Money talks, Petra. He's promised me that they'll go flat out – they're even working on Easter Friday and Saturday, though it'll mean double time, of course. Still, mustn't spoil the ship for a ha'porth of tar. Now, how about some coffee?'

'Get your bloody coffee yourself!' screamed Petra.

Angela sat in the back of the car with Virginia, studying the shape of Sandy's golden hair. It was the sort of result which might be expected if a lion took his mane to Crimpers. He had been more than pleased to add her to the party and have another admiring audience for his new possession, particularly such a pretty one. Angela had, as usual, played upon her youthful charms for all they were worth, and he had seemed most satisfactorily dazzled.

Petra was there under extreme sufferance, but this time with the hopeful expectation that the whole thing might be about to fall through, despite exchanged contracts, and anxious to see the confirmation of her hopes. Something already had fallen through – one of Mr. Hargreaves' men, to be specific, descending from the attic into the bathroom without using the detour of the stairs. As Mr. Hargreaves had gloomily predicted, you never knew what you were going to find and they had found wet rot.

Angela gave a gasp as they left the open, sprouting fields and moved into the trees.

'Gosh! It's enormous!'

The other passengers reacted to her impressed exclamation in characteristic ways. Sandy preened, Petra sniffed, Virginia felt a stab of betrayal. Angela was supposed to be on her side.

'It's ghastly,' she said in a loud, contemptuous voice, trying to hide the fact that she was already afraid.

The house met them with a silent howl of agony, its mouth and eyes open wide. Its window frames had been removed, the broken section of its parapet taken down, its drainpipes stripped ruthlessly away. Its diseased bowels had been torn out and lay in heaps on the open space before the door, now no longer a green, overgrown nature reserve, but a desert of sand, hardcore, plaster, bricks and broken floorboards. A cement mixer churned away all on its own, ladders besieged the walls, workmen crawled across the roof and leaned out of windows with destructive tools in their hands, and a group of busy warlocks tended the great, steaming cauldron of stinking asphalt by the steps.

The banging and shouting of men at work was all around as they entered. Mr. Hargreaves came hurrying towards them, his overalls covered in plaster dust.

'Ah, there you are, Mr. Matheson. Well, we've found a right shambles up in your attic, like I warned you. Your floor is a write-off, we'll have to cut out your joists and put in new ones, and there's a nasty patch of damp creeping up your wall. And I don't know how you feel about it, but it seems to me we're going to have to strip out the whole of your piping and put in copper. That lead in your rising main is in a pretty dodgy state and I don't like the look of your septic tank — it's leaking. I reckon you're going to need a new one, a fibre-glass job, and the manhole cover over your drain was so rusty it broke when we levered it up —'

Sandy strode forward over his warnings, as confident as a man in seven-league boots crossing a minefield.

'That's all right, Mr. Hargreaves, you carry on, just put it all down.'

'I'd like you to take a look up here first —'

Petra followed them as they ascended, listening to the catalogue of disaster with exultation.

Angela danced into the dining room.

'Gosh! What a huge room! It's like a stately home!'

Virginia followed reluctantly. Three men were flaying the walls, attacking the panelling brutally with hot air and scrapers. She stopped and looked around warily, tasting the atmosphere for that strange feeling. It was there. The room was imbued with the healthy presence of modern young men, but it was still there all right.

'Hello,' said Angela to the nearest worker, 'isn't this a fabulous place?'

He looked at her with appreciation.

'Yeah, it's all right, I suppose. You going to live here, are you?'

'No, worse luck. My friend is, though. Gosh, Virge, you didn't tell me it was a mansion. I'm frightfully impressed.'

'Virge?' said the young man incredulously.

'Virginia.'

'Oh, I get it. Virgin for short, but not for long.'

The men burst out laughing and Virginia blushed, dragging Angela out into the hall. Angela was laughing too.

'Oh, Angela, do stop it. Shut up laughing and come and see the awful kitchen. It's really creepy and there's a *horrible* cellar out at the back, just like a burial vault. I'd never dare go in there on my own.'

'Oh, where? Do show me, it sounds super.'

Anglea rushed for the service stairs and Virginia followed her down. The builders had thoroughly colonised the kitchen, but there was no living person in there at that moment; only the deep, half-open cupboards haunted the dark corners, and the clothes rack hovered in the gloom of the ceiling above the range, which was now covered by mugs, paper packets, bottles of milk and a big, enamel teapot.

Angela pulled open the door of the cellar and stuck her head in, squealing with delight.

'Oh, it's awful! I bet it's full of spiders and all sorts of nasties. Hey, there are some old sacks in here, I wonder what's in them? Perhaps it's a dismembered body. Gosh, supposing it were?'

'Angela!' pleaded Virginia. It was in here, too. Frightened, she turned and hurried up the flight back into the hall. Petra, Sandy and Mr. Hargreaves were coming down the stairs.

'This is going to put a lot more on to your estimate, you know. Remember, I put it down in black and white that that wasn't your final figure. There could be a good few thousand on top of that.'

'Now don't worry, Mr. Hargreaves,' Sandy assured him heartily. 'I've got plenty of capital to play with. My present property will more than cover it and until then the bridging loan's completely adequate.'

'Well, if you say so – ' He turned away, shrugging.

Virginia was conscious of the unpleasant atmosphere with her again and took hold of Petra, who was feeling quite happy enough to allow the liberty. She even gave her daughter a pleased, conspiratorial squeeze as Mr. Hargreaves retreated.

'Now come on, Sandy, he's gone, you don't have to keep it up. It's a wash-out, isn't it? Face it, you've bought a huge white elephant.'

'Nonsense, darling, you have to expect little problems on a job like this. Perfectly routine.'

'You don't really mean you're going on with it?' she exclaimed, appalled.

He sighed patiently. 'Well, of course I am. You don't think I'm going to back out when we've got this far, do you? When are you going to realise, Petra, that I know exactly what I'm doing? Now, Virginia, come up and take a look at your room.'

'I don't want to see my horrible old room,' cried Virginia, threat now so tangible in the air around her that she was on the point of becoming hysterical.

Angela leapt out of the service door.

'Oh, come on, Virge, let's see it. I must see it all.' She dragged her up the stairs, giggling. "Virgin for short but not for long!" Hey, that's really funny.'

'No, it isn't,' said Virginia, 'it's just rude. I hate rude people.'

'Which is yours? Wow, is it really? It's amazing!'

She stopped short inside the door, looking across the dirty, echoing cavern of the back bedroom.

The atmosphere in here was appalling. Virginia stood rooted

to the spot, sick with fear. Even Angela suddenly quietened down, though she couldn't have explained why.

'Well, it's quite nice, isn't it? You've got lots of room. Perhaps I can come down to stay – maybe.'

She backed a couple of steps.

'What colour are you having it?'

Sandy strode in holding a sheaf of paint leaflets he had fetched from the car.

'That's what we're going to decide now. What do you think of it, Angela?'

'Oh – great,' she said, looking over her shoulder doubtfully.

'White,' said Virginia, edging towards the door and trying to get around Sandy, 'do it all white.'

'Oh, come on, sweetie, that's a bit unadventurous. How about something nice and feminine? There's a lovely shade here called Fleece – '

'Just paint it white!' shouted Virginia, and rushed out of the door, down the stairs and into the air.

Mr. Hargreaves continued his jeremiad right up to the moment they got into the car. The men were packing up now, and the windows were blindfolded with plastic sheeting.

'You do realise that this rot is going to alter the estimated figure? And then there's the new main into your *en suite* bathroom. I told you that wasn't included. And your demolition job on the outhouses, I'll have to get a subcontractor in – '

'Carry on, Mr. Hargreaves, just carry on.'

Angela sat in the front. Her girlish enthusiasm had completely captivated Sandy and it had been his suggestion.

'Oh, yes *please,* Mr. Matheson. You don't mind, do you, Mrs. Matheson?' The glowering Mrs. Matheson couldn't have cared less.

Virginia was on the point of tears. How *could* she? The whole point of her coming down had been to sympathise and back her up, and there she was, telling Sandy that the house was marvellous and reinforcing all his stupid pride in it.

'Really, Mr. Matheson, I think you're so clever to find a lovely house like that. I only wish my father would do something so exciting instead of staying in that stodgy old flat in Hampstead. And such a wonderful big garden!'

'It's going to need a lot of work to get it in order, of course,' said Sandy, pressing his foot down hard on to the accelerator and cutting up a startled Lotus, 'but that will have to wait until the builders have gone. Thought I might have a tennis court.'

'Gosh, brilliant!'

Virginia closed her eyes and pressed the lids together to stop the tears seeping out. Angela mustn't see her crying. Think of something else, quick.

'Listen, Virginia,' said the young fireman, 'you don't need to trouble about false friends any more. I'm all you need. I'm your refuge, your lover, your husband-to-be, your destiny. I love you, Virginia, and I'll never let you down. And don't take any notice of those animals with their filthy jokes. You're my own sweet, pure Virginia.'

But not for long?

She'd got a pain in her back. She'd noticed it earlier, up in the bedroom, but now it was creeping round to the front, insinuating itself down into her groin, like a cramp.

She opened her eyes wide with sudden excitement. Could it be? That's what the other girls said it was like. All the way from Puckeridge to Highgate, Virginia sat and enjoyed her pain, examined it, greeted it with ecstatic pleasure. As soon as she was home, she ran up to the loo.

It wasn't, not yet, anyway. But it could be, any minute. Oh yes, it really could be. At last.

Sandy rubbed his hands together.

'Well, that was a good day's work, eh, Petra? I'm starving, hurry up and get the dinner on, sweetie. You'll stay, won't you, Angela?'

'Oh yes, Mr. Matheson, I'd love to.'

'You'll have to make do with a fry-up,' said Petra coldly. That child was a tart. She'd suspected it before, she was quite certain now. 'I'm dead tired, I think I'll have an early night. In fact I'm going to go and put the blanket on now.'

'Check the switch, won't you? You really shouldn't have bought the same make again after that near-disaster.'

'They *are* one of your clients, I should have thought that was recommendation enough for anyone. By the way,' she added triumphantly, 'the dishwasher's gone haywire. That's a Taggart's model, too.'

Virginia came down happily, quite ready to forgive Angela, who had now shrunk to a mere equal. Even her fear of Maiden's End was momentarily forgotten. She took her into the living room and sat down on the settee, rubbing her stomach dramatically.

'Gosh, I think I'm going to have a bad time for a change this month. I can feel it coming on.'

It didn't.

Chapter 7

'Daddy? Are you better? You are coming today, aren't you?'
'Yes, Ginnie, I'll be there.'
'Oh, Daddy, I've got so much to tell you. We went down to the house again on Friday and the men have started work on it already. Sandy's actually bought it. I told you it was urgent, but you wouldn't listen.'

Derek closed his eyes and leant his head upon his hand. Oh no, he'd really let her down this time. How the hell had it all happened so quickly? He felt as useless as Petra had always told him he was.

'But what about your mother? I thought you said she was against it?'
'Sandy was doing it all behind her back. Isn't that filthy of him? She was absolutely furious, but I'm afraid she's coming round, because she's stopped arguing. Oh, Daddy, it's still horrible and I'm scared, Daddy. It feels really nasty, and I don't like it a bit. I'm sure something dreadful must have happened there. Can't I come and live with you?'
'Ginnie, I'd love you to, you know that, but your mother just wouldn't wear it. Don't think I haven't asked her in the past, even for short visits, but the answer's always been no.'
'Oh, Daddy, you must do *something!*'
'Look, calm down and I'll try to think. See you this afternoon, anyway.'
'All right. The usual place?'
'Yes, darling, the usual place.'

'Virginia, do stop crying!'

'I *can't* stop crying.'

Derek bobbed agitatedly through Waterlow Park, his daughter following him in anxious little rushes, stopping to snivel and blow her nose and behave altogether like someone half her age. Why did she always have to make scenes? The knowledge that he had let her down very badly, combined with the hellish two weeks he had just gone through, filled him with anger and guilt to the point of exhaustion.

She'd been such a good, happy kid once; he'd loved her so much. But the close tie had become loosened, first by the strains of legally enforced separation, then by his own moral cowardice. Their meetings had become such ordeals that he had found himself shortening them, putting them off, even allowing Petra to cut them down from weekly to fortnightly, because he couldn't bear to look at what he had done to her. Her bewilderment was too painful to contemplate, her desolation too accusing.

It was drizzling with rain. Up at the top of the park, surrounded by Easter Sunday daffodils, Lauderdale House sat on the brow of the hill, looking down over living London through the bare trees. At the bottom, the massed stones of the cemetery lurked behind the hedge.

Her voice wailed behind him.

'You must stop them moving, Daddy. I don't want to leave my house and my friends and you.'

He stopped and faced her, exasperated.

'Virginia, I don't see how I can, it's really none of my business.'

'But *I'm* your business!' she sobbed desperately, gazing up into his face with consciously tragic appeal. He frowned, turning his head away from what he recognised was partly a deliberate performance.

'Look, I'm sure your mother will arrange for you to come up and see me. Perhaps not so often, but now and again.'

'Daddy! Don't you mind?'

'Of course I mind!' he almost shouted.

No, he realised with shame, I don't think I do, really. I still care about her, but her actual physical presence is such an embarrassment. These strained, overemotional meetings give me little pleasure now, and I'd rather remember her as she used to be. She's difficult, neurotic, less easy to love. In a few years' time, when this awful adolescent stage is over, then I shall want to see her. When she's a happy, poised, attractive twenty-year-old with self-confidence and a sense of purpose, when she has no need to cling, when she can sort out her own problems and not keep trying to push them on to me, then I shall enjoy meeting her and even showing her off. But at the moment I've had enough of all this drama — I've got problems of my own, without her constant expectation that I should put hers right as well. How can I, anyway? She's completely out of my hands, legally and practically. She expects too much of me and she's got to learn to stand on her own feet, not whine and cry and demand like this. She can't expect to go on being Daddy's little girl forever.

For the first time, as he looked at the blotched, thin, unattractive face turned up to him so beseechingly, a touch of dislike crept into his feelings for her; he felt suddenly that guilt was being transmuted into blame. It was like finding the key to a puzzle which had been troubling him for years.

Quite unaware of the enormity of his betrayal, he decided that the time had come to put his foot down with Virginia.

He put his arm around her.

'Now look here, darling, I'm going to speak to you straight, as an equal. You're not a child any more, you're nearly a woman. Your mother was married at your age. In two years' time you'll be of age, with your life in your own hands.'

She looked at him with terror, realising that he had drawn himself away from her, that their relationship was about to change irrevocably, that things were never going to be the same again. He was wrong, she wasn't a woman, not even physically. She was an inadequate, frightened child.

'What you must realise is that you're Petra and Sandy's responsibility, not mine. Ever since the divorce I've had practically no say at all in what happens to you. It's cruel and I hate it, but that's how it is. What you've got to do is to put up with things for now. Even if they do move somewhere you don't like, remember it's only for two more years then you'll be free; you can go and live anywhere then, strike out on your own and live as you want to. Until then, you've got to be patient.'

She stared at him with the stunned, begging gaze of an

abandoned puppy in a lay-by, watching the family car speeding away.

'Don't you want me any more?'

He felt sudden irritation and turned his attention to the rapacious squirrel dancing around his feet, leaning down to pet it willingly because it had no claim upon him.

'Of course I want you, but I'm not allowed to have you. I've explained all that. You must start behaving like a grown-up, Ginnie. You're sixteen, for God's sake!'

'Well, I don't feel sixteen, and I'm not grown-up. Don't you understand, Daddy? I'm not grown-up. I'm never going to grow up, I know that now. I'm different. There's something wrong with me. How can I be expected to behave grown-up when I'm not? It's not fair!'

Derek straightened up and looked at her with surprise.

'What do you mean, there's something wrong with you?'

'You know what I mean. It hasn't happened yet.'

'What hasn't — oh! You mean you haven't started —'

'No, I haven't.'

She blew her nose and stared longingly down the hill in the direction of the peaceful, comforting world of the dead.

'Oh, I see.' Derek was intensely embarrassed. This was nothing to do with him and really, he didn't want to know. 'Well — er — what does your mother say about it? Has she taken you to the doctor?'

'No.'

'Well, I think perhaps she should, don't you? Have you asked her to?'

'No. She wouldn't, anyway. She doesn't care.'

'Oh, don't be so silly!' Derek expostulated. 'You must stop wallowing in self-pity, Virginia, it's so unattractive. Look, if that's what's wrong with you, for goodness' sake do something about it. No wonder you're a bag of nerves. It's just a physical problem, not real worries at all. Once the doctor has given you something to get it all moving you'll be a different girl. All these silly fears and fancies will disappear in no time. That's all it is, believe me.'

'Do you really think so?' Virginia asked hopefully.

'I'm absolutely certain. You talk to her. There, now clean

yourself up and we'll go and find somewhere nice. Would you like to go to the pictures?'

'Yes,' she said, brightening up, not least because he had finally offered her something which was his own idea. 'Yes, that would be lovely. We'll walk down to Archway.'

'The car's parked in Swain's Lane,' said Derek.

'Oh, then we could drop into the cemetery for a minute.'

'No, not today.'

'All right, Daddy.' She put her hand in his and looked up with an infuriating, poor-little-girl smile. 'I do love you, Daddy.'

'I love you,' he said shortly.

Derek couldn't face going in to speak to Petra when he dropped Virginia back home. He had no wish to step into what had been his own house and see her and Sandy installed there together. He drove back to Crouch End, let himself into the boarded-off hall of 8, Chaucer Terrace, went up the stairs and opened the tatty sheet of hardboard which was his front foor. The room into which it debouched was a mess, as usual. The washing up was piled in the sink, the papers lay in agitated disarray on the table. He disinterred the telephone and rang Highgate.

'Petra? Derek here. Look, it's about Virginia. She tells me you're moving, and she's been on at me about coming to live here. I've told her you wouldn't allow it but she can't seem to see sense.'

Petra's voice, in the light, restrained tone she always used to him, trickled into his ear like a stream of iced water. He shuffled the papers, eyes picking out disturbing phrases. *'Dear Mr. Blackie, Further to our interview of the 4th inst., I must reiterate that unless...definite confirmation of your... absolute assurances from you... we shall be forced to take steps....'*

'No, of course I haven't been giving her ideas, don't be so silly, Petra – ' his voice became aggrieved – 'no, it's her own idea entirely. What's this new house like, anyway? She seems to have taken against it in the most irrational manner. Oh, is it? Dear, dear. But it's all being done up properly, I presume, it's not a case of camping out or anything? No, no, I thought not.

I'm sure Sandy would want to make himself comfortable, he's hardly the ascetic type, is he?'

He smiled as the icy stream turned into a torrent rushing straight off a spring glacier.

'Well, that's your problem, isn't it, dear? You've made your bed. All I'm concerned about is Virginia. She'll be able to come down and see me? Oh, good. No, I'm sure it's only some silly obsession, I'll leave it to you. Just thought I'd check.

'Look, Petra, there's just one other thing; none of my business, really, but I thought I ought to mention it. I hear she hasn't started her periods yet. A bit late, isn't it? Shouldn't you see someone? Yes, I know that, but sixteen does seem to be knocking on a bit; it could be what's causing all this neurotic behaviour.

'No, don't be so damned silly,' he said in an annoyed voice, 'of course I don't think that all women's troubles are caused by biology, I didn't say anything of the sort. Oh, really, Petra, you are impossible sometimes! Well, if she's that unbearable you'd better go and do something about it, hadn't you? Get her to a doctor quick or you may find yourself having to take her to a psychiatrist, and then you'll really be in trouble!'

Petra put the phone down. So Derek thought he was going to get Virginia back, did he? Some hopes. A fine sort of life she'd have with that useless little jerk. She saw something lying on the floor and picked it up with a tut of annoyance. It was a bra, the one she had given Virginia for her birthday. Honestly, teenagers were just the end — real slobs, all of them.

'Virginia?'

'Yes?' She came in out of the kitchen sucking a Mars bar.

'Did you leave this here?'

'No, I didn't.' Virginia looked at the bra with dislike.

'Well, *I* certainly didn't. I suppose it must have been the fairies,' said Petra wearily. 'Where did you get that muck from?'

'Daddy bought it for me at the cinema. He bought me lots of nice things. You don't buy me sweets.'

'I don't need to, you get plenty of pocket money. You'd do better to spend it on shampoo, from the look of you, when did you last wash your hair?'

'Yesterday.'

'Don't tell silly lies, Virginia, that hair hasn't seen water for a couple of weeks. It's thoroughly unhealthy.'

Virginia slumped down into an armchair and looked smugly pathetic. 'Daddy said I'm not looking healthy at all and I ought to see a doctor.'

'Well, if you're not healthy it's because you don't eat properly or look after yourself, it's not my fault,' Petra said angrily. 'Oh – er – look, darling,' she sat down beside her, putting on a motherly, reassuring expression which didn't come easily to her. 'Daddy did mention one thing – about your periods, actually.'

'I don't have them.'

'I know, that's what I mean. Look, you don't want to worry too much about it, dear, these things are so individual that it doesn't mean a thing. But it is going on a bit, now, and perhaps it would be an idea to see if the doctor can suggest something. Would you like to?'

Virginia dropped the Mars bar on to her lap and turned to face her mother, her eyes suddenly spilling over.

'Oh Pet – Mum – Petra –'

To Petra's intense surprise Virginia burst into tears. She put her arms around her, amazed. 'Darling, I had no idea you were so upset about it. Why didn't you say? It's nothing to worry about, really. Lots of people don't start until they're your age.'

'That's not true!' stormed Virginia. 'All my friends have. I'm the only girl in my class who hasn't. There's something wrong, isn't there, Mummy? I'm different. No wonder I'm so plain and skinny. No wonder nobody wants me.'

'But I want you, so does Sandy. Look, we'll go and see someone about it. You should have said before. I had no idea –'

'Well you should have done!' Virginia sobbed.

'Yes,' said Petra, 'I expect I should.'

She hadn't started until fifteen herself, come to think of it, but her mother hadn't been the sort of person you could talk to. Mrs. Davison was an emotional woman, but her emotion was sexless, even non-physical. Her fear of the body had caused her to deny it, and all her emotion had degraded into sentimentality. Petra, with no intention of following her example, had found her totally useless and gone elsewhere for her sexual education. But she was a modern, unprudish woman. Surely Virginia could have come to her?

'Oh, Ginnie,' she said, full or remorse.

Virginia looked up, her face a red, blubbering mess.

'You haven't called me that for ages.'

'Haven't I?'

'No. Not for years. Not since Daddy went. Oh, Mum — Petra, I do miss Daddy. Why can't I live with Daddy?'

Petra was mortified.

'But you've got me, Ginnie, aren't I enough? I love you.'

'*Do* you?' Virginia's incredulous question made her feel even worse.

'Of course I do, how could you possibly doubt it? Think of all the lovely things we've given you. When have we ever denied you anything?'

'I've often asked for things you didn't give me.'

'When? What haven't I given you? Tell me.'

Petra was shocked, her self-absorbtion suddenly torn away so that her heart stood open to her daughter's needs. All that was required was that the right thing be said, the right request made — a request she was capable of understanding and granting.

It was Virginia's inevitable tragedy that she chose the wrong one.

'I want to stay here in Highgate, and I want Daddy to be living with us again.'

Petra laughed uneasily and stroked Virginia's hair with a careless, automatic, meaningless gesture which was as hurtful as if she had pushed her away. Virginia's spontaneous tears dried as she recognised the involuntary rejection. Even before Petra replied she knew that the moment of intimacy had passed.

'You know that's totally impossible, darling. I'm married to Sandy now.'

'You don't love him,' said Virginia resentfully.

'Of course I love him.'

'No you don't, not now. You're horrid to him, just like you used to be to Daddy. And you don't even like me.'

'Don't be so ridiculous!'

'It isn't ridiculous. You don't. No-one could like me. I think even my friends are really only sorry for me. I'm not likeable, am I?'

Petra was at a loss for words. It couldn't be denied; Virginia was quite outstanding in her unlikeability.

'Well,' she said carefully at last, 'not at the moment, no, but that's rather your fault, isn't it? You don't try very hard to make people like you. But that doesn't mean that I don't love you,' she added hastily, 'I do love you, Virginia, but you must understand that you can't have everything you want in this life, even from people who love you.'

'You do! You get everything you want.'

'No I don't.'

Petra eased herself away from Virginia, frowning, and reached for her cigarettes. People let you down all the time, even the ones you thought were just what you needed, but drink and cigarettes didn't. They were always available.

No, she hadn't got what she wanted. She'd thought money was that, but it wasn't enough. She'd thought giving Derek the heave-ho was what she wanted, but that hadn't given her much more than the satisfaction of revenge. She'd really thought that Sandy was what she wanted at last, but even he hadn't made her happy for long. It was beginning to creep up on her, with slow, inexorable certainty, that nothing would, and the prospect was enough to make her scream out loud. It would be the ultimate horror to have to face, to know that you were incapable of being made happy — that the whole of your life was going to consist of a continual, desperate search for something you were constitutionally incapable of finding. Shaken by her glimpse of the Pit, she made for the drinks.

Virginia made a last plea for attention, in a self-pitying whine which jarred on Petra's nerves like a circular saw.

'I've got a headache.'

Petra dumped the glass on the table and went out into the kitchen. Sandy was playing at washing up, dressed for the game in a silly apron printed with bra and suspender belt, which he had thought terribly amusing when Sam gave it to him for his birthday. Petra, naturally, loathed it. She picked up the aspirins, pushed him to one side and filled a glass.

'What's up, sweetie? Got a headache?'

'No, Virginia has.'

'Oh, poor little love — women's troubles?'

'She doesn't have them,' said Petra angrily, as if it were his fault.

'Really?' Sandy looked surprised. 'But she's sixteen.'

'Yes, she's sixteen but she doesn't have periods. I'm going to take her to the doctor. I should have done it before, but I never thought. She's also dirty and untidy and lazy and depressing and neurotic and a pain in the arse. I don't like her. Isn't that dreadful? I don't like my own daughter. Do you?' she demanded defiantly.

'Of course I do.'

'Liar! Nobody could like Virginia. She's awful. Do you think it's my fault?'

Sandy patted her with a wet hand.

'You're a marvellous mother, Petra. When has she ever wanted for anything?'

'According to her, quite often. To start with, she still doesn't want to move, but I don't suppose for a moment that's going to change your mind.'

'Oh, not that again!' said Sandy.

'Yes, that again. She doesn't just hate the house, like I do, she's afraid of it. I know my opinion isn't likely to make you think again, but surely that might?'

'She'll love it when it's finished,' said Sandy, shutting off immediately. 'Be able to have all her friends down for weekends. It's just her age. They're always funny in their teens, and if she's having trouble with her monthlies it's bound to make her worse. You get it sorted out and you'll see. Hello, what the blazes is this doing here?' He picked something up off the windowsill. Petra looked, then gave a shocked gasp.

'Jesus!'

'Ye-es, a bit tactless of you, wasn't it? Supposing it had been here when we brought them all back tonight? Cause a real laugh, wouldn't it?'

'I'm hardly likely to use *that* in the kitchen, am I? It must have been you.'

'Don't need it, love,' said Sandy with insufferable complacency.

'Well, that's one good mark for me, isn't it?' snapped Petra.

She took Virginia her aspirins, went up to her bedroom and shut the Byo-Rithmic massager away in the back of a drawer.

Then she opened the drawer again and covered it with a pile of underwear.

She sat down on the bed, her stomach churning with nausea. Her daughter was spying on her, intruding into the most secret corners of her life, planning to make her a laughing stock in front of her friends. The realisation was like a physical shock.

The child was *sick*.

Chapter 8

'Daddy, the house is practically sold! A horrible man with a fat stomach and a nasty wife with false teeth and diamonds. Diamonds, Daddy! In the morning! Isn't that dreadful? Mummy said it was really over the top to wear diamonds in the morning, and I said, "Well, I bet they aren't real," and she said, "Oh yes they bloody well are!" Oh, Daddy, please, please, *please* can't I come and live with you?'

'Virginia, I'm busy! Please, darling, don't ring me at the office, I just haven't got time to talk to you.'

'But, Daddy, I'm so miserable. The weather's horrible and all my friends are away and I haven't got anything to do, and it's awful having no-one to talk to in the school holidays.'

'Well, I have got people to talk to, very urgently, so just be a good girl and try to amuse yourself. I really must go now. 'Bye.'

Derek slammed the receiver down and tried to get his thoughts together. He rummaged through the papers, picked one up, put it down, picked up another – he reached for the phone again. The next conversation was even more agitating.

'I'm sorry, Mr. Blackie, they just aren't prepared to wait any longer, you know the deadline passed several days ago. I've done my best, but you really must accept the inevitable. I suggest the only sensible thing to do is to file for bankruptcy.'

'Jesus! Can't you do better than that? You're my accountant, for God's sake, how did you let me get into this mess?'

'I'm not running your business, I can only advise, and it's not as if this had blown up out of the blue. I warned you how things were going in December. Believe me, it's the only way out.'

'The thing is, Mr. Matheson, we can't get on with your sanding until we've got electricity. Mr. Carter couldn't finish laying your cable until all your damp was dried out, and now he's gone off on another job and we can't use power tools.'

'I'll ring him and give him a rocket. He promised me he'd come straight back when you were ready. Don't worry, I'll get him moving. I don't see why he shouldn't work over the weekend.'

'Oh, good.' Mr. Hargreaves' emotion was, again, more personal than professional. It would keep Kevin away from his daughter. ''Bye, then, Mr. Matheson.'

Petra rushed in, ready for bed.

'Sandy, it's that bloody blanket again! Luckily I noticed the smell of burning before it took hold but it's really the limit. We ought to sue Taggart's.' Her angry eyes dropped from Sandy's face to the floor beside his feet. 'What's that by the phone? Look, the carpet's sopping wet. The radiator must be leaking.'

'It's not switched on.'

'What the hell's that got to do with it,' Petra said, 'there's still water in it, isn't there?'

'Perhaps Virginia spilt something.'

Petra, with a sudden horrible suspicion, knelt down and sniffed. No, whatever it was, Virginia hadn't started wetting herself.

'Alistair? Sandy Matheson here. How's things? Good. Oh, you saw the commercials? Good, very glad to hear it. Yes, I think they give the product a really strong identity. No, we filmed it in the boardroom in the Pettifer Tower – wonderful view of the City.

'Look, Alistair, I'm *afraid* we've had a bit of trouble with one of your products – yes, the electric blanket again. George told you, did he? Yes, another near-disaster. Have you checked the production line? Yes. Yes. Well, it could be serious if it's a constant fault, so I thought I'd better warn you at once. No, not at all, you know how near my heart your interests are. . . .'

'Oh, hello, Mr. Matheson. Well, your power's in, and we're starting on your kitchen. You did say you didn't want anything changed, not even your range? Well, if you say so, but it's a right lump of rust. Yes, it's cleaning off, but it'll need to be blackleaded, and I don't know how Mrs. Matheson is going to feel about that. I don't even know if you can still get the stuff...it's poisonous, you know.

'Your dresser's come up quite nice, though, all stripped down and you want it sealed, not repainted, right? All right, Mr. Matheson, I'll keep in touch.'

'Daddy! It's me! Daddy, Sandy says the house will be ready for painting soon. He wants to move down during next term, so I'll have to stay with Angela until my exams are done, but after that it'll be too late, I'll have gone for good! Oh, I can come and live with you, can't I?'

'Oh, for God's sake, Virginia!'

'Petra, have you seen the phone bill?'
'Of course not, you know I always leave that sort of thing to you. How much is it?'
'One thousand and seventy-nine pounds.'
'What!'
'One thousand and seventy-nine pounds, it's crazy.'
'Have you been ringing abroad from here?'
'No, I always do that from the office.'
'Well, you've been ringing Hertfordshire pretty regularly.'
'Don't be silly, darling, it wouldn't come to anything like that. I expect it's just the computer.' Sandy did some quick, approximate arithmetic. 'Eighteen thousand, four hundred units. That's about two hundred calls a day. Ten solid hours of phone calls!'
'But that's totally impossible! It's the computer. I should get on to Telecom.'
'You bet I will. I don't know what's happening to the electricity in this house. The sooner we get out the better.'
'It's going to be *so* much more efficient out in the wilds, isn't it?' said Petra.

It was Sunday night, and Petra and Sandy had gone to the pub. Petra had left in a panic, having found the massager in the hall and hidden it hastily in the cupboard under the stairs. The funny thing was, it appeared to be burnt out.

Virginia was curled up in bed, day-dreaming again.

Pretty, mature, dressed in sprig muslin and a flowered straw bonnet, she gazed up at the idealised man of her longings. A brave young fireman, an ideal, devoted lover. She had given him a name, now – William. Fireman William Strong, the bravest, most daring man at his station, the hero of all his colleagues.

'Come with me, Virginia, I'll give you a proper home and a new life. I'll marry you and we'll live together in my little cottage. It's not a palace of comforts like you've been used to, but there is love there, and it is all for you. Will you mind being married to a poor man?'

'Oh no, no,' she breathed, gazing into his eyes, 'I want nothing but you. I'll work and slave for you. I'll be your loving helpmeet. I'll love you all my life, if you will promise to love me.'

He gave a soft cry and pressed his manly, moustached lips to her face.

(No, not the moustache. Being a Victorian, he probably would have one but the daydream, vividly realistic from long practice, had shown her that a moustache would certainly stick up her nose. Not the moustache.)

He gave a soft cry of joy and pressed his manly, clean-shaven lips to hers. She melted into his embrace.

'Oh, my darling!' she cried. 'My own, brave William!'

At eleven fifteen, the front door banged against the wall. The latest of many such blows finally fractured the hessian wallpaper and a puff of plaster dust burst out of the ruptured skin and fell to the carpet.

The crowd pressed forward into the house, screaming with alcohol-released laughter. God, it was all so funny, so amazingly funny! God, life was *hysterical,* an absolute ball!

'Honestly, darling, I could have died!' Samantha shrieked. 'That great Wally standing there in his socks and waving his pathetic little peashooter at me as if it was Nelson's Column! I just burst out laughing, I couldn't help it. I mean, I expect it was absolutely wicked of me, but really, if you could have seen it! And after all that big, James Bond come-on!'

The door slammed shut. Petra pushed past her friends into the living room and took a quick, nervous glance around before she allowed them in. It seemed to be all right. Chairs, settee, coffee table, bookshelves, the bare expanse of carpet – yes, quite innocent of embarrassment. Better look in the bathroom, though. She stood back to allow the others in, cheering up.

'Sit down, darlings. Sandy, do the honours, will you? I'm just going to make sure Virginia's all right.'

Sam sprawled back on the settee, spreading out her red shoes and black lace legs so that Sandy could see them, and turning her head to smile up at him from within the dense mass of a hairstyle which made her look like James the Second.

'Gin and tonic, please, Sandy. A nice, nice, big one, if you'll trust me with it.'

'I'd trust you with anything, Sam, even my peashooter.'

'Whooooh!'

The screams of amusement echoed round the living room and up the stairs to Virginia's room, where Petra was bending over the bed.

She was asleep, her hair standing up in damp spikes above the quilt. You brat, Virginia, you evil little brat. What have I ever done to you? You do need a psychiatrist. I'll have a word with Zak, he'll be discreet. He'll also be expensive, but it'll be worth it if he can nip this sort of thing in the bud.

She tiptoed out of the room, closed the door and went to make a careful examination of the bathroom, pushing a blameless tube of toothpaste away in the cabinet as if it were an indecency. She went into the lavatory. Oh God! She picked up the book on the seat – *Couples*. Well, that was hardly likely to shock anyone much, but its situation was suggestive and liable to cause a few sniggers. She took it into her room and slung it into a corner.

Yes, she'd ring Zak in the morning.

In the living room the laughter burst out again, surging up the stairs to greet her as she came down.

Sam was curled up in mock embarrassment on the settee, giggling into her hands. Boris was rolling around on the floor in hysterics. Sandy was in the act of bending down and picking something up from the centre of the carpet, with a blush glowing right round to the back of his neck. He stood up, smiling in an incredulous 'My God, what *have* we got here?' way.

'What's the joke?' asked Petra, going across to the drinks table.

'Well, nothing too way-out, darling,' said Sandy in an amused voice which was fairly devoid of genuine amusement, 'but you appear to have mislaid something rather intimate.'

Petra turned, sick apprehension gripping her. She'd checked – where had that bloody child put it? Sandy held out the packet of tampons.

'You don't usually keep these on the floor in the lounge, do you?'

They screamed at her expression. The laughter whirled round her as she grabbed the box out of his hand and made for the door. Before she touched it, it opened and Virginia came in.

She was stark naked. Her sleepy grey eyes stared at the suddenly quietened guests.

'Darling!'

Petra forgot the minor embarrassment in the more urgent need to smother a major one. As she looked round desperately for covering, Sandy stripped off his jacket and thrust it at her. She wrapped it around Virginia, folding it tightly so that her arms were confined to her sides. The jacket was huge and mercifully covered even her thin, immature flanks.

'Virginia, how could you!'

Virginia stood looking straight ahead, her face blank, then stepped forward, the jacket falling open as she moved out of Petra's hands.

'Virginia! Come here!' The room was now hushed except for half-subdued giggles. Petra made a grab.

'Hold on, Petra, don't touch her!'

The young man with a haircut like Frankenstein's monster got up from the floor by the television and came across to Virginia. He folded the jacket around her again, then bent down and looked into her eyes.

'Virginia? Can you hear me, love?' he said in a quiet voice. She didn't respond.

He turned her gently, still holding the jacket closed to

conceal her scraggy little body, and steered her slowly across the room. Petra watched, stunned.

'What are you doing, Rod?'

'Ssh, don't make a noise. Just keep quiet, everyone. She's asleep.'

The hush intensified. The room became so still that a dropped pin would have reverberated like a girder.

Rod Singleton pressed Virginia onwards towards the door, while Petra held it open, the forgotten box of tampons in her hand. He smiled at her reassuringly as he passed, mouthing, 'Don't move.' She couldn't have moved.

They went across the hall.

'Careful, Virginia, we're going upstairs, love. Up you go, now. Right foot up, now the left. Good girl.'

They rose slowly through the silent house, the sleeping girl and the kind young man, like lovers moving towards their tryst.

A low whisper of shocked concern rippled round the living room. Petra came to life. 'I'd better go with them.'

'No.' Sandy's hand stopped her.

'But she's naked, Sandy!' she whispered in agitation.

'That's not likely to tempt him, is it? No, leave it Petra. He knows what he's doing.'

'She be all right with Rod,' said his flatmate, a soft little teddy bear of a man who also sat beside the television. 'He know just what to do. He's a Samaritan. That boy is a darling, a real saint. Poor little kid. This happen often?'

'No,' said Petra, 'never. It's the first time. She's been a bit upset lately.'

'Well, leave her to Rod. He very good at mothering,' he said comfortingly.

Petra looked at him, hurt. It was no comfort to be told a gay was a better mother than you were.

Virginia's head touched the pillow and the duvet was drawn up over her. The sensation flowed into her anxious dream and suddenly sweetened it. She smiled, eyes tightly closed.

'I love you,' she said.

'I love you, darling,' Rod said, kissed her forehead and closed the door behind him.

'Well,' said Sandy jovially as Rod re-entered the living

room, 'I didn't realise you were a do-gooder.'

Petra tossed and turned, the awful scene in the living room playing like a looped tape on the screen of her closed eyelids. She hadn't slept a wink, whereas Sandy was lying there like a great snoring elephant seal. You'd think he'd care too, wouldn't you? You'd think he'd see that it was all his fault – that stupid move, that house. Maiden's End flashed before her eyes, stripped as naked as Virginia and obscene in its evisceration. God, that awful house!

That was the trouble, the move, that and the delayed menses. She'd soon sort that out – there must be pills to bring them on; there were pills for everything, now. Yes, get that sorted out and it would be all right. Poor Virginia. But how *could* she have done *that* to Petra? She must know what she was doing, even if she was ill, and she'd found that thing in the bottom drawer. Oh, how could she? How could she be so deceitful, so intrusive, so viciously spiteful?

She opened her eyes and looked at the luminous face of the clock radio. Four. She'd been in bed for two whole hours and hadn't slept a minute. Presently, the clock on the stairs struck. Five? She checked her wristwatch. The clock radio was wrong, it had stopped. It was whining with electricity but the numerals stood still. Another piece of Taggart's rubbish. She'd make sure that the next piece of electrical equipment they bought would be from a reliable firm.

The worries whirled round in her head. Zak. Yes, she'd certainly ring Zak. And the doctor. She'd definitely ring the doctor. She stared at the window, watching the bar of yellow light from the street lamp shining through the curtains. Perhaps Virginia ought to go and live with Derek after all. There wasn't much room of course, but she might be happier there, it might get her back to normal. Or at the very least it would destroy her illusions about her father and send her running home gratefully, aware at last of how lucky she was. Yes, that really might not be such a bad idea. . . .

The grandfather clock struck six.

It couldn't be, she hadn't closed her eyes. Well, perhaps she had dropped off just for a minute. She was uncomfortable, the vodka was making itself felt – better go to the loo. She summoned up her willpower, rolled out of bed, tiptoed out of the room and down the landing.

As she opened the door, something hit her. It struck her a glancing blow on the side of the head and fell with a single loud bang to the floor. She wasn't hurt, just alarmed, and quickly switched on the light. The object sat before her on the vinyl, solid and round and still.

She edged round it, fury filling her. So it was booby-traps now, was it? The sooner she got Virginia to Zak the better. She put it in her dressing gown pocket, switched off the light and went back to bed. No, she oughtn't to be angry, the poor little beast couldn't help it, she was sick. She hadn't realised. No, she just hadn't realised.

The clock struck seven. Petra woke with a start, the question immediately presenting itself to her mind and demanding an answer.

It had dropped seven feet, it was round and it hadn't rolled. Why hadn't it rolled?

'I thought I might take Virginia breakfast in bed. She's probably feeling a bit off-colour after last night.'
'She's gone out.'
'Out? At eight o'clock in the morning?'
'Yes, I noticed her door was open when I had my bath.'
'But she always lies in for hours when she hasn't got to go to school. Why didn't you say so before? I mean, who knows what she could be doing? She could have sleepwalked again. She might even be out in the street naked!'
'She isn't – her coat's gone from the hook.'
'Sandy, I really am worried. Can't you go and look for her?'
'I haven't finished my breakfast,' he said regretfully, as if he took his meals under the restraint of padlocks and couldn't be interrupted for any reason whatsoever.
'But you're dressed, I'm not. Supposing she's lost her memory or walked under a car? I mean, she's so weird these days, leaving all those things around the house, and she even put a booby-trap on the loo door last night, it hit me. Supposing she's turning violent?'
'Don't be silly, Petra, there's nothing violent about Virginia

– she's incredibly quiet and unassertive, you know she is. And all kids play silly tricks sometimes.'

'Sandy, you really make me mad! She's never, ever played tricks in her life until now. It just isn't like her. And everyone knows that quiet people are often violent inside.'

'Are they?' asked Sandy, intrigued by this new piece of psychological information. It might be a wise thing to bear in mind, when handling deceptively wimpish people. Knowledge, after all, was power. 'What was it? On the door?'

'Oh, one of those alabaster eggs from the bowl in the lounge. Luckily, it only just touched me, but it could have been really dangerous, you know how heavy they are. I'm going to make an appointment with Zak.'

'Good idea.'

'Well, are you going?'

'Going?'

'To look for Virginia.'

He sighed. 'It's totally unnecessary.'

'All right, then, *I'll* go, since you obviously don't care a damn about her!' She saw a book on the worktop; it hadn't been there last night – better check.

'Where on earth did this come from? *The English Gentleman?* Good God, I can't imagine any of that lot last night reading this, can you?'

Sandy's slice of Ryvita stopped midway between plate and mouth. He sat as still as his hand, his face gradually paling while Petra ruffled contemptuously through the pages.

'No,' he said at last, 'I can't.'

Petra flung it down. 'It probably belongs to Boris. You know what snobs these foreigners can be.'

She ran upstairs to get dressed.

Sandy lowered the Ryvita slowly on to his plate, all appetite gone.

It had all seemed so real. That gentle young man looking into her eyes, the kiss on her forehead, the whispered words. 'I love you, darling.' Never before in her dreams, either waking or sleeping, had sensation been so vivid.

She wandered up and down the hills of Highgate for hours, reliving the beautiful moments, trying to understand. It hadn't come from within her own imagination, she was sure. There had been no concentrated effort of will, no shutting out of reality and travelling within, no predetermined scenario to be played out on the glamorous screen of her mind.

It had suddenly come through to her, out of the blue, a real, romantic incident, a contact with real love, reaching out to take lonely, frustrated Virginia Blackie by the hand and draw her into the promised land.

Love did exist, then. Love was possible. Somewhere out there the perfect, gentle, heroic lover might be waiting to find her, to take her in his arms. Perhaps he was longing for her, as she longed for him. Perhaps his longing had leapt, for a moment, across the distance still separating them and touched her own. It must happen, surely, that mystical meeting of kindred spirits, of predestined soulmates.

At ten, the East Cemetery opened and she wandered round it visiting her friends, almost asking them for the answer to her question. You were kind and compassionate, can you tell me where my lover is to be found? You loved deeply, help me to find love.

She stood before Fireman Burton's monument and pushed a daffodil between the axe and the hose. I wanted someone as wonderful as you; does he really exist after all? Is he really the brave fireman I imagined? Do you know? You know everything now, don't you? Tell me.

Petra found her walking up Swain's Lane in a dream, seeming to take seconds to recognise her mother, even when she caught hold of her.

'Virginia! Where have you been? I've been sick with worry.'

'Oh – just for a walk.' The smile faded and was replaced by her usual expression of sulky gloom.

'What did you do?'

'Nothing, just walked.'

'Look, dear, Sandy says he'll take the day off and we'll all go out. Won't that be lovely?'

Virginia looked suspicious.

'Sandy never takes days off. He's a workaholic, you said so yourself.'

'Well, he's going to today, because he's worried about you, and I think it's very nice of him.'

'Where are we going?'

'Knebworth. There are all sorts of interesting things there: a big house, a zoo, a picnic site in the park, an adventure playground....'

Virginia's expression froze into hostility.

'Adventure playgrounds are for kids.'

'Yes, I know, but you'll love all the other things. Would you like Angela to come, too?'

Virginia paused, considering the proposal with the cynical insight of a disillusioned adult.

'Did Sandy suggest that?'

'Yes, he did, as a matter of fact. He thought it would make it even more fun for you.'

'No, don't let's take Angela,' said Virginia.

Chapter 9

The car turned into the High Street. Virginia stared out of the window, watching the bitter wind whipping clothes against the bodies of passers-by. A schoolchild, late from a visit to the dentist, hurried towards her State school. Virginia, with the questionable advantages of a private education, had two more weeks of holiday to fill.

William set her tenderly upon his horse.

(His horse? Well, it had to be, didn't it? He wouldn't have had a car or a motorbike. It had to be a horse.)

Anyway, he set her upon his horse.

'You're coming with me, Virginia. I've got a dear little cottage just off the High Street. We'll be married and live happily ever after.'

'It's a blowy day, isn't it, Virginia?' remarked Petra with forced, anxious cheerfulness. 'Still, it's quite bright. Let's hope the rain keeps off.'

'Yes,' said Virginia irritably.

She put her arms around her lover, while the patient, faithful beast moved rhythmically under them.

'Don't try to race the lights!' said Petra nervously.

Sandy trod on the brake. The horse stopped at the traffic lights. Virginia sighed. You couldn't put Victorian romance into modern surroundings. Forget the horse. Suddenly on foot, he put his arm about her and led her to his cottage.

Sandy turned to face Petra, annoyed.

'Are you going to back-seat drive all the way, Petra, because if you are I'm going back now.'

'Sorry. It's just that you do sometimes.'

The lights changed and the Volvo moved off, past the old shops of Highgate Village.

Virginia studied them closely. She liked that one. William might have known it, not as an expensive boutique where Sam sold Petra exorbitantly marked-up fashions, but as a grocer's, or an ironmonger's, or perhaps as a dairy where he bought the eggs, milk and butter for his simple, wholesome, poor-man's fare. Quickly, she whipped up the ingredients into a delicious quiche, which would have surprised a Victorian working man more than a little.

'Here's your dinner, darling. Oh, how tired you are, how pale! Was it a terrible fire? How many were killed?'

'None, I saved them all. Two little children and their mother.'

'You didn't risk your own dear life!'

'Of course, I was thinking of her poor husband. If it were my sweet Virginia, I told myself, and thought no more of the raging flames and the cruel danger.'

'Oh, my brave, brave William!'

'My own beautiful, courageous Virginia!'

'This traffic is a real pig,' said Sandy, cross. 'Monday's always bad. Why does it have to be a bloody Monday?'

'Well, it was your idea.'

'I didn't choose the day. It was hardly my planning that your daughter should go bananas on a Sunday night.'

'Shut up! She'll hear you!' hissed Petra. 'And she's your daughter as well, isn't she? You've always said she was, anyway. What's the matter, is the responsibility suddenly getting too much for you? Didn't you realise what you were taking on?'

'No,' said Sandy in a low voice, 'I can't honestly say that I did.'

There were roadworks everywhere. They crawled for mile after frustrating mile. In the Finchley High Road, valuable acres of empty road were shut off by cones, with nothing apparently wrong with them and nothing yet being done.

Sandy looked anxiously at the petrol gauge as the expensive, stop-and-start driving took its toll. At last things started to get moving, and on the Barnet by-pass he turned into a garage to fill up.

'I'm hungry,' said Virginia, 'I didn't have any breakfast.'

'All right, sweetie,' he said heartily, 'there's a café over there. You have a good nosh, this is your day. Anything you like.' Better keep her happy.

Virginia ate her way through egg and chips, an ice cream and two Pepsis. Petra chattered across the table with irritating animation, but Sandy had suddenly lapsed into a brooding silence which was totally unlike him.

They stowed Virginia away in the back of the car as if she were a heavy, inconvenient piece of luggage not wanted on voyage, and continued on their way.

'Christ! You'd think they'd grab every chance they could get to pull in the shekels.'

'I'm sorry, Sandy. I didn't know they were closed on Mondays. Let's find somewhere else. How about Woburn, that's open every day of the year?'

'I'm not going to drive cross-country to bloody Bedfordshire on the remote possibility that some tourist trap might very kindly be open.'

'It *is* open. It always is. I just said.'

'You said Knebworth was open.'

'Well, I thought it was. How about Hatfield, then, that's nearer?'

'I've already wasted half a day away from the office and there's only one thing worth doing with the rest of it.'

The car roared out of the blocked driveway of Knebworth House and back onto the A1.

'Where are you going?'

'Where do you think?'

'Oh, Sandy, no, please!' Petra's voice sank to an agitated whisper. 'This whole outing is supposed to be for Virginia's sake and you know how she feels about Maiden's End.'

'I know how I feel about Virginia,' he muttered back. 'I'm not going to mess my life about to suit that neurotic little brat. To think of her, spying into our private lives, rummaging in our drawers, opening our wardrobe – '

'The wardrobe? What did she take from the wardrobe?' Petra felt sick. 'Not the sex manual?'

'Yes,' lied Sandy, 'the sex manual.'

'Where did you find it?'

'On the landing. I moved it before you saw it.' If it had only been the sex manual and only on the landing, but that! She must have known for years; she must have been reading his ridiculous little reference library, laughing at him, even telling her friends. She might even have told Angela! 'Sandy's not really English, you know, he's a foreigner, and he's got all these silly books locked away in a briefcase in his wardrobe which tell him about how to behave and speak and pretend he's been educated at Public School so that he can impress people –' Ouch! It was like being in the clutches of a blackmailer. And now this! In the car itself! The spying, key-stealing little bitch.

The car sped on, Virginia dreaming, Sandy and Petra tortured by their private fears.

Petra studied the map urgently.

'Let's go to Woburn, Sandy. Look, if we turn off at the next junction we can take the A507 straight there. It's not all that far.'

'No.'

'Please!'

Petra sat agonised with despair. What the hell was the matter with him? He'd been so anxious for this outing 'to try and calm Virginia down', and now he was going to do the very thing which might well send her right over the edge into screaming insanity. He'd been perfectly all right until he stopped at that garage and put his V.A.T. bill into the glove compartment.

The turn-off was ahead and he slowed down. Perhaps he was going to Woburn after all. Oh, the relief! Oh, thank you, Sandy! The car slid off the motorway and onto the huge roundabout beneath. They passed the Ampthill turn-off and went on round into the Baldock and Buntingford road. Petra closed her eyes and groaned.

Soon he turned off to the right and into the winding Hertfordshire lanes. Petra let the map drop on to the floor and pulled open her handbag to get at her cigarettes. She rummaged irritably.

'I can't find my fags. I must have left them on the kitchen table. Where are yours?' She pulled at the glove compartment. 'What's wrong with this thing?'

'It sticks sometimes.'

'No it doesn't,' she retorted incredulously. 'Here, give me a hand, will you?'

'Don't be silly, I'm driving.'

'Well, stop for a minute, then!' Her voice sank into a furious whisper as he drove on. 'Sandy, I could kill you! What the hell do you think you're doing?'

'What I want to,' said Sandy grimly. 'I'm doing exactly what I want to do and if you and your daughter don't like it, that's just too bad.'

Virginia, shut off from the low-voiced squabble in the front seat, went over last night's heavenly moment again and again, feeling the hands tucking her in, the lips on her forehead, hearing the soft, gentle voice.

'I love you, darling.'

I love you, I love you. Whoever are you? Come to me again. Let this tedious day be over as soon as possible so that you can come to me again. She looked out resentfully at the brilliant sun which held unwanted daylight hours in suspension. Gallop apace, ye fiery-footed steeds. Who are you, where are you?

Weston, Ardeley, Wood End, Hankey Green. They were approaching the house from the opposite direction and Virginia had no idea where they were going. Petra and Sandy's muttered, agitated conversation didn't penetrate her switched-off ears or her preoccupied attention, although she had caught the word 'Woburn' once or twice. Another boring stately home, with silly, childish funfairs and animals and lots of horrible, boring people.

The car sped through the village, with its pond, pub, cottages, farms and neat skirt of new commuter residences, up on to the plateau, into the track, across the greening expanse....

'No!' Virginia shrieked. 'Not there! Not Maiden's End!'

It was looking better, at least to Sandy's eyes.

The windows were in again and the fanlight over the front door had been reglazed, with only a couple of bars needing to be replaced. The stone had been refaced, the steps repaired. The rubbish had been stacked into a skip – the sixth load – and the workmen were now engaged entirely on the interior.

The new wiring had been completed and found to be reliable, unlike Highgate where the refrigerator had suddenly self-destructed as Virginia walked into the house.

Virginia was shivering.

'Come on, sweetie.'

'Oh, let her stay there! Don't be such a bully!'

Sandy opened the back door, brutal with suppressed anger. 'Don't be silly, Virginia, get out.'

'No!'

'Get – out!'

He pulled her out, pleased by her fear. All right, you little bitch, so you're trying to make me feel uncomfortable, are you? Well, get a load of this, then. See how it feels to be afraid.

'Sandy, I'll never forgive you for this,' Petra whispered vehemently, frightened by his sudden transformation from easygoing, boyish malleability into cruel obstinacy. It was like discovering that you had lived for six years with a complete stranger. She had never seen Sandy at the office.

'Come on, sweetie, come and see your room.'

He dragged Virginia up the stairs, sliding his bulky figure round the ladder on which a painter was precariously perched and pushing her into the big back bedroom.

She was trembling, almost ready to collapse. The presence had been there from the moment she walked into the house. Here, with the ceiling cleanly repaired and the panelling stripped down ready for its insulating modern skin to be applied, she could feel the atmosphere around her like a singing, subliminal note too high for any but the sensitive to hear.

Sandy gripped her shoulder and brought her to a stop, his voice disarmingly jovial while his fingers told a quite different story.

'There, coming on nicely, isn't it, sweetie? It's miles bigger than your room at Highgate. You'll be able to have a proper bed-sitting room and spend as much time up here alone as you want. You'll like that, won't you? I know you don't enjoy being with Petra and me. Don't want to spend time with people you despise, do you? You can lock yourself away in here and we can lock ourselves away in *our* room. I think that might be quite a good idea, don't you? Lock our bedroom door? Understand what I mean?'

His hand suddenly shook her roughly and she looked up at him, shocked. What on earth was he talking about?

He bent down and looked into her face, his big, leonine head inches away from hers. His fair skin was red with anger, his teeth bared in an unreal smile which was more like a snarl.

Outside, Petra's voice floated up the stairs.

'Oh, sorry, did I jolt the ladder? Could have killed you, couldn't I? Honestly, darling, I'm frightfully sorry.'

Sandy made quick use of the last few seconds of privacy. His voice sank to a threatening whisper.

'If you ever do anything like that again, Virginia, I'll tan the hide off you, understand?'

'Do what?' she asked, threat suddenly drawing in from the miasma around her and solidifying into Sandy's hard stare. Silly, laughable, harmless old Granny had suddenly turned into the Wolf.

'You damn well know what!'

He gave her a last shake and went out to join Petra on the landing. Virginia stood there feeling sick. Could he possibly be going mad?

Too terrified to follow him, she glanced wildly round the room. It was bare except for a neat settlement of paintpots, rags and brushes which occupied the centre of the floor. In the corner, a fitted cupboard with a mirror in the door reflected her image with the wavering approximation of old glass.

She'd grown a bit, she was sure – at least an inch. And surely there was a change in her shape? She ran her hands over her sweater, flattening the fabric against her chest so that she could feel the tender swellings over which she had tried the bra only that morning, before putting it away once more in her drawer. And she'd had the pain again once or twice, although it had led to nothing. It must be soon, she was certain, it really would be soon.

She stiffened. There it was again, that atmosphere.

She hurried out on to the landing. Petra and Sandy had gone. The painter was just going into the bathroom, from which voices betrayed the presence of other men finishing the grouting of the tiles.

'Here, Mike, where's my frigging paint-rag? Can't put anything down without it getting nicked.'

'On the pan. Sorry.'

The atmosphere was strong on the landing, too, like a trail of scent left behind by a wild animal. She couldn't take cover in the bathroom, it would look awful; they'd make suggestive remarks she wouldn't know how to deal with.

She pushed herself towards the stairs, eyes fixed on the long, arched window, holding her breath lest she should scream. If I don't show that I'm afraid it won't be able to harm me. If I don't make a sound perhaps it won't notice I'm here at all.

She started down the flight, picking her way round the ladder. If I don't breathe before I get to the bottom it won't get me. Keep my eyes on the window and the trees outside, it's the only place where I'm not likely to see it.

Now the turn of the flight. Have to take my eyes off the trees. Look at the new brass chandelier in the hall. Nearly at the bottom. My lungs are bursting, but I mustn't breathe out yet.

The foot of the stairs, the long stretch of the hall leading towards the open front door. Not far now, not more than fifteen feet. Ten feet, five feet, nearly there –

Her breath exhaled in a rush as she jumped down the steps and ran, away from the invisible thing in the house.

She was still too close, the belt of trees held her in. She ran round the corner, cringing away from the looming cliff of brick hanging over her, and down into the garden, where a rotovator was ponderously turning over the acres of weeds and burying them under newly exhumed soil. She passed it, ran on, panting, then turned at last to look back at Maiden's End.

It stood in its clean, new garb of white sashes and repointed brickwork, the stain beneath the long window fading now that the rising damp had been cut off from its old playground by a renewed dampcourse. Oh yes, it looked all right, sound, cleaned-up and civilised, but as soon as you stepped inside you knew that it wasn't all right at all, it was all wrong.

Her hatred surged up, at Sandy, at Petra, at her helpless, dependent state, at the horrible house.

'I hate you,' she whispered, 'I hate you.'

Her hatred was a live thing, a violent, elemental force vibrating the air around her.

Up in the house, there was a muffled bang.

Her fury gradually subsided until it was merely misery.

Exhausted, she came up past the brick barn which was the only outbuilding Sandy had spared from demolition. It had been tidily rehabilitated and divided into a double garage, a garden tool store and an empty space which Sandy intended to be the changing room for a swimming pool.

Mr. Hargreaves' head rose out of the steps which led down into the basement, his face working with dismay.

'Where's your father, Miss?'

'He's not my father,' she said. Her voice was flat with rejection.

'Mr. Matheson! Mr. Matheson, are you there?'

Sandy came out of the garage. Petra followed behind, her angry expostulations cut off in mid-stream.

'Yes, Mr. Hargreaves, what is it now?'

'That Kevin! Just wait till I get my hands on him!'

'What's he done?'

'He's screwed up your wiring, that's what he's done. I knew he wasn't to be trusted.'

'You didn't tell me that,' retorted Sandy, 'you said he'd do a safe job, I remember quite clearly.'

'Yes, well, he does normally — ' He started to back down the steps, remembering belatedly that his qualms about Kevin were not actually to do with his expertise. 'Anyway, come and take a look at this.'

Sandy followed him down into the kitchen. Virginia, curious despite her fear, crept down the steps and peeped in at the kitchen window. The cellar door was standing open and a blackened mass of metal was falling out of it on to the floor, smoking and crackling with dangerously liberated electricity.

A frightened man stood some distance from it.

'Turn off the mains switch, Bob!' roared Hargreaves.

Bob edged nervously round the fireworks display. There was a metallic clunk and the sparks died. They stood there in the sudden gloom while Mr. Hargreaves took out his handkerchief and mopped his sweating face.

'What the devil happened?' demanded Sandy, surveying the wreckage of several hundred pounds with annoyance.

'Boiler exploded. Suddenly went up like a bomb and all the works shot out. Never seen nothing like it.'

Virginia turned away from the window, smiling. Serve them

right. She didn't care if the whole house exploded. She was suddenly terrifyingly aware of its weight suspended above her and ran up the steps and round to the front drive.

The Volvo was parked over by the gate. She pulled open the door, scrambled in and enclosed herself in the nearest thing to London available. She even pushed down the locking knobs on the windows, then sat there for half an hour in her urban capsule until Petra and Sandy at last emerged from the house, leaving an infuriated Mr. Hargreaves with instructions which totally contradicted his previous ones. Quickly, she released the catches.

As they drove off she pressed her hands to her ears to shut out their irritable bickering, drew up her knees and curled into the corner, forcing comforting fantasy back into her mind. It was hard, the real world was too much with her, but she concentrated desperately and at last he climbed into her window and stood in her room.

'Come along, Virginia darling, you won't have to live in that terrible house. We're going to my cottage.'

Sandy drove back to London, silent, angry and afraid, continuously aware of *The Sloane Ranger's Handbook* sealed in the locked glove compartment.

' – and Sandy said we were going for a day out to Knebworth but it was closed, so do you know what he did? He went up to Maiden's End, even though he knows I hate it, and it's still frightening, Daddy, even with all the new things they've done to it. And Pet – Mummy, said she wasn't going to cook in a kitchen like that and they'd got to strip it all out and put in a decent fitted one, with strip-lighting and a proper oven and an electric hob and a microwave. And Sandy's behaving in such an extraordinary way that I think he must be going mad! All angry and hateful. Really mad! Daddy, can't I come and live with you? Daddy? Daddy! Are you there?'

'Yes, Ginnie,' groaned Derek.

Chapter 10

Petra rang Zak next morning. He was away, his secretary told her, on holiday in the Seychelles. Damn! She rang her G.P. and made an appointment. Well, at least she'd done something.

Virginia went out again as soon as they got back from the doctor's and didn't return until the afternoon, when she immediately shut herself in her room. Petra made one or two attempts to speak to her but her tentative, ingratiating knocking at the closed door produced only monosyllables in reply.

By the time dinner was over she was only too happy to go out to the Flask with Sandy and get that awful child out of her mind for a couple of hours.

She went to the phone again early on Wednesday, exhausted by a night more hair-raising than even Sunday's had been.

'Derek? Petra. Look, it's Virginia. I've been thinking things over, and perhaps it might be a good idea if she was to spend a few weeks with you, or at least until school starts again. She's rather het-up at the moment and it might calm her down. She's so fond of you, you know. What do you think? Could you put her up for a while?'

Derek, newly-awakened, frowzy in unwashed pyjamas and uncleaned dressing gown, stared at the mouthpiece as if it were relaying an unexpected pronouncement from the Sybil of Delphi.

'But you said you'd never let her! I was always asking you to let her stay with me once in a while, you know I was, but you'd never agree. After all these years, Petra!'

Petra pulled an agonised face. Damn! She'd known he'd

make the most of it. She tried to sound calm and reasonable.

'Well, yes, I know, perhaps I was wrong. You see, we've got a bit of bother at the moment, to be honest.' Yes, better be honest. 'We had a day out on Monday and we went down to the house – '

'Yes, she rang and told me.'

'Did she?' said Petra, taken aback. 'Oh. Well, anyway, last night we went out to the pub and when we got back there was another fire just starting. A bit of duff wiring on the stereo, I think, and luckily we got home before it did too much damage, but even so, there's a lot of mess and I'd like her out of the way while we clear things up. Just for a few days, Derek, if you wouldn't mind.'

Derek was stunned, incredulous at this out-of-the-blue appeal for help after so many years of scornful rejection. At last he was on top and he couldn't resist taking full advantage of it. Exultant, he put on a detached, curious voice.

'Well, well, Petra, this is a real surprise. Suddenly you need me. Suddenly I'm useful. Whatever's happened to dear, reliable, infallible Sandy?'

Petra smashed her hand down on to the phone table, furious with humiliation. She laughed in a light, amused tone and reached for a cigarette.

'Oh, come on, Derek, why do you always have to dig at poor Sandy? It's nothing to do with him. No, this is for Virginia's sake entirely. She's in a bit of a state, poor kid, and I don't want her suffering any further insecurity at the moment.

'By the way, I've taken her to the doctor and he gave her a blood test, for the hormone level, you know, but he said there's nothing to worry about, it will all happen in its own good time. That was a really good idea of yours. I'm terribly glad you suggested it, Derek. It was really wise, really, really perceptive. I should have thought of it myself, but you know how it is. One gets so busy and occupied with one's life, and just doesn't see what's going on under one's nose. Still, we're all fallible, aren't we?'

She laughed humbly. My God we are!

'What do you think, Derek? Could you take her for a few days? I really would be most frightfully grateful, if you could.'

Derek listened open-mouthed to the soft soap. There had to

111

be a catch. Six years it was now, since Petra had taken him to the divorce court and the cleaner's, six years of trying to pull himself and his finances together after that Bacchic castration of his masculinity, his self-image, his possessions, his hard-won cushion against life's asset-stripping blows. And never once since had she allowed him to think that he had any rôle to play in Virginia's life; no recognition even of his natural affection towards the child he had fathered — although that action, he had to admit, had been so unthinking, so totally selfish in its aim of immediate physical satisfaction that it contained no more thought for the end product of what he was doing than that of a tom-cat on the crumbling slates above his Fitzrovia flat.

And she had to choose now to throw him the crumbs from her maternal table. All those years of painful longing for his stolen child, and she had to offer him his heart's desire at the very moment that he had lost the wish for it. He had seen Virginia diminish from his beloved little girl into a demanding incubus and now she wasn't his dear Virginia any more. She was alien, unlikeable, even unlovable, a scraggy, sulky teenager with no tie to him except bloodtie. To be honest, he didn't much like Virginia.

'Petra, I can't take her! You don't realise the sort of dump I'm living in. I haven't even got a second bedroom — she'd have to sleep on the couch, or I would. It's really no place for her.' Or for a forty-year-old man, come to that.

Petra was astounded and unreasonably outraged.

'God, Derek, you're selfish! This is the first time I've ever asked you for help and you refuse. So much for all that "I do miss my little girl" crap! Well, we know where we are now, don't we? Just wait until I tell her.'

'No, don't, please,' Derek pleaded, suddenly frightened. 'There's no need to upset her. You don't understand, Petra, it's just that I'm in dead trouble myself. The thing is — well — I've had to file an appeal for bankruptcy.'

'You've what?'

Petra burst out laughing. He had expected no other reaction, but the tears still sprang to his eyes. He grabbed blindly for the remnants of his self-esteem.

'It's just a formality — lots of people do it. Just a way of sorting things out in a tidy way so you can start again.'

'Start again? What'll it be this time, Derek? Double-glazing? Stone-cladding? You've tried them all, haven't you? I suppose there's still steam carpet-cleaning left.'

Derek, unable to speak another word for tears, put down the phone.

Petra looked with disgust at the smoke-blackened state of her living room. It seemed the very symbol of her situation — the potential for unmanageable chaos which lurked beneath her organised, glossy life. The hastily-pulled-out stereo equipment sprawled across the charred carpet. An expensive curtain hung, half burnt, from the rail. The furniture was sodden.

The funny thing was, Virginia had seemed to enjoy the fire. She had stood on the step as the siren approached down the street, crying 'He's coming, he's coming!' and jumping up and down with excitement. Her face had been flushed, her eyes shining as she watched the firemen leaping off the engine.

It had startled Petra at the time, but there had been too much to think about in that fearful moment. Now, she began to think again, going over the obsessive worries of the night. Burnt bed, burnt-out massager, burnt stereo. . . .

The light came on. She turned. Seconds later, Virginia entered the room in her dressing gown, eager and alert, totally unlike her normal morning self. Her eyes gleamed as she looked at the devastation.

'There's no need to turn the light on, Virginia, it's broad daylight.'

'I didn't.'

Virginia clicked off the switch and laughed, full of delight.

'Oh, Petra, wasn't it exciting? I've never seen a fire put out before. Weren't they brave? Did you see that young one with the moustache? I knew he'd be the bravest of the lot.'

'No, I didn't. Who is he then? Do you know him?'

Virginia dropped her head. 'No, I've just seen him about.' He hadn't looked quite as she'd pictured him, he did have a moustache after all, but it was him, her dream lover, he just had to be. He was real. He had been real all the time, just waiting for her to find him. He'd caught her eye and smiled. 'Get outside, dear,' he said, 'it's not safe.' She caressed the lamp which he had moved into the corner, away from the flames.

'Well, it was all a damn sight too exciting for me. We'll have to redecorate quickly before the Liptons see it.' Petra looked up at the blackened ceiling with a frown, then back at Virginia. The lamp was on.

'Oh, Virginia, don't *do* that.'

'I didn't, I only touched it.'

Petra switched it off irritably and turned on her daughter, suddenly determined. 'Virginia, you didn't have anything to do with that fire, did you?'

She looked astonished.

'No, of course I didn't. How could I?'

'I don't know how. I just know that there have been a lot of fires in this house lately and it's usually been when you've been here alone.'

'What a horrible thing to say!' Virginia protested. 'You really hate me, don't you? I don't know why you don't let me go and live with Daddy if you hate me so much.'

'I don't hate you, it just seems a bit funny, that's all. And anyway, I asked Derek about that this morning.'

'Did you? Oh, Petra, did you really?' Her face lit up.

'Yes. He said no.'

Virginia stared. Then the tears welled up in her eyes and ran down her face, with the suddenness of a bucket under a tap spilling over at the brim.

'He didn't. You're lying. He wouldn't say no.'

Petra felt belated compunction and alarm.

'No, I'm really not lying, darling. He said he hasn't room and he's in a bit of trouble with his business. I'm afraid he's just too busy at the moment.'

Virginia's face became a tragic mask, eyes and mouth open like the assaulted Maiden's End. For a moment she was as silent as the tormented house, then a great cry of pain burst from her lips.

It was deafening. Petra clapped her hands to her ears, horrified at the abandonment of her daughter's distress.

'Virginia, don't! Stop it!' She tried to put her arms around her.

'You none of you want me! Go away! I hate you all!'

She stood there in her dressing gown like a demented Wee Willie Winkie, howling with despair.

Petra suddenly froze with terror. It wasn't Virginia, she was used to scenes from her. It was what was happening around Virginia.

About her, like restless grass in the wind, the long pile on the carpet rose and moved. The skirt of her dressing gown swayed with energy, then dragged to one side, pulling the garment away from her body and baring one bony shoulder. Across the pale skin, five red marks started to travel like the lines on an encephalograph.

'Virginia!'

Petra's scream cut across her daughter's cries and brought Sandy rushing into the room, dressed for the office in a grey three-piece suit. Virginia keened on, writhing in her mental anguish.

'What the hell...?'

'Sandy! Look at Virginia!'

Then the lights went on, all of them this time; the centre light, the table lamps and the hooded bar above the picture. The blackened stereo pushed out a tiny tongue of flame and exploded into life, flooding the room with a Liszt Hungarian Rhapsody. The picture fell from the wall.

Soon, the alabaster eggs began to spill over the edge of their pottery basket and fall one by one to the floor. In a fantastic piece of formation dancing, they moved neatly into a circle which threw out quivering waves of vibration across the pile of the carpet.

Virginia started to scream, eyes closed, fists clenched against her face. The dressing gown and nightdress suddenly ripped from top to bottom and fell away, and the red scratches moved down across her naked body like devouring worms.

The music rose in volume, filling the room with a joyous assertion of Sandy's origins, and the flames started to creep across the stereo's whole bulk. He rushed towards it, looking round wildly for something with which to smother them.

With a mocking, jesting offer of cushions, the settee moved forward to meet him.

'The Samaritans. Can I help you?'

The distressed tone at the other end of the line was familiar, but the words completely unexpected.

'Is Rod Singleton there today?'

He paused, then said cautiously, 'Rod 251 speaking.'

'Oh, Rod! It's Petra Matheson. Look, the most ghastly thing's happened. It's Virginia. You were so good with her on Sunday. Could you possibly come at once?'

'What is it?' Rod asked, alarmed. 'She hasn't tried to harm herself, has she?'

'No – well, could be. I don't honestly know. She's got scratches all over her and she's in hysterics – '

'Have you called the doctor?'

'No, it's not like that. Please, Rod, can't you come?'

Rod looked up at the clock on the wall.

'Sorry, Petra, I'm not off duty until ten, and we aren't allowed to leave the Centre before that. I'll come as soon as I finish. Get the doctor, love, and I'll be round as quickly as I can.'

'No, no, not the doctor. You don't understand. Oh God, Rod, it's terrible, we're at our wits' end.'

'Well, try and get her to lie down. I will come, really I will. Just stay with her and try to calm her until then.'

'I *am* trying to calm her but you just don't know what's happening here! It's like hell on earth!'

Petra was near-hysterical herself.

'I'll be there as soon as I can get away.'

'Well, hurry! I'm just – oh God, the table – '

The phone was slammed down.

Rod, shaken, glanced at the clock again. It was twenty to ten. The seven-to-ten a.m. duty was usually a quiet one, and with luck he might get off on time. He looked round the grubby converted living room which regularly had the human misery of London piped into it. On the other line, Mary 198 was hunched over the mouthpiece, gently trying to persuade a weeping over-doser to let her call an ambulance. The next shift would be in any minute; he'd ask them to take over at once.

That poor kid – whatever was up with her? He liked Petra and Sandy, but he had a suspicion that their parental psychology probably wasn't very advanced. They lived on the surface of life.

The bell rang again and he picked up the receiver.

'The Samaritans. Can I help you?'

The next volunteer, a rock musician, pushed the door open the moment after Rod spoke and dumped his guitar case on the table.

'Is that Rod 251?'

'Yes.'

'It's Margaret here. I'm feeling really low, Rod. Bill didn't come home again last night, I know he's got another woman. It's no use, I've tried so hard to get through to him, but he just doesn't seem to care about how I feel.' The voice broke into tears.

Rod grimaced. He knew Margaret of old. This could take hours.

It was nearly twelve before he ran up the path of the Mathesons' house. The front door was on the latch and he went straight in, noticing with surprise the filthy, mud-trodden hall carpet. He glanced into the living room and was appalled by the chaos within. The walls and ceiling were black, the furniture was here, there and everywhere and the stereo equipment in the corner was smothered by a pile of scorched cushions.

He went and shouted up the stairs.

'Petra! Petra, it's Rod!'

There was a rush of feet and Petra appeared at the top, dressed in slacks and shirt and without a trace of make-up on her distraught face.

'Oh, thank God! She's up here!'

'What happened?' Rod asked as he climbed. 'Did she go berserk, or something?'

'Yes, so did everything else. The settee *moved*, Rod, all by itself.' She kept looking round as if expecting the house to collapse about her ears. The grandfather clock cleared its throat and she turned in a panic, staring at the innocent piece of furniture as if it was about to leap upon her like a tiger.

Rod put his hand on her arm, horrified. 'Oh, you poor love, you're in a right state yourself, aren't you?'

Virginia was lying in bed, staring at the ceiling. She hadn't moved or spoken for at least an hour. Sandy stood by the window, drumming his fingers on the pane and glaring down at the park below. His hand ran through his thick locks obsessively, as if he were quite literally trying to keep his hair on. Rod moved across quietly.

'Virginia? Hello, love, what's the matter?'

He sat down on the bed and took her hand in his. Virginia's head turned suddenly at his voice, her face becoming flooded with animation. When she saw him the smile faded and an expression of confusion replaced it.

'Oh, hello. What are you doing here?'

'Petra called me. What's up? Tell me.'

Virginia's eyes moved to Sandy and her expression became sullen. He stared at her steadily, his demeanour a mixture of resentment and what Rod recognised with a shock as fear. He caught Sandy's eye and wagged his head in dismissal. Sandy hesitated, then obeyed, drawing Petra outside with him and closing the door. She fell into his arms and began to cry. The clock whirred and started to strike twelve. She jumped violently.

'It's starting again! Quick, Sandy, let's get out!'

'But what about Rod?'

'Damn Rod, I want to get out!'

She fled downstairs and out on to the step. He followed and tried to drag her in again.

'Not here, Petra. For Petes's sake, everyone will see you.'

Even as he spoke Pat Goodison's face appeared at the next-door bay window and mouthed a concerned inquiry. He gave a bland smile of rebuttal, pulled Petra back into the house and slammed the door. She fled straight through to the back yard. Within minutes, Pat appeared at a back window and repeated her silent question, with full accompaniment of waving hands, raised eyebrows and concernedly inclined head. Sandy laughed merrily at her and dragged Petra round the corner into the sideway, where they stood in close proximity to the dustbin while she sobbed hysterically.

'Oh God, oh God, oh God – '

Her voice rose inexorably towards a scream and he shook her to cut it off before it should reach that attention-drawing pitch.

'Now come on, Petra, it's all right now. Rod's with her and you know how good he is at this sort of thing. Virginia will listen to him.'

'*She'll* listen to him! Do you think the settee will listen to him too? And the eggs and the picture and your bloody stereo? Sandy, do you realise that the stereo wasn't even plugged in?

And the chairs and the plant and the books and the telephone and the lights – are they going to listen to him? Do you think he gets many calls from pieces of furniture? 'Hello, Samaritans, I'm an armchair and I've reached the end of my tether.' 'I'm a stereo and I don't like the things they play on me so I'm choosing my own music from now on.' 'I'm a bed and I keep bursting into flames because I hate the people who sleep in me and want to kill them – "

Sandy shook her harder, trying to silence the wild, farcical ramblings which were not only embarrassingly noisy but were also beginning to awake twinges of nervousness in him.

'Be quiet, Petra, please! The neighbours will hear.'

'Sandy, it must be Virginia. I don't know how she's doing it but I'm sure it's her.' Her voice sank to an urgent, terrified mumble. 'I've heard about this sort of thing. She's stirred something up, something evil. She's invited it into the house because she hates us and wants us dead. Oh God, why? What ever have we done?'

'Nothing,' he assured her, 'nothing. It's probably just some quirk of physics. An electric field, dampness, some fluke of the weather.' He really believed it; anything else was impossible.

She changed tack immediately, grabbing at puny straws.

'Do you think so? It can happen, can't it? Some places are like that. No wonder things always went wrong for me here, I didn't stand a chance. I tried so hard with Derek, you know, but it was all against me. I always knew there was something wrong with this house, I never liked it, right from the start.'

It was the first Sandy had heard of it. Petra's liking for the house had always seemed strong to the point of obsessional. She might regard things as always being against her, but his mind was accustomed to seeing things in the opposite light, and he suddenly saw whatever ailed the house as a remarkably obliging ally. His voice regained confidence.

'Well, we won't be here much longer, darling. We'll bring the move forward. Whatever it is, we'll get right away from it. It's not going to follow us all the way to Maiden's End.'

Petra swung from physics back to necromancy.

'But she might bring it with her. They do, you know, I've read about it. They call it a familiar spirit. She's evil, Sandy! She's a witch! It's all Derek's fault. He's always been a bit round the bend and his mother — God! You don't know his mother, a right cow! She just hates me. Perhaps she's a witch, too. It runs in families, doesn't it? She's probably put Virginia up to it, you know how furious she was when I divorced Derek. She's been planning it for years. She's cursed us. We're all going to die!'

She reached screaming point again and Sandy clapped his hand over her mouth in desperation, struggling with the unprecedentedly agitated Petra while he tried to picture Derek's respectable, upright mother with a pointed hat, a black cloak and a self-driving broomstick. It was unimaginable. At the moment, anything unbalanced about Virginia seemed almost certain to have been inherited from her mother. It was a disturbing thought; he wasn't used to making such bad bargains in the possessions he acquired.

Petra grabbed his hand, gazing up into his face in abject apology.

'I'll sign the contract, Sandy. I'll sign it today. It's all drawn up, isn't it? I'm sorry I've been so difficult about it. You can get on to the Liptons and tell them we're going at once.'

'Not until we've cleaned up the lounge, we're not,' said Sandy tersely. 'We don't want them to see that.'

'Get the painters in tomorrow. I'll start packing. We'll stay with Pat until then, I'm not sleeping here tonight.'

'Do you really want Pat knowing about this? She's quite capable of telling the Liptons herself. You know what she's like — the bionic mouth.'

The side gate rattled and a high, inquiring voice hailed them from the other side.

'Sandy? Are you there? What's the trouble?'

'Nothing, Pat,' he shouted with ferocious gaiety. 'Petra's just a bit upset about the fire. She'll be fine in a minute.'

The gate rattled again. It was, Sandy saw with relief, bolted.

'Oh, poor girl! Can I help with the clearing up?'

'No thanks, everything under control.'

'Well — remember, anything at all —'

Mrs. Goodison retreated, disappointed.

'See?' he said to Petra. She quietened down, sobbing miserably into her handkerchief. 'Come and have a drink.'

'Bring it out here.' She sat down on the dustbin.

120

They were still there when Rod emerged from the house. He looked at the tiny, paved yard, then poked his head round the corner.

'How is she?' Petra asked anxiously, gripping her third vodka and tonic.

'All right.' His voice was carefully non-committal.

'Come and sit down,' said Sandy, suddenly realising the ridiculousness of their hiding place and leading the way to the cast-iron table and chairs. Pat awaited them at the window. He attacked her with a grin which was beginning to show signs of strain and she dodged back with an apologetic smile.

Rod sat down and looked at his clasped hands, which he arranged with studied care on the table before him.

'What did she say?' asked Petra, emptying her glass.

He twisted his fingers, then spread them out in front of him, studying the nails as if they were an idiot board.

'Well?' Sandy demanded impatiently.

Rod looked up with the expression of one who didn't expect to be believed.

'Have you ever heard of poltergeists?' he asked.

Chapter 11

Sandy slammed through the swing doors of the tastefully converted potato warehouse in Covent Garden and up the cast-iron spiral staircase to his office suite. His secretary cupped her hand over the mouthpiece and greeted him with relief.

'Oh, Sandy, thank goodness! I was just going to ring you at home. Skitt and Boom are on the line about the Itsy-Bitsy campaign. You were going to ring them Monday, remember? Can you speak to them now?'

Sandy grimaced. Damn! He'd forgotten all about it. And a new account, too.

'Yes, I'll take it in my office. Where's the file?'

'On your desk.'

'Did Trevor finish the animatic?'

She looked stricken. 'Well, no, you remember –'

'Oh God, yes. How is he?'

'Bad,' she said.

Sandy dealt quickly with Skitt and Boom, then pressed the intercom button.

'Yah, Sandy?'

'Sarah, I'm going to be on the phone for quite a while, so don't disturb me until I say.'

'O.K., yah. You've got Irradiated Meat coming at three, you know.'

'Well, hold them off until I give you the all clear. Give them a drink or something.'

With a tense frown he picked up the telephone. His first call was to a house in Harley Street. When he put the receiver down he was smiling with relief, fully himself again.

He then proceeded to attack the telephone and the people at the other end with determination, bullying and money – the ultimate weapon. The decorator: 'Listen, this is a rush job and I want it done this week. No, don't give me that, you can take a couple of men off that job. I'll pay double time.' The solicitor, the estate agent, the removal contractors, Mr. Hargreaves. . . .
'Hello there, Hargreaves. How's it going? Did you do what we said?'

'Yes,' said Hargreaves gloomily, his hired radio phone to his ear as he surveyed the stripped basement of Maiden's End. Not a trace of the old fittings remained. The kitchen was a bare, plastered room with a half-tiled floor.

'Have the units arrived?'

'Yes, this morning.' The units stood around like smart hotel guests waiting to be shown to their rooms. 'How on earth did you fix that? The last time I had dealings with Littlebow they took six months.'

'Client of mine,' said Sandy. 'Now get cracking, I'm bringing the move forward.'

'But Mr. Matheson – '

'No buts, Mr. Hargreaves, you can do it if you try. I want you all out by next week:'

'Next week!'

The woolly hat was flung down on to the tiles in a gesture of total despair.

By the time Irradiated Meat arrived it was all settled. Everything and everyone had been fixed. If he could have rung God, whom he vaguely pictured before a giant switchboard, pressing buttons marked Earthquake, Pestilence, War, Road Accident and Heart Attack for Mr. Bloggs, he would have done it. Prayer, the method by which less self-sufficient people made the connection, was not in his repertoire. If it had been, he would certainly have offered the Almighty double time for the angel despatched to fulfil the shopping list of Sandy Matheson's requirements.

Finally he rang Petra. She was sitting on the back step, shivering, despite Rod's comforting arm, in the cold wind which had destroyed the April day.

'Phone,' said Rod,

'You get it, I'm staying here.'

'Hello, Sandy, Rod here. Petra won't come into the house, I'm afraid, can I take a message?'

'Just tell her it's all fixed; she can go round and sign the contract. The decorators are coming tomorrow, so she'd better start clearing the room. The move will be next week. How's Virginia?'

'Asleep.'

'Did you give her something?'

'No need, she went straight off. Exhausted, I think.'

'Thank God for that. Here, Rod, you didn't really mean all that crap, did you?'

'Yes,' said Rod, glancing round at the trail of havoc uneasily. There was broken china on the floor.

'Absolute balls,' said Sandy and rang off.

Rod went back to Petra and gave her the message. She seemed hardly able to take it in. She was nursing the vodka bottle and rocking herself backwards and forwards.

'Shall I make some coffee?'

'Don't want coffee. Want another drink.'

'You've had enough. Have a coffee.'

'Haven't had enough, I can still think.'

He went in, put the coffee in the percolator and switched it on, moving round the kitchen on tiptoe. He approached each piece of equipment with careful respect, prepared for anything. As he reached for the china cupboard, there was a rattling within. He stopped, swallowed, then opened the door and caught the mugs as they rose from the shelf.

'Stop it,' he told them sharply, and they submitted to being laid on the tray, although they moved an inch as he released them, making their own choice of position.

The percolator started to bubble, then slide, and he held it firmly on to the worktop. As he removed the jug he felt it give a rebellious tug. He carried it quickly to the tray, on which it performed a mocking jig, then out of the house, where it became still. He set the tray down on the back step beside Petra, breathing fast.

''sVirginia asleep?'

'Yes.'

The china cupboard rattled.

'What's that?' asked Petra, her eyes frightened.
'Nothing.' Rod's hand shook as he poured the coffee.
'I hate this house,' moaned Petra. 'I hate the whole world.'
'So does Virginia. That's the trouble.'
'What has she got to hate?' Petra asked, tears filling her eyes. 'I love her, Rod, I really love her.' She was well into the maudlin stage.
'Well, she doesn't seem to believe that. She says nobody wants her and she's all alone except for – '
' – Derek.'
'No,' Rod frowned, 'there's someone she seems very fond of.'
'You mean she's got a boyfriend she hasn't told us about?' Petra wailed. 'Oh, why does she have to be so secretive? I don't understand it, Rod, it's not as if we were prudes. We'd have been thrilled to meet him. She's just shut us out of her life as if we were total strangers.'
'Well, adolescents do, you know. Everything's so intense at that age that they can't put it into words. I know I couldn't, could you?'
'Oh hell, I can't remember,' moaned Petra, 'it's all so long ago. I'm as old as the hills.'
'Anyway, this boy, she says he's a fireman.'
'A fireman! Good grief, he must be years older than her! I remember now, she mentioned something about him being here last night. God, I'll kill him! A fully grown man messing about with a kid of sixteen. Where does he live?'
'I don't know. She says he's her destiny. She's been waiting for him for some time and now he's turned up.'
'Oh my God,' Petra howled, 'she's off her head.'
'I really shouldn't worry about it, Petra. I think it's completely one-sided – hero-worship from afar. She's built up an enormous fantasy about him and probably never even spoken to him.'
Petra was in a panic. She put down the coffee and reached for the vodka again.
'It's just like me all over again. Did I ever tell you about that, Rod?' The alcoholic tears spilled over once more. 'The only reason I married Derek was because of Virginia, and it was a total disaster. It just ruined my life. I don't want the same thing

happening to my baby. Oh, my poor baby! We've got to save her, Rod. We've got to get her away from him quick. Thank God we're moving.'

'Yes, well,' Rod said doubtfully, 'I think that's half the trouble, Petra. Virginia doesn't want to move. She's terribly upset about leaving here. She's basically very insecure you know, that's why you've got the poltergeist problem.'

Petra screamed and clapped the vodka over her left ear and the glass over her right. There was an alarming clunk as the bottle hit her head, but she seemed completely oblivious.

'Don't start that again, please!'

'But you've got to face up to it, I'm afraid. It's caused by Virginia, and until she's back to normal it will go on happening.'

'She's a witch!'

'Now don't be stupid, darling, of course she isn't. It's nothing to do with black magic, it's something which happens when you've got a disturbed adolescent who can't let her feelings out naturally. I don't know how it works, neither does anyone else, but it's a fact. Probably some natural thing like electricity or magnetism or force fields. Every living thing's got a force field, you know, they've even been photographed. People talk about good and bad vibes − well, it could well be true. We could all be radio stations, in a way. I knew a boy once who could hold his hands over pieces of paper and make them move.'

'Stop it, Rod! Don't talk about it! I don't even want to think about it!'

Rod got up wearily and went inside. You couldn't tell someone something they didn't want to hear, certainly not with a third of a bottle of vodka inside them. He went upstairs, with a great deal more trepidation than he appeared to feel, and tiptoed into Virginia's room.

Her wide-open eyes met him like traffic lights, stopping him in his tracks just inside the door. He was aware of alarm. Her hostility was like a stone wall, as if she had shut herself off from the hateful world within a fortress.

'Hello. Feeling better?'

'Yes.'

'You've had a lovely long sleep.'

'Where's Petra and Sandy?'

'Sandy's gone to work, Petra's downstairs. Do you want to see her?'

'No.' She pulled at her nightdress. 'I wasn't wearing this one. Why did they change it?'

'You were ill.'

'What, sick, you mean?'

'Ill.'

She caught sight of the scratches; scarlet, weeping tracks raised upon embankments of swollen flesh.

'Who did that to me? Was it Sandy?'

'No, of course not,' Rod protested, another hideously unpleasant possibility coming to his mind. He had no illusions about the nasty somethings which lurked in family woodsheds, he'd encountered them all. 'He doesn't hurt you, does he?'

'No, but he hates me. I didn't realise before, but he does. I found out when we went down to the house last time.'

'What happened?' asked Rod, his heart sinking. This was getting worse and worse. Sandy was his *friend*.

'He shook me, and accused me of doing something to his bedroom. I think he's going mad, Rod. I was really scared.'

'Doing what to his bedroom?'

'Don't know. He didn't say.'

'Listen, love, do you remember what happened in the lounge?'

She moved suddenly, as if she had been touched in a painful place, ducking her head down on to the pillow and drawing up her legs. Her eyes fastened on the scratches and she ran her fingers over them.

'I got upset.'

'Because your Daddy couldn't have you to stay?'

'Because he doesn't love me.'

'Do you remember what happened after that?'

Her eyes swivelled sideways at the edge of the duvet, watching the rows of flowers playing hide-and-seek among the folds.

'No.'

'You do, don't you?'

'I think things fell down. I didn't really notice, I was crying.'

'Did you make them fall down?'

'Of course I didn't!' Her voice was scornful, but there was fear underneath.

'I don't mean with your hands. Did you think very hard that you wanted them to fall down, to get broken? Did you feel that you hated them?'

Her hands explored the scratches obsessively. 'I hate everything. Everybody hates me, but they're right. I'm no good. I hate me, too.'

'I don't hate you,' Rod said gently.

She looked at him with the detachment of a scientist observing a white mouse. 'I expect you do, really. You only say you don't because you're nice and it's the nice, kind thing to do, but you don't mean it.'

'You think I'm insincere?'

'No, I don't mean that. Insincere means that you tell deliberate lies. I mean that you don't know how to be anything *but* nice. You have to be hard to hate and you're soft. You haven't got the strength to be nasty.'

Rod winced. Great soft pansy, said his father.

'And you have?'

'I have now. I'm sick of loving people, it hurts. Hating's better.'

'And you hate me.' Rod's voice shook.

She looked at him, right through him, deep into the place where she had wounded him. It felt like a probing scalpel.

'Not all of you. Your voice is nice. It reminds me of someone.'

'What about this fireman? You don't hate him, do you?'

'No,' she admitted, her face softening.

'He's kind, isn't he?' asked Rod, trying to swallow down the lump in his throat. 'You don't think he's soft because he doesn't hate.'

She went silent and sulky.

'Where does he live?' Rod asked urgently. 'I won't tell Petra and Sandy, honest, not if you don't want me to. But I think someone ought to know who he is. Tell me, I'll keep the secret. Just between us two. I care about you, you know. Like you said, I'm soft.'

She saw the tear in the corner of his eye and felt no pity, only surprised curiosity, as if the white mouse had suddenly screamed for help.

'You *are* soft, aren't you? Don't you ever get sick of being hurt?'

'Yes,' said Rod, 'but you get used to it.'

Sandy edged his way past the piled-up furniture in the hall. In the living room, Rod and Virginia were pulling up the carpet.

'Hello there! Everything ready, eh?'

'Nearly finished,' said Rod. 'Have you got any dustsheets? We'd better cover these things up before the decorators get scraping.'

'Don't know, old man. Not my department. Ask Petra.'

'I've put her to bed. She passed out.'

'Oh. How are you, Virginia?'

'All right.'

She rolled away at the carpet, as withdrawn and contemptuous as usual. You would have thought that the morning's events had never happened. Sandy looked at her uneasily. She pushed past him and went out.

'How's she been?' he asked Rod.

'Pretty normal. Very quiet and monosyllabic, but that's Virginia, I gather.'

'You think she'll be all right now, then?'

'No, I don't. She's only got to get upset and things could start up again.'

'Oh, don't be so silly, Rod. It was just a fit of hysteria, that's all. Get her down to the country and she'll soon be running around like a normal kiddie, enjoying the fresh air.'

Rod felt extreme exasperation.

'Look, Sandy, Virginia's not a kiddie. I know she looks like one, but she's anything but. You've really got a problem here and it isn't going to go away.'

Sandy looked at Rod's slim, graceful figure. He reminded him of Trevor. The thought produced a surge of fury.

'Well, what am I supposed to do about it?' he demanded.

'You could listen to her more. Find out what's bothering her.'

'How can I listen to her when she won't even talk to me? She treats me like a piece of furniture.'

'You mean she throws you around the room?'

'Don't be so bloody stupid! There's a perfectly rational explanation for all that, I've been thinking it over. It's that radio tower down the road. Those things always muck up the electricity in the neighbourhood.'

'How about the stereo bursting into flame?'

'It was still smouldering from last night.'

'With a Hungarian Rhapsody?'

'Electricity's funny stuff. You get these freak incidents, and there was thunder about this morning.'

'Shit, Sandy!' shouted Rod. 'Do you never see what you don't want to? Have you no perception of what's going on outside your own narrow little interests? Do you think the whole world is a huge chess game with you controlling both sides?'

Virginia came back and started to sweep the bare boards.

'That's a good girl,' said Sandy heartily. 'Make a nice little housewife one day, won't she, Rod?'

She ignored him. Sandy had missed his lunch and he was hungry.

'Is Petra going to cook soon?'

'I've got a casserole in the oven,' said Rod. 'I'm a nice little housewife myself.'

He didn't stop for dinner.

Virginia said goodbye to him without meeting his eyes. He gave her a few last urgent words as he left the house.

'Don't hate, Virginia. It's wrong and it's dangerous. You'll harm yourself as well as other people. Any fool can hate. Believe me, loving is better and stronger. It takes courage to love people and give them another chance.'

'I do love,' she said.

'Yes, I know, but you must be careful; don't put all your eggs in one basket – that really is the way to get hurt. No one human being is capable of taking on sole responsibility for your happiness. Won't you tell me where he lives?'

She shook her head.

'Listen,' said Rod desperately, 'here's my phone number. If you want to tell me anything, anything at all, just ring me. Any time. Please, promise me you will.'

She took the scribbled-on envelope without looking at it.

'I might,' she said, and dropped it among the Crap Mail on the chiffonier in the hall.

Angela called that evening. Virginia was on her way up to her room, leaving Sandy to do the washing up. He had expected that she would do it and her refusal had made him angry, but he hadn't pushed the point. Virginia had felt spiteful satisfaction as he reached for his female disguise.

'Hello, Virge,' said Angela chirpily. 'Just thought I'd drop in.' She was wearing a royal blue satin blouse, and a huge cerise bow flopped around on her stiff, gelled hair. 'What's all the upheaval for? Are you moving already?'

'No, we've got the painters coming. We had another fire.'

'Gosh, did you? You do have exciting times here, don't you? I wish our flat would go up in flames, it's really draggy.'

Virginia glared at her as she poked around the stripped living room, exclaiming at the mess.

'Wow! It's just below your mother's bedroom, isn't it? Lucky they weren't both killed.'

'Was it?' said Virginia.

'Where are they? Out at the pub?'

'No, Petra's upstairs — she was drunk,' said Virginia with icy contempt. 'Sandy's in the kitchen, doing his little woman act.'

'His what?' screamed Angela, rushing through. Sandy turned from the sink, displaying his frilled pink breasts. Angela went into sycophantic hysterics.

'Oh, Mr. Matheson! Oh, that's brilliant!'

He laughed, his spirits rising.

'Well, must dress the part, mustn't I?'

'Oh, yes! It's a hoot. Here, can I help? You shouldn't be doing that, it's a woman's job. Give it to me.'

She undid the apron and lifted it over his head, simpering with mock modesty as her hands touched his hair.

'That's very sweet of you, Angela. Sure you don't mind?'

'No, of *course* not.'

'Well, let me dry, then. Don't usually have to drudge like this, but the dishwasher's broken down again.'

'Oh, don't worry, I'm quite used to it.' She'd done it only five weeks ago.

Virginia left them to it. They didn't notice. Sandy was enjoying the sight of Angela in her plastic, artificial underwear and the subtle vibration of sexual attraction was already humming between them.

She went upstairs and shut herself in her room. Her bed was unmade. She sat down on it.

There was a high, delighted squeal from Angela down below, and Virginia felt a rush of anger. The bed gave a creak, then a slight jump.

She gasped and her eyes opened wide. The bed lurched.

She started to tremble, terrified, but a wave of sexual excitement suddenly weakened her and prevented her from moving. Her breathing became shorter and faster.

Seductively, the bed started to rock.

Petra woke with a headache.

Sandy woke with a flood of joyous, amazed recollection and lay smiling at the ceiling. Well, well, who'd have thought it? Bit dodgy, though. Under-age, probably. Hope she'll have the sense to keep her mouth shut. He glanced at Petra. Yes, of course she would; he hadn't, he had discovered, been the first.

Virginia awoke, terrified.

She curled up beneath the duvet, her hand clasped over the bite marks on her arm.

Chapter 12

Petra stayed just long enough to let the painters in, then fled the house. She went straight to the solicitor's and signed the contract, then killed time around the shops before returning at midday, still nursing a hangover. There was a big bruise on the side of her head. She couldn't for the life of her remember how that had happened.

She went into the living room and tried to smother her dread by a few minutes' bright conversation with the painters. Yes, it was an awful mess. Yes, they'd been very lucky to discover it in time. Yes, they were moving. Yes, it was all rather a rush. Yes, yes, oh yes.

'Would you like coffee or something?'

'Well, the young lady's already asked us,' said the elder man. 'She's making us a cuppa now.'

So Virginia was up. She'd got to have a talk with her. She'd got to find out about this man she'd fallen for. She wanted to ask her about yesterday. She wanted to get to the bottom of her misery, to penetrate the secret world which had spilled over so disastrously, to put it right, to stop it happening again.

Deeply apprehensive, she went into the kitchen.

'Hello, darling, feeling all right?'

Her voice was weak and shaky. She was no longer just worried about Virginia, she was frightened of her.

'Course.'

Her daughter's flat put-down was like a slap in the face. As she arranged the tray she pushed past Petra in a way which was very near to being downright rude.

'Darling, about yesterday. Would you like to talk about it?'

'No.'

'Are you sure? I want to help. I'm your mother, after all. I care about you.'

Virginia turned a contemptuous look upon her.

'Virginia, you don't hate me, do you?'

Silence.

'Give me a hug.'

'No thanks.'

'Please, darling. Tell me everything's all right between us.' Her voice was pleading.

'Don't be so yucky, Petra.' She made the tea.

'That for the painters?' asked Petra stupidly. 'Soon get things straight again. It might be a good idea to move, after all. This house doesn't seem to like us, does it?'

Virginia's hostile eyes swivelled to hers. Petra backed away as her daughter picked up the tray and left the kitchen. She looked around quickly, to see if anything was moving. If she hadn't felt so ill she'd have had a drink. She opened the back door and escaped into the yard.

The painters were getting on — the speed with which they were working had the full impetus of money behind it. Already the whole room was cleaned down and Bill, the elderly, balding one, was up on a trestle, giving the first coat of emulsion to the ceiling. Jason, the young one with the curly perm and drooping moustache, was undercoating the woodwork. Painters always seemed to come in contrasting pairs, one quiet, dull and unattractive, the other extrovert, talkative and sexy. It was as if they were purposely arranged that way, a marriage of opposites like a comedy duo.

'Tea,' muttered Virginia. Jason laid his brush on the paintpot and wiped his hands down his overalls.

'Bless you, darling, you've saved my life.' He gave her a smile so scintillating that she felt herself blushing. Gosh, he was good-looking! She responded with a shy grin, then fled in confusion. In her room, she went to the window. Below, Petra pottered miserably around the yard in her greatcoat, doing clumsy, inexpert things to the flowers, despite the cold, drizzling rain and the biting wind. Virginia shuddered.

Surely that couldn't have been William? Surely his longing couldn't be so brutally violent that it could actually scar her?

Was love really like that?

She stripped off her clothes and examined the bites and scratches. Oh no, surely not!

Presently, she started to dress again. The bra, the waistslip, the chemise. The bra was still too large, but there was more fullness in her breasts now, and the fit was better. She put on a new pair of tights. She took out her new dress and slipped it over the pretty underwear. She made up her face and brushed her hair. She put on perfume and hairspray and jewellery. She studied herself anxiously.

Voices floated up from the yard.

'Hello, Petra. You absolute heroine, gardening in this weather.'

'Hello, Pat. Just getting straight before the move.'

'I see you've got the painters in. Was there much damage? You were dreadfully upset, weren't you?'

'Well, it was quite a mess, but nothing structural.'

'When do you go?'

'Next week. Sandy pulled out all the stops and got everything moving.'

'Oh, my goodness, I had no idea! We're going to miss you so much. You've been lovely neighbours.'

'We'll miss you, but you must come down and see us at Maiden's End. We'll be having a house-warming party.'

'Oh, lovely! I'm dying to see it.'

Virginia's painted mouth dropped open. They couldn't be, not already. They hadn't said a word to her about it. Oh no, not when she'd found him at last!

The vibrant waves of distress flowed out of her and struck against the walls of the room. She started to cry and the force built up, reflecting back and back upon itself until the room was charged like a battery. The furniture absorbed it, the molecules vibrating within until they jarred against each other like a family of squabbling siblings shut up in a tiny flat.

'Oh, I hate them!' cried Virginia.

The molecules jumped. The furniture started to rock, groaning with the weight of the energy, then crept slowly away from the walls, advancing on her as if drawn by her longing for her lover. Her eyes widened and she froze with fear.

'William?' she whispered. 'Don't frighten me, William.'

Something broke, with a sharp, explosive crash. She spun round and saw the shattered mirror. As her head turned another crash came. The ghetto blaster lay smashed on the floor, its entrails exposed. Something moved past her head.

'No!' she screamed, and the precious photograph of Derek dropped behind the dressing table.

'Oh no, William, no!' she sobbed. 'Don't be so cruel!'

She rushed to pick it up. It was unharmed. She had heard the glass shatter, heard the crack of the frame, yet it lay in her hands whole and undamaged.

And at that moment she heard the voice.

It was only a sibilant whisper at first, coming from the corner of the room. No words, no recognisable timbre, even, just a continuous hiss, like a simmering kettle. But soon it became clearer and louder, the sibilance backed by a low, rumbling murmur. The two sounds merged and became one, as if emerging from a badly-tuned radio, rising and falling with the cadences of speech but without the clarity to be understandable.

'William?' Her knees weak, she sat down on the bed.

Her voice was a high, frightened squeak. It wasn't like William, the soft, gentle, soothing words she had heard on Sunday night. It was deep and harsh, with the insidious tone of the seducer, one of those dirty old men who spoke to you in public places when you were on your own.

'Virginia.' It increased in clarity, as if being tuned by invisible fingers. 'Virginia.'

'Yes?' she whispered, trembling. This wasn't William, he wouldn't sound like that. Her teeth were chattering, her body shivering so much that the bed rattled. She got up and started to back towards the door. The bed continued to rattle.

'Go away,' she said, starting to cry again. 'You're not William. I don't want you. Go away!'

The whisper became indistinct again, hissing in the corner of the room like a snake.

She found the handle and opened the door, rushed downstairs and out into the garden.

Petra turned from the fence as her daughter, in full sexual war-paint, flung herself into her arms.

They were packing. Side by side in the disordered bedroom, Petra and Virginia pulled garments from drawers and cupboards and threw them into suitcases. They worked frantically, casting frightened glances around them, too terrified even to speak. Virginia's hands trembled as she tried to pick up the soft, elusive cloth with fingers which would not grip. Petra, her head throbbing with nausea, sought blindly for the sponge bag. She ran out to the bathroom to fetch toothbrushes.

Immediately the whisper started again.
'Virginia! You're a wicked girl, Virginia.'
'Mummy!' she shrieked.
Petra burst through the door.
'Virginia, you're no good, you're a wicked girl.'
Then it started to abuse them.

They grabbed every garment in sight and thrust them into the cases, listening with horror to the obscene words. They were being stripped naked, everything they had thought safely hidden within their own minds being dragged out and sneered at. They avoided each other's eyes, scarlet with shame, as their intimate secrets were ruthlessly revealed.

Goodness, does Mummy really do that!
Good God! I never realised Virginia knew about that!
At last, they pulled the bulging cases together and ran helter-skelter down the stairs. Jason poked his head out of the living room door.
'What's up?'
'Nothing, we're late for something.'
They rushed out of the house. Petra opened the car door and flung the suitcases on to the back seat, where the contents of one spilled out. Virginia climbed in, hysterical.

Down in the hollow below Hampstead Heath, they drew up before a block of dirty, looming mansion flats. Petra found the right bell and pressed it with a shaking finger. A surprised voice within gave them permission to enter.

They bundled into the clanking, old-fashioned lift and rose within the deserted shaft of the staircase.

Mrs. Parker opened the door, her face lit up by a curiosity which was as ever-present as Angela's.

'Hello, Mrs. Matheson, fancy meeting you at last. And Virginia, dear, what a lovely surprise. Come in.'

She ushered them into her lounge – a graceless, badly-proportioned late-Victorian chamber which appeared to have been the victim of a redecoration project by a woman's magazine.

'Do take a seat.'

She perched on the edge of a reproduction balloon-back chair and took up a self-consciously ladylike pose, crossing her ankles and clasping her ringed fingers in the lap of her neat, Damart dress.

Petra had never met her in the flesh before, nor wanted to. The Parkers were the sort of people she usually avoided – dull, respectable, as square as geometry.

'Would you care for a drink?'

'Oh yes, thank you,' said Petra gratefully. Damn the headache, it might stop her shaking. Mrs. Parker rose at once and tripped to the door.

'Coffee or tea?'

'Oh – er – coffee.'

She glanced round the room longingly. There wasn't a bottle in sight. Her heart sank.

Mrs. Parker stopped short, a coy smile illuminating her face. The Mathesons were rather smart people, weren't they? Sophisticated. 'Or perhaps you'd prefer something stronger?'

'Well, yes, I really think I would.' Petra's tongue was practically hanging out.

The excited hostess opened a sideboard drawer and took out a key, then applied it to the cupboard beneath. With a triumphant flourish she produced a bottle of 'Senorita' sherry.

Jesus! A sick headache and cheap sherry! She took it, though, gulping it down with a speed which gave Mrs. Parker a shock. Dear me, these smart people! She topped up the glass politely.

'Mrs. Parker, you know you very kindly agreed to let Virginia stay with you until her exams were over?'

'Yes?' Mrs. Parker smiled graciously, conscious that it was indeed kind of her. 'Angela's looking forward to it so much.'

'Well, I wonder if I could possibly impose on you a bit more and ask you to take her earlier? We're moving sooner than we thought and it would be less of an upset for her if she could get settled in before term starts. I'm afraid it's an awful imposition on you but – '

'Oh no, not at all!' exclaimed Mrs. Parker. 'We'd be only too glad. So you're off very soon, are you? Angela was just thrilled to bits with the house. She said it was a really elegant home. She went on and on about it, and how you were going to do it up. We were really quite curious to see it by the time she'd finished.' She paused expectantly.

The desperate Petra took the hint.

'Oh, you must both come down. Not just yet, I'm afraid, but we'll certainly arrange it during the summer.'

'Really?' Mrs. Parker exclaimed with delighted surprise. 'Oh, I never thought we'd actually get an invitation. Thank you so much! Yes, of course Virginia can come. When did you think? This weekend?'

'Could she come today?'

'Today!'

It was obvious Mrs. Parker was unaware that such arrangements, or any arrangements, could be made so quickly. Visits had to be settled well in advance, to allow the essential cleaning, re-arrangements, shopping and routine of exactly planned meals to be organized.

'I'm afraid the room is rather dusty.'

'Goodness, that doesn't matter,' Petra said quickly. 'She can sleep on the settee, if you like.' She gestured at the piece of furniture in question, then did a double take. It was a short, hard mound of overstuffed dralon, fenced round with carved mahogany.

'Oh goodness, no!' Mrs. Parker protested. Sleep in the lounge? It was positively Bohemian. 'No, no, I'll get straight down to it. It will only take a few hours to turn out the spare bedroom. The mattress will need turning, of course, and I expect if I shampoo the carpet now it will be *nearly* dry by tonight – '

'I'm afraid we're giving you an awful lot of trouble,' Petra said, not caring a damn. If Mrs. Parker had insisted on re-painting the room in three hours before allowing Virginia into it, she would still have allowed her to do it.

'Oh no, no!' Mrs. Parker waited for Petra to withdraw gracefully and was appalled when she didn't. Mrs. Matheson seemed quite ignorant of the rules of polite behaviour by which everyone always said the opposite of what they meant. 'Really, it's no trouble,' she said anxiously, meaning that it was.

'Well thanks, Mrs. Parker, that's very kind of you. I'll run down and get her things from the car.'

Virginia sat in the echoing, pregnant silence of Petra's absence, staring at the carpet. Mrs. Parker gave her an encouraging smile.

'Well,' she said at last, finding her smile unanswered, 'your mother's having a busy time, isn't she? Quite a panic. I expect you're looking forward to getting down to your lovely new home.'

Virginia looked up with a despair in her eyes which startled her. She was a very plain little girl, not a patch on Angela. And Mrs. Matheson was such a lovely woman, too. A bit flashy, but beautifully turned out. Quite a beauty, in fact. Poor Virginia's father must have been a very undistinguished-looking man.

Petra's finger on the bell removed Mrs. Parker to the hall and Virginia, alone in the high, over-furnished room, felt immediately afraid, looking around her in alarm. No, please, no. Don't come again. Don't follow me here, please.

'I'll put it here for now, shall I?' said Petra, dropping the suitcase on the highly-polished parquet.

'Of course,' said Mrs. Parker. She picked it up at once and carried it down the long corridor into the spare bedroom at the other end of the flat, observing that there was something hanging out of the lid. You'd really have thought Mrs. Matheson had just thrown everything in higgledy piggledy, with no regard for creases. She supposed Virginia would need to use the iron, as soon as she'd unpacked. She'd better set up the ironing board, though it was rather inconvenient on a Thursday. She wouldn't be using it herself until next Tuesday and it would get in the way while she was cooking the dinner. Disturbed, she returned to the lounge.

Petra was giving Virginia an unusually emotional farewell kiss.

'Are you going to be all right, darling? If you want to get in touch with me I'll be at Marjorie's. You know the number, don't you?'

'Mummy!' Virginia grabbed hold of her. Mrs. Parker was surprised and rather offended. Virginia started to sob, and Petra held her tight, murmuring 'It's all right, darling, really it is. I don't know what it was all about, but you'll be all right now. It can't happen here.'

'What can't happen here?' Mrs. Parker asked, suddenly suspicious.

Petra switched on a bright, electric smile and beamed it at her across Virginia's head.

'Nothing, Mrs. Parker. It's just that we've had a bit of trouble at home with a silly fire, and Virginia was rather frightened by it.'

'Oh, how dreadful! Was it a terrible mess?' Mrs. Parker pictured the disastrous results of such a domestic tragedy — soot, smoke, disorder, hassles with the insurance company — the poor things!

'The painters are in already,' Petra assured her. 'Goodbye, Mrs. Parker. Excuse my rushing off like this, but there really is such a frightful lot to see to, you know what moving is like.'

'Indeed I do,' said Mrs. Parker sympathetically. 'I'll never forget how it was when we moved in here. I said to my hubby then, "Never again, Sylvester, never again. We're staying here until they carry us out feet first."'

She tittered. You had to be a bit daring when you were with smart people. Death wasn't something that was usually considered a subject for levity in her circle.

Petra burst out laughing and she felt pleasantly flattered that her little joke had been so appreciated. It was merciful she didn't realise that the thing which had provoked Petra's hysterical mirth was her husband's hysterical name.

'Goodbye, darling,' said Petra to Virginia. 'We'll be going down to Maiden's End this weekend and I'll give you a ring to see if you'd like to come, all right? Don't give Mrs. Parker any trouble, will you?'

'Of course she won't, bless her,' said Mrs. Parker generously. 'She'll be as good as a little lamb, won't you, dear?'

'Yes,' said Virginia with desperate sincerity.
But will he?
Down in the car, Petra collapsed over the steering wheel with her fist in her mouth and started to scream.

Virginia lay tensely in bed, the flowered bedside lamp still switched on. It was ten past one and she had been in bed since eleven, but she hadn't once dared to close her eyes. As she slid down beneath the pink cellular blankets, she had found herself automatically turning to her daydream but had come to with a shock of fear, shutting off the entrance to that dangerous, well-trodden path of escape from reality, lest the opening of the gate should allow him through.

The room was high-ceilinged, and shining damask curtains hid the window which looked out on to Hampstead Heath. She wished it looked out on to the street, with comforting streetlights and passing cars. Mrs. Parker had opened it before she tucked her in but the instant the door was closed Virginia had leapt out of bed and pulled down the sash, shutting out the dark, mysterious waste with its whispering trees.

He couldn't be there, though, could he? He lived in her home, drawn into her room by the pulsating thread of her erotic longings. He had no reason to come to the Parkers'. He wouldn't know she was there. He might search her bedroom at home, pushing her furniture around, shaking her bed, smashing her belongings with inexplicable spite and whispering his cruel messages, but he would find her gone and soon slink back to wherever he came from.

There was a tap on the door.

Virginia froze, staring at the pink barrier.

The tap came again.

'Go away!' she cried.

There was a pause, then the door opened slowly, and a surprised Angela appeared around it, hair tousled and face naked of make-up as in her innocent, termtime schoolgirl guise.

'You all right, Virge?'

'Oh, Angela! I didn't realise it was you. Sorry.'

'Who did you think it was?' asked Angela curiously. 'My Dad with designs on your virtue?'

Embarrassment and revulsion flooded Virginia's mind.

'Don't be so disgusting! Honestly, Angela, you really are tacky sometimes. You've got a really dirty mind.'

'Oh, all right,' said Angela huffily, 'if that's how you feel I'll go. I saw your light on through the fanlight above my bedroom door and I thought you might be feeling home-sick.'

'Oh! That was kind of you. Yes, I am a bit. Come in and have a talk. I can't seem to sleep.'

Angela closed the door and came tiptoeing towards the bed.

'Gosh, it's cold, isn't it? Do you think the spring's ever going to come this year? Just listen to that wind outside, really creepy. Is that why you closed the window?'

'Yes.'

'I did mine, too. Makes you feel as if it's coming to get you, doesn't it?'

Virginia closed her eyes in panic.

'Here, can I get into bed with you?'

'Course.'

They snuggled down together, giggling at the conspiratorial intimacy of sharing a bed. Virginia was so relieved that she almost began to like Angela again. He wouldn't dare to come with her here. Her eyelids began to droop; she was really very tired indeed. Angela started to chatter, quite unaware that Virginia was already slipping away from her.

'When is it you're moving, Virge?'

'Next week.'

'Gosh, that's a bit sudden, isn't it? How on earth did Sandy manage to arrange it so quickly? My mother says moving takes months and months, and that's why she's never going to do it again. Still, I suppose he's really brilliant at business and draggy things like that. A real whizz-kid, if you can still be one at his age, though he doesn't look over forty, does he? I bet he could fix anything if he set his mind to it. Your mother's ever so lucky to have someone like that. Must make you feel sort of safe, as if everything was under control. I like men like that. Wayne's pretty forceful, actually, but he's only nineteen so he hasn't got Sandy's savoir-faire. Do you fancy Wayne, Virge?'

'No,' said Virginia, wishing she'd shut up.

'Oh, you do! You know you do,' teased Angela. 'I've seen the way you look at him.'

'I don't,' Virginia protested, coming reluctantly out of the

fog of impending sleep. 'Don't be so stupid.'
'What's wrong with him, then? Go on, tell me.'
'He's rude and he's noisy and he's rough,' said Virginia, mentioning all the things which seemed to epitomise Wayne's compelling masculinity. 'I like proper, mature men, not silly boys who think being witty means saying arsehole.'
'Have you got someone older, then?' Angela mocked.
Virginia was silent. Angela turned over tumultuously in the bed and raised herself on one elbow, looking down into Virginia's face. 'You have, haven't you? Gosh, you old slyboots! Who is he, one of the school gardeners? I saw you staring at them that day we were playing netball. Who is it, the thin one with the pigtail and the nice big bump?'
'No!' said Virginia. 'Who'd want a nasty lout like that? I wasn't staring at him, anyway. He's got no manners.'
'Oh, yes, I remember. He asked if you'd like a quick one in the bushes.'
Virginia wriggled with furious embarrassment.
'No, I know who it is,' Angela continued happily, 'it's that man down at Maiden's End. "Virgin for short but not for long."'
'It isn't! Shut up, Angela. If I was going to find someone it wouldn't be a pig like that. I'm particular.'
'Yes, you are, aren't you? You don't know what you're missing, Virge.'
Yes I do. I've got an idea now. It must be like that, being scratched and bitten and taken over.
'Virginia.'
Virginia dived under the clothes, trying to smother the scream which was building up in her throat, pressing against the inside of her nose, filling her head with a pressure like steam. Angela raised her head for a second, then dropped it on to the pillow. The voice had been very quiet.
'Wayne's really passionate, sometimes. When we went home from the disco on Saturday he – '
'Virginia.'
'What's that?' Angela listened, a surprised expression on her face which suddenly became awed respect. 'Virge! You've got a man in here, haven't you? So that's why you were awake! Gosh, you should have said! I wouldn't have dreamed of butting in. Who is it? The older man you were talking about?

Where's he hiding? I'll go at once, of course. I won't say anything about it to Mum, but I really don't think you ought to risk it again. I mean, it's frightfully daring of you but if she ever found out – '

'You're a dirty little whore, Virginia.'

They gasped in unison, shock striking them like a blow to the solar plexus.

Virginia's body started to tremble uncontrollably.

'Go away!' she cried. 'I don't want you! Go away!'

It laughed then, the most horrible laugh they had ever heard, deep, catarrhal, dirty. Virginia felt Angela start to shake too. The voice wasn't coming from the wardrobe, or from behind the curtains, or beneath the bed, or anywhere but the empty corner by the bed where there was nothing to hide in but a low bookcase containing a few bound volumes of *Golden Hands*.

'You dirty little tarts!'

Angela burst into tears, the water flooding out of her wide, blue eyes and splashing down on to her baby doll pyjamas. She raised her arms and clasped them protectively across her full breasts.

'Go away!' shrieked Virginia. 'Go away! Go away!'

'You first, Virginia, then her. You first.'

'No!'

Angela gave a wild, terrified scream as Virginia was torn out of the bed beside her and flung across the room, in a high, graceful parabola which suddenly slowed as she approached the opposite wall. Then, incredulous, she saw her stop just before the impact and descend to the floor, as slowly and sedately as if she was being carried in someone's arms.

Virginia collapsed in a heap on the damp carpet, screaming with terror. 'Leave me alone! Leave me alone!'

The invisible teeth closed on her shoulder and she knew with absolute certainty that this was not, *could* not be William, or anyone or anything worthy of being loved.

Angela suddenly erupted from the blankets with a startled cry and was hurled against the bookcase. They both started to shriek, hurling their hysteria across the bedroom and receiving it back from the other stronger, more charged, more potently irresistible, so that if they had wanted to stop they could not have done it.

'I like dirty little girls.'

This was no ideal dream lover. This wasn't William, no heroic fireman or heroic anyone. Whatever she had conjured up by her longings, it wasn't anything lovable. It was something so repulsive, so dirty, that her response to its advances could only be abhorrence.

Chapter 13

Mrs. Parker stood trembling on the doorstep like an outraged pink jelly, her rambling, stereotyped phrases punctuated by nervous sniffs.

The taxi ticked out in the street, swallowing up money, while Angela's white face peered out of the window and gnawed at her polished fingernails.

Sandy recognised her with a jolt of terror. She'd talked. His eyes questioned her frantically and she shook her head. He swallowed with relief and tried to take in what her mother was saying. Sorry to disturb so early – do so regret – have to re-think the arrangements – had no idea that Virginia – Angela so sensitive – not fair to expect her to be exposed to – really *not* what we had expected – hubby's health not all it should be – quiet life, regular habits –

He looked down at Virginia, standing beside Mrs. Parker with her suitcase, like a couple of rejected parcels returned to a mail order house.

'She *what*?'

' – quite out of control – screaming – throwing herself about room – damaging bookcase – tearing bedding – feathers from pillow – poor Angela – hysterics – '

Virginia's wide, desperate eyes drilled into his.

' – could she just – word with her mother – so sorry to let her down – really wasn't to be expected that – '

'My wife's not here, I'm afraid. She's staying with a friend.'

' – well, please tell her – very, *very* sorry but – hubby really shaken up – not good for heart – must get back to him – '

She backed out of the gate, the verbal diarrhoea continuing

until the taxi door slammed. Sandy watched it drive away, then looked with sheer hatred at the dumb, petrified child who stood frozen to the doorstep like a dwarf Lot's wife.

'You little bitch,' he said.

She stared at him, shaking with nerves. He put out his hand and pulled her into the house.

'I want Mummy,' she said.

'She's not here.'

'I want Mummy,' she repeated, tears coming to her eyes. 'I want my Mummy,' she wailed.

Through the open living room door, Jason sang along loudly with the radio.

'Shut up! Don't you dare make another scene with people in the house!'

He drew her down the hall and into the kitchen. She stumbled along behind him, whimpering, 'Mummy, Mummy, Mummy!'

With the door closed, he shook her like a dusty doormat. 'For Pete's sake, Virginia! What the hell do you think you're playing at?'

'I want to go to Mummy! Where's Mummy?'

'At Marjorie's.'

'I want her! I want her!'

He ran up to the bedroom, snatched up the extension phone and stabbed his fingers at the buttons as if he was putting out those tearful, terrified, accusing eyes.

Marjorie poured Petra another vodka and a G. & T. for herself. She held the glass cradled in her pudgy, bronze-taloned hands and glanced curiously at Virginia, standing over at the other side of the big Georgian room and staring out of the window at the bare, tossing trees on the Heath.

'What the hell are you going to do with her now?'

'Can she stay here with me?' pleaded Petra. 'It's only for a few days until the move. She can share my room and I promise I'll keep her quiet.' Petra's explanation had been understated to the point of dishonesty.

'Supposing she does it again?' Marjorie challenged. She didn't want any tantrums here.

'She won't, I promise. I'll make quite sure she doesn't.

She'll be all right, Marjorie, really. I'll ring Zak now, if I may.'

'I don't think he gets back till the weekend,' said Marjorie, her grey eyes hard and hostile.

'Oh hell,' moaned Petra. 'Well, perhaps I'll take her round to the doctor and get some tranquillisers or something.'

'I've got some Librium,' said Marjorie. 'I've a few left over from the divorce. Give her a couple now.'

'Oh yes, thanks!'

Petra crossed the room and put her arm around Virginia, with the experimental caution of one approaching a strange dog.

'All right, darling?'

'Yes.'

'Marjorie's getting you something to calm you down. You'll take them, won't you?'

'Yes.'

'As long as you keep calm it'll be all right,' Petra assured her. 'Rod said so. It's just caused by your getting upset, he says.'

'What does he know about it?' Her body was tense beneath Petra's fingers. Outside, the trees danced, hurled themselves backwards and forwards, grinding and writhing with pain. I must keep calm, I must try to keep calm.

'I don't know. He seems to know about a lot of funny things. I suppose it's all those good works he goes in for.'

Virginia looked again at the Heath. It was terrifying, a battlefield of agonised turbulence. Marjorie came back into the room, rigid with resentment.

'Here, Petra, give her these.'

Virginia gulped down the capsules.

'I suppose I couldn't have some, could I?' Petra asked anxiously.

'Better not with booze. If you lay off it for the rest of the day you could take a couple tonight. Or I could give you some sleepers. They're good – knock you out cold for hours.'

'That's a good idea,' said Petra, relieved, 'and we'll give Virginia some too. Yes, I'll stop drinking now.'

But at ten o'clock that night she was still sitting on the leather Chesterfield, staring with feverish, glittering eyes at the gas logs, hunched over her glass.

Marjorie, her plump face harder than ever beneath her short, curly blonde hair, stared across at Virginia, who was watching television with the earphones on. On the screen an American policeman was fighting crime with all the amoral violence of a psychopath. The blood glowed crimson through the pale pastels of the elegant room.

'Isn't it time she was in bed?' said Marjorie with distaste. She didn't like children, particularly troublesome ones.

'Yes – sure – course – think I'll go too. Can I have those sleeping pills?'

'Don't be bloody stupid, Petra, you've been on the vodka since this morning.'

'Oh, just one, please.'

'And have you being carted off in an ambulance? No thanks.' That had happened to Marjorie's husband. Oh no, not again, thank you.

'I'm all right, Marge,' said Petra peevishly. 'I must have something.'

The doorbell rang and Marjorie rose. 'That'll be Boris. Come on Petra, get Virginia upstairs, I don't want her wandering around while he's here.'

She went out to answer the door. Petra drained her glass, pulled herself up, lurched forward and put her hand on Virginia's shoulder. She turned, languid with tranquillisers, and took off the earphones. The muted, four-lettered abuse of the upholder of law, order and decency sprang out of them like the savagery of a wild animal in a distant forest.

'Time for bed,' Petra enunciated carefully.

'I don't want to go to bed!' said Virginia, terrified.

'S'all right, I'm coming too.'

'Can we leave the light on?'

'Course.'

Boris and Marjorie fell apart as they passed through the hall and started to climb the stairs. Petra glimpsed them like a film seen from the back of the top circle.

'Night,' she said, smiling vaguely. Must keep up appearances. Marjorie swam forwards, hand outstretched.

'Here you are – for Virginia, remember, not you.'

Something slipped through Petra's fingers like dust and bounced away down the stairs into the distant screen. The image of Boris dipped and then drifted towards her, past her.

'Here, darling. Give you good night. You go out like a light.'

Virginia took them gratefully. Yes, please, oblivion. Shut it all out; the night, the terrors, *him*.

Upstairs, she took off her dress and shoes and swallowed the pills down quickly, then got into bed. Petra was moving aimlessly round the big, panelled room, studying it as if from an immense distance. Sanderson prints smothered beds and armchairs, frilled around cushions and stools, looped extravagantly over windows and fell in heavy, lead-weighted folds to the carpet. The pleated shades of lamps cast striped patterns on to the deep pink cloths on the occasional tables. Above, the distant ceiling swayed in a strange, exotic world of mouldings and shadows.

Outside, the wind howled past the windows, and away on the Heath, a tree creaked and clashed its branches. Virginia curled up and pulled the blankets over her head. You can't come with Mummy here, she'll look after me. You can't come, you can't come. Her eyelids closed.

Petra was having trouble with her bracelet. She couldn't get her fingers round that silly little catch. She tried again, felt the bite of the tiny knob and tried to pull it back, but the nail tore and the supple, linked metal slid round to the back of her wrist again.

'Sandy,' she muttered, 'come and get this bloody thing off.'

She tried again, irritated. Stupid thing. Where the hell was Sandy? The bracelet slid round and round in the most infuriating manner. It was really absolutely essential that she take off that bracelet. She couldn't go to bed with that bracelet on. Perhaps she'd have a cigarette. Settle her a bit.

She lit up and sat down in an armchair. The room swam before her, tipping and sliding, sometimes receding to the end of a tunnel so that she was about to be engulfed in blackness, then suddenly reversing its direction and rushing back like an express train, to strike her about the head with a roar of floral chintz, rose pink Duplon and pleated lights which sang like bells.

Time drifted on, long extended time. Petra smoked and brooded. My life has been spoilt, destroyed. I'm a victim.

She tried to focus her eyes on a light on the floor. Silly place for a lamp, someone'll knock it over. More time passed. Behind the glow, in a sudden cameo of clarity, there was a face on a pillow. A very plain face with untidy hair around it. God, what a plain face. It was asleep. Best thing to do if you look like that. Better shut out the world, the world won't want to see you.

God, what a stupid place to put a lamp. Down on the carpet like that, gleaming and gleaming and getting brighter, creeping out into the room. It probably had something to do with that plain little girl over there – there was such an obvious connexion between them; stupid and in the wrong place. Look at her now, she couldn't even stay put in bed, had to rise up and move around in the air like a bird with no nest to go to. Really, how absolutely stupid she looked.

Petra laughed helplessly. God, that was funny! There she went, flying through the air, landing on the floor by the closed curtains.

The curtains billowed out into the room then fell over the sleeping child on the floor, closing their folds around her like a shroud and drawing her into the recess of the bay window.

There, she'd gone. Good riddance. Night, night, plain little girl. Her hand found the strip of metal and sought once more for the clasp. Couldn't go to bed until she'd got that off.

The room rushed towards her again, bringing the glow from the floor dazzling into her eyes. She closed them to shut it out.

Petra came to with a jump. The room swayed, then settled, the lamps diminished into puny glimmers by the shaft of daylight intruding through the frantic shaking of the floral curtains. Not her curtains. Where was she?

Someone was screaming behind them, on and on in terrified hysteria, while a cold blast of air gusted into the room. Oh yes, of course, she was at Marjorie's. She staggered across and dragged them apart.

A child's contorted, shrieking face looked up at her from within the open window seat. The lid had been thrown back. There was glass everywhere and the fine glazing bars of the sash window had been forced out into the cold April morning, as if straining desperately for the freedom of the Heath.

'Don't put me in a coffin! Don't bury me! I'm not dead! I'm not dead!'

'Of course you're not dead! What on earth are you doing in there – er – Virginia?' Yes, that was her name.

'He buried me! He buried me! Don't let him bury me, Mummy, please!'

Petra helped the frantic child out and back into the room, the effort sending waves of nausea over her body. She lowered Virginia into the armchair, then stared with consternation at the large patch of burnt carpet in front of it. Oh my God! Marjorie will kill me. I must have dropped my cigarette. And the window. Oh my God!

Virginia was still screaming, gasping shrieks like the last struggles of a stuck pig. She huddled into the chair, a skinny, plain little girl in her underwear, while Petra looked at her with distaste. She reminded her of someone – someone she had seen quite recently, or perhaps it was just someone she had seen in a dream. Someone she had found terribly funny, though she couldn't think why. Think it out later. Just try to shut her up. Heavens, her slip was torn and there were new marks on her shoulder – scratches, bites. She was howling into the expensive chintz, the bleeding scratches staining the fabric.

Marjorie, standing in the doorway, made herself heard at last.

'Petra,' she said with fury as she looked at the shambles in her beautiful spare bedroom, 'get that bloody child of yours out of here!'

Petra, clutching her head, looked pleadingly at her. Then she spread her arms, trying with a vain, pathetic gesture to hide the mess. 'Sorry,' she said, 'sorry, Marge – very sorry.'

Behind Marjorie, Boris, in a bright silk dressing gown, hovered like a piece of corny East European kitsch. Transylvania, he came from. Transylvania! God, how she hated East Europeans. All that phoney glamour and romantic possibility and let-down.

'Very sorry, Marge,' she said again, then vomited on to the incinerated carpet. Virginia continued to scream. 'It's all right, darling,' said Petra between retches, 'Mummy's here.'

Petra tried everyone. She searched Marjorie's address book

for the numbers of mutual friends, greeting them with false, febrile gaiety and asking for temporary accommodation, just for a few days. Terribly sorry to be a nuisance, but the house was just *chaos* with the decorators in.

Zoe was just off for the weekend. Marina had got the in-laws coming. Babs had the builders in too, extending the conservatory and putting in the new bathroom.

Samantha was in the boutique, up to her neck in the rush of weekend custom.

'The spare room? God, no, Petra, you know I've got Damien coming this weekend. Frightful drag, but I have to take my parental turn.'

Tom had to get a book finished, the bloody publisher was nagging; solitude was essential. Fabian was just off to the Canaries to film and taking the family with him. Terribly exciting, darling; see you when I get back; be only too glad to help then.

Lucinda's bell rang for ages. She answered eventually, then there was the crash of something being knocked over.

'Hell! Sorry — who'd you say?'

'Petra. Lucinda, could you possibly put me and Virginia up tonight?'

'What? Can't hear. Sorry, bad line,' mumbled Lucinda. 'He's not here — gone to the States — back next week.'

Drunk again. She always went on a binge when Paul was away. Forget it. Petra slammed the phone down.

All those so-called friends, who had spent so many noisy, after-pub evenings in her house, full of boisterous affection and reiterated 'Darlings'. A fat lot of good they were in a real crisis.

Derek was out. His office number was answered by a clipped voice. 'No, he's not here. This is Miss Jenkins. I've just called in to pick up my things. No, I don't think so. He could be at his solicitor's. Oh no, it's Saturday.'

She started to cry with frustration as she searched once more through the book. Marjorie tapped her foot impatiently.

'Hurry up, Petra, I want to phone the builder.'

'Sorry, sorry,' Petra apologised. 'Won't be long now. Where's Virginia?' she added nervously.

'In the kitchen, can't you hear her? Sounds as if she's talking to herself.'

She rang Zak hastily. Not back yet.
Desperately, she turned yet another page. Dino Zucconi, Rod's flatmate. Oh thank God! Yes, of course, Rod. No answer from the flat and not at the Samaritans.
The door burst open and Virginia rushed in.
'Mummy! Mummy! He's here. I heard him.'
'Shut up!' Petra shouted in panic. Hastily, she gathered up her coat, handbag and suitcases and pushed her daughter out of the room before her. 'O.K., Marge, we're off now. Sorry about the mess. We'll pay for the damage, really. Just send us the bill.'
Virginia was crying bitterly as they got into the car. She was desperately frightened, she had flown to Petra for help and her mother had shouted at her.
'Sorry, darling, but you really mustn't talk about all this in front of other people. They'll think you're telling the most frightful lies.'
'But it's true, it's true! You know it is. You heard.'
'I know I did, but it's our business. No-one else must know about it. They'll think we're quite mad, don't you see? What did it say?' she asked, her voice quavering.
Virginia blushed. 'I don't want to tell you,' she said.
They fell into embarrassed, horrified silence and sat there in their rejected isolation. In the busy, friend-populated world of Highgate, their only place of refuge was their own car.
In the tense silence, Virginia's terror attacked her body like lethal germs. She shivered uncontrollably, felt cold, felt hot; her head ached, her throat was sore with screaming. It attacked her brain, sending electric signals darting wildly from one cell to another to illuminate their meticulously stored memories: Miss Hibbert's sorrowful face; Angela snuggling up to Wayne; Derek holding her small, infant hand as she laughed up at him; Petra sulking over the washing with her hair in a 1970s waterfall of straight, silky black; Granny Blackie beaming at her indulgently as she opened a long-ago Christmas present under Petra's contemptuous, critical eye; the clock out on the cold winter pavement; Rod sitting on her bed with hurt tears in his eyes.
'Rod didn't think we were mad,' she said.
'I rang him. He's out.'

Virginia's disturbed brain flashed on, sending the vivid pictures speeding across her consciousness. Sandy bending over her with angry eyes and shaking her; 'Virgin for short but not for long'; 'Do you have bad periods, Virge?' 'I love you, darling'; 'You dirty little whores!'; Rod pressing the envelope into her hand, 'Ring me any time. Promise you will.'

She wished she had. Oh, if only she had!

'He's probably at the cemetery. He works there most weekends.'

'Does he? You mean he's a gravedigger?'

'No, of course I don't! He guides visitors round.'

'So he *has* got a job.'

'He hasn't!' Virginia shouted, infuriated by Petra's stupidity. 'It's voluntary, like the Samaritans.'

'Oh.' Petra couldn't grasp all this business of working for nothing. It seemed a funny way to spend your time.

'He might be there,' Virginia insisted nervously.

'Well, I suppose we could go and see,' said Petra.

Chapter 14

Below, beyond the Halicarnassan mausoleum and the great cedar tree, the close-planted crop of stone spread away downhill among the bare trees, to disappear into the invisible depths by the crumbling chapels. Everywhere the brilliance of daffodils broke through the ground like golden promises. In the midst of death, we are in life.

It was odd, thought Rod, that he should find it so comforting. If anyone had told him fifteen years ago, when he was a frightened little boy with his head under the bedclothes because there was definitely a ghost on the landing and a skeleton in the wardrobe and a dead body under the bed, that he would one day find a huge, melancholy old cemetery the most beautiful, peaceful place in the world, he would not have believed them.

And this particular cemetery, too, with its infinite store of macabre anecdote; the thousand upon thousand of closely stowed coffins, the grisly exhumation of poor Lizzie Siddal so that her husband could retrieve his rashly given gift, the sick cavortings of the perverted in the overgrown chaos during the years of abandonment. The visitors enjoyed those stories with all the fascinated curiosity of people who lived in a time when death was a dirty word, and when even doctors, who should have known better, couldn't face up to its inevitability and allow their weary patients to slip away unmolested into rest.

He, who had been so terrified of the modern world's taboo in his childhood, could now bring his sandwiches up here and eat them on the terrace above the catacombs, alone and yet not afraid. It was very odd.

Perhaps it was because its creators had felt so at home with death themselves. They hadn't thrust it away, putting off acknowledgement of its existence until it was unavoidable. They hadn't pushed the newly-dead out of their homes into the decent obscurity of chapels of rest, to be seen again only in concealing polished overcoats for a painful hour before they were whisked away behind curtains and reduced to hygienic ashes.

It couldn't be thrust away in those days; it was not distant but ever-close. Death was everywhere, right out in the open, inhabiting the busy cities and quiet villages as ubiquitously as the modern, everpresent reality of the tax-gatherer, claiming his dues. You paid up and prayed to be spared further payment, but always he would come again, demanding more, more, more. A friend here, a child there; a mother, a sister, a lover. How could you deny the presence of one who lived beneath your own roof, like an occasionally glimpsed lodger, who was the invisible playfellow of your children and the lurking adulterer who stole your wife from you within your own bed?

And, wisely, they had not denied him, but accepted his presence and sublimated their bereavement into ritual. Like Egyptian pharaohs, they prepared their eternal homes well in advance, even building some of them in forms which would have blended into that far-off place and time, behind a great stuccoed gateway of lotus-shaped pillars.

Those with the Victorian love of mediaeval splendour laid their coffins within the Gothic catacombs beneath his feet, rows and rows of them, like family photographs arranged in an album. They came there on their formal Sundays and examined them through the thick, glass panels, where plush, brass, wax lilies and china angels furnished the private little parlours. It was surprising that they didn't put lace curtains in those tiny windows. Perhaps some of them did; nothing would surprise him.

Regularly they came, on ceremonial outings to that second family home which would house them all one day, perhaps very soon. The train of well-dressed and well-scrubbed children stared solemnly at the coffin, or the vault, or the stone, or the great carved monument and were instructed in the

Great Reality. Here is your grandfather, my dears, and your great-grandmother, and your aunts and your uncles, and your poor little sister Florence. Give her your flowers and blow her a kiss and pray for goodness, so that you may be with her again one day.

There had been so much sorrow expressed here, and yet also so much robust self-confidence, even pride and pleasure. They proclaimed their worldly success with carved professional emblems and professional addresses, like huge, permanent business cards, so that the visitor would be aware that commerce was still being carried on and take his custom there.

It was a pity, really, that this celebration of death had largely disappeared. It seemed to Rod that there was more comfort to be found in these flights of fancy than in the private, shame-faced scattering of ashes in an obscure corner of a crematorium. If Dino died he would want a place to come and remember him, a place to express love with flowers, words and stone.

Some would probably consider it unhealthy, all this, even necrophilic, but surely it was healthier to celebrate than to deny?

He leant over the broken parapet, breathing the fresh, mild air that brought spring with it at last. On his right, a short wing stuck out from the end of the catacombs, brick showing through the broken stucco, a rusting iron door lurking behind trails of bramble; the infectious diseases vault, wherein scarlet fever, typhoid and cholera lay entombed with the bodies they had ravished, never, ever to have their embrace disturbed; the germs of cholera could still be lethal after two hundred years. Even there, there was privacy, peace, uninterrupted repose.

A straggling trail of people came up the Egyptian Avenue into the circle of catacombs round the cedar and consolidated into a clump outside a vault. He glanced at his watch. His next tour was at two o'clock. Better go.

He walked the length of the terrace, stepping over the deep, wide cracks awaiting repair, down the steps and along the painstakingly cleared path. The new bark litter was soft and yielding under his feet, and to his right he could hear a volunteer party working in the undergrowth. He took a detour.

'Found Mrs. Bilston yet?'

'Not yet, but we've uncovered the inscription on that big table tomb.'

Rod peered, the fascination of new discovery filling him as always. You never knew what you were going to find – another Victorian worthy, another piece of forgotten history, another useful anecdote for the visitors.

'The family grave of Archibald Westlake of Pinkerton House, Essex and No. 16, Abinger Place, Bayswater. Also of Mary Jane Westlake, relict of the above, and of Peter Westlake, aged twelve years, and of Jemima Westlake, aged three years, and of David Westlake, aged three months – '

The rollcall of the slaughter of innocents disappeared down into the mud.

'I'll look them up in the records,' said Rod. 'Do let me know as soon as you find Mrs. Bilston, won't you? He's getting really impatient. At least one letter a week, now. He actually rang up this morning, all the way from Texas.'

Mrs. Bilston's great-grandson was very keen to trace her and to receive a photograph of her grave. He had the place for it all ready, right in the middle of the piano in the lounge of his ranch.

At the bottom of the cemetery Rod ran down the broad flight of steps, through the semi-circular arcade and into the open space behind the chapels. The party had already been let in the gate and were standing waiting by the War Memorial.

'Good afternoon,' he called cheerfully, looking them over as he approached. Usual selection. Tourists, committed locals, elderly ladies and gentlemen with time to sightsee, a group of young people in jeans, a beautiful dark woman with a little girl.

'Good Lord,' he said, astonished. 'Fancy seeing you here.'

Petra hurried forward and whispered urgently. 'Can we speak to you, Rod?'

'Well not for long, I'm afraid, the party's just starting. Is it Virginia again?' He looked at her anxiously, apprehension causing his stomach to sink. Goodness, she looked awful!

'Happened again, has it?'

'Yes, worse than ever. A voice, too. I heard it, Rod. It was filthy, absolutely evil. Please help us.'

A voice! Oh no, he was way out of his depth here. They needed a priest or a medium.

'Sure, but I'm afraid you'll have to wait till I come back.'

'What, here?' Petra looked round with horror. 'How long will you be?'

'About an hour, longer if they ask a lot of questions. Sorry, but I must – there's no-one else to do this tour. Look, come with us, if you'd feel better.'

'It's a bit gloomy. Don't fancy it, to be honest. I hate this sort of place.'

Rod turned towards Virginia and she rushed forward, her face contorted with erupting tears.

'I'm sorry I didn't ring you,' she said. 'I'm sorry I was rude. I was horrid to you. I thought it was all right, but now I'm so scared I don't know what to do.'

The other visitors stared from afar.

'It's all right, darling, don't cry,' said Rod, pity flooding through him. 'You'll be quite safe here.'

'Will I?' she asked, her voice strangled by tears. 'Will I really? Will I be safe?'

'Yes, safe,' he insisted. 'This is a good place. Nothing can hurt you here. O.K., everyone,' he called, 'this way.' The party moved off, Petra and Virginia clinging to Rod like limpets.

Their anxiety seemed to invade him at once. That was the trouble with being sensitive to other people's misery. It leaked into you, took you over. He summoned up his Samaritan training and tried to be detached without losing compassion.

He made his first stop halfway up the path from the steps, gathering them around him like a flock of curious sheep and giving them a résumé of how and when the cemetery was built. 1839, he said. The parish graveyards of London were overcrowded and insanitary, and there had long been an outraged movement to get something done about it. Charles Dickens, you may remember, had vividly illustrated the horrors of those graveyards in *Bleak House,* with barely-covered coffins and disease infecting the houses built close to the churchyard walls. His family were buried over there, in fact, his parents, his wife, his sister-in-law Mary, who was, of course, the inspiration for Little Nell, also his little daughter Dora, although he himself was buried in the Abbey.

They turned in the direction of his pointing finger, murmuring with interest. He glanced at Petra. Her eyes were closed and she looked quite green. No, this sort of place definitely wasn't her.

'The first burial was made in May, 1839, a Mrs. Elizabeth Jackson of Golden Square, Holborn, over there to the right, and in the following years many hundreds of individuals and families bought plots and vaults and built family mausoleums. The prices ranged from two pounds ten shillings to as much as two hundred guineas, which was an enormous amount of money in those days. The graves were lined with brick, and all coffins had to be lined with lead for hygienic reasons, to prevent the dangerous and explosive gases of decay from escaping, particularly when the graves were opened for further burials.'

Petra gulped.

'In fact, one of the very interesting books the Friends have published about the cemetery, and which can be obtained at the bookstall, has been subtitled *Victorian Valhalla*, and that really is a very apt way to describe it. Everyone who was anyone came to be buried here, or at one of the other great new cemeteries around the capital, such as Kensal Green, Abney Park and Norwood.'

Petra was looking terrible. He hoped she'd stay the course.

'And now we'll move on, up to the most impressive area of the cemetery. It was very much admired in its time, and people would come and promenade here, as if in a park. It's the Egyptian Avenue, the catacombs and the Circle of Lebanon Vaults.'

Look at her! She mustn't be sick, not here!

Fortunately, Petra was aware of that, too. She turned and fled, running down the path in the direction of the way out. Virginia looked after her, panic stricken, and started to follow, then turned back and grabbed for Rod's hand. He took hers and pulled a comical face at the surprised party.

'Hello, got a deserter already,' he said. 'Don't usually bore people so quickly.'

They laughed kindly, their faces expressing instant interest, eager to reassure him that he wasn't being boring. He wasn't, they were hooked.

Rod glanced down at Virginia and smiled. She stared up at him, the personification of desperate trust, thrusting the whole weight of her misery upon his shoulders. She might have been one of those earnest, supplicating angels among the ivy, beseeching salvation.

Poor little devil. Poor, rich, spoilt, unloved little wretch.

'She's all right,' he whispered. 'Don't worry, love, we'll go and find her in a minute. I think she's feeling a bit Uncle Dick.'

'She's hung over,' said Virginia with bleak acceptance. 'She often is.'

'Yes,' said Rod, embarrassed. 'You O.K.?'

She nodded.

He turned back to the curious faces of the party. He tried to release his hand, but Virginia held on. The party looked even more curious.

'Someone's a bit nervous,' he explained. 'All right, Virginia, hold on if you want to.' They laughed again, relieved that he knew her, and followed him up the hill, deeper into the city of the dead. Rod was sweating.

He nearly stopped at the Druce tomb, but remembered just in time that the story of that bizarre exhumation wasn't likely to do much for Virginia's precarious state of mind. The others would have to forego that intriguing anecdote. He went on to the great, mournful dog in the thicket near the wall on to Swain's Lane, and started to tell them the heart-warming, if bloody story of Tom Sayers, the bare-knuckle prize fighter, and his devoted pet. They loved it. Even Virginia seemed to melt at the pathos of the story and looked affectionately at the animal which had followed its master in a carriage all of its own. She had never been in the West Cemetery before; it was the available solitude of the East Side which attracted her. Other people would have got in the way of her communion with the safe, peaceful dead.

Rod continued his tour, making hasty bowdlerisations so that Virginia shouldn't be too disturbed, changing his carefully planned itinerary so that it ended up as a mere précis of the interesting place the people had come to see. He chose all the happy stories: the famous, successful authoress Mrs. Henry Wood; George Wombwell's beautiful, tame lion; the founder of the Carl Rosa Opera; Mr. Maple the shopkeeper;

Mr. Collard the pianomaker; the good, liberal Reverend Maurice, with his charitable belief in eventual salvation for all. He started to lead them off the path towards the victim of the *Princess Alice* river disaster, then thought better of it and merely pointed out how work was being continued along that side of the cemetery, and how beautiful it was all going to be eventually.

One of the elderly women slipped and plunged her unbooted foot into a deep puddle, to the alarmed concern of her husband.

'Sorry,' said Rod, 'we haven't dealt with the drainage here yet.' Their understanding was surprisingly generous. Nice people. Thank God they were such nice people.

Eventually, uncomfortably agitated, he dumped them back at the gate, gave his usual appeal for funds to keep up the restoration work and offered the collecting box from the Portakabin. The coins and notes poured into it, accompanied by enthusiastic thanks.

'Gosh, that was fantastic,' said one of the young people, a punk-looking young woman who nevertheless spoke in the accents of Roedean. 'I suppose we couldn't go round again?'

'If you like,' said Rod. 'The next party is just up there, by the grave of James Selby, the coachman. I'm sure the guide won't mind you tagging on and you could learn a whole lot more information. We all do our own thing, you know.' And you'll probably get a lot better value, this time.

They scampered up the steps, eager for more. Suddenly totally exhausted, he looked down at Virginia, attached to his hand as if it were an umbilical cord. In a rush of empathy he felt her fear, her pain, her isolation.

'All right?' he asked.

She nodded. 'Where's Mummy?' Her voice had the flat hopelessness of one who didn't expect to find her. He looked round. Beyond the immense cast-iron gates, Petra's drooping head stared in at him, resting against the cool metal.

'She's over there. We'll go and talk now.'

Heavy with the weight of unwanted responsibility, he led Virginia back to her mother.

Rod and Dino's flat was in Upper Holloway, on the third floor of a Victorian terrace above a greengrocer's. It had a kitchen, a bathroom, two bedrooms and a sitting room which looked out on the busy street, although its altitude spared it the full impact of the noise and fumes.

The sitting room was painted white and furnished with the careful, tasteful charm of people who were visually aware. The common male tendency to blunder around in a state of myopia was absent. There was no careless, unnoticed mess; books were efficiently housed, papers tidily stacked, surfaces dusted, plants trimmed and watered. It looked bright, cheerful, organized and loved.

Petra and Virginia sat at opposite ends of the soft, cushioned settee, looking none of those things. The recital of the last few days' events had been harrowing, and the fact that Rod had believed it hadn't been comforting, it had merely served to confirm its reality.

Rod began the difficult task of trying to explain.

'Look, you remember what I told you about poltergeists last time, Petra? How they're caused by a build-up of energy?'

'Yes, vaguely.'

She was smoking, the big, Portobello fruit bowl at her side already polluted by a mess of ash and stubs. There were no bona-fide ashtrays in the flat; Rod and Dino didn't smoke.

Virginia was pressed deep into the hollow at the corner of the settee, playing with the tie-and-dye cushion, running her fingers over the design and along the straying veins of colour. She hadn't been still for more than a few seconds together since they'd arrived.

'You see, children have enormous amounts of it, and produce even more when they're approaching puberty. If for any reason the energy gets blocked and they can't express it, it can burst out in the form of psychokinesis – the movement of material objects by the agency of the mind. Poltergeists behave rather like naughty children, which is completely understandable if you think about it; after all, if the child concerned is troubled, then the bursts of kinetic energy are very likely to be expressions of their own repressed anger. So they throw things around, break them, cause damage by fire and water and electricity, play spiteful jokes on the people around them – in fact, they behave exactly like rebellious, angry children getting their own back.'

'But it was horrible, Rod, you've no idea how awful it was. That awful voice. What was that if it wasn't a ghost?'

'Well, to be honest, I don't know. Perhaps it was Virginia talking in a trance, or something. Anyway, it's all probably much more common than we realise. Unless it's so violent that it's unignorable, people keep quiet about it because they're frightened and ashamed. But it does stop when the crisis of puberty is over, that seems to be quite certain.'

'It said things – horrible, filthy things. And it knew things which Virginia couldn't have known about,' said Petra, feeling herself grow hot with excruciating memory. 'Explain that if you can.'

'Well – E.S.P.?' suggested Rod weakly.

He was floundering, he knew that. He just didn't know enough. He was an amateur playing around with something that was potentially very dangerous indeed.

Virginia's face was twitching. Rod watched her restless activity, the ageing frown on the pale face, the eyes searching for meaning in the maze of the printed cushion.

Be still, he willed her, be still. Don't let the energy build up like that. Don't store up fuel for the fire. Please, Virginia, be still.

He could sense that energy, teasing him, nudging him, sending its power across the room to probe at his own defences. He breathed deliberately, building up the calm wall of Yogic protection about his own soul. It was so terribly familiar, that restlessness, so reminiscent of experienced disaster. He felt remembered fear and immediately was aware of the energy intruding into his mouth, his nostrils, his ears. He closed his eyes, did the breathing exercises again and felt his defences close.

Petra whinged on, angry and resentful.

'You don't expect this sort of thing these days, do you? I mean, for God's sake, we're all rational people, aren't we, it's not as if we were bloody uneducated peasants. This is the 1980s, for God's sake. If you ask me, it's something evil, like in *The Omen*. Did you see that, Rod? Really scary. And did you see *The Exorcist*? God, that was frightening! I didn't believe a word of it at the time, but now! If you ask me, that's what's happened to Virginia.

'I mean, she's hardly a happy, laughing little ray of sunshine, is she? I mean, what does she expect, the way she behaves? I've told her to get out and enjoy herself like I did, but she just sits up there in her room and sulks and broods, so it's no wonder something like this happens, for God's sake.'

Rod saw Virginia's hands clutch the cushion and felt the wave of power flood out of her and strike him. For God's sake shut up, Petra. For *God's* sake. For Virginia's. Do you really believe in the power you call on with such facile repetition? I do. For *God's* sake shut up.

'Yes, well, let's stop talking about it now,' he said quickly, 'I think Virginia ought to calm down and forget it for a bit. Let's have something to eat, or a cup of tea or something.'

'But I thought you were going to tell us what to do,' Petra complained. 'I mean, I'm an intelligent woman, Rod, you know I am, but this is way beyond my experience and you did seem to know all about these things when we called you before.'

'Yes. Right. And what I do feel very strongly is that it's important that we get some positive thoughts into our heads. Concentrate on feeling happy and hopeful and – and – loving.'

'Loving! Jesus! What's loving got to do with this?'

Everything, thought Rod, absolutely everything. If you *were* intelligent you'd know that. You'd have realised long ago that love was the most important thing in the world, and given it to Virginia. She's love-starved, you silly, shallow woman. Life's nothing without the knowledge that you're loved. Until you feel loved you walk through life like an automaton, wondering what it's all about. Love her, can't you? Throw her a line. She's drowning.

Like I was, till I found Dino.

'Virginia needs to be loved,' he explained.

'You don't believe I do?' Petra said, offended. 'But I do, Rod, terribly. Virginia, you know I love you, don't you? I mean, just think of all the things we've given you. I mean, for God's sake – '

Virginia started to writhe, pushing her head down on to the cushion.

'Please, Petra, do as I say! Calm down! It's important, really it is.'

For God's sake, for Virginia's sake, for Love's sake, calm down and think. Quick, or it will happen again. There it was, over there beside poor, agitated Virginia, the stirring of the leaves of the maidenhair fern. He seized Virginia and pulled her up.

'Yes, of course we love Virginia. Now you stay there, Petra. We're going to get us all a bite to eat. You calm down and relax and think nice, peaceful thoughts.'

He pulled the child out of the room, away from the infection of her mother, down the corridor to the kitchen.

'Do *you* love me, Rod?' Virginia asked.

'Of course, I want to help you. But you mustn't expect too much of me, you know. I'm as weak and fallible as everyone else. We can none of us love as we should, I'm afraid.'

She stared at him, trying to understand what he meant.

He plugged in the kettle, ran his eyes over the contents of the cupboard and pulled out the makings of a snack meal. He put a saucepan of water on to boil.

If only he could think himself into her place, see her personal vision, understand things from her angle. Did she feel unwanted and unloved? He had only guessed that that was the case. Was he right? It was so important that he should be right. Being wrong was dangerous.

She was still staring. 'You mean you want me to go out with you?'

He turned, smiling, amused but kind. 'No, not that sort of love. It takes all forms, you know, it doesn't just mean sexual love.'

Didn't it? She'd thought it did. That was how it had seemed. Sandy and Petra loved her by buying her things; expensive placebos until she was grown-up and attractive enough to receive real love.

Oh no, don't say she was attracted to him? Poor little brat. She was sixteen, wasn't she, not the child she seemed. Don't say he'd done it again.

It was one of the most painful aspects of Rod's sexual inclination that women sometimes fell in love with him. He was attractive; tall, slim, good-looking. It had happened before, and he had suffered agonies of guilt and self-recrimination when he had to disillusion those poor females. It wasn't his fault, really it wasn't. He'd never encouraged them in their hopes. He couldn't help it if they'd mistaken his natural friendliness for something else. He didn't want to hurt anyone, let alone poor Virginia.

'I thought you loved someone else,' he said quickly, 'you know, the fireman. Don't you love him anymore?'

Her face blanked. 'No,' she said, 'that was a mistake. He wasn't there, really.'

'Wasn't there? What do you mean?'

He emptied the spaghetti into the boiling water and poured oil into the pan. Spaghetti, that was quick, easy and palatable. He reached for the garlic.

She was dumb. He adjusted the gas taps, took a quick glance at the oil and water, then knelt down in front of her, grasping her hands.

'Come on, Virginia, I won't laugh at you. You must tell me.'

Her head drooped and the tears ran from her eyes.

'I made him up,' she sobbed. 'I thought about him so hard that I thought he was real, but he wasn't. It was just *him*, that horrible voice. Oh, Rod, won't anybody nice fall in love with me, ever?'

He embraced her, even as he saw with terrified, angry recognition the force thrust the kettle off the worktop on to the floor, spill the flour out of the jar and hurl the staff of human life towards the wastebin.

'Bloody little whore!' it shouted gleefully.

Chapter 15

'Shut up!' shouted Rod.

It laughed. The pan slid across the stove and tipped, pouring the boiling water on to the floor at his feet and dumping the dead, brown sticks of spaghetti against the oven door. He jumped back as the scalding drops spattered up his legs and stung them like a swarm of angry bees.

Virginia fell on to the floor, screaming, then enclosed her head in her arms and whimpered like a puppy. Rod crouched down to shield her with his body as the destruction continued. Plates slid off the rack and crashed one by one to the floor. The frying pan started to whirl round and round on the gas jets. The window was thrown up, then down, then up, dancing repeatedly on the frame with a regular thump, thump, thump.

'Go away!' Rod protested. 'You're not wanted here!'

'She wants me.'

'I don't!' Virginia shrieked. 'I wanted William, not you!'

'I am William.'

'You're not, you're not! William's good.'

'Good, good, good,' it teased, catching the silly word like a ball and bouncing it back and forth between the walls.

'Who are you?' Rod demanded. 'Tell us who you are.'

There was a pause, filled with heavy, catarrhal breathing.

'You ashamed of who you are?' Rod taunted it, so angry that the fear was almost stifled.

'No!' The shout was practically human in its indignation.

'All right, then, who are you, and what do you want?'

'Her. She's ready.'

'You can't have her. She doesn't want you.'

He was feeling more in charge now. He had got some sort of contact established. Yes, he remembered, that was how you played it.

The breathing continued. It coughed, choked, groaned.

'We don't want you,' Rod repeated, cradling Virginia's head in his arms. 'Go back where you came from. Leave her alone. Nobody here wants you.'

Immediately, it seemed to become angry again. The cupboard door banged. The salt dispenser on the wall emitted a soft, white shower, flooding down into the frying pan and sending a fountain of spitting oil over the stove.

'And stop that!' Rod told it, gaining in confidence. 'Who do you think you're impressing with these childish tricks? Not me, certainly. I think you're pretty stupid.'

It gave an angry shout and the shelves above the worktop suddenly wrenched themselves away from the wall and hung trembling on the last inch of the screws. Rod pulled Virginia into the corner behind the door, away from danger, and started to shout too, furiously angry.

'And that's stupid, too! You're ridiculous, do you hear, just plain ridiculous. Anyone can do that. Anyone can smash things up and break and destroy. You're like some pathetic, useless little vandal who hasn't the talent to create and has to make do with destroying. You can't create, can you? You can't make anything.'

Virginia was fainting with terror, pressed against Rod's thudding, leaping heart. Her hands moved across his sweater, as if seeking buttons. He gasped, trying to drag air into his spastic lungs, conscious of his human body's many betrayals and mortifications. The sweat ran down his face, neck and back, his limbs shook, his bladder nagged with the humiliating imminence of incontinence.

The objects on the shelf above the stove began to move down on to the worktop. An egg-cup, first, settling itself comfortably on the tiles, then a packet of Earl Grey, then a spoon. The peppermill, the colander, three jars of herbs. Together, they did a little dance, then built themselves into a totem pole, each object balanced on the other, the colander on top, the egg-cup at the bottom.

'I made that,' the voice said, and laughed at its own cleverness.

'Not bad,' said Rod ironically. 'Now how about putting it all back and clearing up the mess? That'd impress me a lot more.'

It grumbled irritably, the volume diminishing to a hollow rasp.

'What?' Rod asked.

'No fun.'

'No fun? Oh, being constructive isn't fun. No, I don't suppose it is for you. You only thrive on destruction, don't you? I know that,' he continued, his anger getting stronger and stronger, 'and I despise you, do you hear? I despise you. I don't think you're clever or impressive or even frightening.' Oh, Rod, you liar. 'The best thing you can do is get back to where you came from, you're wasting your time here.'

The pile of balanced objects crashed down, as if it had been struck by an invisible hand. The window shot up again, rattled violently, then shattered. There was silence.

Rod waited in misery, arms clasped around Virginia. He'd got to go to the loo, he was bursting, but he daren't leave her yet. Hold on, hold on. He could have cried with the pathetic weakness of his flesh. The silent seconds ticked on, became minutes and remained empty.

Far away, there was a muffled, questioning voice, like a radio heard from next-door. He closed his eyes, rested his forehead on Virginia's bowed head, felt the sweat pour off him and into her thin hair. Angels and ministers of grace defend us. Hail Mary, full of grace. Oh Lord, by thy great mercy, defend us from all perils and dangers of the night, or the afternoon, or any time.

Petra came to find them. She walked down the long corridor which connected the front and back of the deep, old building and tried the kitchen door. It opened about six inches then stopped with a judder. There was an apprehensive gasp.

'Rod?'

Relieved, he laid Virginia gently against the wall and rose to his feet. The door swung open with the next push.

'What was wrong with the door?'

'I was behind it.' He pushed back his hair. It was ringing wet.

'Is it all right if I use the phone? I ought to let Sandy know where we are. God, what's the matter with Virginia?'

She fell on to her knees beside her daughter and shook her. 'Virginia! Virginia!'

'It happened again,' Rod said flatly, too exhausted to bother with softening the message. He waved his hand at the wreck of the kitchen. For the first time, he noticed that the handmade tiles they had taken months to find were all cracked.

'You were right after all. A spirit seems to have got in.'

'But you said it was nothing to do with ghosts!'

'Well, that's what the books say,' he defended himself.

'Books? I thought you knew all about it.'

'I never said that,' he protested. 'We're all ignorant, we're just groping in the dark. We're like a deaf, blind man in a fairground completely unaware of the activity around him until he's actually touched. And even then he hasn't the faculties to recognise what it is.'

'You mean the books are wrong?'

'I don't know! Experts have been wrong before, haven't they? It's possible, that's all I can tell you. I suppose that once the ground has been laid by the physical results of human misery, lost, malevolent spirits could get in and build upon it. Like a neglected common cold turning into pneumonia. Perhaps Virginia's attracted it. Perhaps she's psychic.'

'Well can't you *do* something?' demanded Petra.

They stayed the night, huddled together in the wide bed in Dino's bedroom, while the two men tried to find ease in Rod's single divan.

Dino, returning from the restaurant in Hampstead where he was a waiter, had been devastated at the destruction of his beautiful kitchen.

'Sorry, Dino,' said Rod wretchedly, 'they'd nowhere else to go.'

'Yes, sure.'

Rod felt the silent jerks of Dino's body against his shoulder. He was crying. He put his arm around him.

'Oh, I know, I know, but I couldn't turn that poor little kid away. She's so alone. I like Petra and Sandy, they're really good company, but I'm afraid they're just not natural parents.'

'No,' said Dino. 'We have good times with them, they are good company, but all on the surface. No depth, no insight.'

'I tried to tell Petra what was wrong, but she honestly couldn't see it. Thinks that all kids need is comfort, luxuries. Things. She thinks she's a good mother, you know. She really believes it.'

'All parents think they are good.'

'Yes.' We've always done our best for you, Rodney. We're only doing what's right. You'll thank us one day.

'Parents do bad things to their kids all the time.'

'And never even notice,' said Rod.

No, Mother can't stay with you, Frank, you mustn't be a baby, there's nothing there. Now, now, Rodney old chap, be a man. Boys don't cry.

They do, they do. I cry. Frank cries. Dino's crying.

'Some people, they don't deserve kids. Others, they can't have them. That's how it is,' sighed Dino. 'Tomorrow I go to Mass.'

'Will you tell the priest?'

'Yes, I think perhaps I tell the priest. You come?'

'Virginia may need me.'

'I pray for her. I pray for all of us. I light a candle, four candles.'

'Yes, please do that.'

From the next room came the crash of glass. Rod sat up in bed. Oh God! Angels and ministers of grace . . .

Sandy called next day at nine, cheerful and totally corporeal. Petra led him up the six flights of stairs, spilling the bad news into his ears all the way to the flat.

'We've been up most of the night, Sandy. Just one thing after another. You should see the state of poor Dino's bedroom.'

'Oh, for God's sake, Petra, can't you control that daughter of yours?'

'But it isn't her, really it isn't! It had nothing to do with her. She was in bed beside me, and the clock smashed to the floor and the pictures fell down.'

His mind shut at once.

'Well, the decorators have finished so you'll be able to come home tonight, and she'll be all the better for a day out. All ready?'

'What?' Petra's face became blank.

'The house. Maiden's End. We're going down there, don't you remember?'

'Oh. But surely – I mean, not now.'

Rod, grey-faced, was rubbing at the pale, oyster carpet. He looked up as Sandy entered.

'Hello. Petra tell you?'

'Virginia again, eh?'

'No, not her,' said Rod, 'the poltergeist. You remember, the *poltergeist*. I explained it to you. Virginia's the focus, Sandy, and she needs help. What are you going to do?'

'Take her out for a day in the country.' said Sandy, producing his complete answer.

'No,' said Rod with grim patience, 'what are you going to do about all this?' His hand indicated the carpet, the wall. Stains. Stains like blood.

'Threw things, did she?'

I give up, thought Rod.

Sandy sat down on the settee, with the grace at least to look apologetic.

'Look, don't worry, we're going to get her seen to. I think you said Zak would be back today, didn't you, Petra?'

She stared at him in despair.

'Sandy,' she begged, 'you know very well it's not as simple as that. Didn't I just tell you? Please, please, please, don't shut off like that. It's real, horribly real. Look!'

Desperate for evidence, she picked up an antique Worcester plate from the table and thrust it under his nose. There was a hole right through the middle, a clean, round hole.

'One minute it was on the wall, the next it was like that,' said Rod. 'I saw it happen. My mother gave it to me when she was emptying her parents' home.'

All right, Beatrice, let the great poof have the pretty little piece of china if he wants it, though I should have thought he would have preferred that shotgun of your Father's. Bloody good gun, that, nearly as good as mine.

No, Daddy, don't shoot the rabbit! Don't Daddy, don't!

Blood, blood. All up his clean, white, lovingly painted wall.

175

Virginia flitted into the room like a distracted wraith, touching things, pulling at the books on the shelves, running her hands through the pot of ferns on the windowsill. She was humming under her breath, a strange, catchy little tune which stopped and started like a badly wound tape, nearly reaching the end of a phrase then blanking out, starting again at the same point, stopping. She darted from one place to another like a restless insect, touching and caressing, as tense as a wound spring.

'Hello, sweetie.' Sandy's eyes darkened as he watched her. She didn't answer, though the fey smile faded from her face. She reached towards the plate in Petra's hand and thrust her fingers through it, wriggling them on the other side.

'Right through,' she said. 'Right through the middle. Bang, bang, you're dead.'

'Been wrecking the happy home again, I see,' said Sandy. She stopped short, gave a silly, high laugh, then began to cry. It was a long time since Rod had hated anyone as much as he hated Sandy then.

'Real psychologist, aren't you?' he said angrily.

'What do you mean?'

'Really know how to handle people.'

'Well, I should hope so, in my line. That's what selling's all about. Now get your coat on, Virginia, we're going out.'

'No,' she cried rebelliously, all gaiety gone. 'I want to stay with Rod.'

'Couldn't he come?' Petra asked anxiously.

'If he wants to. You'd probably enjoy it, actually, Rod, wonderful place. Appeal to your artistic nature.'

Rod didn't miss the snide allusion. How could he ever have liked this man? He hesitated. He didn't like the thought of Virginia alone with those two. Self-centred hysteria and wilful blindness were no companions for her in that state. It would be like shutting up a bag of gunpowder with a lit fuse.

'Yes, do come, Rod,' Petra begged. Virginia, sniffing, was running her hands over his shirt, seeking non-existent brass buttons. He looked down at her. He had intended to go to the cemetery that afternoon. 'All right.' She smiled at once, the tearful mood changing to euphoria with irrational speed.

'Rod's coming, Rod's coming,' she chanted.

'You do realise where we're going, don't you? The house. Do you mind?'

The shadow fell again.

'I don't like it,' she whispered, 'it's frightening.'

'Sorry, Sandy,' Rod said firmly, 'she can't go there if she feels like that. She can stay here with me.'

Virginia laughed out loud. 'I'm going to stay with Rod!'

'You are not,' said Sandy with angry obstinacy. 'Rod can come with us if you want, but we're all going down to the house today, whether you like it or not. You're going to live there soon, and the sooner you get rid of this silly phobia the better.'

'Sandy!' Rod was consumed with outraged disgust, but to his surprise Virginia continued to smile.

'I won't go in,' she announced pertly. 'I'll stay in the car and hate it, hate it, hate it! Then I can come back here with Rod!'

It was seconds before Rod realised with horror what she meant, that she had completely misunderstood him.

'I'm not going to live at horrible Maiden's End, so there! I'm going to live with Rod.'

He didn't even try to disillusion her. She probably wasn't going to live there, she was almost certainly going into a mental hospital. Sufficient unto the day.

The structure was sound, the roof watertight, the new plumbing gushingly operative. A few expensive, double-time workmen scurried round putting final touches to the hurried and therefore botched renovation; another customer was complaining furiously about being let down and the badgered Mr. Hargreaves wanted them all out today, ready to start at Radwell on Monday.

In the bathroom, a roll of carpet was leaning in the corner; in the drawing room, the harassed man from the soft furnishing shop in Stevenage had left an aluminium ladder and a tape measure; down in the basement, Petra looked at her glorious, wickedly expensive workplace.

Sandy's untouched country kitchen had been torn out and carted away in the skip to be dumped in a disused quarry near Bedford, and the streamlined room before her was in total accord with the aspirations of modern Highgate. Well, this wasn't where she'd wanted to live, but her London friends would be coming down and they'd certainly be impressed. Even Marjorie hadn't got a Littlebow kitchen, despite her merchant banker ex-husband. She'd stopped worrying about expense long ago and had decided to sting Sandy for every bloody penny. It was the top-price range – the Country Kitchen range.

Real oak doors. Real brass handles. Hand-carved architraves on top of the cupboards, quaint, turned spindles along the edges of the shelves and a generous electric hotplate beneath a copper hood. Within the recess, the cracked red bricks had been made good, plastered and covered with expensive Spanish tiles which looked exactly like old, red bricks. She gloated, suddenly lifted out of her fear by the sheer luxury of it all. All right, she'd give it a go.

Within its curtain wall of trees, Maiden's End sat scarified, modernised and tamed.

And yet, its unpleasant aura was still intact. The old walls remained beneath the modernisation, extruding their uncomfortable secrets. Virginia had felt it at once, even outside in the drive, and immediately become defensively aggressive.

'I'm not going in,' she challenged Sandy, 'it's not my house, it's yours. You can come and live in this silly place if you want to but I won't. Rod and I are going to stay here in the car, see?' She leant back in the seat, infuriatingly unco-operative.

'You are not!' said Sandy angrily, pulling open the door. 'You are going to stop behaving like a spoilt brat, Virginia, and show Rod round your new home. What do you think, Rod?' He became unctuously charming. 'Splendid, isn't it? How old do you think, seventeenth-century? I expect you know all about that sort of thing, with your sensitivity to the aesthetic.'

'No, I don't think so,' said Rod coldly, despising him, hating him. 'Perhaps 1760ish.'

Definitely not seventeenth-century. They still had nice, pitched roofs, then. God, it's ugly. People go on about the glories of Georgian architecture, but how did countrymen feel when these square, featureless boxes went up in their villages? The man who built this didn't give a damn about beauty, proportion or fitting in with the landscape. Philistinism isn't new, it's always been around. The original owner was an aesthetic cretin with no taste, just a belief in practicality like the architect of a tower block, though what was practical about a basement kitchen when there was so much land around? He just wanted to keep the lower orders in their place, out of sight, out of the daylight.

Reluctantly, he followed Sandy up the steps, glancing back at Virginia. She was standing beside the car. He beckoned, offering a supporting hand.

'Who built it, do you know?'

'Yes, a local gentleman farmer. Great man. I'd like to have met him and shaken him by the hand.'

Yes, you would, wouldn't you? You'd have been two of a kind, all money and profit and materialism. Virginia caught hold of his hand and they went into the hall.

It was in its full new glory, with amber walls and white paintwork, the wood of the staircase gleaming with warm, mahogany stain. The banisters were plain and square, not gracefully decorated as good houses of that period were. The floor was patterned with chequers, as on the tables of Renaissance banking houses, a place to tot up the money.

'This is the dining room. Elegant, isn't it?'

The panelling shone with varnish. The utilitarian boards were polished, like a countrywoman's plain face adorned with make-up. The hard, undecorated chimneypiece was like a funeral monument in the cemetery. A huge, elongated table occupied the centre of the floor.

'I bought this last week, from a dealer in Ware. He wanted a thousand for it but I beat him down to eight fifty. A real bargain, don't you think?'

Yes, if you want the left-overs from a workhouse. I know that sort of furniture, it's got its provenance written all over it.

'Where did it come from?'

'Well, the chap was a bit cagey at first, but I got it out of him eventually. It'd been in a barn for fifty years and he'd bought it for a song and polished it up. Came from an orphanage.'

Thought so. Imbued with misery and servitude and semi-starvation.

'Absolutely right for you.'

Sandy strode off and flung open the drawing room door. A long sward of green broadloom covered the boards with its pungent insulation. The whole room smelt of rubber. The panelling had been stripped here, too, and the open-mouthed fireplace seemed alarmed by the resurrection of two-hundred-year-old dead wood.

'We'll have to put our present furniture in here for the time being, although I know it's not right, but eventually I'm going to get some genuine Georgian stuff, perhaps Chippendale, if I can find it. I'm going to do this properly, Rod, I can assure you. I don't suppose you'd approve of anything else.'

Why should I care? This isn't the golden age of architecture. If you got Robert Adam to tart up this house it would still look evil; not even he could rescue it from its charmless brutality. It's ugly, ugly, bloody ugly. Put Chippendale in here and it could well run screaming out of the door.

'Now come upstairs. You want to show Rod your room, don't you, Virginia?'

'No.'

'Oh, come on, don't be such a pain. It's all white, like you wanted it. Like a mortuary, actually, but it's your choice.'

They followed Sandy up the stairs, Rod depressed by the sheer ugliness of their surroundings.

Virginia walked into her room and was practically blinded by the glaring radiance of the white paint. It was utterly transformed — no longer a dim, gloomy cavern, more a shining, virgin temple, with the spring sunlight sparkling off the mirror in the wardrobe. She went in further, testing the atmosphere. It wasn't quite so bad, but it was still there. Through the three coats of paint, the genius loci bled out and touched her. She gripped Rod's hand even harder.

'Is this what you wanted?' asked Sandy.

'Yes,' she said, closing her eyes. She turned and leant against Rod's chest, as if she was trying to hide herself.

'Now come and see our bedroom.'

They crossed the landing.

A big, bare room. A decorator was desperately slapping pink and white Arcadia on to the walls. Shepherdesses slid suggestive, sidelong glances at girl-like shepherds; sheep grazed safely in never-never landscapes. A door led into the dressing room, now containing a glossy bathroom suite of flowered porcelain.

'I've had the whole room replastered. Stripped out the

panelling, it was a mass of rot. Expect you think I'm a philistine, Rod, but you have to be practical. Don't fancy sharing my bed with fungus.'

'What's the matter?' Rod asked as Virginia pressed her head into his shoulder. This was awful, she was behaving like a lovesick woman. He hadn't meant to hurt her, really he hadn't. Oh God, he thought, like poor Saint Wilgefortis, relieve me from my physical attractions, make me harmless.

'I want to go outside, Rod.'

'In a minute, I promise. Sandy'll be offended if I go before I've seen it all.'

Not that Sandy matters to me. But he's my friend, said his civilised self, I've been in his house dozens of times, drinking his booze, enjoying his hospitality. I've got to be polite.

'The attics are up here, behind this door. Another five rooms, just right for guests. I hope you'll be sleeping here soon, and Dino of course.' To Rod's heightened sensitivity, Sandy seemed to sneer as he spoke Dino's name. Sneer? Why should he? There was nothing conventionally moralistic about Sandy. You might find bigotry in the suburbs, but not in that cosmopolitan côterie which was London N.6. Don't be paranoid, just because you don't like the stupid bastard. He can't help it if he's thick as a plank. Try to understand him, as if he was a client at the Samaritans. Don't judge.

He climbed the attic stairs and viewed the low rooms.

'Nice,' he told Sandy.

'We've put another bathroom in here.' Ivory suite, flowered tiles. Very 1980s tasteful.

'Trap door to the roof is up here.'

If Rod hadn't been with her, Virginia would have screamed. Even he blenched when he looked over the parapet.

Don't be a baby, Rodney. Pull yourself together. I've been a bellringer for thirty years and I've never felt afraid up here. Look, there's our house, and by Jove there's your mother, hanging out the washing. Give her a shout. Come on, boy, give her a shout. Bare knees knocking. Mum, here I am, Mum. That's better, don't want to be a coward, do we Rodney. Head up. Stiff upper lip. Show the flag.

'Yes,' said Rod, bracing his jeaned legs against the parapet and holding Virginia tightly. 'Now can we go down? Virginia's frightened.'

On the first-floor landing, Sandy waved a proud hand at the brass chandelier hanging over the stairs. 'Got it at that lighting place in Chelsea. Five hundred pounds, but worth every penny. Perfect reproduction of an eighteenth-century one.'

It isn't. It's Victorian, and not even right for that. It's suburban kitsch.

Sandy pressed the switch and the landing was flooded with light. The engraved glass shades spattered the ceiling and walls with ghostly flowers.

Virginia gave a sudden jerk and backed away from the door to the attic. Rod started to take her downstairs. As they reached the bottom the light went out with a bang and glass pattered down on them like rain. She screamed.

'Damn it!' said Sandy. He tried the switch in the dining room, but it refused to respond. 'Mr. Hargreaves!'

Hargreaves scrambled up the service stairs with the exasperated weariness of a man at the end of his tether.

'Mr. Hargreaves,' roared Sandy, 'get that telephone of yours and ring Carter right now. Do you hear me? Get Carter!'

Even as Rod's imagination was picturing Michael Caine entering the front door of Maiden's End with a bag of tools, he saw that the orphanage table had started to rock.

He pushed Virginia out of the front door before she noticed. At last she smiled.

'Now I'm going home with Rod!'

Chapter 16

Derek waited for over an hour, shivering. It was sunny, but frost still lingered on shadowed grass and the wind was piling up grey clouds beyond the cemetery.

He looked at his watch again. It wasn't like her to be late. It wasn't like her not to ring him, either, but for once he hadn't needed reminding. There was so much time to fill now.

The frantic necessity to keep his head above water was gone, and he had stopped swimming and sunk to the bottom to find himself stuck in the mud of a small, depressing flat in Crouch End. At first he had sat there for hours on end, not even bothering to turn on the lamp when the light faded. Only when the numbness started to pass had he begun looking for things with which to fill the empty void of unemployment; activity, people, friends. Love.

Not sexual love, he had no illusions about that, and anyway, he'd never been very strongly sexed. The hey-day in his blood had peaked in his early twenties, then fallen off rapidly, leaving only consequent complication in its wake. If he had found a partner who was right for him it might have been different. In that case, his moderate desires might have been strengthened by rewarding return and grown, but rejection is destructive. It builds up expectation of disappointment and failure, diminishes desire even as it is aroused and slaps it down into resignation.

Washed up on the dull shore of his forty years, Derek couldn't comfort himself with memories of past pleasures, and there were almost certainly no future ones to look forward to. His sex-appeal had never been much – no more than the superficial glow of youthful health, the universal attractiveness of young men to young women. He knew that the rest of his life would probably be devoid of that sort of love.

But he needed some sort. There were his parents, of course. He hadn't got round to telling them yet. He knew they would be kind, understanding and sympathetic. They would say how unjust it was that someone of Derek's talents should fail, and how business wasn't what it was in their day, when the world was decent and innocent. They would urge him to come back to Herne Bay and make his home with them until the right opening came along. They'd be kind, so kind. So full of pity.

He couldn't face it. He didn't need pity, he needed reassurance. He needed someone who loved him with the blinkers on, who thought he was marvellous no matter what he did, someone who would make him feel big again.

Thank God for Virginia, he had thought.

The clouds came sweeping in over the cemetery and into Waterlow Park. As the first drops fell, he rose and walked down to the gate. He was angry; Petra was playing up again. How dare she deprive him of his fortnightly treat? It was his right, the law said so. It was his last bit of normal life, the only thing he had left, and he wasn't going to stand for losing that as well. Even a worm can turn. Even Derek Blackie.

He had to walk there. One of the first things they'd done had been to ask for his car keys.

Outside the house, he stood and looked at the smart frontage. Bulbs were blooming in the garden, the mahonia was laced with gold and forsythia was turning from yellow to green. It was all his planting, there was nothing new; the only changes were destructive. No white flowers starred the viburnum beneath the bay window – Sandy had cut it down. The bay tree stood brown-leaved in its terracotta pot; it should have been taken inside, or at least been swathed in plastic before the frosts came. The jasmine had gone from the porch; Petra had always complained about the mess it made.

The house was all right, though, in tip-top condition. That was real estate, investment, solid, retrievable money. It was as spick and span as Sandy's bank balance. Wonder what they've done to the back yard. Is it the same? Are there still roses against the back railings on to the park? Is there still Creeping

Jenny scrambling through the lavender under the kitchen window?

And is there honey still for tea? he mocked himself. No, there had never been honey.

He opened the gate.

Only Sandy was in. He greeted Derek with a burst of generous forgiveness which filled him with shock, showed him into what had been his own lounge and encouraged him to sit down on the settee he had paid for. Would he care for a drink? What would it be, old man, Scotch? Seem to remember you always drank Scotch, wasn't that right?

'Neat,' said Derek, in answer to the waved soda syphon. He hadn't seen Sandy for about five years – hadn't wanted to. Must be about forty-five, though he didn't look much different. It had been the final blow to his vanity that Sandy was older than him. Couldn't even comfort himself with the thought that Petra wanted someone more her own age.

'Well now, good to see you, Derek,' said Sandy, rubbing in the salt energetically. 'How's things? Heard from Petra that you were in a bit of trouble, is that right?'

'Yes,' said Derek shortly. 'How's things with you?'

'Fine, just fine.' He grinned.

'Look, I was expecting to meet Virginia this afternoon, as usual. Is she ill?'

'Virginia?' Sandy frowned as if he was trying to remember who she was. 'Had you arranged something, then?'

'It's Sunday,' said Derek, trying to keep his temper. 'It's my day to see her.'

'Oh!' Understanding dawned, a performance which would have graced the stage of the R.S.C. 'God, yes, of course it is. Well, the fact is, Derek old man, things have been a bit hectic here lately. We're moving, you know. She and Petra have gone to stay with friends while I get things organised. They both came down to the house this morning, but then they went back to Rod Singleton's flat for lunch. Nice chap, do you know him? Screaming fairy, of course, but a really nice, genuine chap.'

Unlike you. Derek was fully aware that Sandy was stringing him along, prolonging the agony.

'Where does he live?'

'Down in Upper Holloway. Virginia's got very fond of him lately and she must have been so excited that she forgot all about you. What a bloody shame. Still, they're all the same, kids, aren't they? No thought for other people, too wrapped up in their own affairs. Bloody inconsiderate, but there you are.'

He drank from his glass, screwing Derek across it with a ruthless smile.

Why does he hate me so much? thought Derek wildly. It's me who should feel like that. He's got everything I ever owned, even my daughter.

'Not Virginia,' he said aggressively. 'She's not like that.'

'Really?' Sandy's interested query was loaded with insinuation. Pathetic little twat, it said, you believe that if you want to, but I know better. I live with her. I own her.

'No,' said Derek, beginning to shake with anger. 'The only times she hasn't turned up were when Petra stopped her. Has she done that this time?'

'Of course not, old man. You're way off course there. But I tell you what it might be: she's been a bit funny, lately, very hysterical and upset, even destructive. Don't suppose you knew that, did you?'

'Of course I did!' lied Derek furiously.

'You did? Oh, splendid. Well, you know what it is, of course. Puberty. Not quite going as it should. Things not getting going, understand?'

'Her periods haven't started. Yes, I know.'

'Oh, she told you?' said Sandy, obviously deeply touched by this evidence of family closeness. 'Good for you. Well, they're all the same, these women, you know how it is. Just a seething mass of hormones, poor cows. Seems to have sent her a bit round the bend.'

'Round the bend? You mean she *is* ill?'

'No, no, nothing serious. I told you, just women's troubles. I really feel sorry for them sometimes, you know, it must be hell. Thank God we're not female, eh, Derek?'

Derek got up, plonking his half-finished drink on to the coffee table which had cost him eighty quid, and that was seven years ago. The neat Scotch splashed out on to the polish and he walked away from it, willing it to leave a mark.

'What's the address of Rod's flat?'

Sandy told him with kind sympathy.

'Don't worry, old man, Petra's getting Zak Ziegler to look at her. The psychiatrist, you know. He's a friend of ours, fortunately. That's the nice thing about a place like Highgate, your friends are all so bloody useful.'

'A psychiatrist? That bad!'

'Don't worry about it,' Sandy purred. 'All under control. *Ciao*, Derek, look after yourself.'

He hurried down to Holloway. The rain was coming down in icy, spiteful bursts, flying into his face and forcing it into the shelter of his upturned collar. The greengrocer's frontage was a blank sheet of iron. Beside it, the dirty green Victorian door displayed its metal-framed, type-written cards: 1. M. & H.Georgiou; 2. Ms.Mary Plunkett and Mr. John Harris; 3. R.Singleton and D.Zucconi.

They seemed to take a long time to answer. He rang again, driven frantic by the teasing wind. A vaguely familiar young man in sweater and jeans opened the door at last.

'Hello, Derek!'

'Virginia here?' he asked, shrunken within his coat.

'Yes, come in. Terrible day, isn't it?'

So what? They all are.

His shoes clattered up the stairs to the first floor, to the second, finally, his legs aching, to the third.

It was a nice room, bright and friendly. The faces looked up as he entered, recognising him with startled surprise, as if he had risen from the dead.

'Good God, Derek, what are you doing here?' Petra's greeting was as chilly as ever.

'It's my day,' he said. 'To see Virginia.' She was sitting in an armchair, perched like a doll within its huge comfort, dressed in white trousers and bomber jacket over a vivid pink sweater, and she was wearing gaudy gilt earrings. Her face was radiant.

Rod showed Derek to a seat on the settee and perched on the arm, but immediately she held out her hand to him, with the eager begging she had used to offer to Derek. Rod got up and went to sit on the arm of her chair, looking down with embarrassment. She gripped his hand.

She was in love with him, there was no doubt about it. He wasn't gay, that was just Sandy's spite. A plump, soft little man was fussing with a tray of coffee.

'We'll need another cup, Dino. This is Virginia's father. Derek, this is my flatmate, Dino.'

'Hel – *lo.*'

Oh yes, you couldn't mistake that one. So Rod *was* gay. Poor Virginia, poor bloody kid! His anger welled up at the cruelty of life, at Petra's blind inadequacy as a mother.

'I've been waiting for you, darling,' he said, leaning towards her urgently. 'In the park. What happened?'

'Oh!' she said. Her face suddenly blanked out and she looked at him as if he were an unpleasant shock, nothing more than a forgotten piece of homework. 'Sorry, Daddy, I forgot.'

Derek felt the betrayal like a blow. Even here they had robbed him. Even with her he had been supplanted.

'How did you know we were here?' Petra demanded.

'Sandy told me. And he said Virginia was ill, but she isn't, is she? You look marvellous, darling, I've never seen you look so pretty.'

I've never seen you look pretty at all, until now. Suddenly you're the daughter I've been looking forward to, the one I was going to enjoy showing off, and you're not mine anymore. I've lost you to that handsome young man who's going to be about as much use to you as I was to your mother.

He pressed his claim angrily.

'Right, well, we'll get off now, shall we?'

'She can't manage today,' said Petra quickly. 'Someone's coming to see her. We're waiting for him now.'

'But it's my day!' Derek insisted. 'You know it is. Every Sunday fortnight. You can't put it off at the last minute like this.'

'Bought tickets for something?' Her voice was spiteful.

'It's my day!' he said obstinately, pleading with Virginia for support. She looked down into her lap, her hand still clasping Rod's.

The bell rang.

'There he is,' said Petra. 'I'll go.'

Him? Who's him? Have you procured a whole harem of safe eunuchs to cut me off from my daughter?

The room was full of tension for which Derek couldn't even guess the reason. He had the impression that he was in the presence of a deep, embarrassing secret. Something had been happening and no-one was going to tell him what it was, although it obviously concerned Virginia.

'What's the matter?' he asked. '*Is* Virginia ill?'

She started to wriggle uncomfortably and Derek saw Rod give her hand a comforting shake. His jealous anger surged up again as the door opened.

Derek had never met Zak Ziegler. He was part of the rich, top stratum of Highgate society that he had never got in with and lived in an old house on West Hill which, over three centuries, had housed a Lord Chancellor, a famous novelist, a railway king and a wealthy eccentric who had filled its acres of garden with aviaries full of exotic birds. The largest of these buildings, a stunning mock-Gothic castle decked with stucco pinnacles, still remained, but it now enclosed a heated swimming pool, a jacuzzi and a gymnasium. At a tactful distance from the main house, a Temple of Venus which had been built by yet another owner and used for metropolitan meetings of the Hellfire Club, had been converted into Zak's consulting room and office, a purpose which its lingering ghosts probably felt thoroughly at home with, though the revelations made within its elegant interior would have taught them little that they didn't know already. Mankind's weaknesses didn't change.

Zak was a sleek, dark, handsome man in his late thirties, with the glowing patina of confidence which only money and success can give. He had learnt his craft from a pupil of Freud, and his view of humanity remained Freudian. Adler and Jung and other professional complexions he bowed to respectfully, as befitted an open-minded man, but Freud was his God, his only God. Big Daddy God was dead. He had learnt young that the human race was driven entirely by sex and his whole professional and private experience had served to strengthen his belief in that premise. There were many of his profession who disliked him to the point of fury, but he had never found any reason to adopt their revisionist qualifications of his fundamentalist creed. For him, all drives towards love, hate, power, success, religion, art and science, even all intellectual interests and hobbies, were merely channels for the sublimated sex drive. In fact, all human life *was* sex, in some form or another. Freud himself might have found him a trifle obsessive.

But his patients quickly came to agree with him. If you were paying that much you couldn't disagree; anyone who charged fees so high must know what he was talking about. In their agony of mind, they were only too grateful to grasp the lifeline which offered liberation from their suffering; their agoraphobia was fear of rape (subconsciously desired rape, of course), their money worries were an anal complex, their affection for their mothers was only Oedipal longing, their fear of and revulsion from physical cruelty merely resentment of the fathers who abrogated all sexual rights to their mothers to themselves. All men and women regarded each other, even their own sex, as sex objects, and quite right too, because that was all that men and women were. Once over your prudish shame at that great truth and you were free; able to function normally, to wallow deep down in the comfortable trough with all the other pigs.

His male patients admired and envied him. His female patients adored him. And some of them found, once they had been safely discharged, that he was a bloody good lover.

Petra fluttered, tense with the excitement aroused by his compulsive personality. It had only been once, after a party, before Sandy became her dominant fixation, but she remembered. Nobody ever forgot a close encounter with Zak.

'Terribly nice of you to come, Zak, when you're only just back from holiday, and on a Sunday, too. You're a gorgeous colour. What's it like down there? Thoroughly decadent and sheer heaven, I suppose?'

Zak smiled. It was an attractive smile, he knew it was. People melted when Zak smiled, particularly female people.

'Believe me, Petra darling, Mammon is alive and well and living in the Seychelles. Boring people, of course, but what's new? Lovely to be back in dear old Highgate and picking up the threads.'

'Yes, well, we're frightfully grateful that you're back, I just can't tell you. We'll get out now and leave you with Virginia. You'll tell Zak everything, won't you, darling? No need to be shy, he'll understand. Just give us a shout when you've finished, Zak, we promise we won't intrude until then.'

They rose and evacuated the room, although Virginia hung on to Rod's hand until the last second.

Derek stayed obstinately where he was.

'What's the matter with her?' he asked. 'I'm her father. I don't understand all this. What's going on?'

'Mr. – er – Blackie?' Zak's tone was patronisingly confused.

'Yes.' Derek asserted his identity defiantly.

'Mr. Blackie, I'm sure you'll understand that the relationship of therapist and patient must be exclusively one-to-one. Any interference between them is counter-productive.'

'What do you mean, interference? She's my daughter. No-one has the right to interfere with *that* relationship.'

'You feel aggression towards me, Mr. Blackie?' said Zak, employing the customary psychiatrist's trick of answering every question with another one. His black eyes fixed intently upon Derek, studying this unbalanced specimen through the professional glass window which kept humanity so comfortably at a distance. Paranoid. Alienated. Possessiveness for his daughter, almost certainly of an incestuous nature. Most interesting.

'Aggressive?' said Derek furiously. 'Of course I'm aggressive! This is the one day in a fortnight when I'm allowed to spend time with my daughter, my only child, and I'm left waiting for hours in a cold park and then told she can't come because she's got to see you, a man I've never seen before in my life. Of course I'm bloody aggressive! Wouldn't you be?'

'Now why do you need me to endorse your wishes? What possible difference does it make to you how I feel about it?' Zak purred, his eyes gathering up the scientific information. There was material for an interesting paper here. He'd never done a paper on incest. Perhaps his treatment of Virginia could be combined with that of her father, and then the whole truth about the incestuous nature of paternal love could be studied and analysed and eventually published for the benefit of his professional peers.

'It makes fuck all difference to me,' said Derek, goaded beyond endurance.

Virginia looked startled as her father used a word which, for some reason, she had never realised he knew. That word belonged to Wayne, at his most offensive and most exciting.

'Listen, you,' said Derek, leaning forward and stabbing his finger at Zak in accusation, 'I don't give a damn about you or your patronising questions. All I care about is getting my rights, my right to see Virginia every Sunday fortnight without fail. For just one bloody afternoon every fourteen days, the law and my poisonous ex-wife allow me to have my own child to myself, with nobody else around, and no-one, *no-one* is going to take that away from me. They can take everything else, everything I've earned and owned and stupidly thought belonged to me, but that I will not give up, so take your smooth, fat-cat face out of here and leave Virginia and me alone.'

Virginia, frightened, was also impressed. Oh, Daddy, how wonderful you are. Oh, I was right to love you so much. Why on earth didn't you talk to Sandy like that, when he first started to steal Mummy away from you? Why did you have to leave it so long?

Zak accepted the angry glare of the man before him without flinching. He had faced belligerent patients many times and held his ground. He met Derek's gaze steadily, waiting for his opponent's eyes to drop. They always did, eventually. It was not just that he was the better, stronger, more adjusted man; it was that ingrained respect for authority from which his patients suffered, the crippling conditioning with which they all limped through life, the weakness which he sought compassionately to heal, and yet which he also employed to implant his own code of values in place of that of their sadly mistaken parents. He was a doctor, a therapist, a much read and much respected man whom they were employing at much, much expense. Stand up to him? Defy him? Hold his gaze? How could they, without losing the chance of healing which he could give them?

In the present case, however, he had made an error of judgement. Derek hadn't paid him anything, nor was he going to. Derek hadn't brought his troubles to him; Zak Ziegler wasn't going to pay off his debts or wipe out his bankruptcy or set his business once more on a viable footing. Derek didn't give a damn about Zak. Derek had nothing to lose at all.

Zak held his calm, balanced, carefully non-reproving gaze for a few seconds longer, then, as the expected signs of shiftiness and retreat didn't appear, changed tactics. He sat back and laughed disarmingly, a charming man of the world, a man just like Derek, a chum not an enemy.

'Mr. Blackie,' he said, with a delightful chuckle, 'we do seem to have got off to the most unfortunate start. In fact, I've been so neglectful of the decencies of social behaviour that I haven't even introduced myself. My name is Zak, Zak Ziegler. As you will have gathered, your wife – your ex-wife – called me in to help Virginia. I've been away on holiday, but when I found her urgent message awaiting me on my return, I came straight here to see what I could do. I had no idea that you were concerned in the case, too, and I must apologise again for my discourtesy.'

He held out his hand.

Derek nearly fell for it. Respect for the professions had been stamped into him as indelibly as if done with a branding iron. Nobody in his respectable, small-town family would have dreamed of being rude or even contradictory to a doctor, a lawyer, a schoolmaster or a bank manager. His hand rose tentatively towards Zak's brown, slim fingers, ready to accept him at his own estimation and shake hands upon it.

Then Zak boobed. It would not have been a boob among the class of patient he usually dealt with. It would even have been the clincher, which was why he used it. But in dealing with an ex-secondary modern boy who had clawed himself up by his bootstraps, achieved success then begun to slip back into the struggling penury into which he had been born, in trying to speak to a smarting loser on equal terms, he boobed very badly indeed. He caught Derek's hesitating hand before it could escape.

'I've heard so much about you from Petra, Mr. Blackie. I gather you're in the home improvement business? You're obviously a shrewd man, putting your money into that sort of enterprise.'

It was four enterprises ago that Derek had been in home improvement. The divorce had stripped him of that. With the vestiges of his organisation he had become an agent for stone-cladding. When that firm went into liquidation he became an agent for permanent rough-cast paint. When that failed he tried being an agent for double glazing. Then finally, in extreme desperation, he floated an extremely dodgy piece of whizz-kiddery financed by an extremely dodgy loan-shark, charging exorbitant interest.

Derek rose to his feet.

'Ginnie, do you want to talk to this man?'

'No, Daddy.' She was staring at him as if hypnotised.

'Right. Come on, then.'

She obeyed, scuttling for the door with a nervous but triumphant glance at Zak. Derek sent him a Parthian dart.

'You sarcastic shit,' he said.

Chapter 17

They walked quickly away from the flat, Derek bobbing like a speedboat fuelled by rage. Virginia walked and ran, trying to keep up with his angry steps as they approached the dangerous convergence of roads by Archway Tube Station. Almost without conscious thought, they plunged into the subway and emerged again, turning uphill past Whittington's stone cat. The slope gradually steepened and they slowed until they were plodding along side by side, silently making for their own special place. The rain had stopped and the sun had come out; had it not been for the wind, it might even have been warm.

By the time they reached Lauderdale House they were panting. They entered the park gates and started the grateful relief of the downward slope. Behind them the roaring traffic of Highgate Hill began to recede.

They sat on the long, serpentine row of benches halfway down and looked across London, from higher up than usual so that the shift in perspective seemed to afford them a new, clearer vision. The park was bright with daffodils, the sun shone on the wet, spangled grass. Far away among the jumbled buildings, the Telecom tower appeared to be growing out of a tower block.

They turned and looked at each other, then burst out laughing.

'Oh, Daddy, thank you!'

'That told him, didn't it?'

'Oh yes, you were terrific! Wasn't he horrible?'

'Horrible will do as a description. All right, Ginnie, what's it all about? What have you been up to?'

Her face tensed at once and she turned away from him, looking downwards, looking for peace. He prompted her.

'It's your – your – you know, isn't it? That's what Sandy said.'

She smiled awkwardly, then nodded. 'I expect so.'

'Haven't they told you? Your mother took you to the doctor, I hear. What did he say to make her call in that shrink? Seems a pretty stupid way of handling that sort of problem. What's he supposed to do, hypnotise them into coming on?'

She struggled with the problem of putting the unbelievable into believable words, then gave up and made a quick mental dash for neutral ground.

'Oh, look, Daddy, there's the mad woman! I hope she's not going to come up here. It's awful when she stops and shouts at you, really embarrassing and a bit scary; you feel she might do anything. Oh, gosh, she's got her soldier's hat on, that's always a bad sign. She starts going on about Hitler and licking Jerry and all that. She's coming this way! Let's move, Daddy, quick.'

She stood up and pulled him to the right, where the path slithered away into the bushes. Derek saw the raging, bundled-up figure climbing towards them, hurling fistfuls of bread at the flock of birds which followed her as if she were a cross-channel ferry. An unbuttoned forage cap was pulled down hard on to her head, its flaps dangling around her shouting mouth. As he hesitated, she saw him and shook her fist.

He obeyed Virginia's pulling hand and beat a retreat, wondering what Zak Ziegler could have done for a real nutcase like that. Not a lot, he suspected.

In the green privacy of the path he tried again, drawing her against his shoulder and urging her to confide in him.

'Come on, Ginnie, there are no secrets between us. Have you really been behaving like Sandy said? I'll believe you rather than him. If he told me lunch was ready I wouldn't believe it until I heard the gong. You haven't really been smashing things up, have you?'

'No.'

'I knew you couldn't have. Why did he say you did?'

'Because he won't believe it wasn't me. He's so stupid I could kick him,' she said violently.

'So who was it, then?'

'I don't know,' she said, tears coming to her eyes.

He stopped and pulled her to another seat, settling her safely against his shoulder. 'Is someone trying to get you into trouble? Doing damage and then putting the blame onto you?'

'Yes,' she said. 'Yes, I think that's exactly what's happening.'

'Any idea who? One of your schoolfriends?'

'No.'

'So who?'

'I don't know. I thought at first – '

She stopped struggling and blurted out, 'Rod says it's a poltergeist.' Immediately the word was out she glanced around in terror, looking for signs of retribution. But had there been any, the turbulence of the wind would have concealed them. And anyway, could it do anything out in the open? Didn't it need the confinement of walls, with a build-up of human energy within to provide the raw material for its party tricks?

'What?' exclaimed Derek, not quite sure he had heard right. 'Did you say – now come on, Ginnie, you're sending me up, aren't you?'

'No.'

He floundered. 'You mean things flying around the room on their own? Seriously, Ginnie, tell me the truth.'

She nodded, crying, her eyes fixed ahead down the path. Her body leaned as if the slope was propelling her towards the place which had given her so many hours of solitary peace and comfort.

'Does this Rod know what he's talking about?'

'Oh, yes. He's explained all about it.'

'How does he know?'

She shrugged.

Derek's knowledge of such things was minimal, rooted in the same cinematic fantasies which had instructed Petra.

'Well, all right, what happened then? Did you call it up? Have you and your friends been messing about with black magic or Ouija boards or something crazy like that? Or – oh no, Ginnie, you're not on drugs, are you?'

He seized her by the shoulders and turned her round, searching her eyes for the tell-tale pinprick pupils. They *were* contracted, surely. What was she on? Pot? Coke? Heroin?

Virginia, blinking in the bright sunlight which was affecting her eyes and trying to turn her head away from it, shook her head earnestly.

'No, no, I'm not,' she insisted through her tears. 'I'm not that stupid, Daddy. And I hadn't done anything else, either, except – imagine.'

'What did you imagine?'

'A man. Someone who'd love me. But he was a *good* man, Daddy. He was ever so brave and heroic, and he loved me terribly and we were going to be married. That's not wicked, is it, Daddy? It's not wicked to want someone to love you and think you're beautiful? I know I'm not, really, I'm plain and skinny and I've got no figure at all and awful, thin hair, but I can't help that, can I? It's not my fault.'

'No, you look like me, Ginnie. If anything, that's my fault.'

'Oh no, Daddy, you're much better looking than me. Oh, Daddy, I do so want to be loved.'

'Everyone wants to be loved.'

'So it's not wicked?'

'No, it's not wicked.'

'So why does *it* say it is?' begged Virginia. 'Why does it sneer at me and tell me I'm a – I'm wicked because I imagine what it's like to have a lover? Why does it call me filthy names and make horrible dirty remarks about my body and things which no-one knows about except me? Why does it spy on me and then tell my most deathly secrets out loud, so that I feel I'm never alone and private, not even in the bath or the lavatory? Oh, Daddy, can you imagine how dreadful that is? Can you imagine how embarrassing? Can you think of anything more dreadful than knowing that when you're with other people a voice might suddenly tell them everything you do when you're on your own?'

'Is that what happened?' asked Derek, going white. When she started her outburst he had thought he was at last seeing the mental illness which had brought Zak to her aid, but now, with the revelation that others had heard Virginia's tormenting voice too, he felt so frightened that he could have been physically sick.

My God, who could face such a prospect with equanimity?

What human being was so pure in mind, body and spirit that he would not fear such disclosures? How many monks in their private cells never allowed themselves the pathetic luxury of a solitary grope?

'Has Petra heard it?'

'Yes, in my room. We were packing and it went on telling her all about what I'd been doing, and I've never felt so bitterly ashamed in my life — I felt as dirty as it said I was, as if I'd never be able to face anyone ever again.'

Derek struggled with prurience, in pity for her pain, but lost. 'What was it you'd been doing?'

'It wasn't wicked!' she cried pitifully. 'You just said it wasn't. And I wanted to look nice, so that if he did come he would love me — '

'You mean the voice?'

'No, no, no! The man I imagined. I thought it was him at first, you see. I thought he must really exist somewhere and our longings had reached out to each other and that he'd come for me — '

'How could he come for you if you'd just imagined him? I don't understand, darling, you're getting me all mixed up.'

' — and it went on saying filthy things all the time we were getting ready to leave. Petra was scared to death, I could see she was. Her hands were shaking like anything and then he started calling her names, too, and she just picked up the suitcases and rushed out of the house and we went round to Angela's, but he was there, too, and Angela heard him, and then we went to Marjorie's and he shut me up in the window seat while I was asleep so that I thought I was in a coffin. Oh, Daddy, can you imagine waking up and thinking you've been shut in a coffin?

'And then after that we couldn't find anywhere to go and I kept hearing him whispering very quietly in my ear so that I was ready to scream, and at last we went and found Rod down at the cemetery, and as soon as we got inside the gates it stopped. Oh, Daddy, it was such a relief! It just stopped, like a radio being switched off, and didn't start again until we got back to Rod's flat.'

'What happened then?' asked Derek, sitting with his hands over his face, shaking with the effort not to faint.

'It started smashing everything up. Poor Rod and Dino — all their beautiful ornaments. And the awful things it said about them, you wouldn't believe it, Daddy.'

'Oh yes, I think I would,' said Derek dully. 'What did it say to Sandy?'

'I don't think it said anything to him, but it burnt up his stereo.'

'And what did he do?'

'He wouldn't take any notice.'

'How the hell did he manage that?' asked Derek vehemently.

'Sandy doesn't notice anything he doesn't want to. Everything has to go his way, and if it isn't going his way it just doesn't exist.'

Derek pressed his hands together. The trembling jerked them up and down. His knuckles turned white with his efforts to keep them still.

'Poor Ginnie,' he said, his tight throat distorting his voice into an unrecognisable quaver. 'What's going to happen to you? Maybe I should have left you with Zak after all. He might have been able to do something, who knows?'

'I couldn't have stayed alone with him,' she said, shuddering. 'I hated the feel of him. It was as if there was a cold fog coming off him. He really is wicked, I'm sure. I wonder why the voice didn't say something about him? He must have lots of the most terrible secrets, you've only got to look at his eyes.'

Why indeed? thought Derek. He knew exactly what Virginia meant — his hostility to Zak hadn't just been jealousy, he had felt repelled by the man's personality. There was a lack of humanity about him, a heartlessness. In erasing the weaknesses of his own character, he had somehow thrown out the human baby with the dirty bath water and become a cold, emotionless automaton. That could explain the voice's lack of interest in him. Where was the fun in exposing the shameful secrets of one who didn't believe they were shameful at all? No shame, no power. No shock, no pleasure. No striving towards virtue, no feeling of failure to be aroused because the striving was unsuccessful.

'So who is going to help you?' asked Derek.

The hopelessness of the question seemed to him irrefutable. Virginia was a lost soul, in the hands of a lost, malicious spirit. Virginia was as good or as bad as dead.

'Rod is,' she said. 'I'm going to stay with him.'

'Only until you move.'

'I'm not going.'

'I'm afraid you haven't any choice, darling. Like you said, everything in the world is expected to go Sandy's way. If he wants you to go, then you'll have to. Unless – unless you came to me after all. I've got time to look after you properly, now. I'll get another job soon, I expect, but until then there's no reason why we shouldn't be happy spending time together.' His face lightened. 'Yes, that's a great idea. What do you think, Ginnie? You've always wanted that, haven't you, to live with me?' A purpose seemed to come back into his life, drawing him up from the bottom of the pond and bursting him through onto the sunlit surface, back into the real world.

She looked at him with sorrowful pity.

'Oh no, Daddy, I'm afraid not, not now. You see, it might come again. I don't think it would have done once, because I'd have been happy with you, but now it's all different. I love Rod, you see.'

'*Love* him? But you can't, Ginnie, you can't love a – someone like that.'

'But I'm sixteen, now. It's all right, I know he won't marry me for a long time, not until I grow up and become beautiful, but I don't mind, just as long as I can be with him.'

'He's not going to want you if your voice is going to smash up his flat!'

'But I don't think it will any more. I've been thinking very hard about that all day. It came because I was so unhappy, Rod explained that and how important it was to stay calm and happy and loving, so that the voice couldn't get in, but I didn't believe him. Then, suddenly, when he said he loved me, I realised he was just like the man I'd been imagining, all good and kind and gentle. So I thought, why shouldn't I try loving him? And today I started seeing if I could and at once it stopped, just like that.'

'I don't believe this,' Derek groaned. 'You mean Rod really said that he loved you?'

'Yes, he said that he cared about me and loved me, but not to expect too much from him because he was human and weak. I thought that was beautiful, so modest.'

'Virginia!' Derek shouted. 'You are talking the most appalling rubbish I've ever heard in my life! Come down to earth! I get the impression that you're floating away from me on a huge sea of self-delusion and disappearing over the horizon. One minute you're telling me that you've been having an experience so frightening that it could send anyone sane round the bend, let alone you – '

'Daddy!'

' – and the next you're pushing the whole thing on one side and saying that it doesn't matter at all because a man about ten years older than you, who happens to have been rather kind because of that appalling experience, is the answer to all your problems, that you're going to live with him and eventually marry him. Can't you see that your thinking is completely irrational, and that you're just being a silly, love-sick little girl?'

'You hate me, too,' said Virginia, shocked. 'You despise me. You think no-one could possible love me. You don't care a bit about me being happy, you just want me now because you've got nothing else left. A last resort, that's all I am, isn't it? And because you're too late and I've fallen in love with Rod, you're jealous and want to break it up. You'd rather I wasn't happy at all if I wasn't happy with you.'

'But you *can't* be happy with Rod! Honestly, Ginnie, I'm not telling lies about that. If falling in love with him has made you happy, even so happy that it got rid of that awful thing which has been tormenting you, then I'm glad, I'm glad and deeply grateful. But darling, there's no future for you with him, you must realise that. I mean, like you're always saying, you're not a child. You're not the ignorant innocent I was at your age, you know about people like him.'

'It's only because he hasn't found the right girl, yet,' she said obstinately. 'He's just lonely.'

'Oh, Virginia!' groaned Derek. 'You seem to think that romantic love and marriage is the universal panacea.'

'I'm sure it is,' said Virginia earnestly. 'It's just that it's so difficult to find.'

'You can say that again! Look at your mother and me. Look at her and Sandy. And look at their friends. How many of them do you know who are still on their first marriage, or even happy in their second or third or fourth?'

'It won't be like that for me, I know I can make Rod happy. I've always known deep inside that if I once found love I'd never be unhappy again. I need to love the way I need to breathe. I've got a talent for it, I can feel it.'

Derek tried one last desperate appeal.

'I know. In a way that's what I've been saying, darling. We love each other, don't we? If we were together we could be happy.'

She kissed him.

'I've told you, Daddy, it wouldn't work now. Everything's different. But you must come and see us, Rod won't mind. He's so kind, and he'd want you to be happy, too.'

He walked home. It was two miles, but if he had had the car he would still have needed physical activity to relieve the turmoil in his mind.

He had so often regarded her blind adoration as more of a pain than a pleasure, feeling burdened by its intensity, pushing it to one side so he could get on with his life. He had found her irritating, embarrassing, troublesome, but always he was looking forward to a future, more manageable Virginia, a pleasure to come, seeing the relationship as something which was going to turn out all right eventually. Even in his moments of real exasperation at her demands, he had never wanted to get rid of her altogether. It wasn't her he was rejecting, only the trouble that went with her. And the only reason he had rejected that was because the ability to deal with it had been taken out of his hands. He'd never expected that the final maturing of Virginia into a person whose company he could enjoy would coincide with the bestowing of her now-desirable love on another.

It had all happened so quickly; he had had no warning at all. Most fathers were allowed to see that step coming and let go gradually, and also to let go from a position of strength. Even when their daughter first fell in love with some remarkably unattractive youth, the father-daughter love was not destroyed. There was room for the two sorts of love because they *were* two different sorts.

But Virginia didn't seem to know that; she regarded all love as one and indivisible. All emotional eggs were put into one basket.

That full basket had been given to him in the past; not just given, but thrust upon him. Here you are, Daddy, take it all, the full burden of my life and my needs and my love. It's all for you and you must give everything to me. When she found love she expected everything from it, from him, from an imaginary lover, from the first young man who showed her any affection at all. Immediately the basket had been snatched back from Derek's hand and delivered into Rod's and there it sat, in hands which, Derek was sure, were so unwilling to receive the gift and carry the burden that they would sooner or later let it fall and smash her whole life.

He climbed up into his flat, looked at the mess, thought of Virginia playing house and bringing homeliness to it with her eager affection. He thought of the bright comfort of Rod's flat and Virginia's happy little figure settled into his chair. He thought of the utter emptiness of his own life.

Virginia pressed the bell. The thundering sound of feet on the stairs culminated in the throwing open of the dirty green door.

'Virginia!' Rod exclaimed. 'Thank goodness! Zak said your father had taken you away by force, but we thought that was probably a bit of an exaggeration. Are you all right?'

'Yes,' she said, smiling up at him. 'Daddy and I just needed to have a talk and straighten things out. Poor Daddy, he's so unhappy now. We'll have to see what we can do for him, won't we? Perhaps we could invite him round for a meal. You wouldn't mind, would you?'

'No,' said Rod, taken aback, 'but you won't be here much longer, will you? Sandy says you're moving on Tuesday.'

'But I'm not going. You told him that it wasn't good for me to live in a house I'm afraid of, it might bring it back.' For a second her smile faded, then she remembered the need to keep up her defences and it returned, the bright, blank, childlike beam of a new convert to a religion with all the answers. 'As long as I'm with you, it can't come again, can it, Rod?'

'Can't it?' he said. 'What happened last night, then?'

'I was unhappy then, now I'm not. Like you said, if I'm happy I'm safe. Oh, Rod, I'm so grateful to you! You're so good and kind and wise. I never, ever thought I'd be so lucky as to find someone like you, not in my wildest dreams. You'll look after me, won't you? I won't be a nuisance. I'll help around the flat and do everything you tell me.'

'But – '

'And I'll always love you, Rod, always.'

'Virginia!'

'Always!' she promised, her eyes shining.

And she stretched up on her toes, put her arms about his neck and kissed him.

He wanted to die.

Chapter 18

'Petra! Petra! Look!'

Virginia's cry woke her with a start. She shot up into a sitting position, pulled the covers up to her chin and looked wildly round the room.

'What? Where? What's it doing this time?'

She waited with dread for the objects to start moving, for the wardrobe door to slam, for the bedclothes to drag back, for the voice to start.

'Has it spoken?' she whispered. 'What did it say?'

'No. Look!'

Virginia sat laughing on her side of the bed, the sheet turned back. Petra looked.

'Oh, Mummy, isn't it wonderful? I'm grown-up! I'm grown-up at last!'

Ten minutes later, Petra finished seeing to Virginia and pulled on her dressing gown. She went down to the bathroom and washed, then examined her puffy morning face in the mirror. She did that every day and it never looked very encouraging. She had finished up Rod and Dino's vodka by five yesterday, and then got another bottle from a pub as soon as it opened. It was on the bedside table, much diminished.

Zak had taken her out to dinner and she had been very late home. Remembering, she smiled, then studied her face with more urgency, noticing the open pores. A face-pack and astringent pads on her eyes, that was what she needed. It was no wonder she was looking so haggard with what she'd gone through these last few days. Thank goodness Virginia had started at last – didn't that stop poltergeists? She tried to remember everything Rod had said on their first evening at the flat.

She heard his bedroom door open and went out into the corridor. 'Rod, can I have a word?' She whispered in case Dino was still asleep. He seldom got home from the restaurant until well after twelve and usually slept in.

'Yes, sure, Petra, come into the lounge.' He followed her down to the front of the flat, catching the smell of her body as they went. His mother had smelt like that when she got out of bed — sour and musky. It hadn't bothered him when he was small, but when adolescence brought knowledge he had started to shy away from her in déshabillé. It was the association with his father — the smell of married intimacy. But his mother had never smelt of stale drink and stale smoke.

Petra sat down on the settee and relaxed in her undress, quite unaware that he might find it repulsive — no other man ever had. He moved away from her.

'Rod, love, Virginia's started. You know, it's happened at last. That's good news, isn't it?'

He felt the blush flood up over him, right from his heart to the crown of his head. He was burning, burning, a mass of intolerable embarrassment. He turned and looked out of the window.

'Oh,' he said.

'It'll be all right now, won't it? Didn't you say that periods stop poltergeists?' she asked anxiously. Her eyes looked restlessly round the room, then she reached across to the coffee table and retrieved her cigarettes. She lit up and lay back with her eyes closed. 'Oh God, that's better. How you can exist without fags amazes me, Rod.'

You slut, he thought, you awful, smelly slut.

The intolerant bigotry of the thought horrified him. He'd never reacted to another woman like that, not even the far more depraved specimens which he had occasionally encountered through the Samaritans. He was appalled at himself. But then, they hadn't been undressed, straight out of bed, profaning his home with their animal femininity.

And Virginia . . . he hadn't realised. Of course, now he came to think about it, it all added up. She was so thin, childish and immature, but at her age she should have already started to menstruate.

'Well, yes,' he said, 'I suppose it might.'

He hoped so. If Virginia was physically mature he didn't want her here, not with the unbearable responsibility for her happiness she had laid upon his shoulders. He hadn't told Petra, or Dino, or anyone about that – he supposed he should have done, but he couldn't betray her trust so cravenly. It would be damnable, in every sense of the word.

He had broken trust once. Frank had begged him not to tell, but his own fear had made him. The result had been cataclysmic. He mustn't make the same mistake again.

'I told Zak all about it last night. He's a wonderful listener, you know. Not like Sandy. He never hears a bloody word you say to him unless it's Yes, Sandy. Of course, Sandy. Oh, Sandy, aren't you bloody marvellous? May I kiss your – '

'You going to leave him?' asked Rod.

'No, I don't think so. At least, not yet. I reckon I can put up with him a bit longer. I've got to, haven't I, for Virginia's sake. She needs a home. Security, that's what she needs, isn't it, Rod? A safe, secure home with no money problems; you see, I did listen to you. You thought I didn't understand, I could see you did, but I'm not half as selfish as you think I am. After all, it's not the first time I've sacrificed myself for her. I needn't have married Derek, my mother didn't want me to at all. I could have got rid of her, it would have been easy, but I didn't. I got married and I had her and I slaved for ten years trying to make a go of things. It wasn't my fault it all went wrong – Derek was such a useless wimp.

'When Sandy came along I could see that I had no choice but to give Virginia a secure background at last. That's why I did it, Rod, really. I could see she'd never have that with Derek and me rowing all the time. Kids know when things are wrong between their parents, and it's bad for them. If there are bad vibes, they pick them up. You may not understand that, Rod, I mean I expect you had a good, solid family background, didn't you? I know you go and visit your parents sometimes, and they must have been married for about thirty years. And you're so calm and well-adjusted; I don't think I've ever heard you complain about anything. It must be wonderful to be like that, but you know, it can blind you to the problems of other people, the ones who haven't been so lucky.'

Rod was picking at the fern on the windowsill, gazing out across the crowded, noisy street, watching the depressed, accepting queue at the bus stop, counting the number of pinnacles on that church, looking at anything except her. What could you say to someone like that? What intercommunication could there be with someone who believed that present happiness meant there had never been unhappiness, that those who didn't talk about their troubles hadn't got any? The only things she was capable of grasping were those which concerned her, and even there there was no insight — just convenient manipulation and re-arrangement of the facts.

'You're going to take her home, then?' he said.

'Well, what do you think? Is she settled down enough? Tell me, Rod, you seem to know how she feels.'

'Nobody knows how Virginia feels except Virginia,' he said with irritation. 'What's the use of asking me? I haven't got the programme to hack into her private thoughts. Why not do something really innovative and actually ask Virginia what she thinks, how she feels, where she wants to go, what she wants to do?'

'Well, hell, there's no need to bite my head off!' said Petra indignantly. 'Anyone would think I wasn't trying. You tell me what's best for her and I'll do it.'

'Ask her!' Rod nearly shouted, turning round from the window with a frayed lump of fern still gripped in his fingers. 'She's not a — a plant like this, just needing to be plonked down in the sun and rain to flourish. Virginia's a person, not a vegetable. Try treating her like one.'

'Hello.'

Virginia stood at the door of the room, wearing a bright, expectant smile, her eyes fixed on Rod. 'Good morning, Rod, did you sleep well? I did. Nothing bad happened at all. I told you it would be all right now. It's all over.'

She moved lightly across the damaged carpet, walking as if she wasn't touching the ground at all. She was wearing a soft blue dress, high-heeled pink shoes, gold necklaces, gold earrings. Her sparse hair had been brushed up into a tuft on the crown of her head and held with a pink plastic clip. Her face was made up. She glowed with pride, aware of the pink and white underwear beneath her dress and the new maturity beneath her underwear.

She came on towards him, the magnet offering itself to the silver churn.

He flinched as she kissed him good morning.

'Virginia,' he said with panic, 'Petra and I were just talking about you. I'm so pleased you're feeling happy, that's wonderful. You must hold on to that happiness and never let it go again.' She nodded excitedly and he went on in haste, 'What I mean is this — you must make your own happiness. You mustn't always be looking for it outside, as if it's something you can only have if it's given you by somebody else. The secret of being happy isn't getting what you think you want, it's liking and enjoying what you've got, what you are. The only person who can really make you happy is you. Do you understand?'

'No,' she said, the smile slipping.

'Well, thank you,' retorted Petra. 'Praise the Lord!'

Rod felt himself grow hot again. What a load of pie-in-the-sky crap. It had felt like the truth when he was saying it, but now he saw its facile absurdity. It hadn't been like that for him, so why should it be for Virginia?

'Anyway,' he hurried on, 'what I — what Petra and I want to ask you is this. What do you want to do now?' Oh no, not that question! 'I mean about going home — just until the move — or — or after that — or — ' he made a despairing gesture. 'Look, forget the stupid questions. You talk, we'll listen. Just tell us quite honestly how you feel about everything.'

'The world, the universe!' Petra declaimed dramatically. 'And if the answer's as simple as forty-two, we'll be bloody relieved.'

It wasn't, of course. It was more like sixteen million, four thousand, six hundred and eighty to the power of eight, over forty-eight thousand, seven hundred and nine, divided by x, multiplied by y, and take away the number you first thought of. Squared. And with knobs on, preferably gold-plated.

They sat there, Petra growing ever more incredulous, Rod more wretched and humiliated, until Virginia's joyous, enthusiastic outburst came to an end.

'Jesus!' said Petra. 'Jesus wept! You want to marry *him*?'

And then the phone rang, bringing to a sudden end Virginia's attempt to let the adult world know what she thought, how she felt, what she really wanted.

'Petra? Are you coming home to do the clearing out?'
'Well, yes, all right. I suppose it is safe now, is it?'
'Of course it is,' said Sandy impatiently. 'Everything's been quiet as the grave since you and Virginia left – which doesn't surprise me in the least. Pity she had to go and smash up Marjorie's tasteful decor. She's brought the estimate for the damage round already, complete with dark warnings that it probably isn't the full sum. Reminded me of Mr. Hargreaves.'
'There's Rod's flat, too, Sandy. You'll pay for that as well, won't you?' pleaded Petra.
'I'll see,' said Sandy coolly. 'How's superbrat now? Did Zak do any good with her?'
'She wouldn't talk to him,' said Petra in a low voice, watching Virginia prattling away to Rod on the settee. She was stroking his hand.
'Wouldn't talk to him? Oh, that's just great, isn't it! I suppose we still have to pay his fee?'
'I don't know,' said Petra, 'perhaps not.'
'Doesn't sound much like Zak if we don't,' said Sandy.
'No.' She could hardly tell him the reason for her doubts.
'Right, well get round here as soon as possible. It's not packing or anything, the movers will do that, but you must sort out the cupboards and drawers and sling out the rubbish.'
'Yes, all right, Sandy.'
'Oh, and I thought we'd have a few friends round tonight – farewell party, you know. I've pushed the furniture back into some sort of order. Ring them up. I'll see to the office invitations.'
'Heavens! You haven't given me much time! How many will it be?'
'Oh, say twenty, maybe more if they bring friends.'
'What are they going to eat?' wailed Petra. 'Oh, I know, there are things in the freezer. If I get them out now they should be defrosted by tonight.'
'Ah!' said Sandy. 'Afraid we've got a bit of a problem, there, sweetie. On Friday morning I found it had been switched off. It was still pretty frozen but I thought perhaps it might be

dangerous to switch it on again. Don't want food poisoning. That was right, wasn't it?'

'Yes, Sandy,' said Petra with gritted teeth, 'you are always bloody well right. Mind you, seeing that it was packed solid, it could have lasted for yet another day without coming to any harm, but let's not quarrel about that. It will at least save us the trouble of carting the lot down to Maiden's End. And what's a few hundred pounds worth of food, with the amount we're spending at the moment?'

Sandy guffawed, not quite sure if she was being sarcastic or not.

'I've ordered the drink. Should be round about eleven o'clock. Well, I must get off now. I left the washing up as you were coming home. And I cancelled the electrician. It seemed more sensible to get things mended once we were in the new house. Be home at seven. The others will be arriving about eight. See you, sweetie. Oh – '

'Yes?'

'I suppose Virginia couldn't stay round at Rod's, could she? Just in case she plays up again?'

'But what about them?' Petra muttered into the receiver. 'We can't not invite them after what's happened.'

'Oh, yes. All right, then. Just keep her in order.'

'I think Rod will be able to do that. I'll have a word with him.'

'Dear Rod. Good as nannies, some of them, aren't they?'

'Virginia,' said Petra as she slammed down the phone, 'you're coming round to the house with me – Sandy's having a party tonight and I'm going to need all the help I can get.'

Virginia twisted her necklace nervously.

'Oh. But supposing . . . ?'

'I thought you said everything was going to be all right?' Petra challenged her accusingly.

'Yes, but – ' Her face lightened. 'Can Rod come? I don't mind coming if he's there, too.'

'I'm sure Rod's got lots of important things to do today, haven't you, Rod?'

'Well, yes, actually.' Like signing on, for one.

'Can't I come with you while you do them?'

'No, you can't, I'm afraid.'

'Will you leave the phone number where you're going?'

'I won't be near a phone,' he said, groaning under the unbearable weight of her devotion. 'I'll be here, there and everywhere.'

'Oh. But you'll come to the party tonight, won't you? Promise me you'll come. And early. It'll probably be all right if I know you're going to turn up at a certain time, and then I can keep happy and safe by looking forward to it, but if you're late I might start worrying where you were and whether you were going to turn up at all, and then it might be able to get in again – '

He stared at her intense, almost threatening gaze, aghast at the unscrupulousness, the sheer blackmail of her love.

'You will, won't you, Rod? What time are you coming? Tell me. Just think of what might happen if you don't.'

Yes, he could see it now. This was why Virginia found it so difficult to get love. When she loved, she ate the loved one alive. She was so starved that she couldn't be satisfied by anything less than total surrender, total sacrifice. She was obsessive, greedy, seeing love as a chain and padlock to which only she must possess the key. No wonder that sick personality had become the prey of an evil spiritual force; it was ready-made for invasion.

Now, although it had ceased its physical use of her neurotic power, it seemed probable that it was still in control. She was, after all, using it as an ally to gain what she wanted. If you don't love me and give yourself to me totally, I'll call it back to take revenge on you. That was what she was telling him.

'I'll be there at eight,' he said.

'No, earlier,' she insisted. 'Come at seven.'

'I can't get there by seven.'

'Seven thirty, then. Promise me you'll be there at seven thirty or . . . ' Her voice was rising.

There it was, just starting, the swing of the lampshade.

'Yes,' he said quickly.

Rod and Dino turned out of Highgate High Street just before seven twenty-five. The restaurant was closed on Mondays. Dino was quiet, his round face pale and tense. He had had a long talk with his priest yesterday, and it had not been particularly comforting. Poltergeists, it seemed, could not be successfully exorcised. They were spiritually pig-ignorant, the lowest of low-grade souls. His hand was clamped into his jacket pocket, worrying away at his beads.

They slowed as they reached the gate and studied the valuable house with the 'Sold' board in the garden. Up in the front bedroom, an eager face looked out and a hand waved. Rod groaned.

'She is waiting for us,' said Dino.

'Yes.'

'How much did Sandy get for the house?'

'God knows. Too much, if I know Sandy.'

'He is a good businessman. Everything goes good for him.'

'He flourishes like the green bay tree,' said Rod.

'That one doesn't,' said Dino as they reached the brown, brittle corpse on the step.

Virginia tore open the door and flung her arms round Rod.

'There you are! I was starting to get jumpy but you turned up just in time! Isn't that lucky?'

'I said I'd be here,' he said. 'Everything O.K.?'

'Oh yes, lovely! I've been working ever so hard getting the party ready. I've made all the butter into little curls and arranged the biscuits in a pretty pattern, and I made Petra buy some of those funny, dead-looking sausages, because I saw one in your kitchen and knew you must like them. Come in and see how nice the table looks.' She pulled him into the living room, the astonished Dino trailing along behind them.

'Lovely,' said Rod, then as she stood waiting, her face full of expectation, realised what else she wanted him to say. 'New dress?' he asked, the words drawn out of him like a tooth.

'Yes, do you like it? Do I look nice?'

'Yes, very nice.'

'Does the colour suit me?'

'Very much.'

'It's eau-de-nil, the new colour for summer. Sam said it brought out the colour of my eyes. Do you think it does, Rod? What colour do you think my eyes are? Petra says they're grey, but I think there are green lights in them. Look at my eyes, Rod, can you see them?'

It was appalling, excruciating. She seemed to have lost all

restraint, to be throwing herself at him in a way which was going to be blindingly obvious to every person coming – friends, neighbours, people he met nearly every day.

It was going to be the most dreadful party he had ever been to in his life.

By eleven thirty, when the closing of the Flask had sent the last influx of friends round into the party, there were at least sixty people crammed into the house. They sat on chairs, tables, floors and stairs. They ate, drank and smoked in the living room, the kitchen, the hall and the garden.

Marjorie and Boris were telling a pleasurably horrified Pat Goodison about the damage to the spare room. Pete Goate, in office suit and Old Etonian tie, was being chatted up by Sam, who knew a good prospect when she saw it. Vickers was trying to convert a socialist librarian to the free market economy. Hummerstone's pin-stripes were running horizontally along the floor of the living room.

Even without music the talking and laughing would have been deafening, but Sandy had borrowed Virginia's record player, and the Beatles informed the assembled company that all they needed was love.

Petra, collapsed on to the settee against Zak's shoulder, gave a reminiscent moan.

'Oh God, this album! It brings it all back. Me and Derek and the baby in this house. I really tried, you know, Zak, I can't tell you how I tried. Just one little phrase from this record and I'm right back there, breaking my heart.'

'Strange how potent cheap music is,' said Zak.

'That's so true. You've got it exactly.'

'Not me, darling, but who's counting?'

On the stairs an actor, a soprano and a writer were talking compulsively at each other.

'Actually, I wasn't all that keen when my agent first rang me. I mean, who wants to be tied up with a soap for years? It's professional suicide to become identified with one part. But Carl said that they'd been considering Johnnie Mills, then decided that he wasn't quite right, then I believe they approached Larry, but he wasn't too well, so I thought who am I to be more proud than a couple of theatrical knights, so I said I'd give it a whirl – '

'Well, yes, that's how I felt about the Countess Ceprano, but I really think they should have given me Gilda, I mean my voice is just ready for it, even Mark said so. But you know how many dirty tricks go on behind the scenes and it went to a little nobody who hasn't been in the profession five minutes. Megan as Gilda, I ask you! She looks more like Rigoletto. All I hope is that she doesn't make a complete fool of herself. I mean, I wish the poor girl all the best, but you know how cruel the critics can be, specially the ones who didn't make it in the business themselves, and really, I ask myself, has she got the guts to take it? I mean, I've had the odd bad notice myself, who hasn't, but I'm too tough to let the bastards get me down – '

' – and not a single, sodding royalty did I see from that book, not after two years' work which ate up the advance in eighteen months. *And* they messed up sending out the review copies so that the *T.L.S.* never even got one at all – '

'Excuse me, please.'

They moved to one side as Virginia slipped coyly past them.

' – and when I tried to get a copy for Alison to take back to America they told me it was out of print! They'd remaindered the whole bloody lot without telling me!'

'Sickening, darling, you must be livid. Of course, the infuriating thing is that my voice has just reached its peak – '

' – and they'll probably sell it to Australia, like *Coronation Street*, so the money could still be trickling in for years after I've had enough and moved on – '

Virginia went into her bedroom and sat down at the dressing table, smiling at herself in the mirror as she repaired her make-up for the fourth time.

Oh, it was wonderful to be grown-up! The self-confidence, the absolute bliss of being a real person. Oh, the ecstasy of knowing that Rod was down there, ready for her to talk to, to sit with, to belong to.

She looked down over the black gulf beyond the window and mentally embraced the city beyond. It seemed full of love, romantic love. No longer did she envy those millions. Down in his flat on Holly Lodge Estate, Wayne could do anything he damned well liked to Angela and she wouldn't care. She didn't need him. She didn't need anyone but Rod. She didn't even need her imaginary lover any more. Her imaginings seemed so childish now and so pale, compared to the reality of a man she could actually touch. Oh, the joy of touching Rod, of planting shy kisses on his cheeks. He seemed shy, too, but of course she couldn't expect him to be very demonstrative yet. She was still only sixteen. But she was changing, she was becoming a woman. Soon she would become prettier and more fit for him to love.

She rose from the stool, her smile growing hard with exultant defiance.

'You can't come now,' she said out loud, 'Rod's here,' and went down to search the crowded rooms for him.

But he wasn't there. Taking advantage of her absence, he had fled to the garden, behind the lilac tree which leaned across the railings into the park, as if it, too, was trying to escape from the bright lights and the noise and the shrieking people. He must go soon, he really must. He couldn't stand any more.

As people drank, their tongues had become more free, their jokes more direct and painful. They weren't being deliberately unkind, but tact had gradually disappeared and an affectionate mocking taken its place. After all, there was no denying that it was funny. That strange, painted little girl hanging on to the arm of a man whom everyone knew was gay, and behaving as if he were her own special property. The remarks to Dino had been hurtful, too, once again not intentionally; but after a certain stage at a party few people can resist making what appears to be a witty remark in order to add to the hilarity, and 'You'd better watch the missus, Dino', produced enough laughter to satisfy any would-be wit.

The iron table and chairs were occupied by a crowd of eccentrically dressed creatives from Matheson Hummerstone Vickers Goate, sharing a joint. Their conversation floated across to Rod in half-heard bursts.

'Anyone seen this place of Sandy's? Is it as fabulous as he says?'

'Must be, he's pouring enough money into it. I suppose once he's got it straight there'll be another party down there.'

'Buntingford's a bloody long way to go for a free drink.'

He could climb over that railing, it wouldn't be too difficult.

'Patty went to see Trevor yesterday. She says he looks terrible.'

'Poor sod. I really ought to go, but I'm not sure I could face it. Who else has been?'

'Zelda and Griff. And Sarah went and took him some flowers from Sandy.'

'Hasn't he been in person?'

'No.'

'That's pretty naff. After all the work Trev's put in for him.'

He'd come back of course. No-one would miss him for ten minutes. Just a bit of peace and quiet.

'Well, I don't think Sandy regards him as the flavour of the month, these days.'

'But Trev's the best bloody artist in the business. He won Sandy an award with that campaign he designed for Hamilton's.'

'He could also have won him something else.'

The voice was full of the smug importance of someone with a good story to tell.

Rod put his foot on to the concrete wall below the railings and drew himself up.

'Rod! Rod! Are you out there? Oh, hello, has anyone seen Rod Singleton?'

'No, love, sorry.'

He climbed over the railings and jumped down into the shrubs. The voices began to fade; he was no longer listening.

'What do you mean?'

'Well, you know, the Plague. Big A.'

'Sandy! You must be joking!'

'Not the usual image of the Hungarian Humper, is it? But I tell you this, darlings, and don't breathe a word to a soul — '

'Of course not!'

' — you remember the office Christmas thrash? Well, about two in the morning I staggered out to the Gents' for a leak. Then I was sitting down in one of the bogs to pull myself together and have a quiet smoke, when I heard someone come in. There was a sort of scuffling noise, and I just peeked out of the crack of the door to see whose turn it was to succumb to alcoholic poisoning, and there he was, our own beloved Sandy, kissing Trevor.'

'Jesus!'

Rod walked down past the tennis courts, brushing the

bushes as he zig-zagged from side to side of the invisible path, hearing the hubbub die away in the distance. Just ten minutes. He'd go back, then. He'd got to get away for a bit. He'd have to leave soon, anyway, he was on duty at the Samaritans at seven — the regular volunteer had succumbed to morning sickness. Just a few minutes.

Out in the street, Derek stood before the jumping joint of the house, on the outside looking in.

Chapter 19

Virginia sat at the window, staring out into the lightening street. Her hands were clasped in her lap, her shoulders were slack and rounded, her hair had escaped from the silver bow which held it and fallen around her face in stringy wisps. Her amateurish make-up had caked into the face of a little girl dressed up.

Behind her, the last few survivors of the party were scattered around the room like litter after a football match. On a chair by the drinks table, the writer sipped a moody brandy and wondered which word would best encapsulate the essence of that awful picture over the fireplace. Incompetent? Puerile? A con?

On the settee, a deeply depressed Dino was being bored to death by Pat Goodison, who was describing the entire menu of a dinner party she had given to a couple of eminent architects.

In a belligerent debating group on the floor by the french windows, the librarian, two creatives and an Irish poet from Belfast were sorting out the Labour Party.

Hummerstone was still on the floor.

In the kitchen beyond, a crowd of alternative artistic rebels were getting remarkably het-up over whether any piece of theatre assisted by the Arts Council could possibly have a claim to street credibility.

Up in Virginia's bedroom, a crowd of advertising executives laughed their heads off at a blue movie on the video. Sandy sat on the bed, grinning vacantly at the screen and mauling Sam with disinterested ferocity; Pete Goate had been rendered *hors-de-combat* by the late arrival of his wife from a visit to Mummy and Daddy in Leicestershire.

Petra and Zak hadn't been seen for some time.

The clock on the stairs struck.

'So for a savoury I fried button mushrooms very lightly in olive oil with garlic and a touch of thyme and served them piping hot with melba toast – '

Dino rose, leaving Pat in full flow, and walked across to Virginia. He put his hand on her shoulder.

'Is late. Why not go to bed? You see him tomorrow.'

Pat, disconcerted, got up with an embarrassed laugh.

'Goodness, is that the time? I must go. Goodbye, Dino. Goodbye, everyone.'

She left, practically unnoticed, to join her sleeping husband next door.

'You mean today,' said Virginia, her voice hard and flat.

'Yes, today, that's right. You go and sleep, Ginnie. He'll come and see you before you go.'

'I'm not going,' she said. 'I'm staying with you and Rod. He promised.'

'No, no, he don't promise. I think perhaps you don't understand what he say.'

'He promised! He said I mustn't go to that house because it frightens me. He said I could stay at the flat.'

'Until the move, darling. That's what he meant.'

'You're jealous!' she said suddenly, shaking off his hand and turning her spiteful face upon him. 'You love him, don't you?'

Dino grimaced, shrugged, put his hands up in a gesture of bewilderment.

'So? Do I deny it? Does Rod deny it? Everyone knows we are gay. You know. Always you know. Why you not understand, then?'

'People change,' she said. 'Some people, they're not really like that. They think they are for a bit, then they find a girl they can love and they marry. Fabian did, remember? Everyone always thought he was gay, but then he married Martha and they've got two children now. Rod will be like that. He'll get more and more fond of me, then one day he'll want to marry me and you'll have to go, Dino.'

He shook his head, full of pity. 'No,' he said, 'no, Ginnie.'

'Yes, yes, yes!' she screamed, leaping to her feet. Her hand shot out, seized a glass from the table beside her and dashed it to the floor. 'He loves *me*!' The hand grabbed another glass and it flew across the room to burst beside Hummerstone's unconscious head. 'He's gone off because he couldn't bear to tell you, because he's too kind to hurt your feelings!' Her foot kicked out and hammered repeatedly at the record player, jolting Richard Clayderman into a startled screech. 'He's mine! He's going to marry me! I want him and I'm going to get what I want! I've been waiting years and years for what I want and nobody's going to stop me getting it!'

She screamed and screamed, her hands seizing everything within reach and hurling it about the room. Dino bolted for the safety of the door. The group by the french windows ducked their heads in alarm, especially the Belfast poet, and up in Virginia's bedroom, Sandy dropped Sam on the bed and lurched to his feet.

By the time he got downstairs it had arrived, sweeping into the atmosphere of hate and frustration around Virginia and gathering the power into itself. A ghastly howling swept from one end of the room to the other, ranging in pitch from a deep growl to a high, shrieking whistle, while in its wake objects were lifted, dragged, hurled, exploded, until the air was a whirling mass of particles, as if a hurricane had passed that way.

'Virginia! You filthy little bitch!' shouted Sandy.

With a scream, she rushed at him and tore at his clothing, her extraordinary strength ripping the revers away from his jacket so that the padding inside was exposed in all its common-or-garden absurdity. She tore his shirt, grabbed him by the ears and shook his big, red, drunken face so that he shouted with pain. She kicked at his shins, hit his mouth, hit him, hit him, hit him...

Too drunk to resist, he fell back on to the floor and cracked his head on the skirting.

A great shout of laughter rang through the room.

'Kill him! Kill him, you little whore! She's a whore, a whore, a whore!'

'Yes, I'll kill him!' shrieked Virginia, the power within her increasing, a volcano welling up into her mouth, her brain, then bursting out through the top of her head. Her hands were drawn upwards with the magma of her subconscious and reached up, up, reaching for the ceiling, gripping the white-hot bulb which had been burning non-stop for eight hours and crushing it between her fingers so that it exploded and sent fragmented needles of glass showering over the room.

'Christ!' shouted the Belfast poet. 'Jesus, Mary and Joseph! She's flying, she's flying!'

Dino was on his knees, praying in agonised, terrified Italian.

The doorway was a mass of pale, terrified faces, drawn in from the rest of the house like matter in the wake of a nuclear explosion. They were pushed aside as another face appeared.

'Virginia!' cried Rod. 'Virginia, I'm here, I'm here!'

The room, dimmed by the breaking of the bulb, was now illuminated by a mass of flaring lights which started near the ceiling and descended slowly to the floor, extinguishing themselves as they touched it. Dino saw one land on his arm and bounce off, leaving a dark, blunt stain. He looked up, still begging his God for assistance, and saw the matches continue to fall, like the sparks from a bonfire. Rod fell to his knees beside him and joined in with good, old-fashioned, Anglican prayer.

And Virginia was floating, high above them all, her arms held wide to receive her real lover, the one she had attracted and energised, the only one who wanted her. She felt the nails and teeth on her again and for a moment greeted the assault with joyous rage, turning away from the human love which had failed her and drawing the warm comfort of hatred into her very soul.

'She's dying for it!' stated the voice gleefully. 'These little whores are all dying for it!'

'Leave her alone!' shouted Rod.

'She wants me. She brought me.'

'Who are you? Tell me your name!'

Up in the bedroom, the sole remaining watcher of the blue movie, too anaesthetised to respond to the urgent stimuli of the real world, studied the busty lady with the black stockings and suspender belt performing yet another eccentric practice on the well-hung male on the brass bed and saw her turn to face the camera with a sly, over-acted wink. She was very ugly. You'd think they'd employ a dolly with a better face than that. The camera panned in to close-up, so that the lady could give the customers the full benefit of her tongue running round her full, red lips. The lips expanded into a smile, exposing broken, blackened teeth, and the heavily-lashed blue eyes shrank into narrow slits, bagged and wrinkled and with the hardened discharge of unhealthy old age gathered at the corners. The blonde hair turned grey. The camera moved in remorselessly until the face occupied the whole screen. The face spoke.

'William,' it said. 'William.'

Never since the disastrous dinner party at Glamis Castle had guests departed so quickly. Within minutes the presumed last, being the confused Hummerstone, was stowed into a car and driven off for delivery to Islington.

Dino knelt beside Sandy.

Rod hugged Virginia, trying to stop the hysterical screaming and the violent struggles of her body.

'I'm sorry, Virginia, I'm sorry. I just slipped over into the park for a few minutes and sat down, and somehow I fell asleep. As soon as I woke up I came straight back. Believe me, Virginia, please!'

It was true, really it was. He'd only meant to stay away for a few minutes, but what with the drink and the exhaustion and the sudden peace, he had dropped off. Now look at what had happened, was still happening.

It was knocking on the walls, shaking the furniture, scratching like a giant rat around the skirtings. The whole room was alive with sound, and the terrifying thing was that they couldn't see the force which was doing it.

'Rod! Rod! Rod!' shrieked Virginia, clawing at his sweater and running her hands over it with that strange, searching action.

'Yes, I'm here. Calm down, Ginnie, calm down and it'll stop. If you're calm it's got no power to work with. Take deep breaths. I'll count for you. One, two, three, four – '

She tried to do as he said, but it was as if she no longer controlled her body. It felt as if there was a battle going on inside her between two separate souls, struggling for mastery. Her limbs jerked while her brain told them to be still.

'I can't,' she cried, 'it won't let me. It's *in* me, Rod, right inside, I can feel it. Oh, go away, go away, go away!' she implored it.

'Dino,' said Rod desperately, 'leave that stupid oaf alone. Have you got your rosary?'

'Yes,' said Dino. Rod pushed it over Virginia's head, but the instant he let go it crumpled itself up against her throat and started to squeeze. She choked. Rod pressed his fingers under the carved, wooden beads and pulled them away from her flesh. The strength of the thing was phenomenal. It was like wrestling with a demon.

No, he knew that this thing was not to be dignified by such a name. It wasn't a prince of darkness, just the remnants of a human being that had lost its body, the only bit of itself it knew what to do with, it had no conception whatever of what to do with its immortal soul. It had probably never even believed that it had one. Its life had been physical, earthbound, devoted to self and its gratification. It had grabbed and exploited earthly life, not used it as a training ground for the one to come. It was lost, confused, angry, with nowhere to go, because it knew of no place, and with nothing to do, because it didn't know that anything *could* be done without a body. It was waste energy, spiritual rubbish, floating about near the places it had known and so desperate to go on living in the only way it knew that it tried to use the physicality of others with which to do it.

If it were not so despicably malicious, he could almost have felt sorry for it. It was like a child who comes to its final school exams and finds it has neglected to learn anything which will enable it to pass them; who hadn't even known that there was an exam, or a university in which to achieve a place.

Its abysmal spiritual ignorance was finally displayed by its tearing the cross out of Rod's fingers and hurling it across the room.

'Get her out,' said Rod urgently. 'It's hopeless while she's in here.'

She fought them all the way through the hall and the kitchen, down the back steps, then, as they sat her down on a patio chair, suddenly weakened, stopped struggling, burst into tears and fell face downwards on the table. They held her while she sobbed, making silly, puerile 'There, there' noises and telling her she was all right now, it had gone, it couldn't get her out here, she was going to be all right.

The window above was thrown up and a body flopped out like a rag doll, leaning over the windowsill and making a high, complaining, keening whine.

'Terrible film,' it wailed, *'terrible* film. Get your money back, Sandy. Terribly ugly dolly – never heard of a dolly called William before – bloody terrible. Even broke the bloody video!'

While they were trying to make sense of this babble, Sandy staggered out of the kitchen door, one hand clutched to the back of his head. He saw Virginia and took a determined stride in her direction, but misjudged the number of steps it was necessary to negotiate before reaching the bottom and slipped down on to the paving in ridiculous, agonising splits.

'Szamár!' he screamed, in part anger and part pain. *'Meg Öllek!'*

'Hello,' said Dino drily, 'I do believe the Magyars are at the gates.'

'Keep your hands off,' shouted Rod, as Sandy pulled himself up and advanced on Virginia. She shrank back against his shoulder, crying louder with fear.

'It wasn't me, Sandy! It wasn't me! I told you all the time it wasn't me!'

He hung over the table, thrusting his pointing finger at her face like a dagger. His face was so contorted that it seemed about to explode. It was the face of a man for whom passion was natural, not the polite, well-bred, English negativity of the mask he had pasted over his true self.

'You!' he said. 'You are going to be locked up! You are going to be shut away until you've learned to behave like a civilised human being! You're going to spend the rest of your life in a place where I can forget you even exist! You're a bloody nuisance and always have been. I hated you from the first moment I saw you, mooning around behind Petra like a useless household pet she wouldn't have put down. I tried to be a father to you, but you wouldn't play ball, would you? All the things I gave you, all the money I spent on you: your toys, your private schools, the expensive clothes which were so wasted on your skinny, ugly body, everything I bought you for six bloody years — you weren't ever grateful, were you? You never thanked me or appreciated how I was trying to make up to you for being such a pathetic little shit. I even tried to love you, but you didn't want to know.

'And how could I, anyway? Nobody could love you, not even Petra. She told me that, you know, before we got married. She told me how you'd always been a burden to her. She said what hell she went through when you were born, and what an ugly baby you were, and how you cried and cried and made a total bloody nuisance of yourself. She said she used to have urges to smash your stupid face in and throw you out of the window or against the wall. She nearly did it once, did you know that? She said you were about ten months old and always whining and grizzling and throwing your food on the floor, and she suddenly snapped and grabbed you up and shook you. But you still wouldn't stop even then, and she threw you into the corner of the room and picked up a bottle — '

'Shut up!' shouted Rod. 'Don't you dare say another bloody word! You're pissed out of your mind! Shut up, you bastard, or I'll shut you up myself!'

'You?' said Sandy, his red eyes turning away from Virginia's shaking, terrified figure on to this obnoxious, effete thing which dared to call itself a man. 'You're an infection! No wonder Virginia's taken to you, you're two of a kind. Useless misfits. I hope you get Aids and die! I hope you give your filthy disease to Virginia, so that she dies, too, and gets out of a world which doesn't want her, which has never wanted her!

'Petra wanted to have you aborted,' he said, turning to Virginia again, 'but her mother wouldn't let her. Went on about the sanctity of human life and all that sentimental crap. You wrecked your mother's life, you know that? She didn't want you. Your father didn't want you, either. He did his duty by you because that's what he was brought up to do — always had to be nice, Derek did, because that's the English sacred cow, niceness — but what he really felt for you was the same as Petra. You were a bloody nuisance, a bloody mistake. You should never have been born. Why don't you die, then we'll all be a damn sight happier!'

Virginia's face was white. She stared at Sandy, not saying a word as the truth of his vicious words penetrated her shrinking soul and received confirmation from her own opinion of herself. She took it all in, without defence, without rebuttal. Yes, she said within herself, he's right, it's the truth. I always felt it was like that. They told me lies for years but I knew. Now at last I'm hearing the truth, that no-one loves me and no-one can love me. I'm a mistake. I'm out of my element. I never felt at home in the world, I belong somewhere else. But where?

And she knew at once; the one place she had ever felt at peace, accepted. No wonder one of them had come for her.

But surely, she thought with terror, I'm not as bad as that? Surely I don't belong with evil, malicious souls who exist only to hurt? I longed for goodness and tenderness and love. Am I so out of tune with reality that even in death I will be lonely, unacceptable and cast-out?

Love, companionship, affection, joy, meaning, virtue – none of those things existed outside her imagination. She had invented them because only she had been weak enough to need them. And now she saw that her gods were self-made and mere idols, with not just feet but whole bodies made of crumbling clay. Love was a lie. Goodness was a lie. All comfortable, comforting things were a lie, a lie, a lie.

And her emotions seemed to die within her. But her body went on living and her brain identified what it saw.

That big, bullying man with the red face – Sandy, her mother's husband. That plump, distressed little Italian – he was called Dino. That graceful, slim, beautiful young man with the illusion of goodness about him, the goodness she had invented and projected on to him because he looked the way she'd thought good people should look – he was called Rod.

Look at them all arguing, shouting, hating. That was reality, that hate, that aggression. They were showing their real selves, acting in the way that real people acted. There they were, down in the gesticulating, angry jungle of the physical world, a million miles away from her and her self-deceiving daydreams. She had nothing to do with it all.

She must go. But there was nowhere to go to, not in this world or the next. The universe she was fit to inhabit existed only within her own imagination. She must go inwards, deep inside Virginia Blackie, seal herself up like a kernel in a hard, uncrackable nut until she was hidden so completely that she would never be found again.

So she just watched them. She watched them rowing and shouting. She watched them coming and going in and out of the house. She watched Dino appear at the window and pull the limp, distressed body off the windowsill and take its weight on his shoulder like a fireman. She watched Rod shouting and shouting at Sandy and giving him a push which sent him back against the fence. She watched Mrs. Goodison's face peeping over that fence at the row which was turning into a fight, and the policemen she called coming out of the kitchen and pulling them apart. She watched and felt nothing at all.

At least, her body felt. It felt it when Sandy broke away from Rod and grabbed her. It felt it when Dino sat down beside her and put his arm about her. It felt the chill of the dawn hours through her thin dress and the shivering of her flesh. It felt Dino's arm being taken away, then a body-warmed jacket being put around it. But her mind felt nothing. She sat absolutely still, watching, watching.

She watched the policemen departing. She watched as Zak and Petra came towards her from the house. She watched their mouths moving and heard the vibration of their voices, but the sounds made no sense.

As she walked through the house between Petra and Rod, she saw that big, angry man at the door and the winking blue light out in the street. She watched the faces of people standing around and the car door opening in front of her. She watched the early morning emptiness of Highgate Village moving slowly past her and the bonnet nosing through a pair of big stone gateposts with eagles on top.

There was so much to watch and it was easier now, when you were outside it, watching with no emotional involvement. You really saw things at last.

A funny building, with pillars along the front and a doorway like Maiden's End, only more elaborate. A room, with beige and white plaster patterns on the ceiling. There was furniture to watch now and high, long windows, a leather settee and a glass coffee table and a big black fur rug. She watched Zak's mouth moving, and stopping, and moving and stopping, and moving —

She watched them all get up and leave the room, their

mouths smiling and moving again before they pulled the door to behind them.

She started to watch the windows now. Outside in the morning sunshine, new green leaves danced against the panes. She got up and went to study them more closely. The greenery was thin and germinal, hardly more than a haze on the dark web of twigs. It waved up and down as if fanning the old wall behind. The top was built of rounded, semicircular bricks like the line of a snake's back, and beyond that there were more hazed green branches.

'Hello, Virginia,' said the voice.

Her emotions suddenly jolted into painful life.

'What happened?' asked Zak.

Rod told them as they stood in the antechamber of the Temple. Petra's huge, frightened eyes turned from one to the other of them as they spoke, her fingers fidgeting restlessly with the catch on her bracelet. The buttons on her dress were done up wrong.

'Its a poltergeist,' Rod concluded, 'a spirit of some sort which is making use of her frustrated energies.'

'There are no spirits,' said Zak with smiling, immediate certainty. 'It's Recurrent Spontaneous Psycho-Kinesis. Just a law of physics we haven't codified yet.'

'Its name is William,' insisted Rod. 'It appeared on the television in Virginia's bedroom. A man who was watching it told Dino. An old man's face, when there would certainly have been nothing of the kind on the video they were watching. It may have started as just psycho-kinetic emanations from Virginia — she's unhappy enough, God knows, poor kid — but then something else took over and used the energy for its own purposes. Has Petra told you about the voice?'

'Yes, yes,' said Zak with confident condescension. 'Hallucinations — it's all part of the pattern. Voices expressing the repressed part of the personality, the part which has been hidden because the persona refuses to assimilate it.'

'But I heard it, Zak,' said Petra anxiously.

'Group hallucination. You're very close to Virginia, aren't you, darling, and you naturally sensed what she was hearing — the biological bond between mother and child can be remarkably strong.'

'I heard it,' said Rod, 'and I'm not her mother.'

Zak's eyes fastened on to Rod, perceiving the rational explanation and rationalising on it for all he was worth.

'But you were, I gather, in some respects *in loco parentis* at the time. You cared about her, you were almost acting as a mother to her, and she was emotionally involved with you and could therefore have imprinted her hallucinations upon your consciousness, because you were in a receptive frame of mind. I'm sure you both believe sincerely that you heard a disembodied voice and I'm not ridiculing you. But you are neither of you familiar with pathological psychology and its symptoms. I do assure you that no matter how astounding these things may appear to the lay mind, there are numerous clinical examples of such phenomena.'

'That's what I'm telling you,' said Rod. 'It happens, over and over again. I've actually met it before. Poltergeist activity is a fact.'

'R.S.P.K. is a fact,' said Zak, 'but its cause is in the brain. There's no need to resort to the paranormal as an explanation. It's physical energy, a manifestation of real, natural phenomena which we have not yet fully investigated.'

'Yes!' shouted Rod. 'That's what I'm saying! It's real! Spiritual, or as you would probably prefer it, *psychological* power is real. We're not totally physical beings consisting only of bodies, we possess mind, spirit, immense forces we don't understand but which are capable of effects upon the physical world. And what happens to that power when we die?'

'It dies too, naturally,' said Zak. 'It is the product of the physical body. Look at it this way: a living body gives off heat, but as soon as it dies the heat starts to diminish and within hours has gone. Everything dies with the body.'

'Does it? Our minds, our personalities, our emotions, our loves, hates, intelligence, our desperate need to find meaning? Are they all just the by-products of biological forces designed to keep us functioning like machines? Look, all we need do in order that the race survive is to eat, sleep, fight off danger, copulate, produce young, bring them up, then die quickly and get out of the way of the next generation. We don't need all those other things, in fact they're a bloody nuisance. What possible biological use is it to feel guilty when we harm other people? They don't matter to our personal survival or our personal reproduction – our selfish genes, as I expect you look at it. Whatever is the use of yearning for kindness and love and purpose, when these things not only don't assist our biological urges, but often frustrate them? Why do we need these things, when they are physically counter-productive?'

'Conditioning,' said Zak with a smile, 'all conditioning. We are trained from earliest childhood in the Judeo-Christian Ethic and are crippled by it. Without it, we would all be happier, more biologically efficient animals.'

'Well, if that's so, why did we develop the Judeo-Christian Ethic at all, or the Islamic one, or any of the religious philosophies which have lasted so long?'

'We are degenerate as a species,' explained Zak patiently. 'We are nearly at the end of our natural span on this planet, and very soon we shall almost certainly destroy ourselves and another species will begin to evolve to take our place.'

'So nature isn't infallible? The great rational force of mindless biology falls down when we start to look for something outside it?'

'Alas, yes,' said Zak.

'Right,' said Rod, furious at the smug expression on Zak's face, 'if all those abstract concepts we long for don't exist, how did we come to conceive them? How can a biological mechanism yearn for a non-existent, non-biological ideal?'

'Because it needs to make sense of itself.'

'But if it's purely physical, it *doesn't* make sense.'

'It feels it does because it needs it.'

'Then if it needs it, it makes sense! The need postulates the existence of the thing needed. We need food and it exists. We need sex and it exists. There are no needs in man which are not answered in the real world. If we need meaning and love and a larger purpose and a spiritual dimension – yes, *spiritual* – then these things exist to answer our needs.'

'For God's sake,' Petra shouted angrily, 'stop all this self-indulgent philosophical crap and think about reality! What about Virginia? What are we going to do about her?'

They had almost forgotten Virginia. The heady intoxication of mental activity had indeed interfered with the physical, biological urge to protect posterity.

And when they got back into the consulting room the window was open and Virginia gone.

'I have,' said Zak, 'a distinct feeling of *déjà vu.*'

Chapter 20

'She's not in the garden.'

As Rod pushed open the mahogany inner doors, Petra broke away from Zak hastily and came to meet him.

Despite the expression of concern on her face, she seemed more her old self, patting her hair back behind her ears, walking with the graceful confidence of the beautiful woman who knows she is. Rod recognised what had happened to her; she had found another strong man to lean on. She had unloaded all her troubles on to him, left him to handle them. She was free of responsibility again.

Zak leant against the desk, hands gripping the edge lightly, a slight smile upon his face. Unlike Petra, he hadn't moved an inch when Rod came in. If there was one thing more than any other which he held in contempt, it was the opinion of others.

'I've got to go. I'm due at the Samaritans at seven.'

'You can't go!' Petra protested. 'Can't you ring them and say you've got an emergency at home?'

'We just don't do that. The only way of getting out of a duty is to send another volunteer in your place, and I very much doubt if I could find anyone this late.'

'Well, at least try.'

'I haven't time. My bus goes in ten minutes. I suppose I could ring round quickly when I get to the Centre, but it's a very long shot. I'll come straight back at ten, Petra. You'll find her, she can't have gone far.'

As he hurried away through the immaculate garden, Petra burst into angry tears.

'Oh *God*, why do these awful things keep happening to me?'

It's just not fair, Zak, it really isn't. It's just one worry after another and there's so much to do at home today. I've got the party to clear up, not to speak of the mess left by that ... And then the removal people will be arriving and I know damn well that Sandy is going to be about as much use as – Oh God, I was absolutely relying on Virginia to give me a hand.'
'Can't you get a friend in? How about Marjorie or Sam?'
'After what happened last night? No-one's going to come near us, not ever again. We're going to be outcasts, absolute bloody lepers. Thank God we *are* moving, that's what I say. At least down in Hertfordshire they won't know anything about all this and we can start again with a clean slate.'
'Are you going to take Virginia or would you like me to commit her for a while?'
'Would it help?'
'I see no reason why drug therapy shouldn't work. I had a similar case a couple of years ago. The kinetic activity subsided very soon after we started sedation, and within six months had gone completely. She's practically normal, now.'
'Practically?'
'Well, the family background was stressful. A bad relationship between the parents, several younger siblings in a disturbed condition and the possibility of abuse, although you can't always believe what frustrated adolescents say about their fathers.'
'But she went home cured?'
'Not home. She was put into care until the foster parents complained about things being moved.'
'You mean it started up again, even after treatment?' said Petra, getting panicky. 'And she's still in a loony bin?'
'My dear Petra, there is no question of that happening to Virginia,' said Zak, avoiding the question with the skill of a politician. 'Now get your coat, darling.'

Rod's bus was late. It was only a few minutes before seven when he pushed open the door of the Samaritans' Centre.
'Tight, Rod, very tight,' reproached the Leader, who had endured a particularly tough night duty and was leaning over the telephone, drinking a long-neglected and nearly cold mug of tea.

'Sorry, Simon, I've been having the most awful bloody time for the last few hours. A kid I know – she's become the focus of a poltergeist.'

'God almighty!' said Simon, rising from his chair. 'And I thought I was getting stick. I've just had some poor sod on the phone for nearly an hour, crying his heart out because he's on his beam ends, his only child has been taken away from him and now he's being thrown out of his flat.'

'There's a lot of it about,' said Rod wearily, easing himself down into Simon's vacated chair.

The phone rang at once. He reached over and picked it up, casting his personal agony out of his mind as he prepared to shoulder someone else's.

'The Samaritans. Can I help you?'

'Supposing she sees us coming and runs for it?' said Petra, leaning forward and scanning the occupants of the High Street with desperate concentration.

'I can run, too,' said Zak.

'Is that her?'

Zak slowed to a crawl beside the teenager. She turned and revealed a furious, frightened face, then shouted something obscene.

'Probably thought you were a kerb-crawler,' said Petra, leaning back as the car gathered speed and continued its way down Highgate Hill. 'Do you think she's gone home?'

'I'll turn off at the bottom and go up via Swain's Lane. She might be making for the cemetery, you know what an unhealthy obsession she has with the place.'

'She might be in it.'

'I don't suppose it's open yet.'

The car climbed the lane with the easy competence of 3.5 litres. The cemetery gates were locked on both sides of the road. At the top loomed the radio tower, hung with circular baubles, its spindly arms thrown up in alarm on either side of its tiny head.

Zak turned right and drew up outside the house. As Petra jumped out and made for the door, Pat appeared at her front window. She was in a dressing gown but still wearing the earrings she had worn for the party. It seemed highly unlikely that she had been to sleep at all.

'Sandy! Sandy!'

Petra's voice echoed through the empty shambles of the rooms. Everywhere was the trail of human and spiritual destructiveness. The back door was open but there was no-one in the garden. She looked up at the gaping sash.

'Sandy! Virginia!'

There was a scrabbling noise from the fence and Pat's head peeped over the top.

'Petra, darling, he's in here. He'd got such a nasty cut on his head that I just insisted that he come in and have it properly seen to. Was it that Rod boy? I saw him threatening Sandy and called the police. I'd never have thought it of him. He's always been such fun when I've met him before. What a terrible end to your lovely party. It was all quite quiet when I left, but in no time at all there was that dreadful noise going on out in the garden. You must have been so frightened.'

'I wasn't there,' said Petra, too anxious to watch her mouth.

'Weren't you? Did you slip out for a minute, then?'

'Yes,' said Petra shortly. 'Look, is Virginia there?'

'No, darling. Has she run away?' Pat's eyes gleamed with excitement.

'No, of course she hasn't run away! She's — she's gone round to Rod's, I expect, to get her things. We've been staying there, you know.'

'Oh, but do you think she'll be all right? I mean, if he's really such a violent man ... I mean, well, I know he's not entirely, well, you know, "normal",' she mouthed, 'but do you think you should have allowed a young girl to be alone with — '

'For Christ's sake, Pat,' shouted Petra, 'mind your own bloody business! Tell Sandy to come here at once!'

It was a very few minutes after Pat's startled face had disappeared from the fence that Sandy lumbered in through the front door, met Petra and Zak halfway down the hall and immediately accosted them furiously.

'Look here! It's just occurred to me: how come when I ring Zak you turn up with him, Petra?'

'Sandy,' said Petra hastily, 'have you seen Virginia? She walked out of Zak's consulting room and we haven't seen her since.'

'What, again?' exclaimed Sandy. 'Does that mean I've got

two lots of fees to pay for nothing? Can't you hold on to your patients? Have you never heard of strait-jackets?'

'Calm down, Sandy,' said Zak, a hard edge coming into his silky-smooth voice. 'I would suggest that the best thing you can do is to go to bed and sleep it off. I might suggest that you give Petra a hand with the clearing up, but I don't suppose for a moment that you will. If Virginia really isn't here we'll get off again and look for her.'

He pushed Petra out of the front door and shut it sharply before Sandy could follow them. His face appeared round it as they got into the car.

'What the hell were you doing with Zak?' he shouted.

Petra was trembling as they started off again on their search, this time turning down West Hill.

'He's murderous, Zak! I won't dare go back to him, I can't!'

'He'll sober up,' said Zak, looking out of the side window at a suspiciously slim young woman striding down the slope. 'What's Virginia wearing?'

'Oh – blue, a sort of pale, greenish blue. You remember, Zak, it was new, and she was showing it off to everyone like a kid at a birthday party?'

'No, I don't,' said Zak, 'I was looking at you.'

'Well for God's sake don't look now,' said Petra, pulling down the eyeshade before her and studying herself in the mirror on its back, 'I look a hag.'

'Stop fishing, Petra, you know perfectly well that you are a beautiful and desirable woman. Is that her?'

'No, she's wearing red. Well, I haven't felt either of those things lately. Sandy would only notice me if I had banknotes stuffed into my bra. Look, over there, some schoolgirls!'

'And all in school uniform. We're nearly at the bottom. Left or right?'

'Left. No, right. Oh, Zak, hadn't we better call the police?'

'Not yet. Give it a bit longer. Perhaps if we go round to Archway. She could be making for the station.'

'What time does the cemetery open?'

'No idea. Ancestor worship isn't my scene.'

'Oh, Virginia, Virginia!' moaned Petra.

'Everyone hates me,' Virginia told herself yet again as she

hurried down the mundane lovelessness of Holloway Road.

'Yes, they do. You don't want them, you want me. I love you,' whispered the voice. It was with her all the time now. It hadn't stopped since she had fled the Temple.

'You don't love, you're full of hate. You scratch and bite. You torment me. You smashed up my room and set fire to my house and tried to destroy everything I feel safe with.'

'Hate's better,' insinuated the voice. 'Hate's comfortable, hate costs you nothing. Don't love people, Virginia, despise them.'

'I do,' she said. 'I'm never going to love ever again. I've had enough of being hurt. I'm going to hurt people before they can hurt me.'

'That's right,' said the voice, pleased. 'You're learning. You've got the secret at last.'

With erotic tenderness, delicate scarlet lines were carved upon her neck.

'Don't do that!' said Virginia angrily. 'I don't like it. I don't want you, go away!'

'But Virginia, I love you, Virginia.'

'Don't lie to me,' she cried, stopping short in the midst of the milling crowds making for the buses and the tube and the daily slog of wage-slavery. 'Love doesn't exist. There is no love!'

'What she say?' asked Fatima Mohammed, pausing for a second in her sprint for the Hop-on bus collecting fares by Holloway Station.

'"There is no love"' said Mary Smith. 'I could have told her that.'

'Poor kid's a loony.'

'Yeah. She's right, though.'

'My Dad says, in his country they don't shut up loonies, they respect them as messengers of God,' said Fatima.

'What God?' said Mary, and dragged her tired, six-month-pregnant bulk onto the bus. 'Highgate Station, please.'

Virginia marched on.

'Why did you pick on me?' she demanded angrily. 'What did I do?'

'You longed for love. Your longing leaked out your vital energy and I seized it. I want love, too.'

'You wouldn't know how,' said Virginia.

239

'No, I didn't know, but I still needed it, and I found it was unobtainable and tried hate instead. It was so easy, so comfortable, like putting on a garment that fitted. And it went hand in hand with lust, which relieved my body. That's the answer, Virginia – lust for the body and hate for the soul. With those two things you can be happy; there's no other way.'

'I was happy loving Rod,' said Virginia.

'Illusion. Love is weak. Love is self-immolation. It's not for souls like you and me who know better than to put our heads into the noose. Lust, don't love. Hate, before you are hated. Use people, or they'll use you.'

Virginia slowed as she saw the young couple smooching in a shop doorway. He was plain and weedy, in leather jacket and torn, dirty jeans. She was uncompromisingly feminist, in ugly, shapeless clothes and a Ms-frizz hairdo. Yet they kissed and embraced.

'I don't want lust and hate, I want love,' Virginia said, and started to cry.

She turned back towards Highgate.

'You're wrong! Learn from me!' whispered the voice with urgency. 'Learn from me!'

The character actress came in at twenty to ten.

Rod put the phone down at a quarter to, gave her a quick appeal about the urgency of the situation awaiting him back in Highgate, then left at the run as she slipped into the chair, full of kind hopes that everything would turn out all right. Her public would have been surprised to see that thin, ugly face showing such concern; she had made her name playing tarts, bitchy housewives, unsympathetic landladies, and finally old battleaxes.

The bus crawled through heavy traffic. Rod fidgeted, pressed his damp fingers together, tormented by memories of the past and fears for the future.

Frank, oh Frank.

He leapt from the bus and down West Hill. He ran through Zak's imposing gates, past the opulent house and up through the garden to the Temple. For the first time he noticed what the figures of Venus and Adonis over the door were doing. Well, well.

Inside, the cool, high antechamber was empty. The secretary's unattended desk stood to his right. The block of filing cabinets to his left was locked and incommunicado. The salacious, precocious putti around the cornice got on with what they were doing, throwing knowing glances over their shoulders at the anxious man below.

Zak was alone. He looked up from the papers and books on his desk, gold pen in hand, smiling.

'Ah, Rod.'

'Did you find her?'

'No. We had a quick look round, but then Petra had to go home to see to the move. I've informed the police, though they weren't particularly interested – after all, she's only been gone a few hours. If she hasn't turned up by the time Petra and Sandy are ready to leave for Maiden's End, I'll give them another ring.'

'I think I should go out looking again.'

'As you wish.'

Above the desk was a Japanese watercolour, very old, very rare and very expensive. Rod's eyes fastened on to it with sudden shock. 'God, that's pretty lewd.'

'Not compared to that,' said Zak, waving his hand at a bas-relief high up on the wall behind the couch. Rod looked.

'It's not physically possible,' he said at last.

'Oh yes, perfectly possible,' Zak assured him, 'if you're in training, of course.'

'The Hellfire Club, I suppose?'

'That's right. The altar was just below it.'

'How can you work in a place like this?' asked Rod, revolted. 'What's the effect on your patients?'

'Very good. Reassuring, in fact. It shows them that they're not as abnormal and perverted as their conditioning has told them.'

'When you think what must have gone on in here, it makes you wonder if there's anything too abnormal or perverted for a human being to have done.'

'There isn't,' said Zak. 'Absolutely nothing. Nothing is so extreme that a human being hasn't done it at some time.'

'Even that?' Momentarily, a terrible, vivid picture of his parents took the place of the entwined stone figures and filled him with nausea.

No, Mother didn't cry out, Rodney, go back to bed at once. How dare you burst into our bedroom in the middle of the night? You will come to my study immediately before breakfast and I will deal with you then.

'Filthy bastards,' said Rod with pain, 'I don't suppose they ever loved anyone in their lives.'

'What, the Hellfire Club? Oh, I don't know. I think it was probably all quite harmless, really. Just the healthy sexual high jinks of men with the means to indulge themselves. No more than what goes on in high-class London brothels today.'

'Which one was it who owned this house?'

'The first Earl of Hilton. Self-made man, entrepreneur, slave-trader, perjurer, fornicator and adulterer. Then peer of the realm and, for a very short time, government minister, until one of his mistresses turned out to have a husband rather more tiresomely conventional than the others'. From then on he added to his other personae those of murderer, fugitive, felon and finally executed criminal. Silk rope, of course. What you might call a full life.'

'And he designed this Temple?'

'Yes. Like most men of his eminence he dabbled in architecture. You could say that this building was his labour of love. He was noted for his virility, you know. Supposed to have had about thirty illegitimate children, and at least a hundred other mistresses who were presumably more careful or more lucky. Particularly fond of little girls, I believe.'

'What was his first name?' Rod asked quickly.

'William. William Capes.'

'How old was he when he died?'

'Oh, quite old. He managed to evade justice for a few years before he was caught.'

'It's him! I bet it's him.'

'Who is?'

'The poltergeist. It's the spirit of William Capes.'

Zak burst out laughing.

'Oh, Rod, for God's sake! Didn't I explain all that to you? There *are* no spirits, only human energy.'

'That's exactly what I mean by spirit, Zak, human energy.'

'But it dies with the body!'

'Energy can't die, it can only be changed into another form.

That's a law of physics, a cast-iron, proved, respectable scientific law — isn't it?' he added uncertainly. Rod wasn't a scientist, and his last contact with the subject had been at school.

'There are *no* spirits,' Zak said, with the calm certainty of a man who knew it all.

The voice whispered insistently in her ear. She started to run, across the road by Archway Station, up the hill, left down Magdala Avenue. At the locked, rusty lower gates in Chester Road she stopped and shook them feebly, seeing the peaceful sanctuary before her, so near and yet so far.

'Virginia, you're mine, Virginia.'

She ran down the road, past the school, past the Snow White cottages of Holly Village, round the corner into Swain's Lane.

Behind the railings, the jumbled, neglected graves were buried under last year's undergrowth, the brown plumes of horsetail covering the ground with a hazy pall. They pressed hard against the railings, those dead, as if they were being squeezed out by the over-populated ground, back into the world they had left so long ago with resentment, reluctance or merely relief.

'Stay with me, Virginia, stay with me. You need me.'

'No, no!'

She ran on, panting with the increasing slope, crying with the increasing fear.

'Give yourself to me and you'll never be afraid or unhappy again. I have knowledge, I have delicious secrets — '

The Swain's Lane gate was locked. She tried it desperately, then continued her way up the hill, making for home.

'They don't love you, Virginia. They don't want you.'

'Go away!'

On the left, the high wall of the West Cemetery blocked off the hard, living world of the lane from the peaceful rest of death. The bricks were smooth and unclimbable, the top was spiked and excluding.

On the right, the park was open. A pair of young men carrying racquets passed into the gate at the top to use the tennis courts.

I wish I was like that. I wish I was attractive and happy and going to play tennis with other young people. I wish I belonged in this beautiful living world.

'This life isn't for you, Virginia, you don't belong in it. You belong with me. Come to me.'

She turned into the road. A huge yellow van was ahead, wedged into the row of parked cars between Sandy's Volvo and Pat Goodison's Metro. It gaped like Jonah's whale and displayed the things it had consumed: the Hülsta fitments, grubby with smoke; Petra and Sandy's bed, up on its side; Virginia's dressing table buried under a strapped-up pile of bedding. The next course of its meal stood ready-served in the road, packed into easily swallowable crates like giant ravioli. In the centre of the pavement stood a dissected long-case clock, its head on the ground beside it, its entrails lying half in, half out of a linen basket from the bathroom.

Virginia stopped short.

'Daddy, oh Daddy! Come back, Daddy!'

The voice gave a howl of anger.

The clock teetered forward and fell with a smash on to the paving stones. A broken splinter of veneer sprang up from the ground and flew at her face.

'Love me!' the voice demanded as the splinter hit her cheek like a dart.

She tore it out and fled, out of the road and down the hill, pursued by the whirling fragments of the shattered clock.

Outside the West Cemetery, a small group awaited the first guided tour.

A man was just opening the gate of the New Ground.

'Virginia!'

She rushed through the gate.

And at last the voice stopped.

Chapter 21

The van was fed up to its back bumpers.

The foreman had a few more uncomfortable words with Sandy about the clock, then the Mathesons' furniture was driven out of the road, headed for the North Circular, the A10 and Buntingford.

Petra, with time at last to indulge herself, sat down on the living room floor and burst into tears.

'Oh, shut up,' said Sandy.

'Is that all you can say? Just shut up? My only child has disappeared without trace and I'm not even allowed to cry about it? You're a pig, Sandy! You're a great, stupid, self-centred, insensitive, Communist pig!'

'I am not a Communist. I have been a card-carrying Conservative for thirty years.'

'You're not paid up, Pat told me!'

'I am a hardworking British capitalist, and the only thing which stands between you and starvation. When did you ever work? What have you done to contribute to the luxury you've lived in for the last six years?'

'What about the house?' sobbed Petra. 'You were quite happy to take that from me, weren't you?'

'It was part of the package,' said Sandy. 'I gave up a very nice flat in Belgravia to move into this suburban semi, and don't you forget it.'

'Highgate isn't suburban! Highgate's about as far up the social and financial scale as you can get without going over the top! Only pseuds live in Belgravia; pseuds and Arabs and drug-dealers and people who never worked for a bloody penny they ever spent at bloody Harrod's!'

'If Harrod's is beneath you, why don't you shop at Mark's and save me a hell of a lot of money?'

'You're mean! Derek never talked to me like that.'

'Poor bloody Derek. He worked his guts out for you, too, and got sod all in return.'

'I don't want to go!' wailed Petra. 'I belong here. I love Highgate.'

'You don't care a damn about Highgate, you just don't want to leave Zak.'

'He's nicer to me than you are.'

'He isn't married to you.'

'And anyway, what about you and Sam?'

'Sam?' He laughed. 'You know Sam, Petra, it doesn't mean a thing.'

'It may not to you, but what about me? Do you think I like it when she smarms all over me while she's fleecing me for her ghastly clothes?'

'You still buy them, don't you?'

'And I know all the time she's been having it off with you and laughing at me behind my back – '

'There's nothing funny about you.'

' – and you've barely touched me for weeks, even though I've been worried sick about poor Virginia.'

'You wouldn't let me touch you.'

'Oh, for God's sake! A real man isn't put off that easily! If you really wanted me you'd go on trying until – '

'Oh, I'm supposed to be psychic, am I? I'm supposed to realise that when you say you don't feel like it you really mean you want me to sweep you up on to my camel and carry you off into the desert!'

'How long is it since you made love to me? What about all those excuses? "Sorry, Petra, I'm feeling a bit dicky, darling; let's leave it. Another time, darling. Tomorrow, next week, sometime, never.!" Of course I went to Zak, you pillock! What did you expect?'

'I had a reason for that,' said Sandy, suddenly sobering. He turned to the drinks table. It had gone.

'Yes, Sam!'

'No, it wasn't that, really. I was thinking of you.'

'Thinking of me? Did you think I'd get worn out by your insatiable lust or something? Were you afraid you'd give me an unmentionable infection?'

Yes – forget it. All right, Petra, you win.

'Oh God, I want a drink!' she cried.

'It's all packed up and on its way to Maiden's End.'

'All right, let's go to the Flask,' said Petra, perking up a bit.

'It's closed.'

'What time does it open?'

'You don't know? You've lived here all these years and you can't remember when your father confessor is available?'

'You can talk!'

There was a polite tap on the open front door.

'Hello? Mr. Matheson?'

Sandy went out into the hall.

A small man in a charcoal grey suit stood hugging his briefcase in the gritty hollow which had once held the doormat.

'Ah! My name's Cohen, I'm solicitor for the Liptons. I gather you're moving out?'

'Of course we are. What does it look like?'

'Yes. Good,' said Mr. Cohen, looking at the bare stairs and the stained rectangle on the wall where the mirror had hung, searching for any signs that a continued sit-in was contemplated. 'Just have to make sure, you know. Right, I'll get off, then. Mr. Lipton's coming in tomorrow morning, all right with you?'

'Absolutely bloody marvellous,' said Sandy.

He returned to the naked cell of the living room, where Petra was still crying her eyes out.

'Shonk,' he said.

'Oh! 'Petra said, rallying at once. 'So you're a racist, too, are you? Oh yes, you Hungarians are, aren't you? A load of pro-Nazi collaborators. There was a programme about it on the box, I remember. Well, let me tell you, Sandy, my parents had next-door neighbours who were Jews, and very nice people they were. When my father died Mrs. Silver came in and spent hours with my mother, and she was a bloody sight nicer to her than any of our so-called Christian neighbours. *And* I had a great-uncle who was almost certainly half Jewish, and a kinder man you couldn't have wished for, so if you think you can indulge your nasty East European bigotry with me you're in for a shock, I can tell you. I don't give a shit what a person's origins are, I judge them on how they treat me and what sort of a human being they are. You Hungarians are all alike!'

'Shut up!'

The marriage was dead, they both realised it. Yet the life-support system of habit kept it functioning.

'Come on, Petra, it's time to go.'

'But what about Virginia?'

'Sod Virginia.'

'You – !'

Another intruder into their private marital grief appeared at the door.

'We've found her,' said Rod.

'Well hello, Rod darling, how's the wife?' asked Sandy viciously.

'A damn sight more lovable than yours,' said Rod in a low voice.

He went into the room and looked down at her, sobbing on the floor. She actually looked human. He softened.

'Virginia's at Zak's, Petra. We found her in the cemetery.'

'Is she all right?' Petra struggled up, trying to wipe her destroyed make-up back into shape.

'No, not really. She was very quiet at first but started screaming when we got her back to the consulting room. Zak gave her a shot. He thinks she ought to go into hospital.'

'Oh no!' Petra protested. 'I can't leave my baby behind.'

'She isn't yours or anyone's,' said Rod. 'She belongs to nobody but herself, and much good may it do her. Look, Petra, I'll take her if you like, me and Dino. I know it's not a good idea, really, but if she's happy with us she can stay for a bit. We'll look after her.'

'Oh will you! I can just imagine how,' said Sandy, spilling his rage out on to the nearest thing to a scapegoat he could find. 'Virginia is our child, Rod, not yours and your boyfriend's. We'll take our own property with us to our new home and deal with her there. Thank you for all your do-gooding assistance. Now sod off.'

I will deal with you later, Rodney. Go to your room.

'Sandy,' he said, 'if anything happens to that child I'll never forgive you. She needs love and patience and understanding, and if she doesn't get them she could be finished. Just remember that.'

'I'll certainly remember you,' said Sandy angrily.

Sandy carried her out of the Temple. She was flat out, nothing but a lump of skinny flesh and bone, a piece of property, not a human being.

As the Volvo drove away from the eagle-guarded gates, Rod gave a cry of impotent rage. 'Edward the Eighth,' he shouted.

'I beg your pardon?' inquired Zak.

'Edward the bloody Eighth! Deprive one child of love and security and you can shake an Empire. Weaken one brick and the house can come crashing down. They're headed for disaster.'

'I've given Petra a good supply of drugs.'

'Drugs, drugs, drugs! That's the modern answer to all problems, isn't it? Pity the Earl of Hilton didn't have a psychiatrist. If he'd been drugged stupid he'd have caused a lot less misery.'

'You're afraid of heterosexual love, aren't you, Rod?' said Zak sympathetically. 'I do understand. Parent problems, right? But it's the greatest power for release and freedom we possess, and only when inhibition isn't present can it do its healing work.'

'Healing work? He was an evil old lecher. Must have been *so* healing for those poor little girls having him put his dirty hands on them.'

'You're thinking of your mother, now, aren't you?'

'No I'm not! I'm thinking of anyone who isn't allowed to love in the way that's natural to them, but has to submit to someone else's way. That's not release and freedom; and it's the most hideous form of slavery in the world for a child to have to submit to a grown man.'

'You're awfully conventional,' said Zak, smiling. 'All right, all right, I know,' he said, holding up his hand as Rod turned on him, 'but homosexuality is only another sort of conventionality these days, isn't it? You're stuck in your own code of behaviour, just like everyone else, and can't accept anything which deviates from it. Some men are attracted by under-age girls, and children have sexual feelings too, so is it so bad if they get together sometimes?'

'Yes, it is. It's not a meeting of equals. It's selfish exploitation.'

'Look, Rod. When William Capes was eventually found, fully five years after the murder, he was hiding out in his sister's house. Nobody knew he was there except for a servant girl who waited on him and was told he was a hermit. Nice touch, that; hermits very much appealed to the sentimental, romantic religiosity of the time. Anyway, the child — only thirteen, I believe — used to take him his meals and talk to him and got really fond of him. He could still charm, you know, even at sixty-three. When the law finally came this girl put herself in front of him and said, "Kill me, before you take him."'

'I don't believe a word of it.'

'It's true!' protested Zak. 'She loved him. He'd given her something her godly, repressed home hadn't — physical joy.'

'And probably warped the rest of her life. You're making me feel sick, Zak.'

'She clung to him all the way down the stairs, begging them not to take him away. In the end they had to tear her off him and give her to Mrs. Maiden to take care of.'

'Mrs. Maiden? For God's sake, Zak, Mrs. *Maiden*!'

The line to Maiden's End was unavailable. Telecom hadn't got round to connecting it yet, not even for Sandy.

Rod didn't own a car. Zak had an evening appointment.

'Have you a railway timetable?'

'Over there,' said Zak. 'Where are you going?'

'Where do you think?'

'I should think the nearest stations would be Baldock or Bishop's Stortford.'

'Oh no! All right, I'll ring Derek.'

'Derek? Oh, Mr. Blackie. But isn't he a bankrupt? Are bankrupts allowed cars?'

'I wouldn't know,' said Rod, 'I've never had enough money to find out.'

He was searching through the telephone directory now.

'I can give you the number of a good taxi firm,' said Zak helpfully, though smiling at this irrational behaviour.

'To Buntingford?' said Rod incredulously. 'Oh, hello? Derek? This is Rod Singleton. Look, have you got a car? No? Right. No, stop moaning and listen. Meet me outside the Firenze Restaurant in High Street, Hampstead, as soon as you can possibly get there. It's about Virginia, she's in the most awful danger. No, I'm not going to explain now, you just do as you're told. If you aren't there in an hour I'll go without you, so get moving.'

He flung the phone on to the cradle and bolted for the door.

'If you could wait until eleven I should be quite willing to take you,' said Zak reasonably.

'Well I can't,' said Rod and ran out of the Temple.

Highgate to Hampstead, though not much more than a mile as the crow flies, is not necessarily a quick journey by public transport. Buses move slowly round Kenwood and the Heath during the Rush Hour and that evening the Spaniards bottleneck was at its worst. Rod abandoned the bus and ran the rest of the way. It was approaching the deadline he had laid upon Derek when he reached the restaurant. Dino's car was parked opposite, facing downhill.

Rod rushed in. Dino started and nearly dropped the loaded tray he was carrying towards the first customers as his arm was grabbed.

'Car keys!'

'Rod! What you doing here? In my coat, of course.'

'Where is it?' demanded Rod urgently.

'In the kitchen. Wait a minute, I get it — '

Rod barged through the slatted swing doors into a hell of steam inhabited by white-crowned, sweating demons.

'Coats!' he shouted. 'Where are the staff's coats?'

A surprised assistant chef waved his hand, then remembered too late that his wallet was in his. Rod ran into the peeling, insanitary outhouse beyond, recognised Dino's padded jacket, rifled the pockets and emerged again into the kitchen, where a large, angry Italian suddenly confronted him with a carving knife.

'You thieving bastard! I kill you! Already I call the police!'

A desperate swerve, then out through the restaurant, catching a glimpse of a terrified couple leaping to their feet and hugging each other. An insane, kamikaze dive into the traffic, then he was opening the car door, looking up and down the street for Derek. He was nowhere in sight. Hurry up, hurry up! What sort of a father are you?

The chef burst out of the door and stepped into the road.

Rod turned the ignition, pressed his foot on to the accelerator and moved off. The North Circular, that was the quickest way, then the A 10.

He drove down Hampstead High Street and Rosslyn Hill, trying to remember which side roads precipitated you into a residential maze and which afforded a quick turn-around. Hampstead Hill Gardens. Yes, he remembered that – he'd gone to a party there. He dragged the wheel to the left, skidded round the long curve, turned into Pond Street and stopped at the T-junction, raging with frustration as the long, uninterrupted line of headlights surged up Haverstock Hill. At last the lights changed and he turned right again, back up the hill past the restaurant. A terrifying mountain of rage was gesticulating outside, with a small, anxious Dino attempting to pacify it.

Rod ducked down behind the steering wheel as he passed. Oh shit! Some damn fool rushing straight across. He might have killed him!

You must drive your vehicle in a gentlemanly manner, Rodney, with proper consideration for other road users. A man who has a road accident is a mere ignorant lout. There is no need for any such thing if you are in complete control of your car and your own body.

Shut up, Father! Shut up, you sanctimonious, self-righteous, inhuman bigot!

He wound down the window and shouted.

'Derek! Come here! Get in!'

Derek stopped as he reached the kerb, turned, opened the passenger door and collapsed into the seat, barely having time to close the door before the car moved forward again.

'What's all this about? I came as quickly as I could. What's happened to Virginia?'

'She's on her way to the very place where that disgusting evil spirit can have her all to himself. Fasten your seat-belt, Derek, we're going to Maiden's End.'

Sandy drove across the track. The corn was inches high now, green and white waves undulating across the dimming plateau in the cold wind. The yellow pantechnicon obtruded through the dark trees like a vandal's splash of paint on sober wallpaper. The useless line dipped up and down between telegraph poles marching up from the dip where Hankey Green lay hidden. A carved board announced the name of this desirable gentleman's residence. The new gate gleamed white. Sparrows dust-bathing outside scattered as the Volvo swept down upon them and flew into the fields, narrowly avoiding the murderous bonnet. Not one followed its natural instinct to fly before it, into the drive of the house.

The removal men were gathered on the steps, examining their wrists with a compulsive nervous tic. They looked restless and uneasy, like imminent trouble at t'mill. The van was closed up and the driver already in the cab, revving up the engine as if making sure it was in good working order for a quick getaway.

Sandy got out and advanced on them with the magniloquent dignity of a king taking his rightful inheritance into his hands.

'All in?'

'Yes, Mr. Matheson. I hope it's all where you want it. You hadn't labelled anything, so we've just had to guess. All right if we get off now?'

'Hold on,' said Sandy sharply, 'I haven't checked for breakages or theft, yet.'

'Theft! Now look here – '

'Come round with me,' ordered Sandy, and entered into his kingdom.

It looked ridiculous. The broken fragments of clock were parked apologetically at the side of the hall. Derek's Victorian chiffonier, which had taken up most of the entrance passage at Highgate and caused inconvenience to everyone who passed, huddled into a tiny corner at the foot of the stairs, bearing the dead telephone and a pile of London directories which Sandy had appropriated. Sod the Liptons, he needed them. On top, a pile of umbrellas and an old briefcase restrained them from flight home. Sandy paused, then picked up the briefcase and carried it with him into the drawing room.

The carpeted, still-uncurtained room contained a minute row of modern fitments tucked to one side of the chimney breast, a mutilated three-piece suite round the grate, a useless heap of stereo equipment, records and tapes by the new radiator and a television dumped between the two front windows, too far away from the seating for the picture to be discernible. The drinks table, covered with unwashed glasses and a great many bottles, offered a hopeful gleam of comfort against the inside wall.

Sandy counted the bottles.

'Where's the Sambuca?' he asked.

'The what?' The foreman looked innocently puzzled.

'Taste good, did it?'

'It broke,' admitted the foreman angrily.

Sandy drew out a notebook and wrote.

'There's a cut-glass decanter missing.'

'Probably in the kitchen.'

More writing. He made for the dining room.

'I'm afraid one of your dining chairs slipped down into the area,' the foreman forestalled him hastily.

The main bedroom looked reasonable, apart from introdden gravel and a scum of fluff kicked up on the new carpet by artisan feet.

Virginia's room looked almost welcoming; her taste for romantic frills and furbelows fitted well into the shining old-world room, and it seemed to be awaiting her expectantly.

In the rest of the huge house, little bits and pieces of Highgate spread themselves around like early arrivals at a party, hoping that others would join them soon and relieve them of sole responsibility for providing congeniality.

'Right,' said Sandy, 'I've listed the damage. Sign here, then I'll send a copy to your boss tomorrow.'

'But — '

'Here.'

When the van drove off the air in the cab was blue, and became bluer when the foreman opened the envelope he had taken from Sandy's hand with the 1980s equivalent of a tugged forelock.

'Shite! Am I glad to be out of there!' said a shaken young

man with a Mohican and swastikas scattered over his denims.

'I'm not sensitive, meself,' said the foreman. 'Do you think he'll notice that dent in the paint?'

Only then did Sandy return to the silent females in the car and lift out Virginia. She was asleep, but came round slightly as his arms tightened upon her. Her eyes half opened and her hands slid across his chest.

'I love you,' she said. 'I love you, William.'

'Where do you want her?' he asked Petra, as if she was another piece of unlabelled furniture. Petra followed him into the house, peering round his shoulder to see if her baby was all right. Virginia was all she had left.

'Better take her straight up to her room. I'll put her to bed and she can sleep through till morning.'

He carried her up the echoing, uncarpeted stairs and into the back bedroom. Petra hurriedly unstrapped the bedding and made up the bed. She put on the fitted sheet. She spread the duvet over it and turned it back. She plumped up the pillows. Sandy stood watching the loathed Virginia, curled up in her pretty-pretty tub chair.

'I'm going to undress her now.'

He left the room and went downstairs to the drinks table. He stood with legs apart before his impressive fireplace, scanning the immense length of his period drawing room and picturing it filled with valuable antiques.

'So how about this, Comrade Marx?' he exulted. 'Power to the bloody people!'

'She said it was a poltergeist, and I must admit I was shit-scared,' said Derek, looking ahead at the rain-soaked desolation of the A10, 'but somehow I couldn't believe it afterwards. You mean it's really true?'

'Oh yes,' said Rod grimly, 'I saw it, and it was the genuine article, all right. All the symptoms. She's desperately unhappy, Derek, and prolonged unhappiness is a terrible thing. Don't let anyone tell you it's a moral force that builds character,' he said angrily as he steered Dino's car down the wet, straight road, 'it's destructive and it attracts destruction.'

'But why should it happen to Ginnie? She hasn't done anything wrong.'

'I suppose the sins of the fathers are visited on the children, and that's not a threat, it's a warning. If you muck up your parental duties your children suffer, and they'll pass their sufferings on to their children.'

'Who are you to condemn?' said Derek bitterly, his guilt surging up painfully. 'You've never been married. You've no idea of the problems.'

Rod swung the car into the roundabout poised above the problem-solving M25, then curved in again to shoot on towards Buntingford.

'No,' he said, 'I've never been married.'

'You're gay, aren't you?'

'Yes. So what?'

'Nothing,' said Derek, shrugging. 'If you're happy that way, good luck to you. At least you don't produce children to suffer for your mistakes. You can keep your failures to yourself.'

'Wives and children aren't the only people you can hurt,' said Rod, his eyes fixed ahead. After a pause he said 'I had a brother.'

'I was an only child myself. I had all my parents' dreams to fulfil.'

'So'd he, he was the eldest. My father gave him hell. The stupid thing was that he loved him, but he wanted him to be perfect; he wanted him to achieve what he hadn't.'

'My father was the same,' said Derek. 'He was a clerk in a council office, but he expected me to rise up into the millionaire class. I couldn't, of course, he'd somehow cramped my horizons. If I had succeeded it would have felt as if I was betraying him.'

'Oh, Father wouldn't have regarded that as a betrayal! Success was everything to him, but you had to do it his way. All Frank wanted to be was a gardener, but Father didn't approve of a job where you got your fingers dirty.'

'Sounds familiar,' said Derek.

Virginia tossed and turned, the drug interfering with her sleep patterns and allowing her neither natural rest nor natural consciousness. Her dreams were filled with strange images; swirling vortices of nothingness, low cries in unknown languages, lost, begging faces mouthing appeals at her through immense distances of time and space. An old man peered out through a window which was not like any window she had seen in her waking life; it was small, barred, too closely barred for a hand to reach through. And yet somehow his hand did come through, elongating into a phallic snake of flesh to press on towards her, for yards and yards, aiming straight at her like a weapon and swelling out into a wrinkled claw at its end.

She stirred uneasily, shrinking away from its approach. Her normal body would have cast off the nightmare and jerked her awake, but it had been robbed of its defences and merely writhed helplessly in its chemical chains.

The hand touched her breast, but didn't stop there. It moved on, down into her flesh, its five fingers suddenly blooming into hundreds. The fingers grew and spread, searching into every part of her body and awakening the nerves to acute life. She was drowning in her own feelings, her body becoming a surging wave of sensation and rising up to the ceiling.

'William!' she cried.

Her eyes opened as she fell back on to the bed with a thump. It was incredibly dark. Even with the curtains closed, her room had never been as dark as this before. Always when she woke in the night there was light to be seen around the edge of the window, where the orange glow of London illuminated the sky outside. And it was so quiet. Where was the distant sound of traffic? Where was the whispering hum of night-long life, the reassurance that she wasn't alone?

She struggled with her sluggish limbs. Gosh, it was cold. Where was the duvet? Her hands groped for it. Beneath her? How did it get there?

Oh, she couldn't see, she couldn't see, and she felt so ill! Her hand reached out for the lamp and couldn't find it. She pulled it back to the home ground of her body and stroked it, commiserating with it for its failure. Gosh, it was *cold*! Sandy had turned the central heating off again, the stupid, mean idiot.

She managed to stagger off the bed and make for the radiator under the window, hands outstretched. They hit wood. Panels. Must be the door. What was the door doing there? She ran her hands along it, searching for the smooth texture of wallpaper, but the door didn't stop. It went on and on. Doors don't go on for that long. I'm still dreaming. What a horrible dream. I want to wake up but I don't seem to be able to, there's something wrong with my brain.

Her knuckles struck and she cried out with pain, then the door started to move at right angles, on and on and on. Her knuckles struck again, and still that awful door stretched away into infinity.

The road bounced with angry rain before the headlights.
'So what did your brother do eventually?'
Rod stared at the road. Puckeridge to the right. Not far now. Pray God he'd be in time. This time, please God.
'He was thirteen and he was bloody unhappy.'
'Who isn't at thirteen? No-one will explain.'
'He shared a room with me. Things started to move when we were in bed. Things broke. He wasn't doing it, I could see that. We were scared stiff. So I tried to tell Father – '
Buntingford ahead. They were doing ninety.
'You mean another poltergeist?' Derek was gripping his seat and staring, terrified, at the black road roaring towards them. The man was a maniac!

Rod slammed on the brakes, skidded, then turned left into the dim lanes. He peered through the windscreen, trying to make out the signposts, trying to keep his mind on them and to detach himself from the painful words he was speaking.

'One night, when we were in bed, there was the most God-awful crashing down in Father's study. Next morning he found all his shooting trophies had been thrown through the window and his favourite shotgun broken. I hated his guns, so did Frank.'

His brother's frightened face was in his mind's eye.

You are a liar, Frank. You have been telling Rodney wicked lies and now you have lied to me. You will go to hell, Frank. There are no demons in this house. This is a godly, righteous home where no evil may enter.

It's true, Dad, really it is! I saw it too! Please help us! I told you about it because we need your help!

Don't try to shield him, Rodney, I won't have you being a liar too. Bend over, Frank.

The car climbed the dark, winding lane up on to the plateau.

Rod searched for the white finger. There! He turned the protesting vehicle into the darkness which hid Maiden's End.

'So what happened?' asked Derek urgently. 'How long was it before the poltergeist left him alone?'

The car stopped at the closed gate. Rod threw the words over his shoulder as he got out to open it.

'I found him in the garden with his face gone. He'd shot himself with one of Father's guns. Unhappiness can be a fatal disease.'

Hands touched her.

'William?' she asked sleepily. 'Is that you? Help me to wake up, William. Take me away to your cottage. Love me.'

'I'm here. Don't be afraid, Virginia, you'll enjoy it. All little girls enjoy it. It's what they're made for.'

Her hands were still moving along the door — she was so tired, so lonely, so afraid.

'You mean love?' she asked hopefully.

'If you have to call it that.' The voice was harsh. Oh, dear heroic William Strong, are you just as bad as the rest of them? Are you changing into a nightmare too?

'William, take me home with you. I'm so unhappy.'

'You are home with me. I knew you'd come.'

Her hands touched cloth at last. The window. She was dizzy, she needed air, even though it was so cold, so deathly cold. The sash sprang up.

The lights of London had gone out. The black gulf extended for ever to the dim skyline. Life had gone and only death remained.

The hands closed upon her.

'Do you have to get drunk *every* night?' asked Sandy testily. He looked down at Petra hunched on the rug in front of the empty grate.

'Yes. So do you.'

'I've only had a couple. It's you who've been knocking it back ever since we got here. Women can't take alcohol like men can, their bodies can't cope with it. You ought to know that by now, Petra.'

'Oh, poor old us! We have ten times the problems that you

have but we aren't allowed the solution that you whop down morning, noon and night because we're not biologically capable of dealing with it!'

'The only problem you've had to deal with this evening is to get me something to eat, and all you could come up with was bread and cheese. With a kitchen like that!'

'Stuff your kitchen! Stuff your ridiculous house! Stuff you! I'd rather have alcohol than you any day, Sandy. I never want to feel your disgusting hands on me again, or feel your great, fat body forcing itself into me, or have to do what you want instead of what I want, or do anything except be a loving mother to my poor, darling Virginia.'

'Oh, for God's sake, spare me the vodka tears! You don't love Virginia.'

'I do!'

'You're a bloody liar,' he said in a low, embittered voice. 'You told me yourself you didn't like her. You can't tell truth from lies, now, can you? You change the facts to suit your own convenience. You just plump for the most appealing angle.'

She looked up, seizing the irresistible advantage eagerly.

'I believe they call it advertising,' she said triumphantly.

There was a thunderous knocking out in the hall. Sandy stood transfixed with astonishment, then gradually swallowed the remarkable fact that people could knock on front doors isolated in the middle of benighted, deserted fields. He went out and struggled with the unfamiliar lock, an iron construction of the size and complexity of a musical box. Nine feet of iron-heavy wood swung back upon its hinges.

The light from the shadeless chandelier streamed out and illuminated two blanched, tense faces.

'Sandy,' said Rod, 'where's Virginia?'

'For Petes's sake!' exclaimed Sandy. 'You just can't leave her alone, can you? I never realised that people like you could be turned on by little girls. She's in bed, of course – Here! Come back!'

They pushed past him and up the stairs, Rod praying as he hadn't done since he left home for university, eight years before. Oh God, let me be in time, don't let me be a failure again, don't let Father be right, don't make another sacrifice to my inadequacy, don't let me be too late . . .

Derek saw the long, yawning window, the bare sweep of the stairs, the high, blank, painted walls. God, what a nightmare of a place.

As Rod opened the door something hurtled out across the landing. Derek spun round and looked down. His own photograph stared up at him.

From the room beyond, a cacophony of sound suddenly burst out. Voices, crashing, laughter, the unmistakable uproar of a wild, joyless party. A party? *Here*?

Terrified, he moved across the creaking, varnished boards into Virginia's bedroom. Rod had turned on the light and the decor hit him like snow-blindness. Rod appeared to be struggling with a small, white ghost — a writhing, whimpering figure which clung to him with one hand and pushed him off with the other — a house divided against itself.

There was no-one else there at all, and yet revelry resounded throughout the room. There was talking from by the window, laughter from by the wardrobe, a stream of obscene abuse from by the dressing table. On the bed, the duvet heaved up and down as if a couple were copulating beneath. Virginia's discarded clothing reared up from the tub chair and floated towards him, the arms of her coat stretching wide to engulf him.

He screamed and ducked as it flapped past his head. The white figure's head jerked up and tortured eyes recognised him.

'Daddy! Oh, I love you, Daddy!'

Another voice roared into the din: 'There is no love but Eros! Love is sex! Love is the body! There is nothing without the body!'

For a moment the wardrobe mirror reflected an old wrinkled face, then shattered. The bed, at the summit of its ecstasy, rose up into the air and crashed down on to the portable television. Stones fell in a sharp, percussive patter around Derek's petrified body, although miraculously none hit him. Stones? *Stones in here*?

Above the uproar a girl's voice rose to a pathetic wail. 'I love him! I love him! Kill me before you take him!'

It was not Virginia's voice. She was sobbing into Rod's shoulder.

'Daddy! Take me home! Take me away, Daddy!'

Her appeal reached Derek through his fear. He lunged forward, grabbed her away from Rod and carried her out on to the landing.

'Yes, I'll take you home. Hold on to me, Ginnie. We're going home.'

More stones whizzed past his ear as he pulled her down the stairs. She was limp now, her bare feet dragging behind her and bumping on the treads. She'll be bruised, he thought, her poor little feet will be bruised. Her poor little baby feet. I should have put on her bootees, they'd have softened the blows. Rod was behind him, panting, pushing him, urging the speed which he was well aware was imperative.

'All right,' he said angrily, 'I'm going as fast as I can. Don't push me, Dad, I'll go at my own pace, understand?'

What the hell was he talking about? Rod wasn't his Dad. He was out of his mind, but this situation was out of anyone's mind. He wasn't in the real world anymore. He was in the world of the subconscious where all life's problems lay unresolved. His body was stumbling down these threatening wooden stairs, but his soul was somewhere else, where the real, real things happened. He was in the good-and-evil struggle which underlay the paper-thin skin of the everyday.

Sandy was standing at the bottom of the stairs.

Derek confronted him with angry confidence.

'I'm taking Ginnie home with me, Sandy. Tell Petra she can set the law on to me if she wants to, but I'll fight it every inch of the way. You just try and get her back.'

'I don't want her,' said Sandy. 'As far as I'm concerned you can tip her down the nearest drain.'

'Thank you and goodnight,' said Derek, and carried his daughter out to the car.

Petra, on hands and knees, reached the hall as the door slammed.

'What the hell was all that row?'

'Derek. He's taken Virginia.'

'He's *what*?'

Sobriety hit her like a bucket of water. She rose to her feet, solved the conundrum of the front door with surprising ease and screamed.

'Derek! Wait!'

Her first husband turned apprehensively.

'Right!' she said to Sandy. 'Where's the money from the house?' Her eyes were crossing, but she only swayed slightly on her feet.

'In the bank, of course.'

'Which account?'

'Mine.'

'When are you going to transfer my half?'

'*Your* half?'

'Yes. In fact I think I'll take the cheque now.' Her hand shot out, palm upwards. The movement upset her equilibrium and she lurched towards the beheaded clock and held on to it, chin belligerently raised. She looked absurdly like a ballet dancer at the barre.

'Now? Don't be stupid, Petra. If you really want it transferred I'll ring the bank tomorrow, but I thought we'd pay off the bills first, then perhaps find a nice little parcel of shares and make a quick killing before we put it in – '

'I want that cheque now, Sandy. I'm going back to London with Virginia and I need money.'

'You're going to Zak, aren't you?' he asked furiously.

'Give me the *money*.'

'With the utmost pleasure,' he said with sudden viciousness. 'You're nothing but a liability for a man in my position.'

She didn't even pack. The instant the cheque was in her hand she walked straight, nearly straight, out of the door and down the steps. He saw her trip and start to fall as he closed the door upon her.

The car drew away. The sound grew fainter and fainter until it had gone altogether and the silence of the house was absolute. Even the whisper of rain against the window panes had stopped. Total silence – echoing, pregnant, roaring silence.

So here was Sandy Matheson with his dream come true at last, in a huge, period house in the middle of black, deserted fields. But he had never intended to be alone in it. He had always pictured it full of fashionable, amusing, admiring people.

The silence was getting on his nerves. He went into the drawing room to switch on the television.

As the sound blurted out he thought he heard a distant laugh. He turned the volume down at once.

'Who's there?' he shouted.

He walked out into the hall and looked up the curving stairs, gleaming in the light of the chandelier.

From upstairs, the laugh came again, then it coughed and seemed to gasp for breath, as if it were being strangled. Sandy suddenly felt ill, conscious of a desperate need to go to the loo. Unfortunately, it was on the upper floor. He was still tossing up whether to risk the proximity of the flight on his way to the service stairs and the new downstairs cloakroom, when the voice managed to catch its breath and speak.

'Young girls,' it said gloatingly.

Sandy's terror changed into relief and apprehension at the same moment. Police. Or perhaps a private detective.

Nasty, but manageable. Derek had found out and brought the man down with him. What a petty, mean little trick. Would you believe it?

'Come here' he shouted angrily. 'Come down here and show yourself. What the hell do you mean by sneaking into my house?'

The voice drew in a hollow, catarrhal gasp and spoke again.

'Delicious, are they not? We are the same, you and I. We know what matters. Money and power and the lusts of the flesh. The sweet, tender bodies of young girls. We are brothers. We are kindred spirits. We are of the same substance.'

'Come down here, you bastard, and stop your filthy insinuations. You can't prove anything, it's just libellous rumour. Where are you? Don't try to hide from me. I'll find you.'

'Oh no,' said the voice. 'We are past finding. We are both lost, you and I.'

And for the first time, right in the middle of the previously empty flight of stairs, he saw the old man.

The tired, elderly car struggled into the outskirts of London.

The light switched itself on for the sixth time and Rod thrust out his hand to turn it off.

'Calm *down*, Ginnie,' he insisted sharply.

'Sorry, Rod.'

He glanced up at the mirror and saw her snuggled up against Derek's shoulder, hooked on to him like a nervous kitten.

Petra had been silent for at least twenty minutes.

'Where do you want me to drop you, Petra?'

She came out of her doze and took in the rows of floodlit semis skimming past the sides of the car.

'Oh – Zak's.'

'But Ginnie can't go there, – I explained that.'

'She's coming to my place,' said Derek firmly.

'She is not,' retorted Petra.

'Yes I am,' said Virginia.

'You are not, Virginia, we are going to – '

'I am, I am!' She gripped Derek in her panic.

The dashboard lights went out and the engine died. Rod used the last impetus of movement to steer the car into the side of the road and turned to face her with weary, exasperated reproach.

'Oh, Virginia!'

And she smiled with amazed relief, suddenly realising the unlimited possibilities of her occult powers.